Geyer Street Gardens

Beneath the Mask of a Hockey Goaltender

Another Story from the Adventures of Harry and Paul

Paul John Hausleben

Cover concept by Paul John Hausleben

Published by God Bless the Keg Publishing
Somewhere, U.S.A.

ISBN: 978-0-9906979-2-3

DEDICATIONS

To: Harry M. Rogers Jr., Jeffrey Scott Pierce, Johnny Cioffi, Raymond Edel, Robert Wexler, George Giordanetti, Michael Dittamo, Anthony Tartaglia, Steven Capuccio, Bruce "The Moose" Baumgartner, Coach Raymond Bossard, Steven Van Dyke, Wayne Cesa, Neil "The Wheelie" Fowler, Aldo Iacovo, Marty DeVoogd, the Centrelli brothers, Greg McDonald, Camille "The Eel" Henry, Henry Jazkot, Mr. Eddie Austeri, Eddie Rusnak, Big Joe Starost, Bill "The Rocket" Campbell, Russell "Jackrabbit" Hayes, Jim Hikibin, P.A. Nichols, Pastor James T. "The Dentist" (he only does extractions!) O'Malley, William Mulligan, number twenty-seven, my dear mother, the old man, Gramps, Dottie, Mr. Pierce, Ronzo, the lip lady, Coach T. Davis, Coach Smithson, and all others, who I may have missed and were either players, members, or supporters of the Haledon Hockey league, other leagues I played in, or I was affiliated with during my hockey career. This novel is for all of you. God bless you all. You gave me so much more in memories and spirit than I could ever convey to you.

This is a work of fiction. Names, characters, businesses, places, events and incidents either are the product of the author's eccentric, strange and unusual imagination or used in a fictitious manner. Any resemblance to actual persons, living or dead or actual events is purely coincidental and it was not the intention of the author.

TABLE OF CONTENTS

"At one time or another in our lives, we all feel as if we have lived an unfulfilled destiny. The truth is, however, that when you stop and examine your life, it is exactly quite the opposite. If you did the best that you could, treated people with respect and gained the respect of others, played the game fair and hard, then you have fulfilled more than you can ever imagine."

Paul John Hausleben

#27

Goaltender

May 2015

ACKNOWLEDGMENTS

Thank you to the following, for helping to shape my hockey career and therefore inadvertently contributing to my own spirit and to the writing of this book. Thanks, and a tip of the goalie mask (with black marker stitches) to Wurtzberg Brothers Sporting Goods in Paterson, New Jersey, Ice World in Totowa, New Jersey, The Tree Tavern, in Paterson, New Jersey, Dr. P.C. Harami, Harry M. Rogers Jr., Jeffrey Scott Pierce, P.A. Nichols, the Haledon, New Jersey Fire Department, Bernard Marcel Parent, Jim Gordon, Sal "Red Light" Messina, Bill "The Big Whistle" Chadwick, Cooper GP59L pads, Bauer Supreme 49 goalie skates, Sherwood goalie sticks, the no bounce pucks, and to number twenty-seven, wherever the hell he is now.

Preface

First off, this is indeed a book about the sport of hockey; however, it is also a book about special experiences in life and how participation in sports contributes to shaping an individual person's soul.

This was the one novel in the collection of my work, books, and the stories of the *Adventures of Harry and Paul,* which I knew that I had to write. It was also the one novel, which would contain the storyline that I knew would be the most daunting and difficult for me to compile.

I have to admit that this novel was a tedious, three-year project, and at times, it became quite the chore to bring all the material together. A number of times during the writing of this novel, I even conceded defeat and tried to relegate the entire project to a simple short story, in which I planned to include in an upcoming anthology.

The underlying trouble in abandoning or downsizing *Geyer Street Gardens,* was that over the years, I have written into the many story lines of the various, *Adventures of Harry and Paul,* numerous references of hockey experiences, games, players, and situations that the two characters of Harry and Paul often speak about, or even more apparent, in the case of the incessant dreamer, Paul John Henson, he thought about during his narrations.

I knew that I needed to write this story in order to "wrap up" all the loose ends and hints of hockey-related adventures. My own idea at being coy, planting hints and tidbits of hockey adventures in the previous materials, as well as leading my readers on, had turned into a bit of a monster!

Still, I knew that this one novel would sum up most, if not all, of the past hockey adventures and fill in some missing years, and parts and pieces in the Adventures of Harry and Paul.

Struggling to find exactly the correct inspiration that I required to compose the storyline for *Geyer Street Gardens,* I performed several site visits to the actual site of Geyer Street Gardens. During those emotional visits back to the old neighborhood, I finally obtained the inspiration that I required for the completion of this novel.

Readers of my biographies might recall that I did indeed play quite a bit of street hockey, roller hockey, and ice hockey within some relatively high-level of hockey competition. Hockey, as well as playing the position of goaltender, is still a huge part of my life. Being a goaltender in hockey is, in my opinion, quite unlike anything else in all of the sports. It combines geometry, profound courage, athletic skills, stamina, flexibility, and frankly, a large amount of stupidity in order to play the position.

The allure is amazing and still to this day, I have never found anything quite as demanding, yet as rewarding, as playing this unique position. It shaped my soul, invoked a certain amount of fearlessness inside of me, and made me look at life quite differently. I think I relive the game, saves I made, and various aspects of playing the position, virtually every day. I have no shame in stating that it consumed my thinking and changed my life. It also provided me with a lifelong respect of a needle and thread.

That shaping of my soul is the main reason as to why I think that I struggled so terribly in writing this novel. I wanted to convey on paper for the reader to ponder those same powerful and deep thoughts about a sport, a simple sport to fans, yet a complex sport to the participating players.

Even to this day, I carefully watch a person's eyes, the habit developed from many years of watching a shooter's eyes, to determine where the player intended to shoot the puck. This practice has been intuitive to me in the "civilian" world, and I must say that has been proven to be rather beneficial several times!

The story lines of the books, experiences and adventures of the fictional character, "Paul John Henson" do actually contain a great deal of factual information based upon my own life, right down to the number twenty-seven being my own uniform number. I tried very hard to be accurate in my depictions of the hockey rinks, the colorful characters, and the lonely life on the road, the pain of the injuries, the brutal features of the game and other aspects of hockey during this era.

It is not exactly a game for the faint of heart!

In reading this book, you will find that I desired to be authentic in my writing, and hockey, in the era, of which is the setting of this book, was a brutal and violent sport. A sport where intimidation and mind control are critical keys to gaining control of a game. Obscene language, as well as brutal violence and wild behavior, were a vital part of that intimidation. Herein these pages, there are some graphic descriptions of the results of some violent aspects of the sport and some obscene language. I apologize for the depictions and language, but I did desire to continue with the authenticity of the novel.

The game has changed quite a bit from those times; it is now a bit more polished and fighting is now not near as commonplace as it had previously been during the era of the 1970s. In the 1970s, hockey was more of a cult sport than it is today, a sport of the blue-collar folks and it certainly was a bit odd, and not very popular in northern New Jersey where Jeff, Harry, and I, grew up.

That is why it was so special to us!

I often shudder to think how we all might have ended up if it was not for the diversion that the love of hockey provided for us in that old neighborhood. There were an awful lot of questionable things and influences that we could have been involved in back then. Hockey allowed, and provided us with an escape, a sport, a safe outlet for our aggression. Hockey really did contribute to the growth of a group of wild, extraordinarily tough and rough New Jersey street kids as they matured and turned into men.

That, dear reader, is the final reason why I had to write this novel. I felt as if I owed the old neighborhood, as well as the sport, the respect, the homage, the tribute, and in a very strange manner, a payback to what it gave my friends and me so long ago.

Without hockey, I have no doubt that I would never have written this book or any of my past books or stories, which I have already written, or will ever write in the future. In fact, I have no idea where I would be right now, or what I would have done without hockey in my life.

I do know that I would not be quite as creaky when I climb out of bed in the morning as I am these days, my face and body would not have certain scars, but my life would have a certain amount of emptiness to it without hockey, and all the sport brought to me.

"Kick save and a beauty by twenty-seven!"

Geez, how I would love to hear those words, just one more time. Yes, one day, before I push up some daisies, I would like to hear them once again.

Yes indeed! I can see it all now. A smelly old locker room, with rubber mats on the floor to prevent your skates from dullin' up. There will be a certain smell in the air. A smell, which I cannot actually classify, but it will be something between musty and downright disgusting. The locker room has to have painted cement block walls, painted in a bright color, such as a bright blue or red. The room will have wooden benches lined up on the walls for you to sit upon and dress into your equipment.

The lights will be dim. You can barely see in there.

I will lace up my ancient pair of Bauer Supreme 49 goalie skates, strap on the steel groin protector, steel cup, garter belt, socks, goalie pants, suspenders, chest protector, shoulder pads, and an extra elbow pad on my right elbow. I need that one, you see, even all of these years later, those floating bone chips in my right elbow, caused by hitting the ice hard while making saves all of those years, well, they still hurt like a son of a bitch.

One of the final pieces of the puzzle will be my trusty Cooper GP59L leg pads.

Full of puck marks, and a few tears too.

Battle scars.

They are made of real leather and cloth, and they smell very similar to how an old mule's ass smells on a hot summer day. They are also very short in comparison to the new pads that modern goalies use these days. You need to be careful; a shot high on the pad can still slip in and hit you hard on the knee or leg. I know that for a fact because I found out the hard way!

I will drag my old ass back into the crease in front of the net, scrape at the ice with the edges of my skates, and make piles of snow on the edges of the net with my goalie stick. You have to make sure the ice is not too tight and make sure it does not have any bumps to cause a tricky hop of the puck.

I no longer have to tie my hair behind my head; age has taken care of that annoying hair.

Lastly, the final piece of the puzzle will need to be in place. My old faithful mask, full of dings and dents, marker stitch marks, as well as the false sense of security which it brings to you. It is the last line of defense between a few stitches and being unconscious, or dead.

My best friend.

I will pull on the old goalie mask; pull it down tight over my face and immediately, a river of sweat runs off the end of my mask and drips down my chest.

Damn, how can it be so bloody hot on an ice rink?

I recheck the straps on my leg pads; crouch, tap the right post with the shaft of my stick to check my distance, and then put my stick out in front of me, straight up with the blade now! I square up to the shooter. My confidence is building. I will stare down this shooter.

There I am in the net, crouching, watching his eyes from behind the mask. The shooter works the puck in closer. He moves quickly from his forehand, then to his backhand. I see him look at the crossbar, then back to the puck and I toe in on my skates to glide out just a bit on the ice. I need to cut down his angle just a bit.

He is going to go top shelf in the net and try to tuck it under the crossbar over my glove hand.

I can tell, because you have to watch their eyes!

Oh, wait! He is a tricky one! I caught him looking at the stick side. Kind of low, really quick. Oh yeah, he is going low on the stick side. Top shelf was a decoy!

I will stop a few pucks; I swear I can still stop a few pucks. Just one more time.

Oh, shit! Here it comes! Low, hard, flat and fast. I see it clearly. The puck has a certain look to it at this speed. I track it and, and, and it is. . ..

"Kick save and a beauty by twenty-seven!"

A dream. Someday, I swear.

Until then, I will write books such as this one and dream of a time long ago, when that old mask, the sprays of ice chips in my face, and the referees' whistle were my best friends.

I hope you enjoy reading this book as much as I enjoyed putting it all together. Thank you for reading it.

Paul John Hausleben

May 2015

Geyer Street Gardens

Beneath the Mask of a Hockey Goaltender

Another Story from the Adventures of Harry and Paul

Prologue

"Tell us again the story, dear Father, of how you and Uncle Harry started playing hockey!" Heather Sarah, Blue Cloud, and Paul William, sat on the living room floor and they all gathered around me while I sat on the sofa in our living room. Our children were now teenagers. They all had grown so quickly. Where had the time gone?

We were all stuffed and happy, after enjoying a fantastic Boxing Day meal of Binky's famous roast beef and Yorkshire pudding meal, prepared from my mum's secret recipes. After dinner and cleaning up the kitchen, we all decided to sit together around the Christmas tree and fireplace on a quiet Boxing Day evening and enjoy the last bit of celebration for the day.

Harry sat in our love seat next to his lovely wife Rose, and my wife, Binky, sat in a chair next to them, while we enjoyed a few drinks in front of a roaring fire. We were going to top it all off with a Christmas pudding sent straight from a distant relative across the pond. A relative who still sent Mum and the old man, my Aunt Lois, my sister, and me, a pudding for a gift every Christmas season.

I had to keep it a secret, but I had a little bit of a time bomb hidden in the cupboard for enjoyment later on, too. That treat was from Ronzo's secret recipe.

I thought to myself, merry Christmas, Ronzo.

While we waited for the pudding to heat, we had all gathered in front of the fireplace and tree to sit and relax.

The Redmond's family dog, Cocoa Two, sat down, barked twice at me and wagged his tail three times.

"See, Cocoa Two wants to hear the story, too. I mean, he wants to hear it also! Can you tell us the story of when O'Malley stuck his stick into the other player's eyeball and the player's eyeball popped out?"

"Who told you that story, Paul William?" Binky screamed as she almost spilled her (shaken not stirred, of course) Martini.

"Uncle Harry told me!"

"Harry!" Rose scolded her husband.

"Oh geez, sorry Rose! Yeah, yeah, yeah, twenty-seven. Tell all of them how it all began for us guys. Tell the story of it all, Paul, as only you can tell 'em."

"Well, I guess. It could be somewhat of a long story, though," I said as I sat up on the edge of my chair.

I took a long swig of Big Boulder beer and looked around at my family and friends. They were all studying my face; it was obvious that they were looking for me to tell the story of how it all began.

I sighed and decided it might finally be the correct time to purge my soul of these thoughts.

"All right, well, you see, there was, or rather there is, this place called Geyer Street. It was just an old, dead-end street, but to all of us in the old neighborhood, it was special. We called it Geyer Street Gardens. It was over by Uncle Harry's house, near Jeff Porter's house too, at the end of John Street. There were these kids in the neighborhood. Let me see now. There was Big Wex, Tags, Jeff Porter, Johnny the Cho, Pooch, Ray Edelski, Big George, Handsome Mike the Italian Kid. . .."

Geyer Street Gardens

Part One

The Start of a Journey

"You know, someday, Paul, perhaps you should write all of these adventures down. You really should. The wonderful stories that you tell, they read as if they are chronicles of your life and of Harry's life, too. It would be a shame if you did not write them all down for readers to enjoy."

"Okay, Binky, I think you are correct. Now that you mention it, well, a long time ago, I actually did write some of them down. Maybe it is time that I should pick it all back up and write some more." I agreed with Binky. I thought to myself, in looking back at all the adventures, I think I will remember them all, but as far as recording them, I had better skip over certain parts. You know, perhaps, not writing all of it down; however, Binky is correct. I think it is time to write a little.

1

The First Save

"Have you returned to visit Geyer Street or the old neighborhood in a long time, Paul?" Binky asked me. I shook my head to indicate that I had not. I looked at Harry and he shook his head to indicate the same answer.

"I think one day that you should go. I think it will help you finally to close the door. You know, to put it all in a final spot within your heart for the last time. A resting place for number twenty-seven. Once and for all."

I thought about her words for a long time until one day when I ventured out. . ..

I knew every crack in the sidewalk. The air even smelled the same. I could not even guess how many years had passed since I had last walked down this street.

It was amazing and sentimental, all at the same time!

Oh boy, I certainly was beckoning the ghosts that always haunt me to pay me a visit now. I swore that I could hear Jeff Porter's voice call out to me and then Harry's voice calling out too. I heard the sound of a wooden hockey puck hitting a stick and the shouts of, "SCORE!"

Harry's brother-in-law, Ronzo Boatmann, was there too. He stuck his head out of the window of the top bedroom of 20 John Street and yelled for us, "To be careful with shooting those damn hockey pucks! Keep them away from my car!"

Then I heard Ray Edelski shout out in his classic, radio announcer voice, "Kick save and a beauty by Henson!"

As I approached the corner of John Street and Geyer Street, I turned around. I could have sworn that I heard the roar of Harry's big engine flying down the street.

I stood there on a cold April morning and breathed in deeply.

My trusty camera dangled around my neck, still bouncing on the cord, moving right and left across my chest. I must have been walking a bit faster than I had realized.

I spun around, looked up and down the street, and smiled. Raising the camera, I snapped a few pictures. First 30 John Street, then a few shots of the iconic 20 John Street, then the Nit-Nat kid's house and many others. Things have changed, they always do. I turned and walked down John Street, past the corner of Geyer Street and John Street, and I stopped dead in my tracks. Andy's Provision store on the corner was now long since gone.

Oh boy, things sure had changed here.

In front of me, it loomed. A plain old, dirty, urban street that was full of dirt, urban decay, potholes and rocks.

A dead-end street, leading to nowhere.

In fact, it actually led to the loading dock of an ugly factory, a factory that was now a lot uglier than I ever remembered it being before. Yet, on this ugly, old street, my life changed.

I felt my back pocket to make sure it was still there. It was.

I smiled, tugged at the hat upon my head and slowly walked up the street towards the spot.

A spot we all knew as Geyer Street Gardens.

"I am bored, youse guys and sick of playing football. I sure wish we could play something else for once. Football sucks," Harry complained as Jeff Porter, Harry M. Redmond Jr., and I all sat on the curb in front of Harry's house at 20 John Street in Haledon, New Jersey.

"Ya need so many guys to play football, and I am sick of passing the football around with just us now," Harry said as he mindlessly kicked the football that was tucked under his foot away from us.

It was late October 1970, and the three of us sat there on the curb on the gritty, urban street, searching for something to do. When you were eleven years old, life required a constant change and excitement, or boredom, crept in very quickly!

"We could see if Johnny the Cho and Ray Edelski were around. If Big Wex is home, then we could have a game of two hand touch," Jeff suggested.

"Nah, I agree with Harry. Football is only fun when we have a lot of guys," I commented while I pushed my long hair out of my eyes and shook my head.

There we sat, three boyhood buddies, on a curb in gritty, urban America. We all grew up together, Jeff and Harry were neighbors, and I lived two city blocks south of them with my front door fifteen feet away from a busy main street. My family's house sat directly on the border between our small borough and the big city of Paterson, New Jersey.

It was a cold and overcast Saturday and the three of us sat around, mulling what we would do with the rest of our precious afternoon. These were the days before video games, when households had one television, you played outside all the time, and you entertained yourself. We rode our bicycles everywhere; our parents did not provide shuttle services to bring you to every event that your heart desired.

It was a different time and place.

Jeff stood up from the curb and looked at the two of us while he said, "C'mon guys, let's not just sit around here. You know, I think we can get into something new if you are up for it."

Jeff Porter was tall and lanky, with long, dirty blonde hair that hung in a bowl cut around his head. Jeff had a trademark; he always wore a baseball cap on his head backwards. Even when we played baseball, since he was a catcher, he always wore his cap backwards. Along with Harry, he was my oldest buddy; we had been friends even before he moved to John Street.

Jeff had one of the most fun-loving families that I had ever met, and the Porters fit right in with the Redmonds and the rest of the John Street gang. Jeff was always good for a laugh, a prank, or some innocent mischief.

"Whatcha got in mind, Jeff?" Harry asked. He was now curious as to what Jeff had in mind.

"The other day, I was riding in the car with my old man, and we went by Buckley Park over there in Paterson by the

Colonial Grille, and I saw some bigger kids playing hockey."

"Hockey! How the heck do ya play hockey with no ice?" Harry looked at Jeff with a puzzled look on his face.

"Nah, nah, nah, Harry, these guys were playing street hockey. They were running around in sneakers on the basketball court. It looked like a lot of fun," Jeff was waving his hands in the air as he described to us the details of the scene.

I stood up and asked Jeff, "Have you ever played hockey? My old man was watching a New York Rovers game the other night on channel nine. I sat down and watched it with him, but I couldn't figure out the rules. The old man fell asleep in his chair, so I bet he didn't understand any of it either."

Jeff contemplated my question, and he answered, "Well, I shot a hockey puck around once with my brother on the Oldham Pond last winter. I have a pair of ice skates that I used a few times, but I have to say, I ain't too cool on how ya really play the game. Paulie, you should know the rules. I think it is sorta like soccer and your grandfather played soccer in England. Ya try to score past the goalie. What else is there to know?"

Harry did not answer, nor did I. We both stood there pondering the question.

Finally, Harry piped in, "I dunno, I do not have a hockey stick, and I never played or even seen a hockey game before."

"Yeah, yeah, yeah, Jeff, you're the only one of us who has a stick. I would have to buy one," I pleaded my case for a lack of equipment.

"Yeah, yeah, yeah, I will give it a try, Jeff. I am up for shooting some hockey pucks around, but I also need to buy a stick," Harry explained.

Harry generally always had some extra money in his pockets. Although none of our families were doing all that well, Harry's family earned just a little more dough than the rest of the neighborhood gang did. This was a rough, tough, old neighborhood in northern New Jersey, and the economy in the 1970s was not exactly the greatest period of economic joy in our nation's history.

Compared to Jeff and me, Harry was more fortunate in the funding department, but that, in essence, was comparing poor, to kind of poor, to really, really poor.

Jeff became energetic, and he was working both of us very hard to convince us that we should try the game of hockey, "If youse guys are up for it, we could ride up to the five and ten in North Haledon, and buy some hockey sticks. I know they sell them. I saw them last week when I was in there with my mom and she was buying some boring ass sewing stuff."

As soon as Jeff mentioned buying something, I searched my pockets for spare change and the best I could dig up was about thirty-five cents. I shook my head and by turning my dungaree pockets inside out, I displayed the predicament that I was about to face, which was my usual severe lack of funding for typical, kid-like ideas.

Jeff and Harry both frowned at me. I never had much in the way of extra dough. Coins did not come easily to the Henson family these days.

Jeff then told me, "They are only three bucks or so, Paulie. Can't ya dig up a few bucks?"

I thought about my funds tucked in a drawer in my bedroom and shook my head because I knew that I was going to come up short. I smiled because I remembered that my sister owed me two bucks from a loan that I had given her a week or so ago. I also knew that a good probe of the cushions in the old man's easy chair might net the rest of the required funds.

I told the guys to wait for me, jumped on my bike and pedaled home as fast as I could. Hockey, hockey, hmm… it might be fun and worth spending some hard-to-find coins on in order to give something new a chance.

After working my sister over for a few minutes, and reminding her of the fact that she just received some extra dough for her birthday, she coughed up the two dollars that she owed me.

Sure enough, a feel or two around the back cushion of the old man's chair netted me a bonanza! Two shiny quarters turned up, along with three thin dimes. I had hit pay dirt, but it still was not looking as if I had enough in the way of funds to purchase a stick.

I jumped back on my bike and pedaled my way towards Harry's house. As I made my way, I ran into my grandfather as he walked back to our house, with a six-pack of Big Boulder beer that he just purchased from Trio Liquor store, tucked under his arm.

"Hello, Paulie boy. Where are you off to this afternoon?" My grandfather asked me as he waved me down and stopped walking.

"Hey, Gramps. Me, Jeff, and Harry is goin' to buy hockey sticks to play hockey with. Us guys want to try to learn how to play."

My grandfather immediately began to shake his head when he heard my words. My mum's side of the family came over from England after the big war and my grandfather was always working hard to teach me "Proper King's English."

He faced an uphill battle while he tried hard to work the poor grammar and New Jersey street slang out of my vocabulary.

"Please, Paulie boy, speak correctly, lad. You should say, today, my friends and I are purchasing new hockey sticks with which to utilize in a game of hockey. We plan to participate together and to learn the rules of the game of hockey while engaging in the contest."

"Oh yeah, yeah, yeah, sorry there, Gramps," I said as I listened to the language lesson, but did not actually learn a single thing.

Gramps shook his head once again as he instructed me, "Where did you learn the yeah, yeah, yeah, response? Your father does not even speak quite as poorly as you do. Now, if you promise to correct this poor manner of speech, I will give you. . .."

Gramps dug around in his pocket for some spare change from his beer purchase. Sensing there may be a way out of my lack of a hockey stick fund situation on the horizon, I jumped at the opportunity to prove my love of "Proper King's English."

I cleared my throat and started over.

"Today, my friends and I are planning to purchase new hockey sticks this afternoon. We then plan to learn the rules of the game and participate together in the game of hockey."

I put the kickstand down on my bike and smiled at my grandfather.

"Why, Paulie boy, that was wonderful. I dare say much better lad, much better indeed, than your previous hooligan-like New Jersey street language. Now continue with the proper and correct manner of speaking, and you will go far in your life. When a person speaks well, the first impression they leave can only benefit the individual. Here are a few bits towards your purchase," Gramps said as he handed me a few quarters from the deep recess of his pockets.

"Thank you, Gramps! I will put this towards the stick. Gramps, do you know the rules of hockey or how to play?"

"You are quite welcome, Paulie boy. No, I do not know much about hockey, but I think it is quite similar to the rules of soccer. You have a keeper. You have a corps of defensemen and their combined mission is to prevent opposition goals. Then you have offensive players who attempt to score. I played a tremendous amount of soccer in England and Wales, so I would think the games are indeed quite the same. In soccer, you use your feet to move the ball, and in hockey, you utilize a stick. I am sure smart, young men such as you and your best lads can figure the game out. You could always go to the library and study the rules there, too."

"Thank you, Gramps! Hey, I will see ya. I mean, yes, I will speak with you at a later date."

Gramps nodded, smiled, and waved as he walked back to our house and I furiously rode away. While I pedaled my bike back to 20 John Street, I thought how that was the easiest seventy-five cents I had ever made!

"Hey, youse guys! I got da dough!" I screamed out as I circled back into the curb in front of Harry and Jeff.

So much for my grandfather's English lesson. After all, when you are a dopey kid growing up in urban New Jersey, your best buddies will not speak "Proper King's English!"

Jeff and Harry must have been confident that I would dig up the money since they both were waiting on their own bicycles to ride to the five and ten store. Our bikes were our prized possessions, and they seldom left our sides. We had thousands of miles on the bikes; indeed, they were our transportation to the world.

Harry and Jeff had the typical "stingray" bikes with banana seats, which were very popular at the time. I rode an English touring bicycle that my grandfather and old man chipped in together for and picked out for my birthday last year. My bike could really roll; it was solid, very durable, and trouble free. I also had a larger frame than the two "stingray" bikes. My bike was set up with some carrying bags and hooks, which we could strap various items to for transporting. Harry and Jeff opted for the "cool" bikes, and I had the more practical transportation. I was stuck in a pattern that would continue my entire life, practical versus cool. Henson; you just are not that cool!

The three of us took off, pedaling our bikes as if we were little whirlybirds toward North Haledon. It was a long ride to the store, a ride, which would take us the best part of an hour or more to arrive there. The five and ten store was in another town, and this store was really the only variety store that we could reach via our bicycles. The only other option would be to jump on the number fourteen bus and ride into downtown Paterson, but that would cost us even more, with us having to shell out some additional coins for bus fare.

Even at our young age, we maneuvered our bicycles expertly through the busy city traffic, weaving and zipping along. All kids in this era could ride bikes better than racecar drivers could navigate on a racetrack. City traffic meant nothing to us. It was just part of the fun.

Up Belmont Ave we rolled, each of us taking turns leading the small pack. We turned onto High Mountain Road and in a few miles, before we even realized it, we had arrived at the five and ten store.

Looking back, I was amazed at how kids our age simply and accurately knew how to follow roads. We paid attention to streets an awful lot more than kids do these days. After all, we did not have computer navigation to guide us!

The store had a small parking lot in front of it, and the spaces were full of cars. This was a Saturday afternoon and I am sure it was the busiest day of the week for this little store. We parked our bikes in front of the store, jumped off them, and confidently walked through the front door of the store. I felt my front pockets of my dungarees to make sure the money had not tumbled out during the long ride to the store. That would have been a tragedy, but not unheard of in my dopey kid history! I was at times a chronic loser of certain things and the old man was always drilling into my head for me to be more responsible.

An older chap standing behind the counter nodded to us

as we walked in the front door to the store.

"Hi there, youse guys. Don't break nuthin ya can't pay for, or I will call ya parents for the dough! And don't even think about five-finger discounts! I watch guys like youse guys like hawks watch for dinner! Got me a bunch of mirrors up to catch ya ass!"

He greeted the three of us as we waved back to him. I thought so much for the kindly part of his personality. Adults were always looking for the negative regarding a bunch of young bucks wandering around a store.

I heard Harry mumble, "Yeah, yeah, yeah, up ya ass, ya old fart. Ya probably blind as a damn bat and don't know ya ass from a hole in the ground."

Harry obviously did not take kindly to the old chap's advice.

This store was the place to be for fulfilling your kid wish list and our heads were on swivels while we cruised up and down the main aisle. The store was a cornucopia of assorted items that ranged from cloth and sewing supplies, household goods, candy, general supplies, toys, and what we were intent on purchasing, which were the sporting goods. Our eyes danced from kites, to spinning pinwheels, to plastic models, to posters of rock and roll stars.

"Hey youse guys, look at this," Harry shouted as he picked up a plastic model of a Halloween monster. "I got to come back and get this! I love these monster guys! They glow in the dark once you put them under a light for a few hours! I can scare the shit out of my sister Patty with this!"

Harry put the monster model down and he now picked up a plastic car model kit. He laughed as he pointed at the picture.

"Hey Paul, look, this is a Putter Classic car like the one your old man has. This model does not have fifty different blue colors though, and all of those rivets and pieces of tape holding the hood on like your old man's car has. It also does not have all those rust spots near the wheels."

Jeff waved his hand, "C'mon, Harry. The sticks are in the back. Don't go spendin' your dough on some other junk and then not have enough to get a hockey stick."

Harry and I followed Jeff while he led us to the rear of the store.

Once more, something else caught Harry's eye as he picked up a kit of a flying kite. Harry pulled the kite out of a store display and laughed when he saw a picture of Dinky the Orange Teddy Bear printed on the kite. Dinky was a very annoying cartoon, which seemed as though it had been on television forever. The obnoxious Dinky sat upon the ground waving, and there he was, with his dopey smile depicted on the kite in full, blazing color.

Harry was still studying the kite and laughing as the two of us stopped, turned, and looked at what he was carrying on about in the middle of the store.

Harry pointed back to us and said, "Hey look, here is that stupid ass Dinky the Orange Teddy Bear on a kite. I can't stand that stupid ass cartoon! I do like the dog that takes a piss on the fire hydrant guy. What is the dog's name?"

Harry put the kite back down, just as some elderly woman yelled out, "Young man! You should be not only ashamed of using that type of language in public in front of ladies such as me, but to insult an American icon such as the beloved, Dinky the Orange Teddy Bear, is disgusting and downright unpatriotic!"

The old bag was standing in front of Harry, shaking her finger in front of Harry's face, and scolding him for his rude, public behavior. She had a hair net covering her blue and silver highlighted hair, a long, pointed nose, and as she wagged her finger in front of poor Harry, a pair of huge clip-on heirloom earrings, which looked as if they were obscure, fishing lures, dangled in time from her earlobes. She stood back after the initial scolding and adjusted her paisley patterned dress that she wore underneath a woolen black overcoat. Even from a distance, we could detect that she smelled like mothballs.

Harry jumped back in surprise at the old gal's roadblock and scolding. He rolled his eyes when he realized that she had overheard his vocal and obscene-laden opinion of Dinky.

Jeff looked at me and shook his head. We could never just make a simple trip to the store. If Harry was involved, there was always bound to be some kind of extraordinary adventure. In fact, it seemed as though my entire life has had some type of wacky supermarket and food store adventures, or some type of other weird shopping experience.

We turned around and made our way over to Harry in a vain attempt to support him in his latest predicament.

Harry provided a meager defense as he put his eyes down and pretended as though he was repentant at his use of such colorful language to describe poor, defenseless Dinky.

He coughed up a phony apology.

"Oh, geez! I am very sorry. I did not see anyone there, and you are right, I should not swear like that in a store."

Harry put his hands in his pockets, kicked his shoes at the store floor a little, and pretended that he was ashamed at his behavior.

Jeff and I we knew better. Harry was no sorrier for cussing in front of the old bag than he wanted to go to school on Monday morning.

However, the old gal bought his contrived sorry act.

"Well, young man, you should be! Are you also sorry for speaking about a harmless character such as 'Dinky the Orange Teddy Bear,' who provides simple joy to millions of little children here in America? We should have more television shows about wholesome subjects on television instead of all those horrible, violent shows, which depict people being killed and shot at!"

Harry continued with his metamorphosis into a repentant, apologetic, young man, "Yes, I do really like, Dinky. I agree those shoot 'em up and killin' shows stink!"

It satisfied the old bag as she lectured Harry one more time, "Thank you, young man. If you are Catholic, you should go to confession and confess your use of such terrible language. I do think you are truly sorry for your public use of obscene language. Otherwise, I would take down your telephone number and speak with your parents. Have a nice day now, young man."

She waved her hand at Harry, nodded her head and shuffled off to the sewing aisle to pick around in the different colored threads, which were, according to a large plastic sign, "On Sale."

Harry nodded, smiled a forced smile, and joined us. He double checked the old bag's whereabouts, leaned into us, and told the first truthful thing he had said in the last few minutes, "Get lost, ya old, fat ass, cow. I would no more give you the right telephone number for my house than I would sit and watch that stupid ass, Dinky shit cartoon. Old busy body, fat ass, saggy breasts, battle-axe." Harry was still mumbling as we turned and once more followed Jeff.

"C'mon guys, now let's get the hockey sticks! Quit messing around with stuff and gettin' into trouble. By the time that we get out of here, it will be too late to shoot around," Jeff waved and led us towards the rear of the store.

Sure enough, Jeff stopped in front of a small wire cage display that was set on the floor near an end cap of the aisle.

"Here youse guys, the hockey sticks are here," Jeff said as he pointed at a collection of sticks inside the display. The three of us stopped and stared at a bunch of wooden hockey sticks stuck upside down in a wire cage. The handles were down inside the caged display, and the blades were facing up into the air, pointing skyward toward the ceiling of the store.

The three of us instantly gravitated towards the cage of sticks. Harry picked one out of the bin first and held it in his hands as he studied it. Jeff and I stood by and watched Harry. Harry held the stick up in the air, turned it around in his hands, shook it, and then placed it down on the floor of the store.

He demonstrated that he was shooting a puck. He then held it back up and studied it again.

"Hey, this blade thing on the end is turned the wrong way. It is backwards. It doesn't feel right."

Jeff took the stick out of Harry's hands and looked at it. He then explained, "That's cuz it is a lefty stick. You bat right-handed in baseball, so you need a righty curve. Ya are backwards and that is why it feels weird."

Jeff put the first stick back in the cage and picked a few more sticks out until he found what he was looking for.

"Here, Harry, this is a righty. Try this one," Jeff said as he handed a replacement stick to Harry. Harry eagerly grabbed it and tried the new stick out on the floor of the store.

Harry smiled and said, "Yeah, yeah, yeah, this is it. This one is good. Now Paulie, you get one too."

Jeff and Harry turned towards me as I studied the sticks. I picked a few sticks out of the bin, studied them, and tried a few. Using baseball as a reference, I first tried to figure out which of the curves worked for me, because I could actually bat from either side of the home plate in baseball. The righty curve felt all right, but I was definitely more comfortable with the lefty stick.

"I need this lefty one, guys. It just feels right."

I then looked at the price tag, saw that it was four dollars, and knew that I was out of luck. I did not have enough money to buy this one.

"Ah no, youse guys. I don't have enough dough to buy

this one. It is four bucks and I only have about three fifty. Please do not forget that there is going to be tax, too."

I was always entering logic and facts into our adventures.

Harry complained, "Ah man, Paul, you are such an old lady. I will lend you some dough! Just friggin' pick one out."

I interrupted Harry as I reached in the bin, pulled out a different-looking stick and held it in the air.

Since Jeff was the resident expert on hockey, and the only one of us that even remotely seemed to know something about the sport, I directed my question towards him, "What's this funny-looking stick, Jeff?"

The fact of the matter was that a red price tag, stamped in large block letters, "CLEARANCE SALE" had caught my eye. The stick's price was only three dollars and with my few extra coins; I could cover this price and any sales tax. The stick had a short handle, with a wide blade that started at the end of the short handle, and continued down into an even wider blade at the bottom of the stick. It was solid, and it felt good in my hands. The blade had no curvature to it; it was just a solid stick of wood. I held it, twirled it, and shook it in the air.

There was something special about how it felt in my hands.

The blade of this stick had a wood burning stamp, with what I assumed to be the name of the manufacturer of the stick on it, as it said, "Sherwood," in black letters on the varnished, tan wooden background. I looked over at Harry's stick, and saw that his label was, "Victoriaville," therefore; I determined that different companies made the two sticks.

"That's a goalie stick, Paulie. That is why it is so wide, to stop the puck from gettin' by ya," Jeff said while he put his hand on the blade and showed us the width of the wooden blade. "I don't think ya want a goalie stick, Paulie. Being a goalie is rough stuff. Everyone is shootin' at ya. Them pucks are dangerous. My brother got hit in the head last winter and he had to get a bunch of stitches in his head."

I heard what Jeff had said and, as I pondered it, I studied the stick and held it in my hands.

There was just something special about this stick that felt so good. I could not explain it, but it had such an appeal to me. I once again spun it, weighed it, and held it in my hands. It seemed to me, as if holding a goalie stick was something that I was always supposed to do.

I looked at my two friends and said, "Well, why not? I guess out of all of us, for us to be able to play, someone has to be the goalie."

Little did I know that this split-second decision, actually based upon a shortage of funds, would have such far-reaching implications in my life. However, is that not how life often really is?

Split-second decisions can always have far-reaching implications in our lives. Sometimes, they are very good and other times. . ..

Harry and Jeff smiled at me. I guess my logic made sense in a strange sort of way. Someone had to be the goalie, so it might as well be Paul John Henson.

Since Jeff already had a stick, and he did not need a new one, we were all set to leave. Harry and I carried our selections up to the front counter and the chap at the front counter checked out our purchases. Harry was first, and he laid his stick on the counter for the man to see the price.

"That will be four dollars and twenty-eight cents, there son. Next time, ya had better be careful of that old gal who prowls the aisles, will ya? I had to listen to her yap for ten minutes about how young people these days have no respect."

The store clerk peered ominously at Harry over the top of his glasses.

"I will, sir. Sorry 'bout that," Harry answered with a

smile as he paid him the money for the stick and received his change.

I was next, and I laid the goalie stick up on the counter, held my breath as he rang up the sale, because I was worried that I did not have enough money.

"That will be three dollars and sixteen cents there, long-haired kid." I exhaled and then paid him the money. Happily, I still had a few extra coins in my pockets.

"Thank you, sir," I answered the store clerk.

"Polite kid for a hippie. I would not think you would be interested in sports with all that hair hanging down there, son. Ya look like a kid who just hangs on the corner and plays very loud rock and roll records all day long. Going to play hockey, huh? Not many hockey players are around here these days. Have fun and be safe. Hockey is a little rough," the clerk said as he leaned on the counter, smiled and put his glasses up on top of his head.

"We will, sir. Thank you," I answered as we grabbed our new sticks and made our way out the door of the store. I was used to the longhair comments by now. I simply brushed them off.

We strapped the sticks up on the frame of my big bike, in the same holders that we used to hold our fishing poles, and we were off. The three of us were pedaling our bikes as if our pants were on fire while we headed back to Haledon. The afternoon was waning now, and we wanted to try out our sticks before it was too dark.

Before we knew it, we were back in front of 20 John Street, parking our bikes in front of Harry's house.

Jeff pushed the kickstand down on his bike. He then ran towards his house and yelled back to us, "I will go get my stick and a puck that I have in the basement. I will be right back, youse guys."

Jeff reappeared in no time flat, carrying his stick and a black object in his hand. Upon closer inspection, we found that the puck was actually not an "official" hockey puck.

Jeff explained how the puck was actually the end of his Christmas tree trunk that he sawed off when it was out at the curb after Christmas. Jeff's older brother, Steve Porter, had given him the idea to make his own pucks to shoot around with on the ice last winter. When people tossed their old Christmas trees to the curb for pickup by the garbage truck, Jeff and Steve sawed the ends off the trunks of the trees into the correct thickness to make a collection of pucks. They wrapped them with some rubber electrical friction tape, which the two brothers hoofed from their old man, and they had a bunch of homemade pucks.

"Well, here we go, youse guys. Paulie, we can use the old warehouse door of Gingert Laces there as a goal," Jeff said as he tossed the puck on the ground and he began to move it along the ground with his stick.

In between Jeff's house at 30 John Street and Harry's house at 20 John Street was an old lace factory. The old factory had a large warehouse door that faced John Street. Since this was a Saturday, the factory was not operating, and the wooden door was down in place and locked. Harry and I watched as Jeff moved the puck along the asphalt of the street, aimed and shot the puck towards the warehouse door.

"Bang!"

The wooden puck made a loud noise as it bounced off the door and rolled along the ground towards Harry.

Harry picked the puck up, moved it with his stick and he tried to shoot the puck in the same manner as Jeff had just shot it. Harry's shot was not as smooth or as accurate, and the puck flew off high in the air and hit the top of the door.

"Thud!"

The puck made a dead noise as it hit higher on the warehouse door and rolled on an edge back into the street.

"Shit! Wow! This is hard to aim. It is a lot harder than I thought it would be!" Harry said as he watched where his shot had hit.

"Go ahead, Paulie. You be the goalie and try to stop the puck from getting behind you. Say, the net is imaginary, and it goes from here on the door, to say . . . this spot here," Jeff was walking in front of the door measuring out an imaginary hockey net, and he tapped his stick blade on the spots on the old door as he explained the boundaries.

I nodded my head and stood in front of the markers that Jeff had laid out.

"What do I do, Jeff? Do I just kind of stand here with my stick and try to stop it? I bet that thing will hurt!"

Jeff looked at me and dropped his stick on the street. "Hey, wait. I know what you need! Wait here."

Jeff ran off to his house once more and he disappeared into the backyard. Once again, he was back in a flash, and this time, he was carrying a baseball glove in one hand and a work glove in his other hand.

Jeff tossed me the gloves as he told me, "Here, put these on your hands, Paulie. It will help you stop the puck and you may not get hurt as much. You have to kind of crouch, sorta like a soccer goalie does. Ya bend over to watch the puck while you protect the net. Here, like this."

Jeff took my goalie stick, put the gloves on his hands, bent over, and faced Harry. I watched and nodded my head while Jeff demonstrated the technique to me. We exchanged equipment, and I stood in front of the door, bent over in a crouch and stared out at my friends.

"Ready, Paulie? Jeff asked.

I said, "Yeah, yeah, yeah, go ahead youse guys . . . shoot one."

Jeff lined the puck up and shot it with his stick. I watched as the puck took off and it headed on an edge towards me. I took my stick and waved at the puck, but I missed it. The puck hit the door behind me, bounced off, rolled past me, and towards Jeff.

"Score!" Jeff yelled out as he smiled at me. "Ya are

supposed to stop it, Paulie."

I nodded my head, but I had already realized that this was not as easy as it looked. Jeff shot another one, with the same result. I reached for it with my stick, but I fanned on it. Jeff's shot hit the door behind me once again.

Now, I was feeling frustrated. I bent over low while I stared with my eyes forward and set my feet firmly. The puck had rolled back to Jeff, and he was ready to shoot once more.

I was ready too.

Jeff swung, and he hit the puck solidly. The puck rose a little off the street and I followed it as it flew towards me. I watched the puck as it approached; I stuck my leg out and bent down to block it. When the puck was close, I put my stick out to block it and, "CLUNK" the puck hit my stick, and rolled away from me.

"Hey, nice save, Paulie, that was great! Ya first save ever! Now ya got the hang of it!" Jeff shouted out.

"Let me try one," Harry shouted.

Jeff passed him the puck. Harry lined it up and he let the shot go. This time I was crouching a little lower and as the puck came to me, I caught it in the baseball glove. I tossed it back out to Jeff. This time, Jeff shot a harder blast that when I tried to block the puck with my stick, I missed it entirely. The puck then caught me right on the lower shin bone of my leg and bounced off.

"Ouch! Oh, geez, man! Shit . . . that hurts!"

I doubled over and jumped around on the street from the pain of the shot. I understood now what they meant, that being a goalie was a little rough!

"Are you all right there, Paulie? Real goalies have leg pads, ya know!" Jeff informed me of that interesting tidbit that he had previously neglected to mention to me.

I continued to jump around a little as Harry laughed at my pain. I refused to rub the sore spot while I was in front of my buddies, but it sure hurt like hell.

"I am good. I am fine. Hey, go ahead and take another shot."

I stood back in front of the door, crouched a little lower, and waited for a shot to come my way. Harry worked the puck on his stick, aimed and swung his blade hard into the wooden missile.

"Bang!"

The puck sailed towards me.

Low, hard, flat and fast.

It was gliding fast along the street and I measured it, kicked my foot out and knocked the puck away with the side of my foot, as I did a little split.

"Wow! Paulie, you are good at being a goalie! That was a great stop and a great shot by Harry!"

Jeff was excited about our performances. The force of the shot and the split that I had performed had knocked me on my backside. I laughed as I rolled over on the cold, hard ground.

I stood back up and I smiled.

My first saves, and I had to admit this was fun. It felt good, as though I was supposed to be playing this game at this time in my life. The three of us shot the hockey puck for hours until it became so dark that we could no longer see that well. I made some saves and Jeff and Harry scored quite a few too. We were all having a great time, and our skills at shooting and playing goal were slowly developing. The game was not an easy one, and I found out several times that the puck was hard and that it hurt.

The one streetlight in front of Harry's house did not provide enough light, and it was time to go home for dinner anyway; therefore, we quit for the night, with the promise to continue after school tomorrow.

I jumped on my bike, strapped my goalie stick on the frame, and said goodbye to my buddies. I rode my bike home with a satisfied feeling.

I loved being a goalie. It was very hard to explain, but I

felt different.

I felt exhilarated, challenged, and in control.

That night when I washed up, I fingered a large bruise and bump that was forming on my leg where the puck had hit me. It was very red, sore to the touch, and swelling.

This goalie stuff was rough, but I knew that I was up to the task. I came from a long bloodline of tough guys, both on my mother's side and on my father's side. My lineage stretched from one side of the Atlantic Ocean to the other, and being a patsy ass was not part of my equation.

Little did I know at the time how this day would change and shape my entire life. This was, in fact, just the first bruise of so many more to come in my goaltending and hockey adventures. I did not know at that time, while I studied the welt on my leg, of how far this afternoon's adventure was going to take me in my life.

But then again, life is one big mystery and we never know what waits around the corner for any of us.

I ran my hand over the sore spot and the rapid, swelling red welt on my leg, and I smiled. It sure hurt like hell, but there was something about it that, despite the pain, made me feel a lot better. It was very hard to explain, but I could tell that I was going to be a goaltender. I leaned back in my bed and sighed, while all the time still staring at the red welt on my leg.

The first save had been the hardest, but then again, I was up to the task.

I just knew that I was.

2

The Birth of the Haledon Hockey League

Ever since our first rudimentary shoot around on John Street, the hockey bug had bitten all of us.

It bit us all very hard.

Hockey was all that we talked about, and it even inspired the three of us to make a very rare appearance at the local library, not to do any schoolwork or homework, there was no way that we would show up for something unheard of such as that! No, in lieu of the pursuit of good school grades, we did instead find a few hockey books, and the research began in earnest on the rules, star players of the past and present, and virtually every other aspect of the game.

When I could sneak the television away from the old man, I would tune in a New York Rovers hockey game, live in black and white, from the garden ice rink in the big city across the river. The New York Rovers hockey club was the local team for most hockey fans living in the Tri-State area of New York, New Jersey, and Connecticut.

At first, it was difficult to follow what was going on with the fast action on the ice, but after watching for a few games, the rules became clearer to me.

I found myself watching the puck and studying the goaltenders while they crouched in the goal. I watched their every move and tried my best to imitate their styles. By watching and studying, the intricacies of the position became clearer to me. I realized that there was a lot more to playing the position than just having the courage to stand in front of the blazing puck while it hurtled towards you. First off, you needed to be a little stupid to stand there in front of the puck. Nevertheless, after that, there was a bit more to it!

There was a science to it, part geometry, and part anticipation, as well as a lot of skill. Of course, these goalies were playing on ice skates. We only had work shoes and sneakers, but one-step at a time.

Virtually every Saturday night during the hockey season, there was a New York Rover game broadcasted live on channel nine out of the city. I began the tradition of settling in (once the old man had fallen asleep in his chair, or he had given up on television) and taking control of the channel selection to watch the hockey games. My dear mum would try to watch the game for a time with me, but she began a tradition that became more important for me.

"I cannot follow the little black thing, Paulie. What do you call it, the puck?" I nodded and Mum continued, "Yes, the puck thing. It goes all around the ice rink so fast it makes my head spin. What is the icing rule again?" Mum was asking and commenting while sitting next to me. She was working very hard at trying to follow the game.

"That is when they shoot the puck all the way from one zone to the other and it crosses the other goal line without a touch or even a chance to touch it, Mum," I explained.

Mum shook her head and said, "Oh, my. It is a bit much. Soccer is so much easier. I bought a frozen Tree Pub pizza today at the Foodworld. Would you like me to heat it up for you as a snack while you watch the game?"

"Sure, Mum. That would be great!"

The Tree Pub was a famous tavern in downtown Paterson, close to the city hall, right smack, dead center of downtown in the city. The restaurant was famous for their pizza, and when the popular pizza eventually went to a line of frozen pizzas, they were a tremendous success. For a frozen pizza, they were great! The famous logo of the tavern was on the box and it depicted a maple tree with full, green foliage and a large, brown trunk. In fact, it was the same logo, which hung over the entrance to the restaurant! The pizza had a nice crunchy crust, tangy sauce, and thick cheese. I loved them!

In addition, the Tree Pub had a sentimental place in dear Mum's heart. It was where my mother and father went on their first date together!

In such a simple manner, a wonderful tradition began of me watching hockey games on a Saturday night on channel nine in our living room at 182 Belmont Avenue, and Mum preparing me a frozen Tree Pub pizza!

Simple, but fantastic memories.

While our hockey craze blossomed and our studies of the real game improved, the three of us continued to shoot and pass our hockey pucks around here and there, both after school and on the weekends. We had a good time, and I noticed as the days went by, our goaltending, puck handling and shooting skills quickly grew more accurate and skilled. I also acquired some more goaltending skills along with a few larger welts on various parts of my body.

Jeff had downplayed it just a bit when he told me that playing goalie was a little rough. It was just a bit more than a little rough.

As October slowly gave way to November, and we wore heavier coats and jackets because of the colder weather, I quickly learned that it was nice to have a layer or two of added protection on my body! Even though I generally disliked wearing heavier coats, I happily wore my old winter jacket when I played goalie, since it absorbed the impact of the hockey puck rather nicely.

It was a cold, Saturday in early November, with a whistling wind and overcast sky, when Jeff made the fateful suggestion and created a plan, which would change our hockey careers and, sometimes, or perhaps, more accurately, our lives, for a very long time.

Jeff had met Harry and me while we stood in front of his house at 30 John Street. As usual, we had our hockey sticks with us, and I carried my baseball glove, an old work glove, and my now very trusty goalie stick. Part of this new plan came as the result of Harry accidentally blasting out the window of his brother-in-law's brand-new Rhino Model 10 Super Glide automobile. George "The Big Spike" Pinia was none too happy with Harry, when a hockey puck went awry as Harry shot around in front of his house one night.

In the interest of self-preservation, Jeff piped up, "Hey, let's go over here in the dead-end over on Geyer Street near the mill. Do ya know where I mean? In front of the lip lady's house and shoot around. That way, we will not blow out any car windows. It is Saturday, and not many trucks go into the loading dock to make any deliveries. First, youse guys have to see what I made with some old wood I found in the garage. I need youse to help me carry them, too."

We followed Jeff into his garage and watched while he handed us four wooden posts made of four-inch-by-four-inch scrap lumber. On the bottom of the posts were flat wooden pieces to act as a base.

Jeff explained his new idea.

"These will be our nets. If we can get some more of the guys to play, then we can have a full game. We will set posts up at each end of the street and we can make our own rink. They stand upright like football goalposts, and if you shoot the puck between them, it is a goal. I found this junk wood, and I made them this morning."

I circled in and studied the posts that Jeff had made and complimented him on the idea.

"Nice, Jeff. Great idea and I like the idea of playing over on Geyer Street because it will give us more room to shoot around."

Harry nodded his head in agreement while studying the

new posts. We picked the posts up, along with our gear, and headed toward Geyer Street.

Geyer Street was a small street that ran from Cook Street, past an intersection with John Street, and then continued on to an ugly dead-end located in the loading docks of the nearby lace and dye mills. There were only a handful of houses on Geyer Street and one business.

On the corner of Geyer Street and John Street was the famous Andy's Provision store. It was a sausage and meatpacking factory. It was on the corner forever, and you could look inside of the side doors and front door on the hot summer days and see the crew grinding up meat and making sausages in long links out of the machines. The owner of the factory would primarily sell his products wholesale to restaurants, but he would open the factory up on Saturday mornings for a short time, in order to sell directly to the public.

We tried our best to stay away from Andy's Provision store for several reasons. One, it did not smell so good on hot days, especially around the rear of the factory, and number two, was that the area in and around the factory had some of the world's largest rats that we had ever seen!

By far, the most famous resident of Geyer Street was an older lady whom we had lovingly (actually, not so lovingly) christened with the nickname of, "the lip lady." I do not think anyone in the entire neighborhood could remember or even knew her real name. For no other reason other than that we were mean and generally stupid kids, we called her that name because she had a large lower lip and spoke with some type of lisp.

As I said, we were stupid kids!

The lip lady lived in the last house on Geyer Street, right before the loading dock entrances. She worked in downtown Paterson, and if I can recall correctly, she worked in a bank on Main Street. She did not drive, and she took the city bus to work every day.

You would see her step off the number fourteen bus at the corner of Belmont Avenue and John Street, and she would slowly walk the few short blocks to her home on the dead-end of Geyer Street. The lip lady had a nice house; it was set back from the road a bit, with a large farmer's porch, a large front yard, and a fence along the entire frontage of her property. That fence played a large role in our plans for the hockey rink that we were about to set up at the dead-end of Geyer Street. She also had an old chicken coop in her yard, although the chickens were long since gone. One of the most unusual features of the property was that it had old, wooden water troughs set into the ground, crisscrossing her front yard. They had, at one time, supplied water and feed to the chickens while they wandered all over the property, in a long, bygone era.

Occasionally, a homeless guy lived in a cardboard box covered with a wooden roof of "borrowed" warehouse pallets at the very end of Geyer Street. He had his humble abode tucked into a far corner of the dead-end, under a tree towards the turn for the loading docks. He was not always there, but when he was, he just sat in the box in a drunken stupor and competed with the rear loading dock areas of Andy's Provision store to see who, or what, could smell the worst.

"Put 'em right here, youse guys. This way, we have the one streetlight on the street in case we want to shoot around when it is dark. We have the lip lady's fence on one side and the rich guy's garage on the other. We have sideboards to check and play the puck off of." Jeff explained while he was pointing and instructing us to where he thought we should place the posts.

Harry and I dropped the posts and studied where Jeff was pointing, and we both agreed that he had chosen the best location. By centering the posts between those two locations under the streetlight, we had indeed made a nice rink. It was just the right length; the width was perfect, and we had the fence on one side and the garages on the other. The garages would prove to be the perfect sideboards to contain the puck and sustain play. You could even use the garages to check an opponent into and give them a solid hit, too. Similar to how they did on a real hockey rink!

The rich guy to whom Jeff referred was a mysterious figure in our neighborhood circles. He was a well-dressed elderly man, who showed up occasionally, and he would open the garages located directly opposite the lip lady's house. Stored inside the garages were old automobiles, including a Model T vehicle, and other fancy, preserved old automobiles of various types, makes, and models. We surmised that he was a rich guy, since he brought along another chap who seemed to be his assistant, or maybe even his butler.

They seldom spoke to anyone, but they would arrive in a black Galaxy 5000 car, similar to the car that the famous mobster Mr. Sal Zucchini would ride around in during one of his rare public appearances in our neighborhood. His assistant would pop out of the driver's door, run around to the rear passenger's door and let the rich guy out. The assistant would pull the Galaxy 5000 inside the last garage and the two of them would stay inside the garages to check out the automobiles. On the rarest of times, they would pull one of the cars out of the garage to either wash the car or go for a ride in it. It did not happen often, but they would show up once in a while.

We also found out the hard way that the garages utilized all kinds of burglar alarms!

We set the posts up, took out our sticks and pucks, and started to shoot around. It worked out very well, with two exceptions. One, a miss of the goal posts, meant a long trip down the street to retrieve the puck, and two, it often was difficult to tell if you had shot the puck between the posts or not. Certain angles deceived you, and without a net behind you to capture the puck, arguments of goals scored became normal.

Nonetheless, it turned out much better than we had expected, and the occasional truck or car that drove through, only resulted in a minor stoppage of play, while we picked up the posts and moved players and posts aside until the vehicle drove by us.

Therefore, it began, a simple dead-end street stuck in a gritty, urban neighborhood became a hockey rink of sorts for three streetwise guys and the best was yet to come!

There we stood, all of us, with hockey sticks, makeshift work gloves for hockey gloves, work boots and sneakers on our feet, standing in a frigid wind on an early Saturday afternoon, in late November.

There was Big Wex, Tags, Jeff Porter, Johnny the Cho, Ray Edelski, Big George, Handsome Mike the Italian kid, Harry and me. We were standing there organizing teams and squads to play our first official street hockey game on Geyer Street. We had spoken about the sport of hockey so much at school that we had successfully lured the rest of our gang into giving street hockey a try.

"I watched the Rovers games just like you and Porter told me about there, long-haired Henson. I know how to play the game. Let's stop talkin' and start shootin'. I like the fights the best, so I cannot wait to start so I can kick some of ya asses," Big Wex stood in the middle flexing his muscles and displaying a substantial body mass.

Big Wex was a huge kid. He had flaming red hair, a large head sitting on a huge frame, but he was a hilarious guy who actually had a great personality. However, when it came to taking part in any games of sport, whether it was football, baseball, basketball, or now hockey, Big Wex would become a little mean and overzealous.

He was fiercely competitive.

We were all friends, but whenever frustration would creep in, Big Wex would ignite his fuse! We mostly ignored his obscenity-laden rants and raves, and his usual swings and misses at us; we knew we could outrun him! He rarely messed with Harry, Big George (who was actually the biggest kid in our whole group) or me, we were actually taller and stronger than he was, but Jeff occasionally, would be a target for Big Wex and one of his tirades. Another interesting thing about Big Wex was that, despite his larger size, he was a very gifted athlete, and he was surprisingly nimble on his feet.

The most gifted athlete in our group was Johnny the Cho. Everyone had nicknames in our neighborhood, and I mean everyone! "The Cho" came from an adaptation of his last name, and often we just called him "Cho." Johnny could play any sport well. He was a solid baseball player, a brilliant ball handling guard in basketball and a shifty little wide receiver in football. I had no doubts that he would be just as skilled at playing hockey!

"Youse guys line your bicycles up in the back of the posts. They may stop the puck from rolling all the way down the road when we miss. All right, I think because the street is not very wide, we should divide into three teams. We can play one goalie, one defenseman, and a winger. We will only play with a centerline that will be offside, so there is no net hanging," Jeff explained, while he organized the teams.

Of course, one team ended up being Harry, Jeff, and Paul John Henson. Another team was Johnny the Cho, Big George, and Handsome Mike the Italian Kid. The last team was Big Wex, Ray Edelski, and Tags.

We all shot around for a long time to warm up and to determine if we even remotely knew what we were doing.

In short order, it was quite easy to see that we did not know what we were doing!

Pucks were flying all over the place, guys were ducking right and left, pucks were pinging off the rich guy's garage, guys were jumping around in pain holding various painful body parts when one or two shots nailed a foot, shinbone or hand, but the more we moved around, the better we played.

One aspect we established right away was that street hockey was not for the faint of heart!

Ray Edelski was a student of all sports. He was, in many ways, the stereotypical coach or manager in his appearance and mannerisms. He always had a clipboard in his hand and he usually sported a pencil, tucked in his ear with which he was always drawing up plays or defensive schemes. He wore his blonde hair long; he had thick eyeglasses with a wide band to hold them on his head, and he was both soft-spoken and well spoken. He was very knowledgeable on a variety of subjects, a good organizer, and he, unlike the rest of us street dummies, remained very level-headed. Ray might have been overzealous with his constant organizing and coaching, and it could wear a bit on your nerves, but one thing that no one would deny was that Ray was a really nice guy.

Ray, feeling the natural need to organize, asked, "We need team names for our group youse guys. We will be the Rovers. How about your team, Johnny?"

Johnny thought about it for a few seconds, turned, and spoke with his teammates and then said, "The Golden Blades!"

It was our turn, and Jeff did not hesitate when he blurted out, "We are the Geyer Street Guys!"

"Nice!" Ray nodded his head in an agreement with our selection. He then made the fateful statement to last all of our lives, "Welcome to the Haledon Hockey League, men, and the first game at Geyer Street Gardens!"

Oh, yeah!

Geyer Street Gardens. The words had a nice ring to them!

The first game began, and the Geyer Street Guys sat the first game out. We would play the winner of the first game. Jeff was the referee for the first game since he knew the rules better than most of us – he became the logical choice. Ray agreed to study Jeff, and then Ray would referee the next game.

There was only one problem, since we had very little equipment; actually, all the poor goalie had to wear for protection, consisted of a work glove, a baseball glove and a stick. Perhaps, because of the limited protection, no one other than me wanted to play the goalie position. I was the only one of us who had an actual goalie stick, and very quickly, the role of playing the goaltending position turned out to be slightly unpopular. A few dings on the knees, a few puck "pops" in the feet, legs and arms, were generally enough to convince you that playing offense or defense was safer.

No one wanted to be a goalie – with one exception. I could not wait my turn to stand in front of the posts!

Big Wex finally conceded to play goalie for one team, and Handsome Mike reluctantly ended up in the net for the Blades. I was surprised that Handsome Mike would risk a nick on his handsome face (he really was a good-looking kid, hence his nickname!) but he rather became a goalie by default.

The first game went well. It had some goals, some minor elbows thrown up a bit too high, a few strategic pushes, some angry shoves and a few minor injuries, but by the third period of the game, it seemed as if we knew what we were doing.

Then again, perhaps, we were just very good pretenders.

Big Wex was into the game, he ranted, and raved and carried on, complaining about every penalty or call that went against his team. Predictably, Johnny the Cho turned out to master the feel of the game rather quickly and he scored a few goals to lead his team to victory.

Now it was our turn!

Some warm-ups for me, some shooting around, and we were ready to play. The Geyer Street Guys versus the

Golden Blades. Our first game together. We started well; I was hot in the net, making a few good saves and feeding the puck out to Jeff, who slipped one or two behind Handsome Mike.

Unfortunately, the game would not last very long. Harry parked his big body in front of me and he was trying hard to strip the puck away from Johnny, but he was really just blocking my view!

I was about to receive a hard lesson in what would become my nemesis in hockey, or more accurately, it is the nemesis of all goalies, a shot known as the screen shot.

I heard, but I could *not* see, Johnny the Cho hit the puck solidly, and I spotted Harry jump out of the way to miss the rising slap shot. At the last second, I caught sight of the wooden missile; it was flat in the air and rising high and fast. I was about to learn another very serious lesson: that catching sight of a hockey puck at the last second was not the most effective way to play the position of goaltender. You tend to block the shot with the incorrect body parts.

While I leaned in searching to find the puck in and amongst the maze of bodies blocking my view, the puck hit me square in the forehead.

BANG!

That was all that I remembered.

The next thing that I recalled was the voice of Johnny the Cho apologizing to me and I woke up to Jeff holding an old tee shirt on my face.

The day was very cold, but my face was warm, which proved to be another lesson in what was turning out to be a very educational afternoon. I came to realize that the warm feeling was always a terrible sign. The warmth came from a solid stream of blood pouring out of my head.

"Hold this tight on your head, Paulie. Push it hard into your head and hold it. Big Wex, get a handful of that old snow over in that pile. Dig down inside so you get some clean stuff," Jeff was administering first aid, while the rest of the Haledon Hockey league stared in on me sitting on the ground.

I was a bloody mess. Literally a bloody mess.

Big Wex handed me the snow, and I took it out of his glove, pulled the tee shirt away and pushed the cold snow into my face.

The snow quickly turned red with blood.

"Ah shit, Paulie, you got this big hole in ya head, with blood gushing out of it, too! Your old man is going to kill ya! I wonder what is gonna hurt worse after he sees ya? Ya head, or ya ass," Harry said as he looked at my face.

That was not what I wanted to hear. Harry had a special way of delivering a roundabout message of doom and discouragement.

I held the snow on the cut for as long as I could stand the pain, and then I tossed the red mess aside.

I looked up at the guys and asked, "Is it bad, youse guys? Do I need stitches?"

Johnny the Cho nodded his head and Big George offered the best assessment of the situation, "Hell yeah. Better yet, ya might need a new damn head there, Paulie. I bet that hurts like a son of a bitch."

It did.

This game was over for now. We suspended play because of the near death of the goalie.

Harry and Jeff gathered up my gear. The guys scattered and jumped on their bikes to head home. As much as they sympathized with my plight, no one wanted to stick around and witness the carnage that was sure to follow.

"Good luck there, Paulie, hopefully your old man does not give you too red an ass along with the mess youse got on top of your head," Big George shouted encouragement, as I slowly walked home with Jeff and Harry helping me hold the blood-soaked rag on my head.

One-step inside the back door of my house was enough to send my poor mum into shock.

"OH NO! WHAT HAPPENED NOW?"

It was a cry that I was about to become very used to as the years and games progressed onward.

"I am okay, Mum. The puck hit me in the head and I have a little cut."

Jeff explained, "We tried to stop it, Mrs. Henson. We put snow on it and Ray's old tee shirt, but it won't stop bleeding."

Mum rushed over and waved for me to take my hand away so that she could examine the cut.

She shook her head and sighed, and then she commented on the situation, "Snow and an old, dirty tee shirt. Oh my, that sounds just wonderful. Let me see here . . . oh no! This cut will not stop bleeding. Thank you, Jeff and Harry, for bringing him home and doing the best that you could. I will take it from here, boys. Thank you."

Jeff and Harry looked around; they breathed a deep sigh of relief that my old man was not home from work yet. They inched closer to retreat, and they made their first steps towards an escape out the back door of my house. I did not blame them. After all, it was in the name of self-preservation.

"Come along now. Let us see if Dr. Salami is still in his office. He might still be open, otherwise, we will need to take the bus to downtown Paterson and bring you to the emergency room at Saint Joseph's Hospital. Wait until your father gets home from the shop! Oh, boy!"

I shuddered at the thought, but at least the old man worked on Saturdays to make a little extra money, and he was not here *right now* for me to face the wrath.

Jeff and Harry bid me farewell and good luck, and off we went, across the street to Dr. Salami's office. Luckily, Dr. Salami had his office across the street from our house. His office was on the corner of Belmont Avenue and Burhans Ave. He had moved in a few years ago and had a successful medical practice. His building was an old, brick building that had the obligatory, second floor office complete with a winding wooden staircase, and the building smelled as if they bathed it in mothballs.

He was from somewhere in the Middle East. He was tall, round, and had a wide smile and dark mutton chop sideburns.

The good doctor was a nice guy. If you met him on the street or in the corner store, he would always stop to say hello, shake your hand, (even if you already knew him!) while smiling and saying, "Hello, I am Dr. Salami" in his charming accent.

We hustled across Belmont Avenue, with me still holding the old tee shirt of Ray's over my cut, the blood dripping from the wound as if it was a little faucet.

Usually, in New Jersey, no self-respecting driver would ever allow you to cross the main road unless it was a red traffic light. Even then, you could stand a chance of them mowing you right over and making a pancake out of you. Unusual compassion set in as Mum waved to the drivers of multiple cars, whose drivers saw her holding this stupid kid up with a bloody rag on his face, and rather than speed up and aim for us, they actually stopped and allowed us to cross the road.

Now, I finally knew the secret to crossing Belmont Avenue! You just have to fake that you are dying!

We were in luck! Dr. Salami was still in his office.

Up the stairs we went, Mum guiding me along the way, and when Mrs. Salami (who worked the front desk for her husband) spotted us, she jumped up from her chair with a loud, "Oh, my!" She then waved for us to follow her.

"Come along, Mrs. Henson! Please put Paulie in this room here. I will get my husband to break away from his patient right away. It is just Mr. Quigley in there with his usual trapped gas troubles."

Poor Mr. Quigley, the entire neighborhood, knew of his trapped gas maladies.

The entire waiting room filled with old ladies with silver and blue hair, bored husbands, and sniffling and screaming kids, grew quiet. The sight of a bloody goalie had stopped them all in their tracks.

Nothing like a little blood and guts to break the monotony of the boredom of Doctor Salami's waiting room.

I heard some little squirt kid say, "That big kid has a giant hole in his head, Mom!"

For a moment or two, I felt somewhat special.

"Hmmm, maybe you should wear a mask like all goalies do when they play hockey, Paulie. Better yet, try soccer, as Gramps suggested."

I nodded at the good doctor's comments as I watched Dr. Salami zoom into my head with a long needle.

"I am not pulling punches. This is going to hurt really, really badly. I first need to numb the area before I stitch it, but hey, after getting knocked around by that puck, it may not be too bad at all."

"Let's see, twelve bucks for stitches. How many did Salami put in your noggin'?"

"Twelve, Dad."

"Damn! A buck, a stitch! Plus, that bum Salami soaked me for an office visit too. Wow!" The old man was scanning the bill from Dr. Salami as he glanced at my head while we sat at the kitchen table.

He continued on his rant, "This hockey stuff is going to cost me a fortune! Next time, duck will ya! You had better go lie down in your bed now. You look a little blue. Joanie, give him a three-finger pour of Big Boulder beer. You need a little protein. Remember, stay away from those stupid Dingleberries. They are way too sweet and give ya a wicked ass hangover."

The old man was coaching Mum on giving me a "pain killer."

"Oh dear, Paul, he is too young for beer," Mum

protested.

"Nah, nah, nah! Give 'em the glass. It won't hurt the kid. Geez, he has a big hole in his head. I will do it!"

The old man took a small glass; held three fingers stacked up next to the glass and measured out the beer while he poured it into the glass.

He then pushed it over to me and said, "Swig that down and get ya wounded, lardass into bed. Don't be listenin' to hockey games all night either. Ya need to rest! I swear there is no rest in any of youse guy's asses these days."

The old man was giving me a free ride! I better take advantage of it and beat it out of here before he changes his mind.

I nodded and sipped down the beer.

It tasted cold and really good.

Slowly, I stood up, put the glass in the sink, and waved to my parents.

I dressed for bed, pulled back the sheets and moved my faithful fox terrier, Skippy; gently out of the way so that I could slip under the covers. Skippy looked up and seemed to do a double take. I guess the big bandage on my head took him a little by surprise.

"Yeah, yeah, yeah, it hurts, Skippy," I mumbled.

I reached over to the little shelf next to my bed and grabbed the headphones for my trusty shortwave radio. Despite his instructions to me, the old man already knew that I would tune in a hockey game. He would forgive me. I clamped the cans over my ears, flipped the on and off switch to "on" and I sat back. I always kept the radio tuned to the station for the New York Rovers games, unless it was Saturday night, when I tuned in Hockey Night in Canada. I leaned back when I heard the whispers of the game in my ears, and I put my head on the pillow.

Man, oh man, my head throbbed.

The announcer cranked it up, "Welcome hockey fans from far and wide, from wherever you might be listening to this evening! Welcome to the garden in the big city, for tonight's game between the New York Rovers and the Philly Comets. It is a packed house tonight in the garden, for this matchup between these two bitter rivals. Rumblehowser is in the net tonight for the Rovers."

I smiled, touched the bandage on my head, and jumped a little at the pain. I thought, 'I bet old Rumblehowser has had a few stitches in his head too.'

Yes, now I was officially a goalie. A real damn wounded ass goalie, with the battle scars to prove it now too.

I leaned back on my pillow and smiled. I had arrived in the class of goalies, who could now count their battles scars and wear them as if they were badges of courage. I fingered the bandages and pressed them just a little to test the extent of the injuries.

Oh yeah, yeah, yeah, it sure hurt like hell, but I sure loved it! I loved all of it!

3

Number Twenty-seven

The next Saturday, I returned to playing hockey at Geyer Street Gardens. My head had healed to where Dr. Salami had pulled the stitches out on Friday. He also instructed me to not only keep my head down, but to keep the cut covered and rub some type of black goo on the cut to speed up healing, minimize the scarring, and take some redness out. The goo smelled as if it was motor oil, but it worked. It became an aroma that, as the years went on, I would grow very accustomed to smelling.

The old man howled and complained when he heard that Dr. Salami had charged ten dollars to remove the stitches, "Are you kidding me? That bum soaks me ten bucks to take out. What the hell he put in! All he did was clip at his head with some scissors. That's it! Next time, I am stitching the kid up myself. I did it in the military when Joe Jenkins cut his hand in a barroom brawl when we were in town on leave! He did not want to go to sick call, so I went and got a needle that we used on our socks and we worked. . .."

I rather gratefully listened to another old man war story to use later on in life when I might need it.

I accumulated a few hundred or so by now.

My head injury was the subject of some talking points at schools all week, as well as the topic of hockey, which had turned into an obsession for all of us. A few of the prettier gals in school, who we now kept just a little closer eye on these days, came over and offered some sympathy for my wounds. In their eyes, I was a tough guy. It seemed as if there was a little side benefit to this hockey stuff.

The plan on Saturday was to resume the game where we left off when the puck knocked a hole in my skull. The resumed game remarkably ended in a tie with three goals apiece.

I played fairly well, and I was not "puck shy" at all after my injury. I was just happy to make it through the game with no additional injuries or cuts.

We kept the game time by one guy watching the time tick away on a wristwatch. It was not very accurate, but mostly, it worked. We played three twenty-minute periods, and the debate raged on at the end of our game, whether or not to add an overtime period or not. We decided to leave it at a tie, and Ray Edelski wrote all the info down on a pad and awarded each of our teams a point each for one tie.

Ray was running the hockey operations and after the first game, we all huddled together and decided that Ray should be the "commissioner" of our league. We needed to have someone retain the statistics, standings, scores, and to serve as the final judge and jury on disputes. Ray Edelski, with his superior organizational skills, was the logical choice and the best man for the job.

The highlight of the day occurred when Handsome Mike the Italian kid, showed up for the second game. He was a little late; he missed the first game, and he arrived just before game time for the second game. He could not ride his bicycle down to Geyer Street because of what he brought with him.

Mike's old man dropped him off at the corner near Andy's Provisions, and we all watched in awe while he carried brand new "official" goaltending equipment with him to the game. He had a plastic face mask, leg pads, goalie gloves, and a goalie stick. Handsome Mike the Italian kid's mom, and dad were both schoolteachers, he lived in a different part of town, they drove nice cars and had a fancy house. I guess after my "incident," Handsome Mike must have told his parents the details of the blood and gore. After hearing of my fate, his old man spent the dough to protect his son's handsome face, and to save money on doctor and dentist bills.

Harry shook his head in disbelief and said, "Holy shit, youse guys. Handsome Mike has real goalie stuff. I guess when he saw Paulie's face get smashed in, he was afraid his handsome puss would end up as ugly as Paulie's face is."

That fact made me feel a lot better about *my* appearance. Harry had a valid point; after all, he had the nickname of Handsome Mike for a reason!

Handsome Mike and the Golden Blades had a major advantage now. It was a lot easier to stand in the front of the posts with the wide leg pads on and stop the puck. The pads covered a lot more of the net than bare legs did.

It was a moot point, but a point that we argued for a long time, all to no avail.

I knew that many wish lists for Christmas in a few weeks would have hockey equipment penciled in on them.

Make no bones about it—these were hard times. Finding some extra money for our families to buy their children some expensive hockey equipment was difficult, but when you grow up poor and tough, you become quite resourceful.

"Do you have any ice packs in the freezer, Mum?"

My mother turned away from the cooker. She stopped stirring her pot of stew and looked at me suspiciously. I could tell the entire world of hockey and goaltending injuries was wearing a bit thin on my mother's patience.

"Where do you need ice for now, Paulie?" Mum asked.

I pointed at my chest and then my legs. I thought it best not to say anything else.

"Paulie, go right now to your room and strip down to just your undershorts. I want to see exactly what has happened to you now."

"Oh geez, c'mon, Mum. It is just a bruise or two and I am too old for you to see me with no clothes on!"

"I did not say for you not to have any clothes on! Paul John Henson! I assure you that you do not have anything I have not seen before. I changed your diaper, you know! I am your mother, and I brought you into this world and I can easily arrange for your quick exit from the same!"

Mum folded her arms across her chest and pointed toward my bedroom. Just for good measure, she planted the dreaded wait until seed in my head.

"Wait until your father comes home from the shop!"

My sister, Dottie, looked up from reading her *Rebellious Teen World* magazine at the kitchen table and she smiled at me. Dottie was three years older than I was, but she knew I was defenseless now that Mum had used my entire name in providing directions.

My English heritage mum was generally not in a negotiating mood at times such as these. Dear Mum was a kind and gentle soul, but you had better not push her kindness too far and mistake it for weakness. She had inherited that traditional English toughness that had changed the face of the civilized world.

I complied with Mum's marching orders, went to my room, stripped down to my undershorts and waited. I stared at the giant red welt on my chest up near my collarbone, and then at the multiple red welts and bruises that dotted my legs. The game had gone well for my team and me, but that puck had a nasty habit of hitting in some terrible locations on your body.

I knew my goose was as good as cooked. I would have to give up hockey and play checkers with Gramps every afternoon. That really sucked, because Gramps would never cut you any slack, and he would relentlessly win game after game. He was the world's greatest checker player.

There was the fateful knock announcing pending doom at my bedroom door. Skippy looked up from his sleeping post on my bed and by the look in his eyes, it seemed as if he had sympathy for my plight.

"C'mon in, Mum," I solemnly mumbled.

The door opened and Mum directed her attention at the latest roadmap of hockey puck impacts. Seldom, if ever, did I hear my mother use obscene language or even some of the colorful, "English bad words" that my grandfather would use. In fact, Mum scolded Gramps whenever he used them around Dottie and me.

Mum gazed up and down at her son's body, shook her head and said, "That bloody awful bloomin' game!"

Wow! I qualified for two English bad words!

"Sit on the edge of the bed. I will be right back with the ice packs."

I had qualified for multiple ice packs! I felt honored.

Mum returned quickly, and she handed me the ice packs. I put one on my shoulder and the other one on the worst welt on my right leg. Mum sat down next to Skippy and stared at me.

"I can tell that you really enjoy playing this horrid sport. Why I cannot imagine, but you do. You have that look in your eyes. I can always tell what is going on with my son by the look in your eyes. They are a window into your soul. You love playing this stupid game. I do not want to discourage you, Paulie, but my goodness, you have certainly inherited your grandfather's courage and your father's toughness and stubbornness. This Handsome Mike the Italian kid . . . my goodness, how horrid! Is that what you really call him?"

I nodded my head while adjusting the ice on my chest and shoulder.

"That is awful to call him such names. I bet Harry came up with that one. Oh well, regardless, what kind of pads did his parents buy for him?"

"Well, they bought him all of them. Leg pads, a chest protector, gloves, arm pads, it is very expensive, Mum. We cannot afford stuff like that."

Mum stared at me and her eyes went down to the red welts on my left leg.

She offered some advice.

"Move the ice over to that one too, Paulie. Do you have a picture of what they look like?"

"Sure, here in this hockey magazine that I bought."

I dropped the ice packs and jumped off the bed. I reached under the corner of my mattress, pulled out a hidden magazine I had dropped my last fifty cents on, in order to buy, and handed it to my mother.

"Put the ice packs back on, Paulie," Mum said as she took the magazine from my hands. "Other young men your ages hide lewd magazines under their mattress and stare at naked females baring their breasts. My son, he hides hockey magazines and drools over goalie equipment. I bet you spent your lunch money on this instead of lunch too!"

I smiled because Mum caught me in her trap again!

"Is this chap here in this leather suit of armor with a mask on his face a goalkeeper, or is he some kind of bizarre goblin of sorts?"

"A goalie, Mum! Yup, he sure is! That guy is Rumblehowser with the New York Rovers! He is my favorite player. Youse guys have to see him play! Oops, sorry for the improper English. I mean, yes Mum."

Looking back, my mother realized that certain aspects of me would never change. She did not comment on my New Jersey slang. Mum studied the picture for a long time. She sighed, and then she handed it back to me.

She stood up and said, "Keep the ice on those wounds as best as you can until supper. Your father will be home soon from the shop. Make sure you wear a sweatshirt to cover all those bruises and marks up so that he does not see them."

Mum went over to my storage closet, opened it up and she moved some clothes around on the hangers. She took an old grey colored sweatshirt and an old pair of dungaree pants and tucked them under her arm. She smiled at me, closed the door, and left the room.

I looked at Skippy and he looked at me. I leaned back on my pillow and sighed. Skippy put his head down and went back to sleep. I guess Mum was going to keep this latest injury wave among the three of us! I flipped the power switch on my radio to "on" and checked for the sports news.

There should be a game on later.

I came home from school one day during the week and Mum was sitting at the kitchen table. My grandfather was sitting there with her, sipping a cup of tea. She had the old sweatshirt in her hands and the old dungarees sat on the table next to her. She had her sewing kit on the table and I could see an old quilt in the mix, too. The quilt was no longer a quilt. Mum had cut it up into various sections.

"Hello, Gramps, hello, Mum. Whatcha doin'?" Gramps frowned at my New Jersey, "speak."

I corrected it rather quickly.

"Hello, Grandfather and Mother. I see you are working on a project." Gramps smiled and chuckled, but he said nothing.

"I am. In an effort to save my son from ice packs, stitches, welts and other injuries, and perhaps, his father too, I have constructed, as best I could, a suit of quilted armor for you to wear in pursuit of that ridiculous position you insist on playing. Here, try all of this on. I cut an old quilt in sections, and I fabricated a chest and shoulder protector inside of this old sweatshirt. I also have sewn some leg cushions inside of the dungarees. It is quite thick, and I am sure it is not as fancy as, sorry Pop, but this is what they call the poor lad, Handsome Mike the Italian kid's equipment, but it is an improvement over what you have now."

"Handsome Mike the Italian kid, eh? That lad Harry must have concocted that rather obnoxious nickname for the young chap. If it is a true description, rather than just a precarious nickname of the sorts, it is no wonder they bought him all of that equipment. I guess they need to preserve his looks somewhat," Gramps observed between sips of his tea.

I smiled at Gramps and his observation and studied the sweatshirt and pants that Mum had handed to me. The inside of the shirt had a thick layer of quilt material sewn to the inside and, sure enough, the legs of the dungarees had the same. It was an instant hit!

"Thank you, Mum!"

I could not contain my enthusiasm for the new equipment. I could see that this would allow me to withstand the impact of a few dead-on puck shots and stand there in front of the posts just as a "real" goalie does.

I leaned in and gave my mother a kiss on her cheek.

"Why, that made it all worth it, Paulie. I hope we will save a bit of money on doctor visits and be able to buy you some proper equipment for Christmas. We will see."

I stood proudly in front of the posts for the next game. The puck hit me dead on a few times in the chest and many times in my legs, and while my poor man's equipment was not as fancy as Handsome Mike's was; but it did the trick! No welts and no ice packs! Thank you, Mum!

Bring the games on! Through ice and snow, cold and sun, we played and the Haledon Hockey League was in full swing! We had a few injuries here and there, nothing too serious; we had a few scuffles between us, and playing whenever snow covered all of Geyer Street was a blast!

The lip lady would stick her head out of the front door of her home, and she would yell at us for "Hanging on her fence," but we did not care. We apologized and played on!

November quickly became December, and soon, Christmas was closing in upon us. Playing hockey outside for endless hours in the cold weather proved as exhilarating as it was difficult for us. My old man gave us the suggestion to rub petroleum jelly on our faces to protect us from cold windburn and the sting of being outside for so long.

He told me, "Do it! It is an old military trick. Ya never felt cold, like when you catch guard duty on a cold winter night at Fort Totten on Long Island, New York. That wind off the ocean is rough in December and January. Ya freeze ya ass off and a lot more, too. Rub this here goo on your pusses and you will be good to go for a few more hours."

It was certainly good advice and another valuable lesson from my old man. Over the years, he gave me more of them than I can ever count.

Slowly, we all were transforming, changing, and the game had taught us valuable lessons. The fact that we organized this all on our own, we created structure and rules, and each of us earned a certain amount of toughness, paid off in our maturation. The toughness was the key point, because it was that aspect that turned into maturity, and contributed to what the game provided us emotionally, as well as physically. We were all turning into a rugged bunch of young men, who were at the peak of physical fitness too!

One Saturday night right before Christmas, the old man was sleeping in his chair and I was enjoying a Tree Pub pizza, while I was watching the New York Rovers on the television. The Christmas tree glowed in the dark, the old man's famous Christmas village was lit up, and it happily broadcasted the pending holiday to all of us, while it glowed there in the darkness.

The old man had worked hard at his part-time job during the day, and he had now earned the right to lift and enjoy a few Big Boulder beers, (he stayed away from

Dingleberry beer, since they were way too sweet) and he had dozed off.

My father was not much of a hockey fan; he did not follow the game or understand it very much. Since I became an incessant hockey fan, he would sit for a few minutes, watch here and there, and even occasionally ask me a few questions, but it was not his bag. Hockey was not very popular in northern New Jersey in the 1970s. It was more of a cult game, with an unusual following of blue-collar type fans.

The old man's love was baseball. He lived, breathed, and worshiped baseball. The New York Bugs were his team and nothing stood in the way of a Bugs game!

The old man stirred and stopped, snoring for a second. I looked over at him, and Skippy, who was begging for a pizza crust, looked over at him, too. He awoke and looked at us and smiled. He played with his hair a little and smoothed it out.

He was still half-asleep but mumbling to me, "Say Paulie, what number does that Rumblehowser goalie guy wear?"

"Well, Dad, Rumblehowser wears number thirty. Most goalies are number one or a number around thirty or forty. Why?"

The old man stirred and pushed the leg rest of his faithful chair closed. He yawned, rubbed at his eyes, stood up and stretched.

"Is he a bum?" He asked me.

"Nah, nah, nah, I mean sometimes he stinks, but he is my favorite player. Why do you ask?"

He then told me, "Oh, I just had a dream about you playing hockey. You were older, and you had a lot of equipment on. Real equipment, like ya, was a real goalie, just as Rumblehowser is. The dream was very vivid. I could see everything really clear. Must have been the beers I sucked down tonight. Anyway, you turned around, and the jersey had a number twenty-seven on the back."

The old man smiled, and then his smile faded. He seemed as if he was pondering something very deeply before speaking.

He gathered his thoughts and continued, rather calmly saying, "Damn dream was so clear. Must have been one of them, promonotions, or whatever they call 'em. So, I guess ya should be twenty-seven from now on."

I was now old enough in my life that I was quite used to my father's chronic mispronunciations of certain words; therefore, I knew what he meant.

The old man walked towards the kitchen. He stopped and smiled at me again, and he asked, "Youse guys winnin'?"

"Nah. The Comets are, Dad. Three to one, Rumblehowser stinks tonight. Like I said, it happens with him sometimes. He loses focus. Not one of his best games, Dad."

"Oh, hey, ya win and lose some along the way. Ya will learn that if ya stick with the game long enough."

The old man wandered off towards the kitchen. I heard the "pop" of a can of Big Boulder beer and a few laughs from the kitchen table as he and Mum chatted about something.

The experience, as well as the words of my father, stuck in my mind. For some reason, it seemed as if he was right on with something here with this strange vision in his dream.

It just felt right.

That night, I borrowed a black-colored marker from Mum's kitchen drawer, a marker, which she used to mark meat wrappers for the frozen section of our refrigerator, and I took it to my room. I pulled out my sweatshirt that had my chest protector sewn inside and flattened it out. While Skippy watched, I carefully wrote in big block numbers the figure, twenty-seven on the back of the sweatshirt. I then wrote my last name in block letters across the back top of the sweatshirt, right above my number. "HENSON."

Little did I know how far that little act, and my father's dream, would take me! My father had provided me with an identity, a nickname, and an additional persona all in one. Christmas morning that year brought me several wonderful gifts, but the one that sat perched under the tree and meant so much to me was a white, plastic goaltender's mask. It was a reasonable facsimile of the "official" mask that Rumblehowser wore!

I feverishly tore it out of the package, held it in my hands and turned it over and over, while studying it.

I was about to experience, for the first time, a wonderful, magical experience. I just did not realize it at the time.

I placed the goalie mask on over my head while my parents snapped picture after picture of me wearing it. I stood there as if I was some kind of dope, feeling as if I had graduated to the big time! In the pictures, you cannot see the smile on my face underneath the mask, but I assure you it was there.

An ear-to-ear smile.

The tag on the gift read, "To Paulie. Love Mom and Dad. P.S. The mask was cheaper than payin' that bum Doc Salami."

I recognized my old man's distinctive language.

That year, we filled our Christmas holiday from school with game after game, all of us sporting the new, fancy hockey equipment that we had received for Christmas gifts. Despite how poor most of our families were, they all must have saved their pennies, because it seemed as if all of our parents were apparently exhausted of the doctor's bills. After that Christmas, I think that Dr. Salami took a little hit on his total revenue.

There was no doubt that we all had taken hockey to a new level. We were all hockey players now, equipped with new sticks, new gloves, new pads, and a new ambition!

The trips to school once Christmas vacation ended included the very important ritual of "puck harvesting." We patrolled the neighborhoods for old Christmas trees that were tossed away to the curbs for trash removal. We carried a handsaw and a bucket with us, and we would cut the trunks off in the proper dimension and thickness to use as a hockey puck, and then toss it in the bucket.

All around Haledon, players of the Haledon Hockey League did the same thing. I bet the trash collection crews wondered why the ends of these trees had cut off trunks!

We carried our bucket full of "pucks" to school; we hid the saw and bucket in a secret location on the playground and then took them home after school. Our combined efforts gave us enough pucks to last the rest of the season! You tended to lose a puck or two here and there, and they would eventually chip, split and no longer be flat enough to be play reliably. Therefore, many pucks were required in our supply in order to last for an entire hockey season.

We played right through the winter, and the cold weather only added to the experience!

The coldest day or the heaviest snow did not stop us. Ice, wind, snow, cold, it was all the same to us. Out, on Geyer Street we battled on.

A bunch of frozen neighborhood kids with petroleum jelly rubbed on our faces—too dumb and too in love with the game of hockey to come in out of the winter. We did not care; it was what we wanted to do.

Attitudes towards snow, cold and inclement weather were a bit different back then. Certainly, then they are right now. People took it all in stride back then. It was just another day, not a cause for panic, or to stay inside and hide under your kitchen table, because the weatherperson on the television waved at a polar wind hurtling down from Canada.

In fact, we looked upon it as an exciting adventure. A

little snow or cold weather did not cause us to stay inside, hiding from the elements.

We grew up tough; we grew up rough, and there was no one who would ever dream of calling us soft! All the goaltenders in our league would agree though, a puck hitting your foot or toes on a freezing cold day. Well, it would send a few stars in your eyes, and sometimes, it was lights out! I would like to have a dollar for every time that I took my socks off after a hockey game, and one of my toenails came off with my sock.

Often on nights when we finished our homework early, Jeff, Harry, and I were shooting around under the lone streetlight on Geyer Street. There we were, shooting the pucks, laughing and practicing, until we were all in some serious trouble for staying out too late on a school night.

Time went by us rather quickly. When you are young, time seems to fly along all too soon.

Spring came, the weather moderated, and the hockey league was winding down. Soon, it would be baseball season!

The Golden Blades led our league in points. Johnny the Cho was a prolific goal scorer, and the Geyer Street Guys proved to be a good defensive team, but we could not score goals! We would lose two to one, or three to two, and seldom did we score more than three goals in a single game. Jeff was a great defenseman, Harry was a good player too, and I battled hard at guarding our net, but offense was not our strong point. We were much better at defense than offense. We sadly finished in last place for the first year, but we would be back!

The battle for winning the championship came down to the Rovers versus the Golden Blades, and the question finally arrived in all our minds. What award would the championship team actually receive?

As usual, when we required something creative, we depended upon the creative genius of Jeff Porter to solve the dilemma. "Real hockey" had the Stanley Cup, but we had the Tremont Cup! On the way home from school one day right before we had the championship game between the Rovers and the Blades, Jeff suddenly jumped to the side of the road, picked up an old, glass soda bottle, and he held it high in the air above his head. He was mimicking the hockey players that win the Stanley Cup when they parade around the ice rink, holding the trophy in victory.

"Look! Tremont soda, youse guys! This is perfect for the championship trophy. I will take it home, clean it up and it will be our trophy!" Jeff held the soda bottle from a famous, local, soda company in Paterson in his hands.

It worked for us!

Forever more in perpetuity, the champion of the Haledon Hockey league won the Tremont Cup, or in reality, their just reward for winning the championship in a hard-fought year was just an old glass soda bottle.

However, do not tell the Golden Blade players that won that first championship in a hard-fought victory over Big Wex and the Rovers that it was just an old soda bottle!

To us, and to them, it was anything but that!

4

Painting the Lines, the Spit Fight and Other Geyer Street Legends!

When you are young, the world moves at an incredible pace. Your eyes are wide open, the experiences of life come in droves, and you work as hard as you can to experience all you can. It sails by in a flash, and there are many who will say that this is the best time of your life.

I am not too sure.

In many ways, it is also what you make of every single day.

All too soon, a group of young, fledgling hockey players had turned into fourteen, fifteen-and sixteen-year-olds, who really knew how to play the game. We all eventually had injuries, after all, stitches, lost teeth, broken fingers, bumps, and bruises were all part of the game. We took it all in stride now; it became commonplace, a part of your hockey life.

We even branched out a bit, and when we saved some extra pennies, we bought ice skates and played pond ice hockey when the local ponds froze over. We also gave some roller hockey a whirl when a few of us had purchased roller skates. The old standby, though, would always be to return to playing street hockey in our work boots and sneakers on Geyer Street Gardens.

More equipment, more experience, a few new players here and there, but much of it was still the same from when we first started playing.

The lip lady would yell at us, "To stop hanging on her fence!" Despite her grouchy demeanor, I still secretly think she was quite lonely, and she enjoyed the hockey action, in addition to the company. I would often catch her sitting on her porch in her chair, rocking back and forth, while she watched us play the games in front of her home. I could have been wrong, but I think she even cheered a time or two, when she spotted an exciting moment, or a goal scored here and there!

As I said, I could have been mistaken, but somehow, I do not think so.

The rich guy would come by on a Saturday when the weather was pleasant, and he would pull his cars out of the garage. He would warn us when he pulled his expensive vehicles out of the garage to stop playing, as a precaution to prevent any puck damage to his precious vehicles. We would always call a timeout and wait until he was safely in the clear before resuming play. I am sure none of our parents had enough spare dough lying around to fork over money to repair any nicks, dents, or other damage to the expensive automobiles that he owned. Just the image of the licks that we would incur on our backsides from our parents if that ever happened was enough of an incentive to stop playing until it was safe to resume the game.

We had two major changes to our games from the initial startup. The first change occurred when we switched from using our deadly wooden pucks to a plastic puck made by one of the major hockey equipment manufacturers for the specific use in street hockey. The puck came in different versions, according to the outside weather temperatures, and while it speeded up the game and minimized damage to property and humans, it still packed a deadly force for the goaltenders. The new puck traveled at faster speeds than a wooden puck did, and because of the increased speed, it still inflicted serious pain and suffering for the goalies.

The second major change came when Jeff built wooden hockey nets. Harry and I helped him; we constructed them out of some scrap lumber we found in Harry's garage. We covered the wooden frame with chicken wire we "discovered" in the rear of the Gingert Lace factory.

Making a random "discovery" of various things in our neighborhood was a sugar-coated description of a much stronger word, much as we utilized kinder and gentler words such as "borrowing" or "reassignment." We did not use the word "stolen" in our neighborhood.

The nets made an enormous difference in our game, and no longer was a goal scored at a strange angle, sure to cause a wild dispute over whether it traveled through the scoring zone or not.

The three goaltenders for each team in our league now, mostly, had full equipment, although I still did not have enough money saved for a chest protector. I still gut it out on the chest region, since my old sweatshirt that Mum had sewn for me had long since worn out and I had outgrown it too. I wore the heaviest coat that I could stand for some protection and work boots on my feet to deaden the blow of the foot saves.

I saved my pennies, used the extra dough for real goalie pads for my legs, and wore my old mask, but I knew I was just a birthday, side gig, and part-time job away from more equipment.

Whenever a puck would strike it, I marked my goalie mask up just as they did in the professional ranks. I took a black marker and made a fake stitch on the face of the mask in the general location where the puck hit against it. Over the years, with more and more marks accumulated upon it, the mask resembled a Halloween monster! We called them battle scars.

The poor Geyer Street Guys were perennial losers. It always turned out to be that we just could not score goals! It would come down to a heated rivalry with the Golden Blades versus the Rovers, and Johnny the Cho and Big Wex became "on the rink" enemies. Johnny could twist a goalie inside and out with his puck handling skills, and although he did not possess a hard slap shot or wrist shot, he knew how to score around the net!

It was pure finesse with Johnny, especially when he was in tight around a fallen goalie. He could tiptoe his way in and around the net, and Johnny just had a special knack for tucking the puck underneath, or above the goaltender. Seldom, if ever, did he score from outside the crease area on a long shot. Johnny was, however, deadly accurate from close quarters.

I knew how accurate he was because he scored a ton of goals on me!

Another thing that had changed over the years was how we had all grown up. I was now tall, lean and lanky; my height approaching six feet three or thereabouts, and my arms and hands grew strong from constant exercise and carrying my heavy goalie stick around all the time.

My blonde hair with red highlights had now grown very long. It was now well past my shoulders and I had the faint growth of a wishful beard and moustache growing on my face. As far as my long hair went, well, I would take a little hair tie, grab it in a big ball and then I would tie it behind my head, pull my mask over the top of my head and hope no stray hairs crept into my vision path.

The old man was always hounding me constantly to shave my facial hair and trim my long mop of hair, but I had steadfastly refused. I had no qualms about being different, and goaltenders had the reputation for being oddballs, as well as more than just a touch eccentric. It seemed as if I fit the bill!

After all, you had to be a little crazy to play the position, where the risk was often not worth the reward. By now, the rest of the league accepted me as an odd, hippie goaltender and now took my rather intense and, often, eccentric behavior for granted. I became an intense student of the game, and while I was not a gym rat, I was working out constantly. I also never stopped studying geometric angles that shooters would take on the net, and I would always be refining and working to improve my goaltending skills continually.

The fact that I was tall, lean, and very quick on my feet turned me into a capable goaltender, and most of the rest of the league felt as if I was the best goalie that they had to face. I still felt that I could be a lot better, and I studied new techniques and new skills of professional goaltenders all the time, all in an effort to pick up tips in order to improve on my style.

Jeff, too, grew tall, lean, and strong. His long reach, combined with his fearless courage to make him proficient at shot blocking and defensive poke checks. Jeff was unbeatable when a shooter took him on with a one-on-one approach. Then he was impossible to get around with his long stick hanging on the end of his long arms.

Harry, well, he was Harry. He had grown up big, strong, and powerful. The best description of Harry's build was that of a fire hydrant. He was about six feet tall now, and solid as a rock, with huge legs and a powerful chest. No longer was it just Big George and Big Wex, who were the largest and strongest of our group. We had all caught up and, in some cases, passed them both by.

We were all growing up.

Jeff, Harry, and I, we did not take any lip from anyone. We may not have won too many, but no one pushes us around!

By far, the most contentious player in our entire league was Big Wex. He soundly disputed everything, and he would not hesitate to raise his fists up in anger when things did not go his way. Mind you, that Big Wex was a tough guy. He did not back down from anyone, and while he occasionally took his licks, he was still big, imposing, and fearless.

His chief nemesis in the world of hockey seemed to be

Johnny the Cho. It was amazing to me that although we were all very close friends, we could, and often would, turn into mortal enemies when playing against each other in a hockey game. Another fascinating aspect of all of this was how the meanest confrontation, laced with physical fights or verbal assaults, would all be forgotten the second we left the game behind us. We were truly hockey players; we assumed that it was typical hockey player behavior and all part of the game!

There was no doubt that Big Wex resented the fact that Johnny always seemed to win at most every game in which he played. Big Wex's anger would fester and boil. He watched all the professional games where hockey disputes commonly erupted with some fisticuffs and intimidation, and he would duplicate that behavior on the rink at Geyer Street Gardens.

One Saturday in late October, when we all were around fourteen or fifteen years old or thereabouts, Big Wex started one of the most disgusting, yet legendary incidents, in the entire history of the Haledon Hockey league.

This was an incident not for the faint at heart, nevertheless, all of these years later; I am hesitant to recall it here in the pages and annals of history. However, no true recanting of the Haledon Hockey league would be complete without mentioning this incident in graphic details!

On this afternoon, Big Wex's frustration with Johnny the Cho had reached the point of no return. The Golden Blades were scoring goals at will on this afternoon, and Big Wex could not stop a beach ball if it rolled towards him. All goalies have days such as these when you just do not have it and everything goes wrong.

Well, Johnny scored his tenth goal of the afternoon in the net behind Big Wex when Big Wex lifted his mask, swung his goalie stick in frustration at Johnny, and laid out a line of curse words a mile or two long.

Some of those words would make a sailor blush, and they still hang over Geyer Street to this very day. In a legendary tirade and parade of curse words, Big Wex called Johnny, as well as all of his living relatives, a few rather juicy words.

Since our team was waiting to play the winner of this game, Jeff was the referee for this game and Harry and I sat on the sideline waiting our turn. Despite the gruesome and disgusting language, we all laughed at the scene. Over the years, we were used to Big Wex's outbursts during games, but what he did next took it to a new level. Big Wex charged out of the net, swinging his goalie stick wildly at Johnny while spewing his descriptions. He chased Johnny the Cho a little, and when he could not catch him, he stopped, sucked in deeply and spit a disgusting blob of who knows what at Johnny. We all watched in disgust and horror while the blob hurtled through the air and "it" landed solidly on Johnny's jersey.

"You damn, rotten, disgusting pig!" Johnny reacted to the mess of sinus related goo, slowly sinking down the front of his hockey jersey.

The game was now on! Johnny the Cho charged Big Wex, and they tore into each other. Fists were flying right and left, more spit coming out of their mouths and a touch of blood on Johnny's face when Big Wex landed a blow to his nose.

I did not wait around for this one; Johnny was too small and clearly outmatched in the grasp of Big Wex. I ran into the melee, grabbed Big Wex and pulled him away, while still shielding him from Johnny, who was swinging in the air wildly in a vain defense.

I heard the lip lady cry out in horror. She ran from her chair onto the porch and into her home. She slammed the door and slid the deadbolt across the door.

It was indeed a little too much to take! I thought for a fleeting second that she ran inside to call the police, but right now, I turned my thoughts to rescuing Johnny the Cho.

Johnny was a player, he certainly was not a fighter, but he vainly held on and tried his best against the much larger young man! However, I knew that if I or someone else did not intervene that eventually, Big Wex would pummel poor Johnny into a bloody pulp.

As I held Big Wex away, he seemed startled at my strength, and he lifted his fists as if he was going to attack me, too. I held him around the waist, and in one motion; I hurled him violently to the ground. He hit hard, tumbled down head over teakettle, his equipment flying in all directions until he rolled to a stop.

The two players, two "friends," (off the rink but certainly not on it) had traded some serious blows. Johnny must have surprisingly also landed a blow or two because I could see a trickle of blood in the corner of Big Wex's mouth as he sat on his backside looking up at me.

I yelled, "All right, cut it out now! This is disgusting! Spitting at each other and beating each other silly!"

Big Wex from his backside position rolled his tongue and looked as if he was loading for a kill shot on me while I stood over him.

I stopped, pointed my finger at him, and said, "If I were you, Big Wex, then I would think long and hard about that one!"

Big Wex's face changed. He peeled back, and slowly got to his feet, and brushed off his pants and backside. I guess my size, confidence, and intimidation factor weighed heavily upon his decision to swallow the proposed projectile. That in itself was rather disgusting, but at least I did not have to resort to choking him. I was not a violent guy, but earned my reputation of being the one guy in our group who you did not want to test.

"Henson, ya are such a goody, goody. You are such a pansy ass! Ya had to run in and be the big sassy-ass hero and save Johnny," Big Wex spouted at me.

"Yeah, well, I am not the one who is sittin' on their big ass now there, Wex. You are."

Big Wex looked at me; he tilted his head and mumbled, "Yeah, yeah, yeah, I did not know youse was so strong, Paulie. Ya tossed me aside as if I was a tissue and I am now weighin' in at two fifty. Youse a strong son of a bitch for sure. I am sorry. That spittin' *was* disgusting."

Big Wex's massive ego took a hit, yet he gained respect, because he was man enough to admit that he had, for once, been knocked on his backside by someone bigger and stronger than he was.

I mumbled to him, "I did not think you would want to tangle with me today, Wex."

I turned to each of them and shook my head while saying, "This is disgusting. Look at both of youse guys. You have gob all over your jerseys and blood all over your faces. Each one of you would not back down. Someone, please, throw us a towel. I ain't touching youse guys to help clean ya off. Ray is going to have to decide on a penalty. The rule book does not cover spit fights. You should both be ashamed of yourselves."

I stood and pointed at each of the combatants. I felt some amount of preaching was in order. My thoughts were coming out, not to make them feel worse than what I could tell that they already did, but to put it all in some type of perspective.

I continued, "You both took the frustration to a new level. Geez, youse guys, yeah, yeah, yeah, we are playin' hockey and it is rough and tumble, but we are still all friends. I would think that above all, we ought not to forget that fact. It's okay to have a push, or a shove, or two and some words. Let's try to settle some differences 'bout a game, but we always need to remember that in the end, we are all friends. Someday, we will need to stand as a team together, so we better learn to get along now."

All the guys nodded their heads in agreement; it seemed as if my sermon had struck a chord with them.

Handsome Mike the Italian kid, tossed them both a torn towel he kept nearby, a towel that he used to keep himself handsome by wiping sweat down during the game. He had torn the towel in half and tossed a piece to each of the combatants. Johnny the Cho caught one end of the towel, and Big Wex grabbed the other one. I could tell that they both felt bad about how the argument had turned into a disgusting display of frustration and demeaning behavior.

While the two opponents cleaned up, and we checked them for serious damage at the bloody sites on their faces, as often happened with our group, it was Harry, who broke the tension with some laughter.

Harry laughed, and he commented, "That has to be the most disgusting display of anything that I have ever seen. Youse guys sure showed your bare asses, and it was not pretty either!"

Hmm . . . I thought that was a typical Harry M. Redmond Junior analogy, but it was indeed an accurate comparison.

Big Wex could not help but smile and then laugh too. Before you knew it, the entire league was rolling in laughter at the incident. Yes, it was disgusting, but it was in a roundabout way, hilarious too!

After a prolonged break, of which we all recovered from the spit fight fallout, Big Wex and Johnny the Cho both cleaned up and we waited for the ruling from Ray.

Ray continued to study the rules. After a careful study, Ray said, "Ah, what the hell, the penalties offset! Shake hands and let's finish the game."

It seemed to work. The two heavyweight champions shook hands, and play resumed. Forever more, the legacy of the spit fight lived on, and it took a good four or five hockey games to pass, before the lip lady regained her courage and reappeared back on her front porch.

"Tonight, is the perfect night, guys. It will get cold soon and we will be out of luck until next year!"

"I do not know, Jeff. I have a feeling that this is against the law."

"Ah, shit! There he goes again, Jeffrey, acting like an old lady. Twenty-seven is forever more, a helpless and hopeless victim of the Old Lady Syndrome. Never will change, I tell ya," Harry waved his hand in the air towards me, discounting my usual efforts at interjecting some type of logic, or even something as important, such as the law, into my argument against our latest scheme.

Jeff looked at me, dropped the paint bucket, roller pads, roller tray, and some paintbrushes down at his feet. He came over, put his arm around my shoulders and he tried hard to convince me to shift gears out of my old lady mode, "Look, Paulie . . . it is a dead-end roadway. No one goes there, except for warehouse workers, the rich guy and delivery trucks. What could happen?"

I had learned over the years of being friends with both Jeff and Harry, as well as a few moments with my old man, that those three words could have major implications. Three seemingly innocent words. Very simple words, forming a simple and direct question.

They were harmless.

Or, so it seemed, they were harmless.

It was as if they came directly from some wise Biblical prophet of old, or better yet, I could picture an old gypsy lady, with a rag over her head, waving her hands at her crystal ball, throwing magic pixie dust into the air and howling, "Oh well, what could happen?"

Meanwhile, the crystal ball on the table in front of her displays a reign of terror in its magnified and warped magical glass.

Despite Jeff's efforts to calm me, I knew better. I felt the Old Lady Syndrome would not allow me to concede defeat so easily.

Pondering our latest scheme for a moment, I needed to offer some more logic to my friends.

"It might be a dead-end . . . but it is still a public road. I do not think we should paint lines for a hockey rink on a public road. If we get caught defacing town property, it will mean the clinker for all of us! I know my old man will not spring for the dough to bail us out. And neither will your fathers either." I added just a sprinkle of reason to my apprehension, "We will miss the test on board feet in wood shop class on Monday! Mr. Brown will kick our butts too!"

When I mentioned school commitments at our vocational school, it seemed as if I crossed the patience line with Harry.

"Oh, shit, twenty-seven! For the love of Pete! Really, really, twenty-seven! Are you really being friggin' serious? With all the crime around here . . . drugs, murders, knife fights, gun battles in front of ya house, mobsters running numbers games, and beating the shit outta guys in dark alleys over by your house, you are gonna tell me that the police are looking for jerks like us who are painting lines on a street to make a hockey rink! A dead-end street that no one drives down, anyway. Where the only residents are the lip lady and a stinky guy who lives in a box, tucked in the center of urban warfare! C'mon Jeff, leave him here! We will paint the lines together."

Jeff looked at me and shrugged his shoulders. Harry grabbed the supplies, waved his hands in the air at me, and he marched off rather angrily towards Geyer Street Gardens.

The plan was to paint with some white paint that Jeff had discovered in his basement, an actual hockey rink on the street's surface. We would paint a centerline, faceoff circles, goal lines and two creases on the surface of Geyer

Street and officially mark the street forever more in perpetuity (or as long as the paint would last) as our beloved Geyer Street Gardens.

I stood watching my two best buddies and teammates stomp off toward Geyer Street. I thought how I could not let them go to jail alone and how peer pressure, when you are a teenager, really was a bit of a pain-in-the-ass. I had to admit that my "missing the test" argument was very lame.

"Hey, all right. Wait up! I will help!"

I sprinted into action and followed behind them. Harry smiled and handed me two long pieces of lumber that we planned to use as straight edges to make our lines as straight as possible.

"I knew you would eventually shake off the Old Lady Syndrome. Maybe someday, they will come up with a pill or something for you to take to cure ya of that shit. Nothing is going to happen, twenty-seven. What could happen?"

Harry put his big arm around me and squeezed me until I felt as if I was in a vise. His grip prevented me from shuddering at the mere mention of those dreaded three words.

It was just about dark now, a Friday night, so there were no remaining work shifts left at the factory. We knew that all the workers were gone for the day; the factory only ran three shifts on Monday through Thursday.

We also knew that only the night watchman remained, and he was already asleep on the chair just inside the loading dock doors. Besides, he parked his car in the front of the factory over on Belmont Avenue and he would never drive out the loading dock; he would go out the front of the factory.

We had lived here so long that we knew all the details, and this well-planned adventure minimized the prospect of someone driving through the freshly painted lines.

We had a good plan.

Under the cover of darkness, we broke the lid off the

five-gallon paint bucket. Harry tilted the bucket, and he poured some of it into a paint tray while Jeff used a broom to clear rocks and stones away and he carefully measured and laid out the lines and format. Harry and I rolled out the centerlines. Jeff laid out the rest of the markings and he instructed us where to place the goal lines while he turned his attention to the net locations and he marked out the creases for the two nets. We had one streetlight above our heads, and a well-lit surface to work with, and the lines were going down crisp and clean.

Our plan was working out well.

"Forget the blue lines, guys, we only ever used the center line for offside. If we add it now, it will be too confusing," Jeff remarked as he marked the final goal crease.

Jeff had already painted the center faceoff circle, and he was just moving over to make some of the small faceoff circles in front of the net, when we heard the fire horns of the fire system for the Borough of Haledon, start to sound off loudly into the night air.

Haledon had an unusual and very ancient system of sounding fire signals for a fire emergency within the borough. Once you crossed over from the city of Paterson, and were in the Borough of Haledon, (where all three of us actually lived) the borough had three or four huge fire sirens, or for a better description, fire gongs to show fire locations.

Mounted in various strategic areas in the borough were these immense fire horns and they sounded so loudly that you could hear them sound no matter where you were located in the town.

Well, mostly, no matter where you were. . ..

Our house at 182 Belmont Avenue was literally the last house in the borough before you crossed into the city line, and it was a little difficult to hear the fire horns. You could hear them, but it was weak with the traffic noise on

Belmont Avenue and the city bus line going up and down the road.

Many a snowy morning, my sister and I would huddle next to the windows, with our ears pressed to the glass, praying to hear the blessed three blasts from the horn, signaling to the joy-filled youngsters throughout the entire world of a school cancellation!

It did not happen as often as we wished it would. In fact, it rarely happened.

Just to add to the weirdness factor, mounted on poles in various areas were fire pull stations to pull for general fires, disasters, and car accidents. I can only imagine how vandals and pranksters would set the world on fire with such a system in the modern age!

The fire horn blasts then cross-referenced to a chart that showed where the fire was located. Every year, my old man would donate some money to the local fire companies, and they would give him a new calendar with a picture of a fire truck on the cover and on each page too. Predictably, and like a fine-tuned watch, every year, the old man would complain that the calendar was "Getting more and more expensive and the paper cheaper and cheaper!"

One cool feature that we all used was the fact that the calendar had the fire horn codes printed on the top of it. It became a pastime of all residents of the Borough of Haledon to listen to the fire horns, count the blasts, and then count the pauses, jump up to check the calendar, and, "See where the fire is!"

I knew the code for the pull box in front of our house was three blasts, a pause, then two blasts, a pause, then four blasts, and I knew the blessed, "three—three—three" for no school.

Other than that, I knew no codes, but Harry knew them all!

In keeping with their usual behavior of salivating over disasters, emergencies, floods and plagues, Harry and most of the Redmond family were walking cross-reference charts of the Haledon fire codes. They had all the codes memorized. It was amazing. Even his little nieces and nephews would stop playing with their trucks and dolls or watching, *Dinky the Orange Teddy Bear* on the television, when the fire signals went off, and you could see them standing there, counting the blasts and pauses on their little fingers and toes.

They would then yell out in unison, "Henry Street and Lee Avenue," and return to playing.

It was an integral part of Redmond family training. Anyway, they all loved disasters and fires. It was in their blood, and that is, a whole other story.

Harry loved counting the codes and then telling all of us where the fire or disaster was located. It was an obsession of his.

As soon as the fire horns went off, Harry shifted into emergency mode. He stopped dead in his tracks, waved his arms over his head, took a deep breath of air, and he yelled, "Quiet guys! The fire horns!"

Jeff looked up from his painting and said, "Yeah, yeah, yeah . . . so what, Harry?"

"Shhh . . . be quiet, man. I got to count 'em!" Harry stood there, still waving his arms in an effort to quiet us, so that he could concentrate. As the horn blasts went off, we could faintly hear sirens roaring off in the distance, fire truck sirens.

Harry closed his eyes, and he was counting the signals, while reaching deeply into the recesses of his mind to a storage area where he kept the secret to the magical codes.

"One, two, three, four . . . a pause. One, two, three, four, five . . . a pause," Harry stood there in the center of Geyer Street Gardens counting aloud the stupid fire blasts.

Jeff and I continued to work on the faceoff circles while he counted. I had to admit, even after these years, that it was a little annoying of Harry to be so obsessed with the fire signals. Jeff shook his head while we worked hard to finish the work.

Harry continued, "One, two, three. . .."

While he stood there, it seemed as though the fire sirens of the trucks were growing louder.

Harry finished counting and the fire horns stopped blasting.

He calmly turned towards us and said, "Four fifty, three. Geyer Street, Brawer Brothers, Dye Company. The fire is, well, shit, damn—the fire is here, youse guys!"

Jeff Porter's eyeballs almost burst out of his head, and I felt my heart jump up into the top of my head.

Jeff dropped the paintbrush on the ground, stood up and screamed, "HERE! THE FRIGGIN' FIRE IS HERE! AS IN GEYER STREET HERE?"

Harry walked slowly over to us and repeated, "Yup, the factory, youse guys. Right over here."

In the meantime, the fire truck sirens were now well, very loud . . . as in right down the street loud.

Jeff ran over to Harry, grabbed him by the shoulders and shook him while saying, "Tell me you're playing with us, Harry! Please tell me that you're wrong! Wrong, wrong, wrong!"

Harry shook his head while he was reiterating his expert cryptology skills with the fire chart numbers.

Harry adamantly stated, "Nope, I ain't ever wrong on a fire signal code! I know that chart like I know every curve in the ass of the cute chick who sits in front of me in my third period English class. What is her name? Oh yeah, I think it is . . . Sandy. I sit there and study it carefully and pray that Miss Brier calls her up to her desk, so that I can watch her walk up the aisle in front of me."

During the entire time, in which Harry was babbling on and on about Sandy's various attributes, the fire engine sirens were growing closer and closer.

"SHUT THE HELL UP HARRY AND RUN!"

Jeff and I had already sprinted off and made a beeline for the lip lady's fence. We could hear the fire trucks roaring down the street now, and with one leap, we dove headlong over the fence and hid in the grass in the lip lady's front yard.

Harry came out of his euphoric fire horn state, as well as he woke up from his daydream of Sandy's glorious backside, and he suddenly realized our fate. He, too, whirled around and ran, dove headlong over the fence and landed with a loud "thud" next to Jeff and me.

Two seconds later, as we watched and cowered in incredible horror and fear, four thousand, two hundred, and sixteen fire trucks, ambulances, police cars, rescue vehicles, and one, of every known emergency vehicle on the face of the Earth, charged by us. I had a vague glimpse of the first fire engine hitting the five-gallon bucket of paint that we had left in the center of Geyer Street Gardens, and we watched in awe, while it spun high in the air, broadcasting white paint over every, single, emergency vehicle, as each one whizzed by our covert hiding spot.

Just to make Jeff and me feel better, Harry leaned over and offered up another wonderful tidbit of fire emergency trivia, "Oh yeah, youse guys, whenever there is a fire alarm at the dye factory, it goes to like six or seven alarms. We should see the city of Paterson soon, and even Wayne Township will send a big pumper down to assist. These dumps are old tinderboxes, ya know. This sucker could burn down about five or six city blocks, ya know."

"Thank you, Harry. That does make me feel a lot better." I could not resist offering Harry some element of praise for the current state of panic deep within my soul. When we saw a police car, double back and shine his spotlight on the road, scan the paintbrushes, trays, and rollers, then the toppled paint bucket, we had enough.

We knew the neighborhood like the back of our hands (Harry knew it like, well, you already know about Sandy and her backside), we crawled across the lip lady's lawn, slipped under the hole in the fence, across the old chicken troughs, and we exited stage left.

I sprinted all the way home. Jeff and Harry jumped over fences on Cook Street and made their way to their own homes, by scooting across various backyards and avoiding the streets.

Escape was within our grasp . . . maybe.

I dashed through the back door of my house. I kept telling myself to relax. Curled up on his bed on the back porch was Pussface the cat. He did not move a muscle when I walked in. The old man must have prepared him a dish of beer and he was either sound asleep or passed out.

We had the only beer-loving tomcat that I have ever heard of, but that once more is another story.

Everything was well; the flash of the light from the living room told me the old man was watching the black and white television and sitting in his easy chair, the sound of the bathtub running water, told me that Mum was washing up. The loud rock-and-roll records blasting from Dottie's room told me she was in there listening to the latest and greatest hits on her 45-RPM player.

I arrived at a safe haven, a port in the storm. There were no policemen or detectives sitting at the kitchen table, waiting to slap handcuffs on me. I had made a successful escape. Now, I just needed to lie low for a long, long time. I should be able to reappear in twenty years or so.

I snuck into my room, changed into my sweats, pushed ole Skippy aside, and tuned in the Rover hockey game on my radio. No knocks at the door, no police cars in the driveway. Everything was quiet.

"Hey, is everything all, right? What were youse guys doing tonight? Huh? Were ya shooting hockey pucks? Are you okay? All ya teeth still there?"

I almost jumped to the ceiling when I heard my father's voice at the door.

I recovered, "Yeah, yeah, yeah, we were shooting around. I am good. I am just listening to the game."

The old man stood in the doorway to my room. He frowned a deep frown, and I heard my breathing increase a little. For some reason, he was lingering.

"Don't you ever get homework from the vocational school? Are those teachers a bunch of bums who allow youse guys to goof off and skate through life?"

"Yeah, yeah, yea. I mean, no. Mr. Fosse is kinda tough on us. He gives us tons of work to do, Dad. I did it all during my study period. I have a test in wood shop class on Monday and a welding test in metals on Tuesday. You went to vocational school. You know that it is not easy. I am good. It *is* Friday, you know."

Now, God gave to all parents, detectors inside of their heads and hearts to detect whenever their dopey kids are into something that they should not be. The old man was first in line to receive his detector, Mr. Redmond was second, Mr. Porter was third, and Mum was in the mix somewhere thereabouts too. Furthermore, all of our parents had signed a reciprocal agreement to allow them to beat our backsides silly whenever one of them caught any of us out of line!

The old man's detector was going off and doom loomed on my precarious horizon.

"You are acting weird! Did you or those hockey pucks you hang around with do something? Did Harry get in trouble today? Did he drag you and Jeff into the mix to try to bail him out? I bet he is in hot water for a squeeze on some gal's backside or did he get caught looking down her shirt or something?"

I had to laugh at that one because it actually could have been true.

"Nah, it is all good, Dad. No trouble. I am listening to the game here. The Rovers are getting blasted by the Chicago Missiles."

At the mention of sports—the old man seemed satisfied. His radar went down and he went to turn away.

"Yeah, yeah, yeah, all those Shercargo teams (The old man always twisted the pronunciation of Chicago) are always tough." He went to walk away but turned back once more. He was not done yet, in his torture of me.

"Hey, I heard all kinds of fire sirens out there tonight. What in the hell was going on? Was the whole borough burning down or what? Did youse guys see where it was? I heard 'em, but I did not count the alarms. I must have dozed off for a spell. Your mother stinks at counting. Do ya know where the fire was at?"

I crossed my toes and my fingers under the covers of my bed, and shook my head while mumbling, "Nah, nah, nah, not really."

Teenagers are, for the most part, quite deceptive.

"Okay yeah, yeah, yeah, just wonderin'. Hey, take the garbage out and walk Skippy before you sack out. Don't wake Pussface. That damn cat sucked down two dishes of beer tonight. Goodnight, chief."

"Goodnight, Dad."

He was gone in a flash and I breathed a sigh of relief. Skippy looked up at me and sighed as he stuck his nose back between his paws. Even my faithful dog knew we had done something wrong.

Daybreak came; I snuck into the living room and checked out the old man's copy of the *Paterson Evening News*. I scanned page after page and nothing.

Wait! Here is something.

"Multiple towns and the city of Paterson respond to a false alarm at Brawer Brother's Dye factory."

I scanned the article for any mention of stupid teenagers painting hockey rink lines, or paint cans spinning in the air, but there was nothing there to implicate us.

"Geez . . . just our rotten luck that after all of that, it had to be a false alarm," I said to no one, but only said to satisfy myself.

I closed the newspaper and smiled.

Upon viewing the carnage, the next day, the best way now to describe Geyer Street Gardens was that it looked similar to the maze of runways and markings on the asphalt at the airport. Tire tracks in white, faceoff circles blobbed here and there, and it had a centerline that went north and south at the same time. The goal creases, well, they looked as if we were half-in-the-bag when we painted them. Rectangles they were not, they were more as if they were overlapping circles.

On Saturday afternoon, while we all stood there in shock and horror at our handiwork and we waited for the rest of the teams to show up, Jeff optimistically offered, "It will wear off soon."

The only other mention of the now famous line-painting episode came from the cunning mind of Harry's brother-in-law, Ronzo Boatmann. One day, about a week after the "false alarm," we were sitting around in the kitchen at 20 John Street. Ronzo was having a Dingleberry beer and shooting the breeze with Harry's sister Linda and with Mr. Redmond too.

Ronzo suddenly offered up, "Geez, I had a few beers over at the American War Veteran's Hall, and my old war buddy, Jimmy Macalister said that he and a bunch of the other firefighters at company number two, spent days and days, compounding white paint off the side of the fire truck. Something about running over a paint bucket over on Geyer Street when they responded to that false alarm over at the dye factory a week or so ago. Now what dumb-ass would have left a paint bucket over there? Musta fell off a delivery truck or something."

Jeff, Harry, and I stirred uneasily. We all shook our heads in guilty unison.

Luckily, Mr. Redmond was lost in an article that he was reading; he looked up from his newspaper and just quizzically said, "What?"

He, thankfully, had not been paying attention.

Linda smiled and shook her head. Ronzo, who obviously knew the culprits, but always had our backs, stood up from his chair, winked at the three jerks standing there shaking in our boots and said, "I asked you if you want another beer, Pop. Ya want a Dingleberry?"

"Nah, nah, nah, please will you get me a Big Boulder. Those Dingleberries are way too sweet."

"Sure, Pop!"

I leaned over to Jeff and Harry and whispered rather cynically, "After all, youse guys, what could happen?"

They frowned at me.

Harry whispered quietly to me, "Yeah, yeah, and yeah. Up ya ass there, twenty-seven."

It always hurt when the dreaded Old Lady Syndrome proved to be correct in a prediction.

Sorry, I just could not resist.

5

The Buckley Park Bruisers

About mid-November of the same year, which the best that I can remember would be in or around 1974 or thereabouts, we had a turning point in our hockey lives. It was a month or so after the paint incident, (in which, we for obvious reasons, preferred to refer to, as the "false alarm") and we were playing our usual hockey game on a Saturday afternoon.

The game was embroiled in deep turmoil, a close game, in fact, a hard-fought tie game that was now ticking down to the last few minutes. During the last few minutes, we all watched when a tall, lanky guy on a worn-out looking bicycle pedaled up to Geyer Street Gardens. He parked his bicycle, stood, and watched our game from the sidelines for quite a while.

Two additional younger guys soon pedaled up on their own bikes, too. They joined the lanky lad, and all three of them now stood on the sideline watching the game.

I would guess the age of the tallest of the guys, to be around fifteen or perhaps even sixteen years of age and the smaller guys, to be a year or so younger. Most us were in and around the fourteen to fifteen-year range, with Handsome Mike the Italian kid, being the oldest of us all, as he was nearly seventeen years old now.

The three of them stood on the sideline, watching our game, retrieving an out of play puck occasionally, but mostly, they were studying the action. Besides our biggest fan, who was the lip lady from her front porch seat, we did, on rare occasions, have actual spectators. We had a few neighborhood gals who might stop by to flirt and distract us, a few younger kids, who dreamed of playing with us someday, the annoying Nit-Nat kids would drift in and out, Mr. Porter, Ronzo or Mr. Redmond, but in reality, spectators, for the most part, were quite rare.

One red-haired Italian kid (they were rare in northern New Jersey) named Steven Cappuccino, would stop by and he was not a bad little hockey player. He was about three years younger than we were, he always brought his stick with him and occasionally, we would allow him to be a practice "dummy." Steven would jump in during a shoot around or practice with us, excited to just be part of the gang. He was such a likable kid, and eager to learn and play, we did not discourage him. Soon, he became a permanent substitute player.

Steven was like a little lost puppy dog, following the bigger dogs around town. During games, he would substitute for an injured player, or someone who was tired, but mostly, Steven loved to hang out on the sideline and wait for his limited chances.

He was a little on the smallish side, would get beat to near death, but he hung in there and he was a remarkably tough kid. All he wanted was to be part of the league and play with the "big guys."

We, of course, in typical New Jersey fashion, when we found a name or a word too difficult to roll off our Jersey-accented tongues, we shortened his Italian last name, and we just called him, "Pooch."

This current game, which had drawn our strange spectators, was a match between the Geyer Street Guys and the Rovers, and Big Wex was in one of his moods. No, he was not lining up for a repeat of the historic spit fight, but he was now irate by the lack of scoring by his leading scorer, a guy we named Tags.

Once more, Tags, actual last name, was Italian in origin,

and it was too long for us to use. Tags worked out much better!

Now, Tags was a slender, somewhat skinny guy, who in the last year or so, had shot up to be tall, lanky and very skilled. He played offense on the Rovers and scored most their goals. Next to Johnny the Cho, Tags was the leading scorer in the league. He was shifty, good around the net, and tough in the corners.

Today, though, we had his number.

I was hot in the net today, making tough save after tough save, and Jeff and Harry had each scored from slap shots from alternating points on the rink.

It was our day today!

Big Wex was ranting from the goal on how he could score on Henson, he could take out Jeff, and how, if he came out of the net, he would take out Harry in the corners. All of his rants were, of course, pipe dreams! He could not even catch Harry, and even if he did, Harry was so big and strong now that taking Harry out in the corners would not happen.

Tags could not take it any longer, and after a few more rants, he turned to Big Wex and told him, "At the end of this period, Ray is going in the net, and your big ass can come out and let's see you score on the long-haired hippie. It ain't easy!"

"Fine, pansy ass. That is fine with me!" Big Wex shook his goal stick in the air and pointed at his teammate. I laughed under my mask because Big Wex was one of a kind, but he was a passionate hockey player. You could never question his desire to win, or his competitive edge.

The period ended, and we took a break.

The tall, lanky spectator, who had been standing on the sideline, wandered over and asked, "Say, long-haired hippie goalie . . . you are a pretty good goalie. Not bad. Who is in charge here with youse guys?"

I stood up; he realized I was taller and larger than he

was. He was studying me and I could tell that. I surmised at this point that he was a hockey player, too.

"Thanks. Ray is in charge. Ray Edelski."

I turned and pointed at Ray, who was sitting with Tags and Big Wex. Everyone was curious now, and the entire gang followed the tall guy over to where Ray was sitting. His two buddies walked over there too, and soon we were huddled up together to listen to what was going on.

"Hey, Ray. I am Jimbo Carlisle, the best center man around here. I play ice hockey, roller hockey, and street hockey. I am the captain of a team and league over by Saint Peter's Church. Do ya know, Buckley Park in Paterson?"

Ah, hah! I vaguely remembered years ago Jeff telling us about a group of players that always played a few blocks over at Buckley Park. Could it be after all of these years?

Ray stood up, he looked around at all of our anxious faces, brushed his pants off and said, "Yeah, yeah, yeah, hey Jimbo. Nice to meet you. I know where it is. It is over by the fountain that they turn on in the summer so you can cool off. Got it. What can we do for you?"

"My team is the best in our league and we all are tired of us beating the hell out of the other teams, so we made up an all-star team of our best players. We call ourselves the Buckley Park Bruisers. We want to play youse guys. We heard youse have been playing over here for years and thought we would come over and check it all out. We want to play. Ya interested, or are you a bunch of pussies?"

Play another team! The thought went through my head like a rocket ship! I never dreamed of playing someone other than our own group of guys!

This was historic!

I looked around and studied the faces of our friends. Harry's eyes were bugging out, Jeff was nervously kicking with his right foot at the asphalt, and Big Wex was rubbing his hands together while plotting a reign of terror. Big Wex had dreams of new and fresh victims to pummel running through his head.

It was a moment of arrival, a moment to put the famous Haledon Hockey League in the record books. We might even become an entry in an encyclopedia after this!

Ray looked around at his league and all the players who considered him our leader.

He swallowed hard, studied our faces and then stammered a little, "Well, I need to talk to my guys here. We never played anyone outside of our league." We all were now nodding our heads, to indicate to Ray not to blow it.

He was stammering too much.

Jimbo and his Bruiser teammates were going to think we *were* afraid of them!

C'mon Ray, shake the cobwebs out of your head.

"What are youse afraid of, Ray? Shit, it turns out that youse guys are a bunch of pussies after all! Huh? Shoulda guessed as much. At first, I did not think ya were cuz, the big red-haired guy in the net seems as if he has a lot to say. Guess that I wuz wrong," the tall center man for the Bruisers was now spouting off and poking hard at us. Upon hearing the reference, Big Wex stepped up.

Oh, oh! Harry and Big George intercepted him and Big George put his arm around Wex and led him away.

"Hold on there, big guy. Save it for the game," Big George was offering some very good advice. "He is just poking at ya to get you worked up."

Ray sensed that our reputations were now at stake and he gauged our reactions.

As our leader, Ray knew that he could not hesitate any longer.

Ray loudly stated, "Hell no! We are not afraid of jackshit. We will play your team."

Ray now put his confidence on the line; he bagged his apprehension, as he added, "Anytime. Any friggin' place ya want, we will play and we will beat ya asses. Where do you want to play? Here or Buckley Park? We play three on three here, because of the size of the street, but we could fit another player and go four on four, including the goalie if ya want."

I was, and I knew that the rest of the Haledon Hockey League was very proud of our leader. Ray would not allow some punk from a few city blocks over to intimidate him.

It was now a matter of pride.

Jimbo smiled widely. He was obviously proud of his efforts. His baiting had been successful. Intimidation was always going to be part of the game of hockey. The teenage banter and dialogue seemed silly, but as I progressed in the world of hockey, I would learn that this type of dialogue in hockey circles would not change much, even between adults!

Jimbo turned to his two teammates and asked them, "What do you think? I say we play here. It has boards and fences, so it is better than our joint." The two teammates agreed, and it looked as if it was going to be a game. It now became time to work the final deal.

Deal making in New Jersey is a way of life, and the best deals come from the ones made in the streets and on the street corners.

This deal was not going to be an exception to that fact.

Ray scanned our faces for confirmation, and then asked Jimbo, "Deal, sucker. What about refs? I want to play all my players. We usually use someone from the team that is not playing to ref our game."

"No sweat. We have this geeky, doofus guy from our neighborhood. He loves hockey, knows every damn rule and then some, but he sucks as a player, so he never plays. Charlie Lumproast is his name, but we just call him Lumpy."

Harry spouted, "Geez, shit, with a last name like that, I can understand why."

We all balked at the thought of utilizing a referee from

their neighborhood.

He could be a ringer!

Jimbo Carlisle sensed our apprehension, so he quickly added, "It is cool. Lumpy is as honest as they come. His old man works at maintenance at Saint Peter's Church and is a troop leader for the Woodman Scouts. They are goodie, goodies."

That seemed to be some type of bizarre qualifier, and Ray Edelski nodded his head in acknowledgement of his ironclad honesty.

"Okay then, we will use Lumpy. But, if he is a bum, we have the right to pull our own guy to ref along with him. And we only play offside with the centerline. There ain't any blue lines. We play icing, and penalties are the same as the big league."

We all scanned the mess of lines on Geyer Street Gardens made from the "false alarm" incident, and you could make out the intended lines much clearer because the tire tracks had now worn off just a little.

Jimbo looked around and he said, "Yeah, yeah, yeah, we got a deal. Say, it looks like a truck ran over some of these lines."

We ignored his observation.

"Ya got ya a deal there, Edelski. How about we play the game on Friday after Thanksgiving? That will be a day off for all of us. It will give us Saturday for a makeup day just in case it rains or snows."

Jeff and I looked at Harry and saw the disappointment on his face. Harry's family had a trip planned to Florida over the holiday, and that meant Harry would miss the game! The team would miss Harry too, between him and Jeff; they were a tough defensive corp.

"Hey, thirty-five, chin up, man. There will be another game. We will beat their asses badly, so they will want a rematch!" I did my best to encourage Harry.

"Yeah, yeah, yeah, I guess. I am going to talk to my old

man about not going." Everyone nodded their head in agreement, but we knew we had a better chance of Rumblehowser from the Rovers showing up here on Geyer Street and playing goal for us than Harry did at weaseling out of a family trip. A trip that his old man had saved money up for a few years in order to go on.

Jimbo Carlisle and his entourage overheard my comments and now that he had sealed the deal, it was time to talk some smack.

He sauntered over slowly, with his minions following his every move. It was quite obvious that not only was he their team leader, and most likely their best player, he was also highly confident and perceived himself to be a tough guy.

"Say, longhair! Did I just hear you say youse are going to beat our asses?"

I looked at him and answered, "Yup. Ya did. Why? Is that a problem for ya?"

I was always glad my grandfather and Mum were not privy to all of these hard New Jersey, accent laden conversations. They might have shipped me back over to Nottingham for some English lessons.

Jimbo smiled at me, got up close to my face and his eyes went back and forth over my eyes and my face.

"I assume you are gonna be the starting goalie for your team. I watched ya. You can stop the biscuit, and ya got balls, but it ain't gonna help ya. I have the hardest slapper ya ever seen, and I will tear your damn head off with my wrist shot. I shoot for the head first, and then I will take out those balls of yours. If ya got a girlfriend, ya had better warn her, since it ain't gonna be pretty for you for a few weeks. She might need to find some other way to keep herself occupied!"

Jimbo's minions laughed awkwardly at his rather lewd references.

I felt a little fire rise inside of me. It started way down

deep inside of me, somewhere near my stomach, and it rose through my body all the way to the top of my head.

For the first time in my life, I felt the fire, and later on in my hockey career and in my life, I would come to know this feeling very well.

I stepped in close to Jimbo. I was taller than he was, and bigger too. It was obvious that he did not appreciate my boldness. I could sense that it was all an act, and he was suddenly extremely uncomfortable. In a roundabout way, I just earned his respect, because I did not back down. Apparently, people always backed down when Jimbo Carlisle called them out. I kept my cool and Jimbo smiled a smirk once again. This chap did not give up easily, and he was brimming with cockiness.

"Kick his ass, twenty-seven! Squeeze his damn throat with that death grip of yours and choke his friggin' eyes out! Let 'em know ya can't scare, twenty-seven!" Big Wex started up in the background, coaxing me on. "Ya lost two teeth last week, and heck, a few more stitches in your head this year will not matter, Paulie. Tell 'em."

I decided to answer the call, "Bring it on, Jimbo. Give me your best shot. I can take it. Groin, head, or any other place."

I stood proudly in front of him. I wanted him to know that he would not intimidate or belittle me. I turned, walked away, and went and sat on the sidewalk in front of the rich guy's garage. I needed to re-tape my goalie stick for the period coming up and cool off a bit. I knew I needed to save the fire that I just felt in my belly for our game. Besides, this afternoon, we still had a game to play.

I was ready.

Jimbo left us with one last insult, "Long haired freak. Long haired hippies aren't goalies. I will shave that hair for you, twenty-seven. My shot will take it all off. No need for a barber for your ass. See youse guys on the Friday after Thanksgiving around noon. Ya better practice."

"Get lost, jackass!" Big Wex, too, could not resist hurling one last insult. Jimbo Carlisle and his sidekicks, with their middle fingers held in unison in the air, all walked over to their bicycles, jumped on them and they pedaled away.

The stage was certainly set now!

After some roundhouse banter amongst us, we remembered that we had a game to resume! The excitement of a game with an actual outside foe had overwhelmed us.

Harry continued some wild protesting about missing the game, but secretly, we all knew he was doomed and there was no way out for him to escape the Redmond family trip.

We assured him that there would certainly be a rematch. My actions in not backing down from smack talking, Jimbo Carlisle, seemed to be a bit of a highlight for my teammates, (we were all teammates now, no longer could we be called league mates!) and our lofty dream and aspirations at the prospect of shutting down a loudmouth such as Jimbo, inspired my teammates to new heights.

I was about to learn an important lesson about being a goaltender. A lesson in that displaying confidence to your teammates was half of the battle!

We finished the rest of the scheduled games for the day. The Geyer Street Guys were flying high after trouncing both opponents today. We had shown steady improvement and Jeff now possessed a mean and wicked slap shot.

No longer was a lack of offense our trouble!

Jeff, Harry, and I were in high spirits and hockey consumed our minds. Harry, of course, still kept a small section open in his mind for the young gals he was currently chasing around, but even he now mostly focused upon hockey.

"Guys, guys, guys," Ray gathered us around after we finished the games for the day.

"Listen up! We need to have a team meeting. I assume that since I am the commissioner, and sorta our coach, that youse guys want me to coach us in this game, too."

Ray scanned our group for affirmative nods of our heads and he listened to a mumbled chorus of, "Yeah, yeah, yeah, of course, Ray."

"Well, since we do not see each other in school any longer, we need to set up a meeting." Ray took his duties very responsibly.

Ray was correct. Most of the gang, now attended college preparatory classes, Handsome Mike went to a fancy, Catholic prep high school up in Wayne Township, and the Geyer Street Guys, well, we all went to the trade programs at the vocational school side of the regional high school for our area. We had spread out since our elementary school days, so meeting for game plans and strategy was not as easy as it used to be.

"How about we meet over at my house after school on Tuesday for us to put a game plan together? I think we need to cancel the games for this week, and practice as a team. We play all the time, but we never practice as a team. With Harry not being able to play, we will need to shift our defense around. We have a lot of work to do youse guys. The game is on and we only have a week or so before Thanksgiving. We do not have too much time!" Ray had a valid point, and we all acknowledged his suggestion, as well as his leadership.

We met at Ray's house on Tuesday and had our first official team meeting. Ray's old man was polite to us and he even bought us pizza as a special treat, and he allowed us to use his basement as a meeting room. The excitement now was reaching a fever pitch.

Ray was into a serious coaching mode, "I think we are all set. We all will agree that twenty-seven will be our goalie. He is the best there is. Not meaning to hurt any feelings here, but we need to win this game guys, and Henson gives us the best chance. Without you on your best game, Paul, we do not stand a chance!"

Ray and all of my teammates turned and looked at me in unison. Harry was sitting next to me and he gave me a playful shove in the back. I looked over at the big guy and smiled. I knew him not being able to play was killing him, but he was there to support us in spirit.

I nodded while I pondered my role. Oh boy, the pressure was on. I could feel my stomach churning a bit with the excitement of the challenge.

There was no doubt that I would make sure I was ready.

Ray continued to point to a chart that he had drawn up on an easel he set up in the center of the room. It had all different types of lines and his shift changes for the game.

Ray was a serious coach.

"With Harry out for his family trip, we have a big hole in defense. If we stick twenty-seven in the net, that gives us Big Wex, Handsome Mike, and Jeff on defense. That is a good defense. Big Wex can move some people out of Paul's vision. Wex can kill the screens from the point and fill in some muscle that we miss with Harry being gone. I will move Big George to offense. His big body can set screens in front of their net and he is hard to move. On offense, we will be good, very good. We have Cho and Tags, and I can shift in if they get tired. I mostly want to concentrate on coaching and moving our players in and out, but I do not mind taking a shift or two."

Ray stopped his strategy speech and looked at Pooch, who was waiting anxiously for Ray to call his name. The kid would not go away, and he seemed to have slowly turned into one of the guys.

We invited Pooch to come along to the meeting. He was small and young, but there was no doubt that Pooch had the heart and guts. He had hung along on the sideline for so long that he was now a part of the team, too.

"Pooch, we may need ya! I can't promise anything, but all I can say is that ya little ass will need to be ready," Ray was serious, and he pointed at Pooch with the pointer stick, he had been using to show us the line changes and shifts. Pooch's eyes lit up, and his face broke into a huge smile. Jeff put his arm around him, and I swear his red hair turned ten shades redder.

Pooch stood up; his hands gripped tightly around his always-present hockey stick; I swear the kid slept with that hockey stick. A hockey stick, which, for some reason, he brought along to the meeting.

As Pooch stood there, he proudly declared, "I will be ready, Coach Ray! I promise that I will not let youse guys down. All I ask is for a shift. Give my little ass just one, damn, shift. I can score, ya know. I am really good at garbage goals around the net. I'm not afraid of no one, Coach Ray."

"Good, well, very good. I will keep that in mind."

This was serious stuff to all of us. It was a moment of arrival, a decisive moment for our team. Arrival, from a place of a handful of kids hacking around with hockey pucks, not knowing what to do with them, to a point where we now knew that we would measure our success by our ability to work together with teamwork.

It was going to be a powerful lesson for all of us, for not only hockey but also in life.

We had played together for years and years. Since we were all ten years old. Now, for the first time, we had a chance to test our hockey skills, our knowledge, and our abilities with an outside foe. We had played teams outside of our leagues in town baseball, football, high school sports, but now it was a strange opponent in hockey. This was different; this was a rite of passage for the Haledon Hockey League.

We could not have had a better coach than Ray Edelski. Ray was a solid player, nothing too spectacular, just steady and reliable. As a coach, he was a student of the game. He devised game strategies, ran a full week of practice, drilled us in positions, drew up set plays, and provided us with an element of confidence. Ray was the first real hockey strategist that ever taught us that hockey was more than just running around and slapping at the puck, banging into people and intimidating the other team by waving a stick in their faces and cursing at them, while calling their mother names. You had to have a game plan and now we did!

The week or so building up to the big game included practices, tension and strategy lessons. It was nonstop hockey chatter.

"What if they dump the puck in the zone? How do we handle the power play? Never dump the puck in the corner . . . and twenty-seven, no rebounds, cover the puck!" This was enough to make your head spin and your nerves unwind!

The week also included a solemn goodbye to Harry as he reluctantly took off for his family holiday. After school on the Wednesday before Thanksgiving, all the Redmonds, Mr. Redmond, Ronzo, Linda, Patty, the Big Spike and all of Harry's screaming nephews and nieces packed up, and were ready to roll to the airport. Just what he wanted to do, walking around a goofy family resort, interacting with stupid, cartoon characters, singing stupid songs, and skipping merrily along in the hot, Florida sun, as opposed to all out, hockey warfare with a smart-ass opponent!

Jeff and I sat on the front steps at 20 John Street, watching the last of the suitcases load up into the trunk of Mr. Redmond's Galaxy 1000 sedan.

A forlorn and sad-faced Harry appeared at the door. "Hey, give it all, youse guys got! I will be with ya. Kick their asses! Kick 'em for me and the Geyer Street Guys!"

Jeff and I stood up. Jeff patted Harry on the back while telling him, "We will win, Harry. We got it!"

I reassured Harry, "I will be sharp and, on my game, thirty-five." We both gave the big guy a hug, and Harry turned to head for the car. He stopped, and turned around while pointing his finger at me, "Not a marble can get by you, twenty-seven. Not even a marble!"

I smiled and said, "I will do my best."

He waved, climbed into the car, and with a big roar, the car pulled away, followed by the rest of the Redmond caravan. Jeff and I stood and watched as they turned the corner and disappeared onto Geyer Street. One piece of us was missing. Jeff and I would need to pick up the slack.

The weather looked good for the day after Thanksgiving. Freezing but clear, and we had a big family get-together for the holiday planned with my grandfather's sister, Aunt Alma, who was visiting from Florida and her daughter, the famous Cousin Pat, joining the celebration. We also had my mum's kid sister, Aunt Lois, and the kind and fun-loving Uncle Ed, coming over too!

That particular Thanksgiving turned into a memorable one at the Henson household. The events leading up to the holiday also were indeed, somewhat memorable.

Once more, that is an entirely different story for another set of words down the road someday!

Because of a sudden unexpected event, we had a change of our holiday plans for Thanksgiving. At the last moment, we ended up sharing our holiday with the family of my sister's best friend, the Zipperelli family.

The Zipperellis were a huge Italian clan, full of fun, joy, and excitement. They were part of the large Italian-American population that lived in northern New Jersey. They cooked up incredible Italian food, made homemade Italian wine, laughed, spoke broken English, spoke mostly in the Italian language and oh yes, the family included a pretty young lady within the fold.

A certain young gal named Miss Maureen Zipperelli. Maureen Zipperelli was my sister's best friend for as long as I could recall. In fact, since we were all just little squirts. She was a short, loud, talkative gal of Italian-American descent, who lived on the other side of the Borough of

Haledon. She was sort of round and plump, as well as she was charismatic, outgoing, and beautiful.

Talkative did indeed, accurately describe her. Maureen could really talk a lot. I do mean talk a lot, as in talking the ears off an elephant!

I was just coming into the age where I gave females just a little more notice, and Maureen vaguely interested me, even though she was a little less than three years older than I was. I could stand Maureen's talking for about five minutes, and then I would need to take off to protect my ears.

In all honesty, let me revisit that fact. I would *usually* take off to protect my ears.

Something had happened when I was with Maureen on Thanksgiving, and despite our slight age difference, I had a feeling she was a little smitten with me.

I had to admit that I enjoyed her company, too.

She was still a bit on the plump side, but she was losing some of her baby fat and filling out to be, well, a shapely and voluptuous gal!

I had not only hockey on my mind these last few weeks, but I had recently also taken keen notice of the amazing attractiveness of Miss Maureen Zipperelli!

As Harry M. Redmond Junior grew older, he also developed a wholehearted and usually dead on, distinctive manner of speaking. Some of it you could certainly consider New Jersey street slang. Some would say it was even a bit on the crude side, but he usually always hit the nail on the head! He especially was talented in his descriptions of the young women that we encountered.

As far as his description of Maureen Zipperelli went, Harry would whistle low, shake his head gently and say, "She has all her parts and pieces in the right places, with just the right amounts, too!"

I certainly had to agree.

In a spontaneous reaction, inspired in part, I am sure, by

my bouncing levels of teenage testosterone and while we were enjoying some time together on that wonderful Thanksgiving Day, I invited Maureen to attend the big hockey game.

She was of Italian descent, her parents and entire family except for her brother and herself, were born in Italy, and as a result, they were huge soccer fans. There were some vague connections between the game of soccer and hockey. The basic concepts of the two games were the same, with nets and goalies and forwards and defense. If you could follow soccer, then the game of hockey would not seem so foreign. Maureen and the rest of the Zipperellis did not know a hockey puck from a baseball, but Maureen did not seem to care. She eagerly accepted my invitation.

I think that she felt it was a roundabout invitation for our first romantic date!

I initially invited her in order to have a cheering section for us, knowing that she would come along with my sister, and the two of them would provide us with some strong fan support. My sister already had told me that she would attend to support the team and her brother. She was, and is, an amazing sister, and our deep connection always told her when something was important to her kid brother.

I could always count on her support.

As I sat and thought long and hard about it . . . that was part of it, but another part was that I wanted to impress Maureen.

I had to admit it, however, perhaps only to myself! Now, as I thought more about it, I hoped that her presence and my sister's attendance did not cause a distraction, but then again, as long as Maureen remained bundled up in a winter coat, you could not see many of her more "distracting parts."

Sometimes, when you are a male teenager on the cusp of manhood, and the initial flow of testosterone is bouncing in your bloodstream, it is quite easy to be painfully honest, especially with yourself.

I slept like a rock after the exciting, but long Thanksgiving Day we all experienced. I woke up a little after seven in the morning and I could hear the bang and rattle of the pots and pans in the kitchen. The old man had taken a rare vacation day from the shop for the day after the holiday, and he was now preparing breakfast in the kitchen.

He had some type of convoluted, Henson family rule that he adapted from his military days of when he was up, and then everyone else had to get up, as he would say, "Out of the rack" too.

I jumped out of bed, stretched, and flexed. My muscles felt good, nice and loose. That was a good sign. I knew how important the leg muscles were to a goaltender. It was where it all began and where it all will end.

Skippy jumped up with me. It was time to head out and let ole Skippy do what all doggies do.

At breakfast, the old man dished out some scrambled eggs, two or three Irish sausages, (as Gramps would say that stout from a saint, something or other's gate and this sausage, were the only bloody good things that the Irish ever made) and a piece of toast.

I eagerly gobbled all of it down.

"Are you full, Paulie? Do you want anything else?" My dear mum asked.

"Thanks, no. I am good. It is going to be a big day."

After all that I had eaten on Thanksgiving, it was a wonder that I had room for anything else. I pushed my chair back and smiled. The breakfast was a good start. Just about as good as you could ever imagine. Mum smiled at me, and the old man waved for me to carry my empty plate to the sink.

My sister turned. She looked at me as she carried her plate to the sink. She had an optimistic look on her face because my sister always believed in me. My sister always knew that I would succeed.

Dottie asked me, "What time is the faceoff, Paulie? Maureen and I do not want to be late."

"I would guess around one. I am not sure. Ray told us to be there by noon. I think I will change and be over there early. I need to be ready. Ya know?" Dottie smiled and nodded her head.

I went to my room and changed. I had a ritual now. It was something I had started and would stick with me for longer than I would ever want to remember. I dressed in tight, thermal underwear to keep the heat close to my body, to keep me loose, and to keep me warm. I pulled on a jockstrap with a full cup protector, twisted it in place, and adjusted it to fit.

Sorry, Jimbo, but I am ready for ya!

I first grabbed a tee shirt, then an old pair of dungarees, and finally, a sweatshirt. I still did not have enough money to afford a chest protector. A few welts on my chest were easy to handle, and they were commonplace. I did not feel them any longer. The sweatshirt would have to do for now. I then pulled a hockey jersey over the top of my head and pulled it tight over my body. It was an old jersey now, dyed in our team colors, the two colors that Jeff, Harry, and I had picked to be our team colors years ago. The Geyer Street Guys wore red and white, with respectively the number five, number thirty-five, and number twenty-seven on our backs.

My jersey also said "Henson" on the back.

The last piece of the puzzle was a small silver cross. Mum had given it to me as a birthday present a few years ago. I had the cross safely tucked inside a white cloth, deep inside of many folds. I took it and placed it in my back pocket.

When you play goal, you learn to pray an awful lot, and accept all types of intervention. Divine or otherwise.

This methodical dressing for goaltending duties was a

ritual, in which, over the years, the type of equipment I put on would change, but the routine would not change for a long, long time.

I just did not know it at the time.

I kept my goalie pads, sticks, and some other equipment on the back porch, and I walked through our kitchen and headed for the backdoor.

"Is Pussface awake and gone for the day, Dad?"

The old man was reading his newspaper and having a cup of coffee at the kitchen table. Mum was at the sink, finishing cleaning up the dishes from breakfast.

The old man put his newspaper down and answered, "Yeah, yeah, yeah, he is out. I let him out early. He ate a lot of turkey and drank a lot of beer yesterday, so he needs to run and work it off. Say, twenty-seven! Good luck and remember to duck, will ya? I do not need any more doctor's bills. Doc Salami has bought two brand new Galaxy 100 cars since youse guys started playing hockey."

"I will try to duck, Dad. Thanks. Doc Salami might be outta luck today."

He smiled at me and waved as Mum shouted, "Good luck! You are not too old or too big to give your old mother a kiss and a hug . . . now, are you?"

"Sure, Mum. Thanks."

I stopped and kissed Mum goodbye, and she smiled as I gave her a hug. Both of my parents seemed to sense how important his game was to me, both in a competitive way, but also in my heart too. I waved, grabbed my equipment and out the door, I went.

For a few minutes, I was alone at Geyer Street Gardens. I thought it would be too early to stop by Jeff's house and see if he was ready to go, but while I just shot a puck mindlessly into the side of the rich guy's garage, I spotted Jeff Porter walking up the street towards me. He had his red and white jersey on and, of course, he had the ball cap on his head turned backwards.

"You ready, twenty-seven? I bet you never slept a wink." Jeff was so eager to join me that he trotted the rest of the way.

"No, actually, yesterday was an exhausting day. It was a strange holiday, but really cool. I slept well, but now—I am set to go. Let me tell you. I am really set to go."

We had come a long way from those first shots that we had all shot together in front of the warehouse door, after picking out hockey sticks in a five and ten store, and now we were ready to face some competition, to see just how good we actually were. Jeff and I passed the puck back and forth for a bit when I confessed. If I could not confess to Jeff and Harry, then whom could I confess to in this world?

"Hey, Jeff, do you know, Maureen Zipperelli?"

"Yeah, yeah, yeah, your sister's friend there. She is that hot Italian chick with the ooh, la, la, shape. Yeah, man. I know her. Ya kiddin' right? Cuz, ah yeah, all the guys know her. Why?"

"Ah, she was over at my house yesterday for Thanksgiving. It is a long story, but her family came over and we all ate together. Well, she is coming to watch the game. She and my sister are going to watch. I invited Maureen."

Jeff smiled and launched the puck harder in my direction. I batted it down out of the air, spun it on an edge and passed it back to him. Even though I was a goalie, I could handle a shooting stick pretty well on my own.

"I am not sure why I asked her, but I did."

Jeff yelled out, "I know why ya asked her. One look at her will tell you why. She always has her eye on you too. I do not know her that well, but whenever I saw her hanging with ya sister, Maureen always glued her eyes on ya ass. Ya, a slick one, twenty-seven, an older, super-hot chick. Wow! Lucky stiff. It will be nice to have a cheering section for us, especially since they are a bunch of hot chicks. I know she is your sister and all, but Dottie is super-hot too."

I looked up and smiled at Jeff. Yes, she was my sister, but it was nice to hear a compliment about her. Dottie was, indeed, beautiful.

Jeff continued to speak while we passed the puck between us. "That was a great idea, Paulie. It will intimidate the Bruisers that we have hot chicks cheering for us."

I turned my mouth up, a little on that comment. I was not very sure of the logic. When you are fifteen or so, screwball logic does manage to infiltrate your life!

Jeff continued to dwell on my good fortune in attracting Maureen's attention, while we passed the puck back and forth some more, "You dog you. An older chick, man . . . that is cool. I shoulda told ya that I heard from some other girls around town that she has some goo-goo eyes for you, Paulie. Hey, maybe if we win, you will earn some kind of, how shall I say, a reward!" We laughed together.

I then looked at Jeff and confidently said, "You mean, when we win!"

Soon, Geyer Street Gardens filled with the players of the Haledon Hockey League team. I suited up in my gear and began warming up as the hour to faceoff clicked closer. I felt good, I felt sharp and despite the cold day, my muscles were loose and I started to sweat. It was essential that I remained loose, so I kept moving, but I remained very careful not to overdo my warm-up routine.

Ray was still coaching us. I swear that Ray ate and slept hockey strategy. He brought along a little pad and marker, and he was drawing up a few more formations and haunting us, to fore-check and back-check as hard as we could, in order to wear them down. Ray was confident that we were in better physical condition than the Bruisers were; part of his strategy was for us to run them down hard, tire the Bruisers out.

There was one problem. Johnny the Cho woke up feeling a head cold coming on, he complained that he was a little tired, his nose was stuffy and his body had some aches and pains. Our best offensive player was not at one hundred percent! That meant that Tags would have to be at his best, and perhaps Big George could knock a few pucks in the net too.

Word of the big game had spread throughout the old neighborhood, and a crowd had gathered to watch. It was amazing how the old neighborhood bonded together, how even a simple street hockey game of the local teenagers played on a dirty, old, dead-end street, gathered support and encouragement from the residents.

The unity was remarkable and how times have changed.

Mr. Porter arrived with his best buddy, Cliffy McWhiffy, the famous obscenity hurler, and leader of the famous Chronic Mispronunciation Guys, to check out the game. Every single sentence that Cliffy said began and ended with obscenities. He did not pronounce most words correctly, and after every sentence; he habitually laughed, three loud laughs.

Every single time.

The ever-present Nit-Nat kids, (their last name was actually, Nitnatirellilini, we just changed it as we needed to, in order to say it faster with our accents) who were generally the most annoying miniature human beings on Earth, ran all over the place. I swear there were more of them every day as Mrs. Nit-Nat pumped out new Nit-Nat kids continually, as if they were on a childbirth production line. I would hate to see what their food bills were like.

Joe Hinky Doo and his old man stopped selling "stuff" on the street corners to wander over, the homeless guy who lived in the box on the end of the street, stood out in front of his "home" to see what the excitement was all about today. He was happy, because the ever-jovial Mr. Porter went over to him, slipped him a few bucks for the holiday season, told him war stories, and brought him a cup of hot coffee and a snack.

Today would provide the downtrodden sad sack, some simple entertainment, and a few simple things. Often, these simple things would mean more than if you gave him a million dollars.

Even the assistant to the rich guy was interested in the game. He stopped our warm-ups, pulled one of the fancy cars out of the garage, and then tucked it safely around a corner of the garage out of errant puck range. He then stood on the side and instead of polishing or checking the vehicle; he stood and watched the warm-ups. He, too, was going to watch the game!

This was a major event in the old neighborhood!

The lip lady was in her glory. After her obligatory yelling at us about hanging pucks on her fence (of which we had no real comment) she then invited all the spectators, except for the Nit-Nat kids, who already were hanging in her trees on the front lawn anyway, to come inside her fence, and watch the game. She had some chairs set up on her lawn; she was making hot coffee, tea, and chocolate, and serving up cookies and other various snacks.

It appeared as if for once in her life; she was not quite as lonely as she usually would have been. She had guests, perhaps, for the first time in longer than she could ever remember.

A simple game, on a dirty, old, dead-end street. On the other hand, was it? It seemed as if to us, and many other people, it was a lot more than just a simple game.

"Hi ya, Paulie!"

The guys had stopped taking shots at me, and at first, I did not know why, until I turned around to see "civilians" had wandered into the deadly zone behind the net. I also saw by the looks on my teammate's faces that something had caught their eyes. I knew that alluring voice, and I turned around to see Maureen Zipperelli, standing next to my sister, behind the net.

Oh, boy!

Maureen had a heavy winter coat on in order to combat the cold day, but she had the front of the coat open, revealing her skintight dungarees, along with a tight, white winter sweater, which adhered to her body like tossed bubblegum sticks to the sidewalk on a hot summer day. My sister looked really pretty too! However, she was my sister!

I flipped my mask up, leaned on the net, and smiled. I needed to play it cool. Cool, hippie, goalie, yeah, yeah, yeah, but in reality, my heart was pounding at the sight of Maureen Zipperelli.

"Hey, Dot. Hey, Maureen. Thanks for coming to watch."

Maureen wiggled over, while the team drooled in awe at the sight of the two gorgeous gals.

Maureen growled seductively, "Of course, Paulie. You are such a cutie. I would never miss it."

She came over and posed a little in front of me.

"Too bad you're all covered up in that equipment and I cannot close in for a better view. I will be ready after the game, though."

She winked at me and wiggled off with my sister to join the rest of the growing crowd on the lip lady's lawn.

Maureen was so aggressive.

Our heartbeats and emotions recovered from the grand entrance of the pretty ladies, and now we had to turn our focus from shapely female figures with jiggling and bouncing body parts back to hockey. We needed to return our focus quickly because out upon the horizon . . . loomed, and appeared, the enemy.

A caravan of the Buckley Park Bruisers appeared, some pedaling bicycles, some walking while holding their hockey sticks and equipment in their hands. Of course, the cocky Jimbo Carlisle led them, and they sashayed into the rink, grinning confidently at the ragtag players and avid supporters of the Haledon Hockey League.

They had a small contingent of fans and supporters, but it seemed as if, unlike us, they did not have a coach. I surmised that Jimbo Carlisle was a player-coach and he would lead and guide them. That made perfect sense because I cannot imagine any hockey coach being able to coach Jimbo Carlisle. His confidence and attitude, most likely, would not be open or conducive to allowing guidance from anyone.

Some of our supporters booed the grand entrance of the Bruisers, with the chorus of heckling led by Cliffy, who hurled his customary, obscenity-laden insults.

This was suddenly turning into a firestorm and legendary event in the history of our neighborhood! I stood there looking around at the gathering crowds of spectators and players, as well as feeling the growing excitement of the hockey match. I thought about how it might just land in the annals of historic events, right behind the Redmond's exploding swimming pool incident and the day when Sal Zucchini and his henchmen visited our neighborhood. That for sure, is another entire story!

After some small talk greetings and unusually pleasant conversation, Jimbo turned into hockey mode, "I hope your old man paid his medical insurance bills up there, twenty-seven. After this game, ya gonna need some medical attention."

I did not answer or even try to acknowledge him; I sat quietly next to my team and taped my stick. I was not about to be sucked into his ploy of rattling my nerves and allow him to get inside of my head. I needed to remain stoic and confident, even if I was shaking inside. I was not playing down to Jimbo's level.

The sport of hockey is rough and tumble and I had already learned that all too often, mind games were a large part of the strategy. It is a game of territorial properties, and the more you can occupy the enemy's territory with the puck in a scoring position, then the better your chance of scoring and winning. To establish your turf, you push, fight, shove and bang to establish camp. If you can intimidate, then the occupancy aspect of the game becomes easier!

Simple game, simple strategy.

The warm-up period before the game is vital to intimidating the opponent. During the warm-ups, each team lined up on the centerline and carefully observed the other team while trying hard to gauge the talents and to discover potential weaknesses. In warm-ups, you did your best to show off your skills by displaying hard slap shots to frighten the opposition goaltender and to show off your goalie's remarkable ability to stop the biscuit. An unwritten rule amongst teammates was that, when you warm-up your own goalie, you never try to make him look bad. My team did a good job and our warm-ups went well. I felt we were very organized and impressive. Ray ran an efficient hockey machine, blowing his whistle, waving at us, shouting instructions, all while he was coaching us in some shooting and intricate passing drills. We looked good.

We were ready to go, therefore, when the Bruisers set up to warm-up their team, we all watched eagerly. Big Wex, Big George and Johnny the Cho, stood at the centerline on our side of the zone and watched rather closely.

We needed to show our own muscle.

When Jimbo Carlisle launched his first slap shot, and it rocketed into the net and just about went through the back of the cage, all of my teammates turned and looked at me.

His shot was the real deal. I saw it and swallowed hard. Jeff was standing next to me while we stood together in front of our net and carefully watched the Bruisers team warming up.

Jeff was leaning on the top of his stick watching the Bruisers warm-up and he leaned in and made an observation, "Holy shit! Damn, Paulie. Ya had better buckle ya mask tight. He has a rocket of a shot." Jeff looked at me rather suspiciously and asked, "Ya okay?"

"I am ready, Jeffrey."

Jeff smiled and tapped my pads with his stick.

"Shit yeah, Paulie. I know you are ready. Your friggin' eyes are burning a hole in ya mask."

The Bruisers were a mixture of tall, short, big and small players. They all seemed very skilled, good stick handlers, and the team had a small, quick, goaltender whose nickname seemed to be "Jackrabbit." The nickname fit him well. He could play; he was fast, cut his angles down effectively, and he seemed to be very experienced. I sensed some of our confidence fading because the Buckley Park Bruisers were a lot better than we had hoped they were.

Lumpy, the referee, stood at the center faceoff circle, a wristwatch on his wrist that he explained also doubled as a game timer. He was wearing an actual referee jersey, and he was fully equipped with a whistle on a rope around his neck. The Bruisers came from a little more of an upscale neighborhood than we did, and it showed in their outfitting and equipment. They all had matching jerseys and fancy equipment and we were all secretly hoping that it was all show and no substance. Somehow, I felt in my heart that they could back it all up.

Lumpy stood at the center faceoff circle while he discussed the various rules with Ray and Jimbo. Lumpy was going to be fine; he looked more as if he was a college student than he was a hockey referee. He wore thick glasses with a black frame that hung on a chain around his neck. His thick black hair combed over in a sweep to the side and some type of greasy goo held it in place. And most importantly, Lumpy was very serious. I felt as if he would control the game; you could tell that he knew what he was doing!

Lumpy waved, and he was ready.

We all were ready.

I jumped in the net, pulled my mask down over my face

and crouched down, ready to go. Maureen, Dottie, Mr. Porter, and Cliffy were all cheering wildly, but I ignored them. Number twenty-seven now focused on the task at hand. I had waited a long time for this day. My heart was pounding in my chest, and despite the cold, I felt a trickle of sweat running down my face and gathering in the belly of the chin of my mask.

Jeff came over and tapped my goalie pads with his stick, as did Big Wex and the rest of the team. Ray started the game with Big Wex and Jeff on defense with Big George and Johnny the Cho on offense. That left Ray, Tags, Handsome Mike, and Pooch on the bench. Lumpy organized the faceoff, checked first with Jackrabbit and then with me. We both raised our sticks to signal that we were ready.

Lumpy checked the time, and Jimbo faced Johnny. Lumpy dropped the puck, and the game was underway! Jimbo won a clean draw; he moved the puck quickly to his right and cut across the high slot. Jeff moved out to defend him, but it was too late. He had wound up and rocketed a slap shot that rose so quickly, I hardly had time to set and square up to the shooter. Already, just a few seconds into the biggest game that I had ever played in and I had made the classic goaltender mistake! I did not square up to my shooter. I lost track of the puck after it left Jimbo's stick and now I lost it within a screen, while I remained flat-footed in the net. I tried to follow the puck, but it was rising harder and faster than I initially thought. The puck blew under Jeff's armpit and beat me cleanly and hard above my stick side, just above my right shoulder.

My heart sank when I heard the puck hit the net behind me.

"SCORE! SCORE! SCORE!"

Lumpy blew the whistle and signaled a goal. The Bruisers screamed and his teammates mobbed Jimbo. A loud groan filled the air from our supporters. Ten seconds into the game and we were already down by a goal.

Jimbo had blown me away.

I had never seen a shot that was so hard.

"Sorry for the screen, Paulie," Jeff apologized as I picked myself off the street.

"C'mon, twenty-seven, ya can't suck today," Big Wex warned.

"My fault, no screen, my fault," I mumbled, while I leaned in hard and buckled down in a tight crouch. I bounced in my crouch, working hard to loosen my back and convince myself that Jimbo's shot was not too hard, not too fast, and that he was not going to eat me alive today.

Whom was I kidding? This was rough. His shot was a bloody blur. I had just lost all my confidence and my stomach was in a knot.

Our fans, even Dottie and Maureen, were stunned and silent. The lip lady leaned on her fence and clapped her hands feebly. I could hear Ray shouting encouragement from the sideline. There was a sense of foreboding that Jimbo Carlisle was going to eat all of us alive, not to mention the rest of the Bruisers, and that I was the main course.

Lumpy brought the teams together for another faceoff, and Jimbo pointed the blade of his stick at me as a threat.

"Here it comes again, long hair! You told me to bring it on, so buckle ya chin straps and grab ya sorry ass because here it comes again!"

The next faceoff was the same result. Once again, Johnny the Cho cleanly lost the draw. Jimbo moved the puck the same way, but this time, just as he moved to the high slot, Big Wex caught him with his head looking down and he leveled him with a hard, but what I thought was a clean body check.

Jimbo went flying backwards, his stick flying in the air. One of his gloves fell off his hand, and he tumbled over and landed hard. His feet left the ground and he must have been airborne for at least five feet!

The puck scooted off Jimbo's stick when Big Wex hit him and it went over the fence on the side of the street. Lumpy blew the whistle to signal a stoppage of play, and he pointed at Big Wex to signal a penalty, too.

Jimbo's teammates seemed shocked that their hero was sitting on his backside and they rallied to his support.

"There ya go there, hotshot! Swallow some blood, asshole! Tough to score when you are lying flat on your smart ass. Hope ya swallowed some of your fancy teeth, too. Bet they are rattling around in ya mouth, ya cocky son of a bitch," Big Wex taunted him.

You could see from the look on Jimbo's face that he was not used to sitting on his backside, nor used to a player confronting him. It had taken some of the wind out of him. Big Wex caught him high and hard, with his head down, and surely it hurt more than just his pride.

"Two minutes for a cross check!" Lumpy yelled out and signaled a penalty to Big Wex!

Oh, no! We were going to be shorthanded, and while there continued to be some jawing, pushing and shoving going on after the whistle; both teams did not want to risk another penalty.

Ray protested the call, but it was too early in the game to get on Lumpy's bad side, so he let it die quickly. Ray changed the line and sent Tags out, along with Handsome Mike, and amid ongoing protests, Lumpy dropped the puck.

The Bruisers won the draw, passed the puck crisply on the faceoff, and we set up to defend the power play. Of course, it was a set play, and the puck went back to Jimbo, who set for the big slapper from the point. I had a clean look this time as Jeff cleared the way, and Jimbo nailed the shot, and on purpose, sent it towards my head. It clipped me cleanly on the face of my mask, high and hard, and the force of the shot knocked me backwards, but I kept my wits. The puck dropped at my feet and I covered it up for a faceoff before a Bruisers' player could knock it loose.

"Next one is into your groin, hippie! The pretty gal over there screaming for ya is going to be crying, too. Ya told me to bring it on. So ya are going to get it now!" Jimbo yelled.

"Geez, that's how you want to play, huh? Head shot, on purpose there, ya jackass," Jeff scolded Jimbo while we were all lining up for the faceoff. "Ya okay, Paulie?"

I nodded my head, but the warm trickle rolling down inside my mask told me that there was a cut to deal with now.

I ignored it.

The puck dropped and after a few mad scrambles, a few hard checks, the puck slipped to a small winger for the Bruisers who had a clean shot at the net while he was standing in the low slot. I had been stuck on one post; I threw myself to the other post and tipped the puck enough with my glove to make the save. We watched as the puck went flying up over the net and it flew out of play.

This time, it was our chance to cheer!

"Nice friggin' save there, Paulie! It is like ya are oncontenshis! HA! HA! HA!" Cliffy yelled out, trying hard to figure out how to say the word "unconscious."

"Buon lavoro," Maureen was yelling.

I was not sure what Maureen was babbling in Italian, but I was sure it was some kind of praise. There was a strange feeling coming from inside of me. I stood tall; I smiled and pulled my mask off. It was a warm feeling, a confidence, and a flow. I was on it now!

"Big save! Nice. Shit, ya cut badly there, Paulie. Under your eye," Jeff said as he looked at me.

"I am good." I took the cloth that held my cross out of my pocket, wiped the blood away, and held it hard on the cut for a minute or two, while Lumpy retrieved the puck. For Jeff to give me an honest analysis of the severity, I leaned towards him.

"Stitches?" I asked Jeff.

Jeff looked closely and examined the cut.

"Could be that ya need at least one. Maybe two, Paulie. I damn sure have seen ya have worse cuts."

"Ain't worried about one or two . . . it can bleed for a bit. Eventually, the cold will stop it."

I pulled the mask back over my head and was back in the game. That was it; the Haledon Hockey League was in the flow now, too. The hit by Big Wex had evened the score, and it had changed the entire tone of the game.

Up and down, we went for two solid periods. Body checks, clean shots, big saves by both goalies. Jackrabbit was good, and Johnny the Cho, Big George, and Tags were trying as hard as they could to score, but he had a solid defense in front of him. It was hard to manage a clean shot or to catch them out of position.

Jimbo Carlisle was growing frustrated. His cockiness was now gone, and Big George was punishing him at every chance he had, all in a slow progress to take a little toll on Jimbo's body. I stopped Jimbo's hardest and most accurate shots now, and the set plays they had, we now were wise to and they no longer worked as effectively. One or two times, I was beat, but Jeff saved me on one with a big shot block and Big Wex leveled a Bruiser in front of the net, and allowed me to make a kick save on a tough angle shot.

Between periods, Jeff managed to stop the bleeding a little on the cut under my eye, and the lip lady was kind enough to give Dottie and Maureen a bandage to place on the cut and help to slow the blood flow for now.

Handsome Mike the Italian kid, suffered a stick to the eye. It was sure to be black by the morning and well, he will have to be a little less handsome for a few days!

The battle scars were now adding up on each side, as the game toiled on and on, in a hard-fought struggle for both sides.

About two minutes into the third period, we were still only down one goal to zero, when Ray called out a play to Johnny and Tags, who worked a perfect give and go, and Johnny slipped the puck neatly under the Bruisers' goalie. We all went wild! We had finally tied the score!

"HELL YEAH! IT IS ABOUT DAMN TIME YOUSE JERKS SCORED! HA! HA! HA!" Cliffy hurled obscenity after obscenity into the air, while Mr. Porter failed in his efforts to shut him up. Dottie and Maureen wildly cheered, Joe Hinky Doo celebrated with a "smoke of a suspicious nature" behind a clump of tall shrubs, and even a few of the Nit-Nat kids, stopped throwing rocks at the lip lady's cat in order to cheer for us.

Ray came off the bench to play a little offense because Johnny the Cho was running out of gas. It seemed as if his head cold was worsening. We had played the game hard and clean on both ends until there was finally no time left in the game. Lumpy blew the whistle and waved his hands. The game was over and it ended in a one-to-one tie!

"Sudden death overtime!" Lumpy yelled out.

It had been a brutally tough game. Both teams were evenly matched and players were cut, cold, bleeding, sore and tired and now we had to suck it up for just twenty minutes more, or until a goal was scored.

"Ya okay there, twenty-seven?" Ray asked me as we all sat with our backs on the rich guy's garage door and we all tried very hard to recover our senses and muster our courage.

"The cut is bleeding badly again. For certain, I think ya need a stitch or two."

"I am good. A little hard to see now. I think the cut is swelling. My eye closed a little. I am good, though."

Ray nodded and coached us for a last hurrah.

"C'mon, youse guys. They are just as tired as we are. Suck it up for a little longer. Look over at them! They are hurtin', bleedin', and just as cold as we are! C'mon, guys!"

"I can't go, Ray. I can't breathe anymore. I feel like fever is taking my body over. Shit, I am sorry, Ray. I got to sit out," Johnny the Cho was gassed, and he looked terrible. "This head cold is too much now. I feel like shit and I can't stop shaking like a leaf. And this cold weather is not helping me much. I am sorry, youse guys. I got to sit."

"You look like crap too," Big Wex commented.

We were stunned.

Our best scorer, sudden death overtime, and Johnny the Cho could not go.

"I need a few minutes too, Ray. I am cramping a little here. This dry and cold weather sucks, it gets inside of you," Tags was shaking his head and holding his legs.

We were out of players . . . all except for one.

Ray looked up and down at his worn-out team and his eyes stopped on, Pooch. The little red-haired kid jumped to his feet, grabbed his stick, and shouted, "I am ready, Coach Ray! I will not let youse guys down!"

Big Wex howled with a protest, "Shit no! Ya can't put Pooch in now, Ray. One damn mistake and it is over! What the hell are you thinkin'? This is sudden, damn, death, Ray!"

Ray looked around nervously, but he had very little choice. The game was restarting. Lumpy was blowing the whistle and calling us out for the start of overtime.

The pressure was on.

Ray's eyes went back and forth. . ..

Our coach spoke his options aloud, as he struggled with his decision, "I could put Handsome Mike on offense. Or I could go in, but I need to coach this overtime." Ray stomped his foot as he made his decision! He turned and adamantly said, "Nah, shit! Pooch, you're in the game. Give me five minutes, Pooch. Run them to death. Ya legs are fresh! Five friggin' minutes Pooch, that is all I ask . . . until Tags can go back in!"

Ray grabbed Pooch by the shoulders and shook him.

"Stay in position, Pooch. Don't cheat or get caught deep in the zone. Listen to me!"

Pooch nodded, and just before we all trotted out, Ray grabbed Big George by the shoulders and whispered to him, "Set a screen, George! If and when you get a chance, set the screen. Jeff can shoot from the point. Set your feet in front of the goal and dare them to move ya big ass outta the way!"

Big George nodded, and we all went out for the faceoff.

Big George and Pooch on offense. Handsome Mike the Italian kid, and Jeff Porter on defense.

This was it. This was all that we had left. A ragtag, makeshift group of players.

Our supporters were going crazy now, drowning out the small contingent of Bruisers' supporters. Everyone was leaning in now. The rich guy's assistant even clapped, cheered, and stood next to the homeless man, who cheered wildly for us too.

Big George seldom took faceoffs, but when Lumpy dropped the puck, he was on it, and he surprisingly beat Jimbo cleanly. His superior weight and muscle pushed forward, and the puck sprung into the offensive zone.

Sometimes, you need to listen to the coach!

Every player on our team did exactly what Ray Edelski warned us not to do.

Pooch took the bait worse than anyone else did. He was so eager to capture the puck and create a scoring chance that he cheated too deep into the zone in anticipation that the puck was clear of the Bruisers.

It was not.

A defenseman for the Bruisers captured the puck. He lifted it high in the air, and it dropped in perfectly on the centerline, right where Jimbo Carlisle was waiting.

Ray screamed from the sideline, "GET THE HELL BACK! GET BACK!"

Jeff realized the sudden turn of the play, and he made a

last second, gallant dive for the puck, but it was too late. Jimbo was in the attack zone! He was free and clear, one on one on a breakaway.

Here it came down to, ironically, in sudden death overtime, Jimbo, versus number twenty-seven.

I crept out to cut the angle down, and I tapped the side of the right post of the net hard with my goalie stick, to measure how far out I had crept. The tap provided me the measurement that I needed, and I now knew that I had the exact angle I wanted.

Harry's words echoed in my mind, "Not a marble can get by you, twenty-seven. Not even a marble!"

I shut it all out. I could not hear the screams from anyone, not Maureen, or Dottie, Mr. Porter, or Cliffy.

No one.

I did not hear the coaching from Ray on the sideline or the screams from Big Wex telling me to come out of the net and try to beat Jimbo to the puck.

It was a feeling that I was in, and I came to call it, "The Flow."

Later on, in my life, it would serve me well.

Right now, I trusted my instincts.

My goaltending book told me to watch the shooter's eyes, and I bounced between Carlisle's eyes and the puck. He went to his forehand, and then to his backhand, and his eyes looked low on the glove side. Then, I saw his eyes lock upon my stick side low, and I surmised that is where he was going.

Guess, Paul. Just friggin' guess.

Jimbo flipped to his backhand. I jumped to my stick side low and leaned in that position.

I guessed . . . correctly.

I had come out just far enough and taken away the shooting angle to all, except that one location. Jimbo's shot was soft; he tried hard to put a trickle touch upon his shot, and he assumed it would slip underneath me. He assumed wrong. The puck hit very softly on my stick and it landed in a dull "thud" at my feet. I watched as Jimbo's momentum took him out of the play and he tumbled behind the net.

Jeff recovered, he finally made it back, and he came in sliding hard and fast on his knee pads into the crease in front of me. He stopped and rolled when he saw that I had made the save and I was planning to handle the puck with my stick. I kept my balance and my wits, looked up and saw Pooch and Big George standing free at the centerline!

All the Bruisers, except for one defenseman, had pinched in since they were thinking that it was a sure goal, and they had guessed wrong and ended up trapped deep in the wrong zone. Pooch tapped his stick hard on the asphalt, coaxing me for the pass, and pass the puck I did. A perfect pass!

The puck landed crisply, right smack on his blade!

Two on one—the other way!

Ray screamed, "Set the screen, Big George! Set the friggin' damn screen!" Big George set up in front of the goalie and the Bruisers defenseman tried desperately to move the big guy, but it was to no avail.

"Shoot the damn puck, POOCH!" Ray Edelski screamed.

Poor Ray was going to burst a blood vessel, have a stroke, or perhaps, a combination thereof!

Pooch crept in, and just past the left faceoff circle, he lined it up and let it ride. Pooch hit it perfectly, the puck was low and hard, and right at the last moment, Big George jumped in the air and the puck passed under his feet, and it blew by the fallen Bruiser's goalie!

After that, it was a blur.

All I remember was Lumpy blowing the whistle and signaling a goal!

I heard Jimbo Carlisle scream, "NO!"

And that was it! The game was over!

Fans and players alike mobbed the beloved rink, and

everyone mobbed, knocked over and buried poor Pooch. I saw the lip lady jumping for joy, hugging and kissing Mr. Porter. Cliffy was hurling loud obscenities and hugging Dottie and Maureen. The Nit-Nat kids ran all over like little tornadoes, and the homeless guy went over and shook hands with the rich guy's assistant. And, of course, Joe Hinky Doo broke out another, "smoke."

The honor of Geyer Street was intact! The celebration was on!

It was a madhouse on the street! Pooch was a hero! The little red-haired Italian kid had won the game.

Jeff looked up at me; he repositioned his famous ball cap on his head, wiped his face and smiled as he said, "Holy shit, Paulie. Damn! Well, Jimbo, he can now kiss my royal ass. Like you do, I think that I have royal blood somewhere on my mother's side. Pooch just won the effin' game!"

I lifted my mask off my face, trickles of blood from my cut rolled around inside of it as I tucked it inside the top of my leg pads. I felt my back pocket to make sure the cross was still there.

It was.

Jeff and I quickly embraced, and then we ran to greet the rest of our team.

When we finally could let poor Pooch up from the ground, as we peeled him up and out from under a crush of his teammates, I noticed that tears of joy ran down his cheeks.

"I told youse guys that I could shoot! I knew that I could score!" Pooch screamed jubilantly.

Maureen reached me, she hugged me and there in the middle of the rink as my teammates admired my good fortune, she let me have a big kiss right on the ole kisser! My first ever!

"Oh, Paulie! You need to have that terrible cut taken care of quickly. It is bleeding badly now. I will kiss your pain away."

Oh geez, I thought. I hope the guys did not hear that one.

Maureen was so aggressive.

Maureen was screaming something in Italian, and Pooch was answering her in Italian. All I could understand was, "Viva Italia!"

After she was finished smooching me up, and turning my feelings inside and out, she then ran up and gave the very embarrassed Pooch, the hero, a kiss on his cheek! He turned even redder than usual!

When the celebration died down, we all lined up and, just as is the custom in the big leagues, we all shook hands with the Bruisers.

Jimbo Carlisle reached me; he smiled and shook my hand fervently. He then hugged me and his embrace was very sincere.

"Hey, nice, damn game, twenty-seven. Sorry about the cut there. Nuthin' personal. You are the best goalie that I have ever seen or played against. Ever. Ya, a hippie and a long-haired freak, yet man, ya can play some damn hot ass goalie. Fearless and a little stupid, man, that's what ya are. No one ever stops me on breakaways. I bet someday that you will make it big. Then, I will have the honor of saying at least that I faced ya and scored one on ya!"

"Thanks, Jimbo. You are the best shooter I have ever seen. Good luck to you."

Therefore, it ended.

The game of a lifetime. A game full of memories.

A game, which turned me from a boy playing around as a goalie, into a young man who loved the challenge that the position brought not only to me physically but also mentally.

The game experience had changed me forever.

We all sat and talked for hours about the game and celebrated our hard-fought victory. Maureen, my sister, Mr. Porter, and Cliffy hung around too. It seemed as if everyone felt the emotion of the win. Before we knew it, but we surely all felt it. The day grew colder and darker and it was time to head home. We all parted, tired, worn out, cut and sore, but winners!

I walked home with Maureen and Dottie and when I walked in the back door, the old man took one look at me and said, "Oh, geez! More money! This time, let me try some butterflies on that cut. Eat your heart out, Salami, ya bum!"

I think the presence of Maureen, and the sympathy and testimony of my sister, softened the old man up just a bit. Maureen stayed for dinner and she talked all of our ears off. She, too, had caught hockey fever. It was going around now. I think the old man wanted to use some butterflies on Maureen's mouth for a bit of time.

The old man used some butterfly sutures on my cut and Mum made me sit like a dope with an ice pack on it to take the swelling down.

After dinner, Maureen called her father to come pick her up, and we sat together on the front steps of 182 Belmont Avenue and waited for Mr. Zipperelli to arrive.

"I am a little cold, Paulie. You could come a little closer and keep me warm, you know."

"Okay, Maureen," I said as I wiggled a little closer and Maureen snuggled right up against me. She was soft, and she was snug too, and she smelled like Heaven on Earth.

"So, when is your next game?"

"I dunno. I will let you know. Did you enjoy it?"

"Enjoy it? It was the most exciting game that I have ever seen! You were great! I do not know how you stand in front of that puck thing. It must hurt."

"Oh no," I sputtered like a boastful idiot.

"It does not hurt a bit," I said as I fingered the cut under my eye.

Maureen stared at the cut under my eye and the swelling, and she laughed.

"You are such a shitty liar, but such a cutie, too!"

She then leaned in and gave me another kiss. This one was a lot longer. Maureen always smelled a little like garlic, but I did not mind.

Maureen was so aggressive.

Mr. Zipperelli's junky old car pulled into our driveway and he honked the horn loudly. Mr. Zipperelli stuck his head out the window and shouted in his broken English, "Haya younga Paulini! Congratoolaytioninis ona yooseaa guysa winni biga gamarini!"

"Thank you, Mr. Zipperelli!"

"You better call me!" Maureen shouted as she ran towards the car.

I stood up and yelled back, "Call you, what?"

She laughed, smiled and said, "You and that dry sense of humor. You know what I mean, Paulie."

I waved as she tore away in her father's car. Mr. Zipperelli drove like a wild man.

That night, I climbed into my rack and every single muscle in my entire body ached. It felt as if a freight train had run me over, yet I never felt better in my entire life.

We had a rematch with the Bruisers a few weeks later. We played on a bitter cold December day over at Buckley Park. We had Harry back, and Johnny the Cho was feeling full strength and fully recovered from his illness.

However, it was not the same as the first game was.

The magic was gone compared to our first meeting. We had better players, stronger players. Ray was a better coach, and we cleaned them up. A shutout! A win by the score of five to zip.

Time would pass, and my goodness, there would be so many more hockey games, so many more adventures, so many more cuts, bruises, stitches, ice packs, saves and goals. Not too many of them ever matched that game on Geyer Street Gardens on that cold November afternoon for pure, heartfelt joy of competition and hard-fought victory.

On that windswept afternoon, a group of teenagers turned from boys to men, and we learned that with teamwork, you could achieve almost anything that you set your mind out to do.

Oh yes, and I learned that a kiss and a few hugs from a pretty gal on a bitter cold day can be somewhat inspiring and warms your heart too!

Geyer Street Gardens

Part Two

Harry and Paul

The Hockey Players

1

Only Two Remain

Sadly, time and life passed poor Geyer Street Gardens by. It faded into obscurity and transformed back into a dead-end street once again. Even those crazy white lines finally faded away.

Only the ghosts remained.

The only remnants of the Haledon Hockey League left were the three original guys who started it all, Harry M. Redmond Junior, Jeffrey Scott Porter, and Paul John Henson.

Most of the players in the league went on to attend college; some moved away, some remained in the area, some even got married early in their lives, but mostly, they lost interest in playing street hockey.

However, for three boyhood friends, the hockey dream remained, and in many ways, it even grew.

We graduated trade school; we found jobs; we learned to drive and bought trucks and hot rod sports cars. We met young women, fell in and out of love, and grew into young men.

Outside of hockey, we had many adventures. Dear reader, it would take many, many pages to document all that happened to us and all that we experienced. Someday,

I will do my best to fill it all in. For now, all I can relate to you are the many stories of these wild hockey adventures, where they brought us, and where they led us.

Jeff, Harry, and I all continued to play hockey. We picked up games with a semi-pro street league that played all over northern New Jersey. Some older guys we had met invited us to join forces with them, and we actually earned some prize money when we won a few games. We also played on roller skates, in some roller hockey leagues in both New Jersey and some across the river in New York City. The roller leagues in the city were rough and tumble leagues. They were full of blood, fights, guts, referees who took payoffs to look the other way, and games with no hard and fast rules. There we were, Jersey guys wandering across the river and slowly, our reputations for being formidable, "hired gun" type hockey players grew.

We were the New Jersey trio with two big, tough-guy defensemen, accompanied by their long-haired hippie, goaltending sidekick. It was quite interesting.

When ice formed upon the ponds and northern New Jersey experienced long, cold winters, we skated and fooled around with pond ice hockey. Ice hockey, now that brought us to another level entirely.

As the years passed, and we grew older, another byproduct of growing into young men turned out to be the introduction of many young women in our lives. Harry dated too many gals for me to keep track of! He always had a multitude of young women chasing him around, and he required a scorecard to keep track of them all.

I was very low key in my romantic life. Harry was my polar opposite. In actual comparison to Harry's romantic schedules, every male in America would be jealous! Harry was, in fact, a terrible womanizer. He constantly juggled multiple relationships simultaneously.

However, the one constant in my romantic life was Miss Maureen Zipperelli.

My sister had moved to the west coast to take a job in California, and even though her best friend was gone, Maureen was always around. Maureen was my most avid supporter and my only fan club member. She showed up at many of our street and roller games to watch me play, and we had a special, but somewhat undefined, relationship.

We often double-dated with Harry and his revolving cast of different loves and whenever I had some rare extra coins in my pocket, Maureen and I went on solo dates. Maureen was great fun; she was gorgeous to look at, and she seemed quite attached to me. I cannot say that I objected to that fact. It was just that I had this magnificent dream of playing professional hockey, and to be involved in a serious relationship with a young lady did not quite fit that dream at the moment.

Looking back now, I was only fooling myself.

At the time, I might have been trying hard to convince myself that this was just a casual relationship, a passing fancy, but the actual truth was, it was indeed a lot deeper than just a casual attachment. Maureen and I did actually spend more time together and I had to admit, she was very special to me, but I tried very hard to convince myself not to fall in love with her. I had to keep telling myself that I was not in love, and that this was just a fleeting romance of sorts, a good friend to spend time with, just a companion.

I felt as if it was nothing very serious, but despite my efforts, as so often is in our lives—the truth is often hard to face. Maureen made no effort at all to hide how she felt about me, and she clarified that she wanted to turn our relationship up a few notches.

The fact that she was older was of some concern to me. Mum and my friends thought it was silly, since she was only a little less than three years older than I was. Harry would outright tell me that I was acting like an old lady and that I was crazy!

"Maureen is gorgeous! She is a knockout! Are ya

kiddin'! What a body on that chick! Besides, she is crazy about you, too. I would take her to a dark room. . .."

Well, you get the picture, and I am sure you can fill in the blanks.

Harry was bombastic, gregarious, and somewhat overwhelming, but he really meant no harm. Harry's advice in the pursuit of females could be sometimes overzealous, and at times lewd, but he tried his best to convince me to shake the "Mr. Nice Guy" image, or as he often would label it, "The Old Lady Syndrome."

I also had to admit that Harry's observation of Maureen's appearance was indeed quite correct. Maureen was gorgeous, and as she grew a little older, she had lost all of her baby weight and while she was still a bit on the curvy side; she was fantastically shapely and well; I am not ashamed to say that Maureen Zipperelli was very attractive, alluring, and an extremely sexy young lady! She was a captivating woman, with dark features and a sultry allure that followed her everywhere. Her voice was full of soft seduction, a faint Italian accent mixed with a New Jersey twang, and her smile could melt your heart. I was the envy of many men when I was lucky enough to go out on a date with the gorgeous and captivating Maureen Zipperelli on my arm. She *was* a knockout!

I did not say that I was not interested; it was just that I had some other things on my mind too, and a full-time, romantic commitment to a gal was not high on my list at the moment.

Looking back, I must have been crazy.

For Jeff, however, it was a different situation. He had met a gal in our last years of school, who was a year or so younger than he was. What we all thought was a casual relationship had turned into a serious romance. The romance was the real deal, and Jeff slowly spent more time with his gal, Debbie, than he did with his two boyhood buddies.

Harry and I did not blame him; Debbie looked a lot better than the two of us looked! Jeff and Debbie eventually married, but that is also a different story.

As time marched on by us, our worlds changed, and the normal progress of life occurred. Jeff Porter moved on, and before we knew it, Jeff too, put hockey on the shelf. Soon, only two players remained of the Haledon Hockey League. Harry M. Redmond Junior, the bombastic and charismatic number thirty-five, and his best buddy of all these years, Paul John Henson, who most people knew as number twenty-seven.

Oh, oh! Look out, world!

A turning point in our world of hockey came about in and around the year 1975 or thereabouts. A local investor built a full-scale hockey arena and ice-skating venue in the town of Great Falls, New Jersey, about two towns outside of where we lived.

A hockey shrine! A golden land on the horizon. They called the arena Ice Land, and to Harry and me, it became our second home. We quickly learned by skating public skating sessions, you could meet many young ladies, and we drooled over watching "real" hockey teams and leagues play on "real" hockey rinks!

We also recognized the need to learn to improve our skating abilities. If we had any hopes of taking our street and roller hockey skills to the ice, then it was imperative that we learned how to improve our ice-skating skills. We never doubted that we would succeed, and within a short period of time, we would become accomplished hockey ice skaters. Harry and I truly believed that we could achieve anything that we set our mind to. We looked upon this as just another challenge, just another obstacle.

Therefore, we skated, and we skated, and we skated. . ..

"I have my eye on that full set of goalie equipment, thirty-five. I just have one trouble. It is an awful lot of dough. I need to raise another three hundred dollars or so,"

I explained to Harry while he stood on the front sidewalk, and I sat on the front steps of his house at 20 John Street. Harry fiddled with the latest gadget from his new hobby of photography, as he pointed his new and very expensive camera in the sky and adjusted the focus on the lens while we spoke.

It was April 1976 or thereabouts, and I was once again lamenting to Harry about a common trouble for me these days, which was a severe lack of funds. I did have a decent job, working as an electronic and electrical technician, but it did not pay anywhere near the wage, in which Harry earned working as a welder in his dad's metal fabrication shop. Harry always had a good amount of extra dough in his wallet. His main trouble was that he sometimes spent it a lot quicker than he earned it. The camera was just another example of his expensive spending habits.

"Yeah, yeah, yeah, well, you just dropped what? Four hundred buck-a-roo-skis on those goalie skates. Geez, c'mon, twenty-seven, think, man! Ya bought top of the line skates, in fact, professional skates. Ya could have saved a few bucks and bought a step down, but I guess it is not worth it. Those pucks in the skate boot must hurt like a son of a bitch."

Harry waved his hands in the air at me; he was working hard to make a point.

"Yup, they do. Break your foot and toes too. It is not worth it to go cheap on a skate. Yes, they were expensive, but how much was the new camera, Harry?"

At first, Harry frowned at me, and then he quickly covered his tracks.

"Yeah, yeah, yeah, but I worked a great deal with the guy, and I got this puppy for a forty percent discount."

Harry seemed as if he had an air of sympathy for me. He let his camera hang down on the strap around his neck; he wandered over closer to me and leaned casually on the fence in front of his house, next to the step where I was sitting.

"Look, twenty-seven, ya gotta go and work a deal with Wurtzberg Brothers downtown. Ya know, maybe pay them off on time. If ya want to be part of that goalie clinic in the fall of this year, then ya need to shake ya ass and you had better have the equipment by then. I thought that Dottie knew the big shot owner guy at Wurtzberg. Ya know, from when she worked downtown for that big deal, lawyer guy. Maybe she can make a few calls for you and work the deal. Call ya sister out there in Californiah-a-roo-ski and have her set the deal for ya. Ya sister is a hot chickee poo, those Wurtzberg boys will hear her voice, and it will spin them there, beanie Hanukahs, or whatever ya call 'em on their heads and they will be ready to deal. You have to learn how to work deals, twenty-seven. That nice guy stuff holds you back. I have to teach you everything!"

This was a typical Harry speech, full of passion, yet in a roundabout way, good advice.

I ignored his usual criticism of me and said, "I can do that, Harry. I will give Dottie a shout and see if she can call them next week."

"Great! And as a bonus, well, you are in luck, because as usual, I have come to the rescue with an incredible money-making opportunity for us!"

I shuddered at the mere mention of a money-making opportunity, because this usually meant some type of impossible mission, or some kind of looming disaster on the horizon of Harry and Paul.

Harry suddenly stood up, and he quickly snapped a picture of a bird flying across the road, with the ever-present camera he now carried constantly around his neck.

The Redmonds were famous for the various, as we called them, "phases" that the family went through. The story of the famous Redmond phases, I will strategically leave for another set of words down the road, but right now, the entire Redmond and Boatmann families were firmly entrenched in a photography phase of their lives. Harry, as well as every single Redmond and Boatmann family member, now carried cameras and lenses, extra film in camera bags, tripods, and other camera accessories wherever they went.

"I think that was one of those rare white and grey speckled zippy birds! I got one helluva picture of it too. Gonna sell it and make a shit ton of dough."

I watched as the bird, which appeared to be an ordinary city pigeon, circled and landed on the roof of the Gingert Lace factory next door.

"Harry, please, it is just a pigeon. Anyway, what is this opportunity?"

"Nah! That was no pigeon. I have seen them rare birds on that show on television. Ya know, the show is sponsored by that disgusting Dingleberry beer."

I simply sat there and shook my head without even commenting. Sometimes Harry was too much.

"I know rare birds! Ah, man! I need more film! I might have missed that shot." Harry was feverishly checking his camera while winding some type of lever on top of the camera's body.

"This hobby is costing me a fortune. I need the extra dough to buy more camera stuff and still save for that fancy car I want to buy this summer. Yeah, yeah, yeah, I met this weirdo named Len Starrett, or it might be Ben Carrot. I can't remember which it is, but anyway, I met him while welding some counters at a diner over in Bergen County. He saw how big and strong I was, and he asked me if me and my buddy had a truck and we wanted to make some extra dough delivering appliances."

Harry looked at me for a response and all I could think of to ask was, "Why, is he a weirdo?"

"The guy is a nervous wreck, twenty-seven. He fidgets all over the place and has this big knot thing on his forehead. It is some kind of growth or something."

"Well, maybe he has a medical condition, Harry. You should be more sympathetic."

"Nah, nah, nah. He is a whack job, Paul. He owns an appliance store over in Rock Glen, and he is looking for some guys to help him on the weekend. He says he will pay us big time. It sounded easy."

"Oh, geez. I do not know about that, Harry. You need to have insurance to go into people's houses and perform work. What if we were to damage something? We could get sued."

Harry rolled his eyes at my predictable response and he started in on me, "Oh geez, there you go. You know, for a pauper, a guy down to your last friggin' nickel, you sure are fussy about your methods of income. The Old Lady Syndrome and Mr. Nice Guy are taking over your mind! Sue, you for what? An old piece of junk truck that barely runs, and a pair of new goalie skates. It is not like ya own anything that is worth a shit, twenty-seven. Soon, you will be on your own, and no offense, but your old man will kick your ass out soon, anyway. He is tired of paying for stitches! Dr. Salami can retire on your head repairs alone."

"By the way, I have my own medical insurance now. You might be correct in the fact that I own very little, but you have stuff!" I hit Harry where it hurt. "They could take your cameras and the Takajunky is not a bad car." At the time, Harry drove the Japanese made 1971 Takajunky Model 10, and once we fixed it up and put a new engine in the car, it was not a bad set of wheels.

"Ah geez, twenty-seven! Stop acting like an old lady, will ya? You need the money for goalie equipment. What choice do you have? Relax, Paul! It will be a piece of cake. After all, how bad can it be?"

There were those words again! It was such a common theme for me now that you would think I would not allow it to bother me any longer. Those few words were the ultimate kiss of death. Now, all Harry had to do was cap it all off with his famous grand finale saying, "After all, what could happen?"

Harry jumped up and pointed in the sky at what was obviously an ordinary civilian airplane coming down to a landing altitude for a final approach to Newark Airport.

"Look! I think it could be a UFO, or one of those secret military aircraft! Your old man told me how he read about them in his 'Dark Secrets' magazine. I am gonna sell one of these pictures these days and make a fortune."

He put his camera up to his eye and snapped away. I did not have the heart to remind him that he just told me he was out of film. Harry was always so dramatic over ordinary things. The ever-present camera was a bit annoying. I knew that I just had to last it out until the next phase came along. The phases were a roll of the dice; you needed to take your chances to see if the new one was an improvement over the previous phase. I had to admit that "photography phase," while annoying, was a tad bit better than, "opera phase" proved to be.

While I shook my head, I heard him say, "After all, Paul, what could happen? I told Ben or Len that we would meet him at his store on this Saturday around two in the afternoon when we get off our regular jobs."

I sat back and sighed.

We were doomed. How do I get myself into these messes? Oh, wait! Yes! I know. Harry M. Redmond Junior.

"Youse, two guys will do fine. Big and strong. The long-haired guy there must be six-foot bijillion or so. Do you have a truck?"

"Sure, sure, sure, we got a truck, Ben!" Harry and I stood in the center of the sales floor for Len Starrett's Appliance Store in Rock Glen, New Jersey. Harry was down to the final nuances of negotiation on our latest money-making opportunity.

"It is Len not Ben, there Barry."

"Nah, Harry is the name there, Len. And this here long-haired, muscular guy is Paul John Henson, the best long-haired hippie, hockey goaltender in all the land!"

Len Starrett looked up at me and frowned.

"A hippie hockey player named Pat? I hope you have a backup plan there, Henson."

"The name is Paul, not Pat."

"Oh yeah, yeah, yeah, got it, Paul. Why do you have a camera around your neck, Barry?"

"Oh, yeah, yeah, yeah, well, look here, Ben. I am just about a professional photo-ge-raffer you know. I never miss a chance at a snapshot. Big buck payoff for the right photo, ya know! The money shot!"

Len's eyes went up and down on Harry and he shook his head.

"Yeah, yeah, yeah, whatever. Good luck with that shit. Sounds kinda hit or miss to me. Ya had better not hang ya hat on that dumb-ass idea. Anyway, here is the address. It is a twenty-six cubic, side-by-side box going in, and a side-by-side box coming out. I do not care if you junk the old one for scrap and make a few bucks on that, too. The folks are Jewish and they should be back from their temple by now. The delivery is over on the eastside of Paterson. Use the big, wide staircase, the other one is narrow and tight. It is a piece of cake delivery for two big, strong jerks like youse guys are. Fifty bucks is what I pay. Miss Goldblatt is the customer. She will write you a check for. . .." Len glanced down towards a metal ticket book that contained sales slips and he confirmed the dollar amount.

He then continued to give us instructions, "Yeah, yeah, yeah, she will write a check for seven hundred and ten bucks. Bring it here, and I will give you the fifty bucks. The box is sitting behind the store. Load it up and get lost. There is also an old hand truck back there for youse to borrow. I called her and told her youse dopes are on the way."

The entire time he spoke, Len Starrett fidgeted and fussed with nervous tics and habits. I also could not help but focus my eyes on the giant knot on his forehead. It looked as if he had a baseball stuck in his head. It was obvious that the poor chap had some type of medical condition.

"And remember, I know all about youse guys, Barry. I checked Pat and youse out—so do not even dream of taking off with my fridge and selling it downtown Paterson in some dark, back alley!"

Harry waved his hands in the air in typical Harry fashion when he wanted to make a point, and he told Len, "Cool your jets, Ben. You have been reading 'Dark Secrets' magazine too much. Twenty-seven here. He is a choirboy. They chucked both of us out of the Forest Scouts when we were kids, but that was because they associated him with me. Other than that, he is clean. He doesn't even cheat at Warship. I cheat like hell and move my ships all over the board."

"Yeah, yeah, yeah, me too, Barry. Ya can cheat for the first few minutes, then it catches up with ya."

"Yup. So, tuck the knot on ya head back in and don't worry. We got it, Ben! Let's roll, twenty-seven."

Harry tore the paperwork out of Len's hand and we marched to the rear of the store. I pulled the van next to the curb and stared at the largest, most immense refrigerator box I had ever laid my eyes upon in my life.

It appeared to be the size of the State of Wyoming.

After struggling with the weight and size, we managed to wrestle the refrigerator into my van. We also loaded up the hand truck to help us move the appliances. The engine protested, while it crawled over to the east side of the city of Paterson, the rear end of my poor wreck of a van was just about scraping the pavement and the old beast burned two quarts of oil on the four-mile trip into the city.

Harry pointed at a large house on the corner of a main drag and a side street.

"Here it is, twenty-seven. Two, two, four, East Matzo Ball Street. Ben wasn't kiddin' when he said this was the Jewish side o' town. Look, there is a driveway, pull around to the back, and I will jump out and check it out. One, two, three, we will be out of here in time to skate tonight and I can see if Joyce Dilber is over at Ice Land. I hope she wears that tight blouse with the plunging neckline tonight!"

I stopped the van and shut the engine off. Harry jumped out, and he walked over to the rear door while I climbed out of the van, opened the rear doors and waited. Harry was knocking and knocking, and as usual, he was growing rather impatient that the person inside was taking too long to answer the door. Harry was last in line to receive his patience gene.

He was about to be rewarded for his persistent knocking.

Suddenly, the door swung open and a young woman stood in the doorway. Not an ordinary woman! No, no, no, that would have made this job normal and not too much in the lives and the adventures of Harry and Paul can ever be normal.

Why break the mold now?

There, in front of Harry . . . stood a movie star!

His life was about to be forever altered.

I guessed her to be about twenty-five to thirty years of age, and she was an absolute knockout. There was no other way to describe her. She was stunningly gorgeous! Long, brown hair tumbled over her shoulders, and her hair fell in alluring waves upon a tight, white sweater that enhanced her rather large chest region and perfect female form. She wore a tight, black miniskirt that would not allow her to bend over even a sixteenth of an inch before revealing to the entire world all the physical features that the good Lord gave to her. She wore knee-high boots, polished to a deep, black shine that gave the perception that her legs ended somewhere close to where the Moon orbits the Earth.

Oh, boy! Even with his back to me, I could see the steam blow out of Harry's ears and out the top of his head, while the big guy struggled to speak, "Ah, ah, Miss Golden Flapper, or something like that . . . ah . . . we are from Ben Carrot's store and we have a thingy for you. . .."

"Why, hello there, big boy," Miss Goldblatt said while flipping her hair, tugging at her plunging neckline and posing seductively in the doorway for Harry.

"I think you might just have something to give me. Something, ohhhhh, to cool my stuff down. I am soooo hot!"

That was it.

Harry's knees gave away, and I knew that I needed to run over there as quickly as I could and hold him up. I knew that Harry required some type of non-hormone driven intervention.

I made it just in time. I propped the big guy up by his shirt collar, and leaned in.

"Hi. I am Paul, and this week-kneed chap is Harry. We have your new refrigerator. Can we see where the kitchen is, Miss Goldblatt?"

"Oh sure, honey." She stepped aside and opened the door for us as she wiggled towards a set of steps leading up into a kitchen. "Wow! You are one good-looking, long-haired guy! I love all the blonde hair and a touch of red in there too. You are movie star quality. Where have you been all my life, handsome? C'mon in. The kitchen is this way . . . all of my other rooms, including my master bedroom, with my bed full of silk sheets are down this hallway."

I heard Harry exhale and groan in pain a bit. Harry's eyeballs were rotating around in his head. I swear his left eye went clockwise and his right eye, counterclockwise. I watched as his legs wobbled, but he somehow managed to follow me up the stairs. In fact, he recovered from the lack of oxygen quite nicely, and he tried to push ahead of me when he realized that Miss Goldblatt and her miniskirt were leading us onward and upward.

Miss Goldblatt pointed at the old refrigerator and explained, "Right here, big boy. This old refrigerator is coming out and the new one will slip right on in here. I have cleaned out all the items inside and stored all of it in coolers until you big, strong, handsome bruisers bring in my new one. Let me bend over here and show you some of what I have packed in here."

Miss Goldblatt sauntered over to the coolers and was preparing to "show us" when I blurted out, "No, no, no, we understand! We need to get to work now."

Harry struggled to speak as I elbowed him to shut his trap, when he weakly said, "I could take a peek with ya there, Miss Golden Flapper!"

"Oh well, maybe later then. What else can I do for you?"

Oh boy, we successfully maneuvered through that situation, just barely. It was going to be one challenge after another with this adventure. I thought about how I should ask her work-related questions and see if we can survive this episode. Yes, there we go. That seemed as if it would be a good strategy.

Let me give that a whirl or two, "Thank you. Is the staircase we just came up the best way in? Len at the store told us there was a big, wide staircase and that one in the rear is narrow and tight."

She smiled at us and seductively lowered her voice into a hoarse rasp as she said, "Well now, we cannot have handsome young men such as you and Harry are, being all narrow and tight as you bring it on in, but I am afraid that the front stairs are much worse. The rear steps are the way they brought this one in years ago, and it is the best way. Besides, you would not want me to make it easy for you now. Would you?"

She stopped speaking, smiled, and flipped her hair over her shoulders.

Harry coughed and choked, and it looked as if the big guy was going to pass out. What a piece of work this chick was turning out to be. Everything she said had some dual meanings and hidden sexual innuendos!

Well, my first go-around on that conversation did not work. I needed to cool these jets quickly, so I worked up another bit of job-related conversation, "Okay now. Well, we need to measure the path here. I think both of these doors will need to come off."

"Baby, you can take off whatever you need to get it in!"

Oh, geez! I walked right into that one. She turns everything against us! Harry held onto the wall, in order to prevent himself from falling over. Sweat poured from his forehead and all his other bodily orifices. Slowly, some recovery occurred within Harry's hormone imbalanced mind, and he seemed to recover enough from Miss Goldblatt's constant seductive wares to put a few words together.

Harry suddenly blurted out, "I will get the measuring tape, the hammer, and the, the, the . . . measuring tape!" He bolted down the stairs and out the door to the truck. Wait! I am not staying here alone with this simmering mound of molten female lava.

"I will help you, Harry," I said while I bolted down the stairs behind Harry.

"Hurry back, boys. You do not want my *things* to overheat now!"

Harry nearly collapsed at the doors of the van.

"Holy tamales, twenty-seven! She is gorgeous! This is unreal! I am going to die of heart failure! Did you see those legs and that short miniskirt? Where do her legs end? In Australia? What is with all the hints? My goodness, I cannot even breathe any longer."

"Okay, okay, calm down now, Harry. She is as phony as

a three-dollar bill."

"Yeah, well, shit no, twenty-seven! Those parts of her don't look too phony to me!"

"Focus, Harry! Not on her, but on the job. This refrigerator is heavy. Concentrate on anything but her."

"Ha! Ya are a damn dreamer there, Paulie, or I swear ya going blind. You won't be able to play goal anymore if ya can't see her bazookas."

"Let's just get this refrigerator out of the van and get that old one out. You need to breathe deeply and hang in there."

"I am good, I am good," Harry said, while trying hard to convince his wobbling brain that Miss Goldblatt had no ill effect upon him. He stood there holding his chest while trying very hard not to hyperventilate. I thought about how this adventure might be just a little more than the big guy could take.

We worked hard at removing the two doors of the house off the hinges in order to provide us a little more room to maneuver. I took the exterior door off the back entrance and Harry took the door off that led from the back staircase to the kitchen. This would not be easy. The stairs twisted and turned, and then we had to carry the appliance up a little staircase of four stairs before finally reaching the kitchen.

I do not know what staircase that Len Starrett looked at, but I had a strange feeling he had snookered us. No one else wanted this job, and I was now certain of that! Len had pawned it off on the two of us! The entire time, while we measured and planned, Miss Goldblatt posed and worked poor Harry M. Redmond Jr. into a mad frenzy of testosterone turbulence with her wild conversation.

I took the doors off the old refrigerator, measured the width of the refrigerator, and then I measured the width of the entrance and staircase.

Geez, we made it by one inch! You talk about a close

shave.

We strapped the old refrigerator on the old hand truck and inched it towards the staircase. It weighed about sixty-two bijillion pounds, and we slowly moved it along the floor, until we ran out of flat real estate. It was now time to move it down the stairs.

The entire time that we were working, Harry was jabbering up a storm with Miss Goldblatt, trying his best to impress the young gal. He was laying the flim-flam on really thick!

"Yeah, yeah, yeah, between my buddy Paulie and me, we can do anything! Paulie is a friggin' genius. He works on electrical systems, air conditioning, heating, motors, and he can fix most anything. I can fix plumbing, roofing, I do a little cabinetwork . . . you know, most anything. Gotta tell ya, Miss Goldblatt that, I am virtually a professional photo-ge-raffer too. I would love to take a few snapshots of you."

"Oh, my! That is so good to know, Harry. I could certainly pose for you and show you . . . a few things. I also need someone to do repairs here. You know, I do not have a man around this old house to help me with all of these pesky repairs. I am all alone and so lonely all the time."

Oh geez, I could not see Harry with the mountain of a refrigerator between us, but I could only imagine by listening into the obnoxious banter going on what his face looked like right now.

We inched the refrigerator closer, and we went down the first step, then the second step, then down another. I was on the bottom of the hand truck working the weight down one step at a time, and Harry was on the top holding the handles of the truck, so that it did not come flying backwards and crush me.

It was a good thing that we both were big, strong guys! One turn and then another. It cleared by just a whisker, and the weight was tremendous! Oh boy!

"Oh, Harry! Just look at your bulging muscles!" I could

hear Miss Goldblatt spewing ego-boosting drivel to the big guy. "What else do youse guys do? I need so much help around here! If you could only imagine how lonely it is – when you are so alone. I need someone to fix my shower. Maybe later, you could help me with aiming the nozzle. I could be in there and you could adjust it for me."

I felt the hand truck shake a little and all the weight come down upon me.

OH, NO! OH, NO!

The big guy was faltering under the seductive hints of Miss Goldblatt! The shower comment had buckled his strength and Harry had folded like a cheap camera.

"Harry! C'mon, stay with me, big guy! Easy up there! Concentrate, Harry! Concentrate! We only clear by an inch down here! I NEED YOU TO PAY ATTENTION TO ME NOW, HARRY!" I screamed in vain, while desperately holding back the weight of the refrigerator and trying to make the precarious turn.

I heard Harry tune it up for another round of mindless blabbers. He was lost in a haze of alluring seduction, a web of sexual intrigue spun by Miss Goldblatt, and the fate of his best friend on the bottom of a bazillion pounds of metal was the last thing on his mind. He must have let go!

"Oh sure, Paulie and I are experts in showers. We also do masonry work, we fix car engines, and we. . .."

That was it.

Despite my strength and size, the sheer force and weight of the appliance overpowered me. My legs gave out, the refrigerator went flying backwards, and it knocked me clean over, and pushed me right out of the doorway! I caught myself and recovered. My goaltender flexibility assisted me in recovering, and diving back quickly to the doorway to try in a vain attempt to grab the refrigerator.

Alas, it was too late.

BOOM! BOOM! BOOM!

The wayward refrigerator crashed down one stair at a

time. It was now a missile that I could not stop!

I helplessly watched in horror, while the appliance crashed down the last steps, went clean through the sheet rock of the porch wall and blew out the side of the house!

"Oh yeah, after all, what could happen, Paul?" Harry's prophetic words once again came back to haunt me. "Insurance? We don't need any damn insurance!"

Harry did not miss a beat. The big guy could sell ice to an Eskimo!

While I sprawled in vain along the bottom of the steps, and stared at the impaled refrigerator, he turned to Miss Goldblatt and calmly said, "We also specialize in sheetrock repairs and painting, too!"

Miss Goldblatt peered around Harry and looked at the scene. A long-haired hippie, covered in sweat, sprawled along the base of her staircase, and about half of her old refrigerator impaled into what used to be the sidewall of her back porch.

She smiled and said, "Well now, I guess you two big, handsome men will need to repair that wall and fix all the other things around here that need attention. Feel free to work without your shirts on because it does get so hot around here sometimes!"

"Oh yeah, yeah, yeah, don't you worry, Miss Golden Flapper, Paulie, and I can do anything!"

"That is what I am counting on, Harry!"

"Say, once we have finished repairing your wall, could I take a few photos of you, Miss Golden Flapper?"

"Sure, big boy. Should I keep my clothes on? Or do you want me in a more natural state?"

Oh geez.

Remarkably, and thankfully, Miss Goldblatt's seductive rhetoric was harmless, and much to Harry's chagrin, I was correct in my assessment of her rather phony outward approach. She was putting us on most of the time, other times, I was not so sure! It turns out that she was an aspiring actress from a very wealthy family and she was desperately trying to crack the theatre scene in the big city. She never could turn off the acting!

We managed to install the new refrigerator without further incidents; we repaired her wall and sheetrock as well as repaint the back porch.

Over the next few weeks and months, Harry and I went over to her house often, and repaired many of the items that Miss Goldblatt required repairs on around the old home. She paid us handsomely, (in cash) and when you became used to her unusual "approach" and took her with a grain of salt while she practiced her acting lines, she actually was great fun to be around, besides being very easy on the eyes too!

I was very careful, in the interest of self-preservation, not to mention Miss Goldblatt to Maureen Zipperelli.

We did have a slight, water related incident when Harry lost his concentration while underneath her kitchen sink repairing the trap on the waste line one day. Miss Goldblatt, wearing one of her famous miniskirts, leaned over the sink with Harry underneath it. And well, it was nothing that a few hours and a wet vacuum could not clean up.

Harry obtained a few snapshots of her and while they might have been a little risqué, much to Harry's sheer disappointment, they never went over the line. Harry had Miss Goldblatt's picture on the wall of his bedroom for years. He would sometimes forget to remove it and hide it when one of his steady gals came over to "visit" him, but mostly, it provided us with fond memories of the now famous "refrigerator" incident and a very eccentric, but quite an entertaining and gorgeous woman.

Between Len Starrett throwing us part-time deliveries, (of which we actually became very good at, we could have done without the stove that went up the fire escape, but that is another story!) and the money that we earned from fixing up Miss Goldblatt's rickety old house, I had enough dough by summer's end to purchase my ice hockey goaltending equipment. Harry had enough dough for his new camera equipment and a new sports car. Despite working for Len Starrett for most of that summer and into the fall, he never stopped calling me, Pat, and Harry, was forever more, Barry. Then again, Harry always called him Ben Carrot, so I guess we were even.

We had quite the summer that year, and the adventures during that summer alone would fill many pages of books. Someday, I promise, dear reader, I will find the time to tell of those adventures, but for now. . ..

It was also a turning point for me as a young man, a point in my life, where I first felt the pain of a lost romance, the pain of love gone wrong. It was a pain that I would experience many more times and even deeper in the next few years. I could never deny how I felt about Maureen Zipperelli. She was special to me. She was the first woman that I ever shared my body with and parts of my soul too, and I held her near and very dear to my heart. Yet, despite my feelings, I could not bring myself to commit to a long-term relationship right at this point in my young life.

Hockey was first in my heart, and I needed very much to chase this crazy infatuation for as long and as far as it would take me.

Maureen sensed that and the pain that I caused her forced her to make a decision, of which I knew caused her great unhappiness too. Sadly, Maureen Zipperelli and her family moved to Italy at the end of the summer of that year. We had spent a wonderful Labor Day holiday together with Harry and his, on again, and off again, steady gal, Miss Joyce Dilber, and then, shortly thereafter, Maureen was gone.

I never saw or heard from Maureen Zipperelli ever again. However, I often thought of her. I often pondered and wondered how her life turned out and, in all honesty, I have to admit that forever more; I will never forget her gentle touch, her fun-loving personality, her sultry voice, and those kisses laced with a touch of garlic and red wine. I am sure that some lucky guy, who had his head screwed on tighter than I did, recognized her as the rare and precious gem that she was, and was not foolish enough to let her leave.

Maureen may have left my life, but she will always remain in my heart and I will always have many fond memories of her and of our time together.

"Is this equipment here, what you are looking for, twenty-seven?" Mr. Wurtzberg asked me.

I stared down into the pages of a hockey equipment-merchandising catalog that Mr. Wurtzberg was holding in front of me. I was inside of Wurtzberg Brother's Sporting Goods store in downtown Paterson, New Jersey, drooling over pictures of new goaltending equipment.

"We do not have many requests for hockey goalie equipment, Paulie. I am afraid it is not my area of expertise."

"No, no, no, this is it, sir. It is the same equipment that Rumblehowser of the New York Rovers wears."

Mr. Wurtzberg looked up at me and stared over the top of his eyeglasses that he had down close to the end of his nose. He asked in his heavy New Jersey Jewish accent, "Rumblehowsahhh? What the hell or who the hell is a Rumblehowsahhh? Sounds as if he could be Jewish. Is he a good Jewish boy, Paulie?"

"I do not know. He is the goalie for the New York Rovers. But, hey, Mr. Wurtzberg, I would like to purchase these leg pads, the set of goalie gloves, the white mask, the shoulder pads, the red socks and the chest protector. I have the dough now. Oh yes, I need the jockstrap, the garter belts and the goalie cup and groin protector, too."

Mr. Wurtzberg looked up at me over his eyeglasses again and he smiled while telling me, "Ya better get those jockstraps and groin things if you are hell-bent on playing this position, twenty-seven, especially at your age! I have to order all of this, Paulie. It will take a week or so for the order to come in. I will call you when it arrives in the store and is ready to pick up. Do you want to pay upfront? I will give you such a deal if you do. Since you are Dottie's brother, and you just bought those fancy goalie skates from us, I will give ya ten percent off on top of that deal too."

"Sure, sure, sure, I have the cash here, Mr. Wurtzberg."

I pulled out my wallet and handed over more cash than I had used for any other transaction in my entire life! He smiled at my eagerness and the prospect of the cash.

"How is Dottie doing out west, Paulie? We miss her smile, and her buying ski equipment from us. Such a pretty woman. If she were Jewish, I would marry her! I so enjoyed her calling us up the other day to ask us to work a deal for you. She is a cutie for sure, and once I hung up with her, I called you right away and left a message with Mum to make sure you knew that we would take good care of you here on these prices."

I smiled and recalled that once more, Harry's deal making advice had paid off handsomely. He was amazing.

"She is doing well, sir. She might stay out there. Who knows, right? I really appreciate the discount here and you working with me on this equipment. It took me a long time to save this money and let me tell you . . . some hard work too!"

"Well, it is our pleasure. Please tell Dottie, I said hello and please give her my best once again, twenty-seven. I love that gal."

"I will do that, Mr. Wurtzberg. I will."

He handed me my sales receipt. I waved goodbye and left the store. When I reached Main Street, I stood there and breathed deeply. I looked over at City Hall and had to run to catch the Haledon number fourteen bus back to Belmont Avenue. I had this euphoric feeling that I was no longer a pretender. That I was now a real goalie. My dream of attending the ice hockey goaltending clinic at Ice Land in a few months grew closer. As I sat on the bus, watching the gritty city pass by my window, I smiled ear-to-ear.

Look out, hockey world; here comes number twenty-seven!

2

The Clinic

I purchased my goaltending equipment, and finally fulfilled my dream by signing up for the long-awaited ice hockey goaltending clinic.

I know that Harry, as well as all of my other friends and family, certainly were glad that I finally enrolled in the clinic and they no longer had to hear me talk about it! Over the past few months, I drove them crazy with my constant chatter and excitement about the clinic.

It almost seemed as if I was in a dream, while I stood in the middle of rink number one at the Ice Land Arena in Great Falls, New Jersey. It was a Saturday evening in late October in 1976, and I stood there dressed in my new, and barely broken in goaltending pads and equipment.

Over the top of my new chest protector and shoulder pads, I wore a red and white practice jersey, with a stenciled number twenty-seven on the back (embroidered numbers were too expensive) with my last name in small letters. Earlier in the week, I had bought the jersey for an inexpensive price at the pro shop in the arena. The jersey was on a special discount, because no one in New Jersey wanted the colors of a big-league team in Michigan, but I did! It was the color combination of the original Geyer Street Guys.

I felt as if I was inside of a suit of armor.

The key to the armor I currently had flipped up and tucked back on my head. It was my goalie mask. The last line of defense, my protector, and what would be, in many ways, my disguise. Next to Harry, my mask would become my best friend. Forever more, it was my trusty white fiberglass, goaltending mask, and the same make and model mask that my hero, Rumblehowser, wore.

I already enjoyed flipping my new mask down and hiding behind it. It just felt right, and no one could actually see whom it was that was hiding behind the mask, or what I was feeling. Paul John Henson no longer existed. All people knew now was a goalie wearing the number twenty-seven, and that was just fine with me. As the years went by, I would come to hide behind the mask more and more. It provided me more than comfort—it actually gave me an alter ego of sorts.

I stood in line with about twenty other nervous goaltenders. Some of them were my age, some older, some shorter, but only one or two who were taller than I was, and we all shared a bond. We were there to play the position that some say presents more challenges, both physically and mentally, in all the sports.

I nervously scanned the lineup.

Not a single goalie was smiling, and all of us had new equipment shackled to our bodies. We wore shiny, new masks without dents or nicks or fake stitch marks, and we had pads stiffer than boards strapped on our legs. We were "unbroken in" rookies! It seemed as if we were in a leather factory with all the brand-new pads glowing in the lights of the rink.

One of the main reasons that I had signed up for this clinic was the outstanding reputation of the instructors. One of the instructors was the famous, retired big league player from many years ago, Gordon "The Eel" Gurney, who played for the Rovers and a few other teams in the 1950s and 1960s, and was actually a member of the Hockey Hall of Fame! He was a center iceman, famous for having a deadly accurate backhand shot, which was almost as hard and accurate as his forehand shot! To think, right in front of me, was an actual professional hockey player, a Hall of Famer too!

The other instructor, who was the actual goaltending coach, was the famous Jim Hikibin. Jim was a well-known person at Ice Land; he managed the on-site skate shop and pro shop and played semi-professionally in the Tri-State metro-area circles.

He even floated back and forth in between Canada and the United States, flirting with junior leagues and other higher-level leagues. He was, in my eyes, a true and actual goaltending legend!

Jim skated out onto the ice surface, followed by Gordon. They were professional players! A dream had finally come true for number twenty-seven!

"Welcome, men! By the time, we are finished here, all of you, or at least most of you, will be able to do this and your girlfriends will still be ya gals!" Jim shouted across the ice to us as he skated towards center ice. He was wearing full goaltending gear; complete with leather leg pads, he wore worn out pads, all frayed and stained, unlike all of us in our stiff, "newbie" gear!

Jim skated, almost at top speed from the faceoff circle at center ice and while we watched in awe, he slid hard into the net on his skates, cut hard, he turned back and jumped in the air in front of us, while performing a full-out leg split to duplicate a split save.

Everyone in our line grabbed our groins in pain. Just watching the incredible display of flexibility was a bit painful.

Jim popped up unscathed from his rubbery display and smiled while proudly proclaiming, "The key to being a great goalie is flexibility and the ability to skate better than any other player on the ice. Therefore, first, we bend and stretch with all of this stupid equipment on, because you cannot be without it, so you might as well learn to live in it, and then we skate. We will skate, and we will skate. And when you hockey pucks are sick of it and want to quit, then I will let you skate some more. Until Christmas, we will skate and flex, then maybe in the last few clinics. We will actually let you play some goalie and face live shots. All of you had to sign the medical claim, disclaimer. Now, mark my words that some of you will get hurt when you face a few shots from Gordon here. For those who survive, the next clinic in the early part of next year will be pure goaltending. Not now though. You losers look like wooden soldiers standing there."

Jim turned and pointed at Gordon, who had set up an obstacle course of orange cones on the ice, and Gordon was slowly weaving on his skates in and out of them.

"So, men, toss your goalie sticks aside, make sure you have your numbers on all of your equipment! That includes your sticks, too. No sticks to help balance ya! Hands folded in prayer behind ya backs, your weight forward, never backwards, now get out here and . . . LET'S SKATE OUR ASSES OFF!"

He blew his whistle loudly and off we went. A team of stiff wooden soldiers was an excellent description of us. Slowly, we wove in and around the cones under the watchful eye of the two instructors. A few goalies slid out right away, losing an edge or two on the newly dressed ice. I made my way fairly well, with good balance, but no speed. I just wanted to concentrate on staying upright. Rather quickly, I found out that it was a lot easier to skate at public sessions when you had to impress gals than it was to work your way through these cones, with your hands behind your back, wearing all the equipment. I had thought that I was a pretty good skater, but I quickly learned that I was a bum. After we went around about ten times, Jim blew the whistle and he made us skate in the opposite direction about ten times.

All the time that we were skating, Gordon and Jim would skate alongside us. They were watching, teaching skating techniques and providing tips to the goalies along the way. One or two goalies were superior skaters; they zoomed in and around the cones and left us in the dust.

A few more of us tumbled down here and there; I lost an edge on one of the last cones. My ankles were screaming at me! I quickly scrambled back on my skates and wove back into the line. After skating for what seemed as if it were forever, we all lined up and did flexibility exercises, with Jim leading us.

It was a long night for the first clinic. We all left the ice, tired, sore and quite shaky.

While undressing from our gear and showering in the locker room, I overheard the complaints and mumbles from a few of the goalies who just wanted to play in the net. The drills did not bother me. I knew I had a long way to go to reach my goal. I was not Canadian, or from Vermont, or Michigan, where the ice remains on the ponds for a long time in the winters. I was a New Jersey kid from the streets, a product of street hockey and roller games.

This ice surface was a big step up and a long way from Geyer Street Gardens!

I needed to learn to skate.

I knew I could stop the puck when the time came to do so; right now, I needed to learn how to take the next step to being a goaltender and not just a reflex-oriented, reactionary, puck blocker.

This would not be easy; nothing worthwhile is ever easy. It always entails hard work, sacrifice and dedication, to a dream, to the honor in your heart and the passion you feel in your soul. I had worked most of the day at my regular job, but I paid all of this money for lessons and equipment, worked hard to get here, and I was not about to fold up on my dream.

I did not miss a single minute of the clinic.

I buckled down and performed all the drills, worked out on my own, started a running and walking program and set my mind to being the best skater of all the goalies at the clinic. On weeknights and on the weekends, I worked out with light weights, stretched, and ran a few miles. The old man helped me out on some of my workout drills. He was an outstanding baseball player in his day and even if he did not find hockey at the top of his interest list, my father was quite the athlete. He invented some reflex drills with a tennis ball that he would toss at me, to keep my eye and hand coordination sharp and my reactions peaked.

I was now intent on zooming in and out of those cones too, and not losing a single edge. Improving my skating was now my focus. I wanted to feel as natural on skates as I did when I walked on the sidewalk. It was difficult, but slowly, I could feel some progress, my flexibility improved and my balance and edge on my skates also saw a marked improvement.

One day after the rink time, while we were dressing in our civilian clothes, one of my fellow goalies came over and sat down next to me in the locker room. I was always polite to people, but mostly; I kept to myself and concentrated on my training during the clinic. Outside of my small circle of friends, I was never overly social.

"Hey, there, number twenty-seven, how ya doin? I am Denis Beauchamp." He stuck his hand out to shake mine and I stood up and shook his hand. "Wow! Ouch! A big, muscular guy. Ya, do not look as big as what you really are. Ya know, when you are on the ice, or when you were sitting down there?"

I recognized this chap as the goalie who zoomed around on his skates in all the drills. He was the best skater in our group, and it seemed as if he was an experienced goalkeeper—unlike the rest of us rookies. His pads were worn, which I realized was a good indicator that he had played a good bit.

"Oh sorry, Denis. I am Paul John Henson. Twenty-seven works too. In fact, that is what most people call me, anyway. I did not mean to shake your hand so hard. I have been working out."

"Yeah, man. I can tell. Hey, do not take this wrong, but you just do not seem to fit the stereotypical goaltender mold." He pointed at my longhair, which was now past my shoulders. I usually kept it tied up behind my head while I played, but now that I had showered, it was hanging down loose and long.

"I have to say that you are the most improved skater out there. The first day you really sucked, all stiff and wobble ass, but now, I think you have almost caught up with me. Keep up the good work. I hope you can stop the puck too. I am dying to get into the net."

Denis rolled his eyes a little to emphasize his point, and then he continued with his rant.

"This endless skating and drill shit sucks big time. If we do not have a little net time soon, then I will quit. I grew up in upstate New York, near Canada. I know how to skate! I also am not ashamed to say that I am the best goalie here. I only signed up for this clinic to meet people and see if I could learn a few tips. I can stop 'em. Jim is all right, but man, I want to take a few shots from Gordon. He is old now, always drunk off his ass and washed up, but I want to stop him a few times, to show him how good I am. He still has connections to the big time, ya know."

I thought how confidence was good, but I would be a little leery of calling a former professional player who is enshrined in the Hockey Hall of Fame, such as Gordon Gurney was, old and washed up. This Denis Beauchamp chap was, in my opinion, a bit too cocky. My old man always taught me to play confidently, try to win, but always play humbly too.

"I know that I do not look the part Denis, but I love playing goal and after all, someone has to be different. Thank you for the compliment on my skating. I have been working hard, but I noticed that you are an amazing skater.

We might get a chance in the net next week. Do you remember that Jim told us to make sure we all had our goalie sticks? It is the last clinic session, anyway. No reason to quit now, Denis."

Denis sat down next to me and started to untie the laces on his goalie skates. "Oh, wow. I did not realize that. You are right. 'Bout time, eh? Well, hey, we will see."

A few weeks later, at the beginning of the last clinic session, we skated out to the center of the rink and we all watched carefully as Jim and Gordon set up a line of orange cones. Jim was not wearing any goalie pads on his legs, but I could see that he was wearing his goalie equipment on his upper body, under his jersey. He also was carrying a shooting stick and not a goaltender's stick.

"Oh, geez. More boring drills, twenty-seven," Denis complained as we stood on the side of a line of cones. "I am itching to show everyone what I can do."

"Maybe, but they are set up differently this time, Denis. Check it out. Jim has a shooter's stick, too."

I pointed my goalie stick toward a line of cones, which now started at the red centerline, went through the neutral zone, and ended with two cones on each point of the blue line.

Jim skated to the middle of the zone where the cones were set up and he stopped.

He bellowed out, "Here is the moment you have been waiting for men! Goalies line up in a row on the goal line in the right corner and left corners. Split 'em up now, even numbahs on each side of the goal, men."

Jim pointed to each side of the net to organize us into equal groups. This drill was vaguely familiar to me; it seemed as if Coach Ray Edelski ran a drill just like this drill many, many years ago.

"I need a new goalie to skate hard into the net each time that I blow the whistle. The old goalie, ya gotta, move ya ass out of the net, skate hard, and go to the back of the line.

We flip each time, ya know, alternate sides. Skate in and out, hard and fast. This will be hard and fast, a drill that does not stop. We move fast and we shoot hard. Throw the loose pucks back out to us in the center here. Practice your passing! Masks down from now on, heads up, and buckle those jockstraps men, grab ya ass and adjust your cups. You may note to be careful of what you wish for in the future!"

Jim and Gordon both picked up leather bags and tipped them over. It seemed as if about four thousand hockey pucks fell out and tumbled in all directions.

"Now, here we go, twenty-seven. Finally! Watch and admire! Look at all these patsy-ass goalies here, trembling in their skates. Not me!" Denis spouted off while pulling his mask down over his face.

I smiled, pushed back my hair, and pulled my mask down. I reached behind my head, tucked the ponytail of my hair under the mask straps, and clicked the last buckle. The goalies all followed Jim's instructions, (even the grab our asses part in order to make sure it was still attached) and we skated into our positions on each side of the goal.

I stood in line about halfway down the right side of the rink, Denis of course, in his eagerness, pushed his way to the front of the line, and when Jim blew the whistle to indicate the first goalie was up, he cut a hard edge and barreled into the net. He crouched down and tucked into a classic goaltending position in front of the net. His stick was down, his gloves and arms in a perfect position, and his head was up. He was perfectly square to the shooter. Nice stand-up style. Denis Beauchamp looked as if he was a professional goalie!

Jim grabbed a puck and Gordon followed behind him. The two instructors skated slowly through the cones and then split at the blue line. Gordon stopped, aimed, and blasted a rocket of a slap shot that tucked neatly into the top corner of the net. The twine of the netting in the goal rippled with the force of the puck hitting it and the puck bounced out as if it was a rifle shot.

Denis never even moved or saw the shot coming!

So much for being too old and washed up.

Denis would not have a chance to set himself or recover, because Jim deftly handled his puck right away. Jim watched the first puck roll across the slot in front of the net, and he then wove past his cone into the lower slot. He ducked a shoulder; he faked looking long side to the net and then fired a wrist shot into the short side past Denis.

Denis flopped and spun around like a top. So much for that classic style.

Professional talent had blown him away. I had never seen a performance like that one. The force of the shots and the skill in which they placed the pucks in the net was amazing. They were as if they had the skills of surgeons, and they just sliced poor Denis up into little pieces. Denis hardly stood even a chance.

I chuckled under my mask. Jim Hikibin had nailed it dead on when he said, "Be careful of what you may wish for men!"

Jim laughed a bit at the performance of Denis and yelled out to the group, "Wow! Not too good, hotshot. That sucked big time. That was a perfect display of shitty goaltending. Now, go back in line and lick your pride a bit. Next goalie! Skate out hard, hotshot! Stay square to the shooter! Remember to come out and cut an angle or good shooters will eat you alive, no matter how good your reflexes are!"

Denis skated out with his head down, and he was not as talkative as he had previously been. He may have wanted to excuse himself and head for the restroom to clean out his drawers a bit after watching that slapper blow him up.

The next goalie skated into the crease and he did not fare much better. He came out of the net, way too far, and Jim skated in, ducked and danced, and put the puck in an open net. Gordon did the same, just with a little unique twist on his shot, but the net rippled with the same force as it did before when the puck hit behind the goalie. These shooters were making all of us look silly.

"NOT TOO FAR OUT THERE, GOALIES!" Jim Hikibin screamed.

Gordon smiled, but he had nothing to say; it seemed as if the two instructors were also tired of the drills and were rather enjoying eating us novice goaltenders alive.

Jim dropped his gloves, blew the whistle and coached us on the finer points of cutting down angles, staying square to the shooters, covering the net and positioning. He blew the whistle and the next goalie was in.

Same results, then the next one, then the next one. All the same, results because we could not stop beach balls rolled towards us.

The score was instructors about forty, and loser, rookie, goalies zero. Jim grew a bit frustrated; our ineptness was confounding to him. Not one goalie had made a single save yet. I was about two goaltenders away in the line for my chance when Jim blew the whistle, waved his hands and stopped the drill.

"HOLD ON! HOLD ON! You guys really suck. You look like a bunch of clowns! You are just not getting it. Give me a second here and let me slip on the gear to show something." Jim skated over to the bench where his pads, gloves, and mask were, and quick as a flash, he had strapped his pads on his legs. He skated in the net and yelled to the nearest goalie, "Hand me your stick. Now watch. C'mon, Gordy, give me a few."

Gordon "The Eel" Gurney said very little.

He did not need to say anything because Gordon let his stick do all of his talking for him.

All of us, including Jim Hikibin, were about to receive valuable lessons that even at an advanced age, with a little nip or two of whiskey running through his veins, a professional hockey player who was enshrined in the Hockey Hall of Fame, was there for a very good reason.

The first shot blew Jim away in the top, right-hand corner of the net, then the second shot beat Jim on the stick side low, then a puck slipped in on the short side, and for a grand finale, Gordon skated in and turned Jim upside down, while neatly tucking a backhand shot under the fallen, Jim Hikibin. This was not exactly what Jim had in mind when he decided to show us how we were not, "Getting it."

"WAIT! Hey, you goalie! Number thirty ovah there. Please go and get my stick over there. This stick sucks. It does not feel right!"

Ah, yes! The old, wrong stick excuse!

A goalie skated over to the bench, retrieved Jim's own stick, skated back and handed it to him. Jim pointed at Gordon, who was laughing quite hard now, and Gordon proceeded to beat him on three additional shots, before Jim finally appeared to have made one save . . . no, he got a piece of the puck, but it still trickled into the net behind him.

The stick did not help him.

"We get it now, Coach Hikibin!" One goalie could not help but yell out. Jim saved his face a little, as he raised his mask and laughed too.

"Well, you do know now why his old ass is in the Hockey Hall of Fame! They put ya in there, Gordy, for a good reason! But you could see the basic idea that I had. Right, men?"

Wow, I thought. I did not really grasp what it was that Jim was trying to teach us, other than lying on your ass, spinning around like a top and letting pucks score in the net behind you.

We did not want Jim to feel worse than he did, so we all feebly nodded in agreement in order to humor him. Jim took off his leg pads and tossed them aside, blew the whistle, and restarted the drill.

The goalie, standing next in line in front of me, turned to the goalie behind him and said, "Ahh . . . you go, my, ah, my pad strap, is loose here."

That goalie promptly turned to me and said, "Ahh . . . you can go twenty-seven. Mine are loose too, and my skates need tightening too. I have a bad nick on my right skate blade."

I skated out hard and fast.

Into the net I went, whispering the entire way, "Not a marble can get by you, twenty-seven. Not even a marble!"

To gauge my angle and distance, I tapped the right post behind me with the shaft of my stick. I was right where I needed to be, a foot out of the net, well within my comfort zone. This did not differ from the stance I used on the street or in roller skates.

The ice no longer mattered.

I was finally in the goal.

Jim picked a puck up; he studied me for a second, took two long strides, and then he rifled a wrist shot off from the high slot that was high on my stick side. I followed it rather easily, and it hit squarely into my stick glove. Oh, oh, a rebound! I spotted Jim's eyes. I had made a save, but I had given up a terrible rebound and Jim was hell-bent on making me pay. He burst on in and for a fleeting second, I thought about skating out and trying to beat him to the puck, but I realized it would be futile.

Jim captured the puck and then tried to leave me dead on the left post. His eyes were looking at the open net. I flew across, stacked my pads, and stopped the puck dead on. I slid across and covered it with my catching glove, then tossed it to the corner.

"NICE! FINALLY! A damn friggin' real ass goalie! Great saves there, long-haired goalie guy!" Jim screamed, while he turned away from the goal hard, and he skated back out to the blue line. My fellow goalies were now cheering wildly for the first saves that anyone of us had made during the entire drill!

I did not celebrate because, well, Gordon had picked up a puck and he was now closing in on me. I relaxed and crouched. Once more, a quick tap on the post told me where I was. I was not yet used to the crease markings on the ice surface to gauge my distance from the net, so I tapped twice just to be sure. Good, stop and glide on your skates, twenty-seven. At first, I thought he was going to shoot from the point, but then I realized he had dropped his shoulder to gauge my reaction. I glided out on my skates, squared up to him and then backed into the net a hair. I looked at his eyes, just as I always did, for a clue to where he was thinking of placing the shot.

A strange thing happened, that in all my countless hours of playing goal, never happened before. When I looked into Gordon's eyes, he was looking at mine! He did not even have to look at his stick in order to handle the puck! It was second nature to him; it was as if the puck was part of the blade of his stick.

Oh, oh, twenty-seven, your ass is grass now!

That plan will not work on this professional player. You are facing a professional shooter. A player who was the best of the best! This was not Jimbo Carlisle, or Johnny the Cho or some roller hockey, meathead tough guy from Queens, New York. This was a professional ice hockey player, and he was going to eat you alive!

I was going to have to rely on pure reflexes. First, Gordon went to his forehand, then to his backhand, then he dipped his right shoulder, and I knew to stay put. As quickly as I could even set my skates, he flicked a backhand shot that was harder than most slap shots into the top shelf, exactly opposite of the way his shoulders had dipped! I went into a full split, and with a whisk of my stick, I caught the puck with the end of my goalie stick and it tumbled lazily over the crossbar and fell behind the net.

I fell backwards, but quickly jumped up and landed on my skates. Gordon still did not say a word, but he smiled, skated by me and tapped my pads with his stick. I could tell that he appreciated the save, but I wondered if he had eased up on me on purpose.

"SAVE AND A BEAUTY! NICE WORK LONG HAIR. FINALLY, WE HAVE ONE FUCKIN' GOALIE AMONG THIS SORRY ASS BUNCH! TWENTY-SEVEN, MAKE SURE YOU GO KISS YOUR OWN ASS, BECAUSE YOU JUST STOPPED GORDON HALL OF FAME GURNEY!" Jim Hikibin yelled out, while tapping his hockey stick on the ice as a salute. He waved for the rest of the group to join him, and soon the echoes of hockey sticks "clapping" for me resonated throughout the ice rink. Jim sure was an excitable chap who did not pull too many punches or mince many words, but his enthusiasm was contagious.

"Next, sorry ass punk victim! Ya up, goalie!"

I skated over to join my fellow goalies and landed squarely amongst a round of hearty backslaps, as well as congratulations. This was a feeling that I had never had before.

It was wonderful.

"Ridiculous saves there, number twenty-seven," Denis Beauchamp said to me later in the locker room, while we dressed in our civilian clothes. The last clinic was now over. "You are a fantastic goalie. Where did you learn to play goal like that?"

I smiled and said, "On Geyer Street Gardens. Where else!"

"Where? Geyer what? Where the hell is that? Some shitty ice rink around here?"

"Oh, yeah, yeah, yeah, kinda. You would not know about it. I guess that I have played around here and there."

"Well, good luck to you, twenty-seven. Maybe I will see you around. The next clinic won't have me in it. I am good enough. I don't need any clinics with washed up old guys shooting at me."

I shook his hand and smiled. What a cocky guy this Denis was. He just did not get it, or his pride was hurt too badly. I think it was a combination thereof.

"Good luck to you too, Denis. I will see you around a rink someday."

Denis left, and I was now alone in the locker room.

I was finishing dressing and after pulling on my civilian pants; I sat down on the bench and I started packing my equipment bag. I was a bit surprised when the door to the locker room opened and I saw Gordon Gurney walk into the room. He looked at me and smiled widely as he walked over to me.

I stood up as he approached.

"Hello, Mr. Gurney. It has been a pleasure to be in the clinic, sir. I learned an awful lot. It has been my pleasure to meet you, too."

He walked over to me and stood next to me, a little wobbly, his worn face wrinkled and showing scars of a lifetime of collisions with hockey pucks and sticks.

He spoke in a gentle, Canadian burr of an accent, "No, the pleasure has been mine there, number twenty-seven. I am ashamed to say that I don't even know your actual name. All I ever heard you called was either long hair or twenty-seven. I can say one thing; you are a big, tall, strong guy. You do not look so big on the ice. Do you hunch or something, eh?"

I laughed while saying, "I don't know, sir. But it seems as if everybody tells me that."

"Call me, Gordon. Your name?"

"Oh yes, sorry. Paul John Henson. However, everyone just calls me Paulie, or twenty-seven."

He motioned for me to sit down and he settled in next to me. He was old, a little bent over. He groaned a bit while he sat down. I surmised that a lifetime of playing hockey without modern equipment would do that to you. No one wore hockey helmets or other types of fancy equipment in this day and age! In fact, masks had just become standard issue equipment for goaltenders.

I was in awe. I was sitting next to a hockey legend!

He spoke again in his thick Canadian accent, "You from around here, Paulie? You speak as New Jersey, as I speak Canadian."

"Yes, Gordon. Paterson and Haledon, New Jersey."

"Nice. City kid, eh?" He nodded and continued, "No wonder. I can tell you are a fearless son of a bitch. Tough guy. Say, I wanted you to know that I was not going easy on you out there. I fully intended on tucking that puck top shelf, Paulie. That is a shot that I rode to the Hockey Hall of Fame and you stopped me cold. Damn impressive."

"Thank you, sir."

"Shit, it was remarkable. No one stops me on that shot. I watched you tracking my eyes, somewhat uncanny for a goalie to watch me so intensely. Damn sure was amazing, actually. Forgive my language. Hockey gives you a trash mouth. Unfortunately, it is a byproduct of the game. Luckily, I speak little, and when I do, it is with a purpose. I was very impressed out there. It kinda floored me that you made that save. Where did you learn to play goalie like that, eh?"

"On the streets in our neighborhood. A place called Geyer Street . . . it was just an old dead-end street. But we made it into a shrine, a hockey rink that we called Geyer Street Gardens."

His eyes grew squinty and a little intense. He seemed to be deeply wandering his own past.

"Nice. Street hockey guy, eh? We call it shinny in Canada. Same sorta game. My rink was Oak Hills Lane. We broke a lot of windows. A lot of 'em. I bet you broke a few too, eh?"

"A few."

"Ya a sharp lookin' chap. Ya got a girlfriend?"

"Had one . . . but none now. I want to keep my head in the game."

"Oh, well. Ya are better off, eh? These women will take you down the tubes. You give them your hearts, and they just steal your life, and tear you apart worse than the hardest slap shot ever could. If you find a good woman, who is a prize, who loves a hockey player, especially if she knows what icing is, then hold on to her. I dare say that, if she knows offside rules, and she enjoys a glass or two of Scotch, then I would marry her ass!"

He rolled his eyes, smiled and laughed a bit; I enjoyed the fact that this was a rare moment that Gordon shared in some levity. I decided that I should smile along with him.

He then added, "Yup shit, I am not even sure that I know what the rules for damn icing these days are, but anyway, a good woman, well, appreciate her and never let her go, ever."

I did not know how to answer him; therefore, I simply nodded in recognition. It seemed as if he was speaking from more life experience than I could ever dream of, at this point in my young life.

Gordon continued, "Just sayin' one athlete to another, but that is some build on you. Especially for a goalie. Ya muscles have muscles. You must have rocked that lassie's world. Ya lift heavy weights?"

"No sir, light weights only. I do a ton of flexibility drills and some other drills that my old man invented for me. Oh, yeah, yeah, yeah, I do run every day."

I was a bit embarrassed, and I quickly pulled my shirt on over my head.

"Natural athlete, eh? Wow, kinda figured that. Ya drink a lot?"

"Just some beer. I rarely, if ever, drink any whiskey."

"Good, stay away from the hard stuff. It will be the death of me now. If you are a'wonderin' why I am in the Hockey Hall of Fame and I am here coaching clinics in

New Jersey instead of coachin' in Canada, or sittin' on my old ass takin' in the money, well, you can just look in the bottom of a whiskey bottle and you will find the answer, eh? Mark my words, twenty-seven. Someday, this hockey world will be a blur. It will haunt you day and night. It is like some kind of damn disease the way it will invade your soul, and you will want to dull the aches and pains and chase away the memories. Age?"

"Almost twenty."

"You love playing goal, eh?"

"Oh yes, sir. It is all I think about these days. I love the challenge. It is so difficult and very demanding. You can make fifty saves in a row, and then allow one goal, and all that anyone recalls is that one goal. Besides, I can stay in the net and no one knows who I am. It feels as if you can be a good guy and a bad guy at the same time. It is very lonely and for some reason, I am fine with that fact."

Gordon laughed and then he said, "Damn, never thought of it that way, but all you goalies are weird sons of bitches."

Gordon wiggled a little on the bench. I saw the pain in his face, and he held his lower back a little, as he moved around in an effort to become more comfortable on the wooden bench.

He looked at me and the tone of his voice grew a little softer. "I need to tell you this, twenty-seven. You need to work more on your skating. You improved on your skating a great deal from the first day of the clinic, but you have some long ways to go yet."

I nodded.

"I tell you, Paulie. I have to tell you this. I faced a million goalies over my lifetime. This is why I wanted to come in and chat with you a bit, cuz you floored my old ass a little out there on the ice today. I know that goalies such as you are, well, they do not come around too often. I only have seen a handful over my career. You have a chance. It is so hard for an American to break in these days, but I am telling you to stick with it. You are an amazing talent, great reflexes, courage, friggin' fearless, ass bastard ya are, and you have a hockey sense that I seldom see in goalies anymore. I think you are the real friggin' deal, kid. I am not just blowing smoke up your ass either. I speak little, especially when I speak with a young man, so count on it because I do not spew any bullshit."

"Thank you!" I became over excited when I heard his remarks.

He stood up slowly and placed his hand on my shoulder. It was then that I caught a faint whiff of whiskey.

Hard living within this world of hockey.

"I hope to see you next clinic."

"I will be here, Gordon. I cannot wait! I am going to play all the games that I can with my best buddy, Harry. He is a defenseman. We skate all the time."

"Good, good. Keep skating, twenty-seven. Keep skating until ya ass is draggin' on the ice. Sleep with your skates on your feet. Take 'em off only when ya have some pretty lassie in bed with ya. You would not want her to know you are an eccentric goalie."

I laughed at his wonderfully dry humor. Gordon was a quiet man, who actually had a depth of emotions that I seldom had ever experienced in a man until now.

He smiled and instructed me, "When ya ass is draggin', then suck it up and skate some more. Okay?"

He tapped my shoulder with his hand and said, "Hey, twenty-seven, keep ya head up and the straps buckled tight. We will see you in the next clinic then, eh?"

Gordon spun around and he wobbled a bit, but he steadfastly made his way towards the door. Then he stopped, and he turned around to face me while saying, "This place, called Geyer Street, Paulie. It is a shrine to you and some other lads. It is holy, a kind of sacred ground, eh?"

I felt a chill go down my spine.

I then smiled so widely that I felt as if my face would break.

"Indeed, it is, Gordon. No doubt."

He nodded, smiled and softly said, "I knew it."

The door opened and slammed behind him. I continued to pack my equipment bag while sitting alone in the locker room. I took the cross out of my back pocket and tucked it safely inside the bag.

When I left the locker room, the lights glowed very dimly over the rink. All that remained now was the Zamboni ice machine with a lonely maintenance man steering it as it glided around out on the ice surface.

There is a smell to a hockey rink, a certain atmosphere that I even to this day know, but I just cannot describe.

It is in my mind's eye and my senses forever.

I stood there next to the rink for a long time and watched, and then I made my way out the front door.

I could hear Harry's voice loud and clear in my head, "Not a marble can get by you, twenty-seven. Not even a marble!"

3

A Chap Named O'Malley

Time marched on, and the next clinic, in the late spring of 1977 or thereabouts, went just as well as the first one did for me. I received plenty of one-on-one instruction from Gordon Gurney, who seemed to have taken me under his wing. When we would have scrimmages, if the play was down in the other zone, he would pick a puck up and shoot on me. He was always giving me tips and teaching me all the time. It was a tremendous opportunity for me to meet him at this point in my life. To work one-on-one with a player enshrined in the Hockey Hall of Fame was unbelievable to me; it was a dream that came true.

Harry and I played wherever and whenever we could. We played on the ice in pickup games, and as ringers for some organized teams that paid us in cases of beer or with a ten spot or two. We did not care, we would play for anything, or just play for free because we just wanted to play hockey. Some hockey clubs, who knew of our reputations, would pick us up and they would ask us to play for them. Often, it was on the ice, or on roller skates in the rough and tumble roller leagues in New York City or over in Connecticut, or just on the street with only the two of us.

At this point, hockey was hockey.

Harry had grown into a monster. His chest was as wide as a beer barrel; his legs were strong and powerful. He was a solid, but somewhat slower skater; however, no one was tougher in the corners or along the boards. He also possessed a mean, hard slap shot that would ride low and hard on a goalie.

I knew. I had the scars and bruises to testify to it.

We had countless adventures on and off the ice, and Harry's whirlwind romantic life continued. His longtime girlfriend, Joyce Dilber, was serious. Then it was off, and then it was on again.

It was quite exhausting indeed.

Since Maureen Zipperelli left, I did not have many dates with the ladies. Here and there, Harry and Joyce would fix me up with a gal, but I never seriously dated anyone after Maureen.

However, looking back, that is dutifully incorrect; there was always a nagging memory, of which I tried very hard to remove from my mind. In all honesty, in fact, *there was* a short-lived but powerful romance with a wonderful gal named Renee Gorman. It was unforgettable, emotional and heartfelt. Actually, in all honesty, it might just have been a once in a lifetime meeting and an indescribable love affair between two very different persons. Once again, I used hockey as an escape, and buried the memory of Renee and what we shared deep inside me and covered it with layers of hockey memories.

For me, these days, it was a simple routine, hanging out with Harry and the Redmonds, working hard at my full-time job and playing hockey. It was what I did, and as I matured and grew, a transformation occurred within me. I became quieter, calmer, and more relaxed. I studied things; I did not become uptight or angry very easily, or speak randomly. I became introspective. Playing the position of goal made me who I was. It was so much more than about winning or losing to me; it became a part of my soul.

Maureen Zipperelli had told me in a very insightful manner before she left that, "It is so much more than just the sport of hockey for you, Paulie. It is about playing the position of goalie, in how you can face challenges of not only the game, but of life, and what it brings to your spirit when you win, and in some cases, when you lose. You are such a deep thinker, and a caring and wonderful person, as well as a complex young man, Paul John Henson. You give so much of yourself away all the time. I wonder when you have time for yourself. I think you regain your soul when you hide behind that mask. The ice is where you are always the most comfortable, Paulie. It is where you can hide behind that goalie mask, and no one really knows who the real Paul John Henson is."

She was correct.

I missed Maureen . . . she was a special gal.

I had finally decided to sell my old van in March 1977. It was time to seek out a new identity. The old man backed the van into our driveway. He put a "FOR SALE" sign in the window and he sold it in one hour!

I bought an old jeep that I had my eye on for a long time. The MJ-17 jeep had been at the corner gas station near my house on Belmont Avenue for quite some time. I made the owner of the station, who was my old friend, Vince Baroni, an offer for it and he accepted the deal. I loved the jeep. It had some miles on it, but it fit my image. I even sprung for some extra dough and ordered a special license plate from New Jersey. The license plate proudly proclaimed, in block letters, "GOAL27."

"This is a good gig, twenty-seven. I managed to get them to cough up twenty bucks for you and twenty for me, too. If you shut them out, they will toss an extra five bucks in for ya. Look, we just have to play this wimpy ass team here and move on in the playoff tournament. I heard there are some scouts here from the Metropolitan Hockey League looking for players for some fall leagues. It will be our chance for someone to notice us! The team we are playing for sucks, but the first team we have to play is the Christian Skater's Hockey Association. Must be a bunch of Bible thumping wimps."

It was late spring in 1977 or thereabouts, and Harry and I were dressing in our hockey uniforms and equipment for a playoff tournament game for a team out of central New Jersey. The team required a few more players and, most importantly, they needed a goaltender. No one these days wanted to play the position of goaltender. Goalies, it seemed, were in a very short supply. It made sense; you needed to be half-crazy to play the position!

This was a typical tournament; there were many of them spread out throughout the year, especially around the Christmas holiday, a sponsor puts up some money, teams pay to enter the tournament, the teams can walk away with some pocket change and a silly trophy for wins, and the arena, and the sponsors are both very happy. These competitions were very popular years ago, and hockey clubs found it an easy way to get some exposure for their players, or their various causes. The tournaments were typically "round robin" in playing format and elimination, but not always. This tournament was a single, round robin tournament.

The team we were playing for today had asked us to join forces with them a few days earlier, and I scrambled to be available for the game. Harry had met them along the way, with his many connections as he worked a deal for something, somewhere! He was very difficult to keep up with these days.

I tucked the cross in the back pocket of my thermal pants, pulled on my goaltending pants, flipped my suspenders over my chest and back, and pulled them tight.

"Never underestimate a team, thirty-five. Peter cut the ear off the Roman soldier. Chances are that hockey is a means for them to draw attention during the tournament to their Christian mission."

I pulled a banana out of my equipment bag, sat down, and peeled it open. I took a few bites when I was conscious of Harry staring intently at me.

"Really, Paul, really . . . a friggin' banana?" Harry said with disdain in his voice.

I looked at him, then at the banana and said, "What? Yeah, yeah, yeah, it is my new ritual for the pregame. You know, it helps with potassium. I sweat five pounds off a game, so the potassium helps to stop the terrible cramping."

Harry shook his head and laughed, "You are a weird one, twenty-seven. Geez, man, there is no manly way for a guy to eat a damn banana! Can't ya switch to oranges or tangerines?"

I laughed at Harry's observation. He certainly brought a unique perspective to everything.

Harry stood up and pulled the ugliest red hockey sweater that I had ever seen, over top of his equipment while shaking his head and answering me, "Whatever. We will wipe them out. Your sweater is there on the bench in that packet. Remember, you are now a Red Jersey Devil. You know, the monster that is supposed to live in the Pine Barren swamp down there in lower Jersey. That's what we are today."

"You have got to be kidding me, Harry? The Christians against the Devil!"

"Nah, nah, nah, not *that* Devil. This *other* one. It is a New Jersey legend, ya know. Hey, I will meet you on the ice. I want to get out there and show off while skating around in the pregame. The joint is packed, and there is this cute twigeon coming that I met in the frozen food section of Foodworld the other day. What a caboose she was towing on her train! An Italian chick. I can't remember her name. I think it is Daisy, or Iris . . . nah, it might be, Rose. Some kind of flower name. See ya out there."

I shook my head and finished dressing. I pulled the ugly jersey over my head. Harry was one of a kind, and sometimes, I prayed to the good Lord that in his ultimate glory and wisdom, he created only one of him. The world might not be able to take any additional Harry M. Redmond Juniors running around.

I took to the ice and as I glided around, loosening my legs, and testing the ice and my skate blades, I glanced around at the crowd. A packed crowd sat in the stands of Ice Land Arena, which seemed a bit unusual for me. It was an early Saturday night start, with a six-thirty faceoff time. Oh well, I thought. Maybe it was not so unusual. Six thirty was not a bad time. The tickets were inexpensive, and perhaps, this was a popular and inexpensive entertainment for families on a Saturday evening.

I skated in the net, crouched in my stance, tested the glare of the arena lights, checked my angles and prepared to go to work to earn my whopping twenty dollars. As I scuffed the ice in front of the net with my skates, I continued to notice banners, signs and other strange things about the crowd. I read some of them aloud to myself as I worked the ice in my crease.

"Jesus rules! Beat the Devil down! Send the horns packing! Go, O'Malley, savior of our hockey world! Only the Lord saves more than our goalie does!"

Oh, oh, even in the weird world of semi-professional hockey, this one may rank up there. Hockey and Bible fanatics!

Harry skated by, stood next to me, and asked, "Whatcha think? Do I look super cool? I tried to skate fast, so my hair blew behind me in the breeze. I don't see that gal in the stands, but I did not realize how packed this joint would be. So, how did I look?"

"Great, ya looked great, very nice. You looked great . . . like a movie star. An arena packed to the rafters to see the Christians crush the evil Devil. I dunno, thirty-five. Did you check out the signs? I think these fans of the Christian Skaters are taking this a bit too seriously."

Harry looked around and nodded, "Bunch of whacked out, crazy ass lunatics." Harry pointed at the one banner and said, "They even have an icon to save them. I wonder who this O'Malley asshole is?"

We conducted a short warm-up period, and Harry's painful assessment of the Red Jersey Devils was correct. This team did stink, no shooters, poor skaters, a clueless guy serving as a head coach and general disorganization within the entire hockey club. The addition of the two remaining members of the Haledon Hockey League did not seem to elevate the team to any lofty status, either. This game was beginning to give me an ominous feeling.

I was a little sorry that Harry had involved us with such a horrible team, since I connected more with the Christian team than I did this haphazard collection of so-called Red Jersey Devils. Deep down, I was a spiritual person, and my own beliefs were very important to me. I did not wear my thoughts on my sleeve or advertise my beliefs, but I had constant faith in God's plan in my life.

Besides, when you play the position of goaltender, you tend to pray a lot for protection, as well as divine intervention!

In addition, to top it off, the Christian Skater's Hockey Association had cool uniforms, with a white background and gleaming gold crosses emblazoned across the front, with a superimposed "CSHA" in black, embroidered letters.

Our crummy, cheap jerseys only had our numbers and names written with a black marker on the back of them. It was a throwback to the old days!

I stood in the net for the National Anthem, and the rowdy crowd was very respectable during the song. Once the song ended, then it became quite a different story.

A loud chant of "O-O-O-MALLEY, O-O-O-MALLEY," broke out and echoed amongst the Christian team's faithful fans.

Both teams squared up for the faceoff, Harry skated by and tapped my leg pads with his stick, while he mumbled his customary and usual encouragement, "Not a marble tonight, twenty-seven. Not a marble."

I nodded to show that I was ready to go, and the referee dropped the puck. A center with blazing speed won the draw cleanly; he split straight down the ice for the CSHA and closed in on the blue line. The Red Jersey Devils looked as if they were skating in sand and the CSHA players were now equipped with jet engines.

I crept out of the net, while Harry screamed to his defensive partner to take the center iceman, as Harry slipped back in front of me to pick up the wingers. The defenseman for the Red Devils tried to spin on his skates, and he lost his edge and fell head over a teakettle. As he fell backwards on his ass, the right-winger for the CSHA took his stick and chopped it viciously across the legs of the falling player. It was a disgusting tomahawk slash and chop. I heard Harry screaming for a penalty, and I glanced at the officials for an arm in the air to signify a penalty or a whistle for a stoppage, since the CSHA had possession of the puck.

Oh, oh. No call. Homer refs! I could smell a payoff a mile away.

It was now three on one, with only Harry back on defense. The back-checking offensive players of the Red Jersey Devils were useless. They were such slow skaters that they still were stuck in the center faceoff circle.

It did not matter; Harry and I had played together for so long that I knew beforehand the three on one strategy that Harry would use.

I would lean towards the open players and Harry would force the puck handler and the play to the outside and attempt to neutralize the pass. The left-winger made the pass to the center iceman, Harry barreled over the left-winger and crushed him, and the center looked to pass to the slash master player, who was now free on the open wing.

Instead, at the last second, the center iceman decided to shoot a hard slap shot, in which I easily tracked, gloved and held for the faceoff. The slashing maniac barreled into the net and came down with his stick on the back of my glove with a vicious two-hand slash. Even after the whistle, he chopped and chopped as if he were a madman at my glove.

"Whoa, whoa, cool it, pal. Play the whistle there, Mr. Slashy. My hand has leather on it, but it is still going to hurt being stuck in your face or my stick will fit very nicely up your ass crack," I yelled at him while protecting the back of my hand from his wild slashing with my goalie stick.

I then jumped up on my skates, stood up and pushed the overzealous jerk away from me, in which he promptly glared and raised the butt end of his stick to jam it into my gut!

So much for my theory of a night of family-oriented entertainment.

This was going to be an ugly night.

Harry came over and leveled Mr. Slashy with one crushing blow and that was it! Bedlam ensued, as the slashing player and his teammates scrambled around us and pushed, slashed, and tried to butt end our entire team.

The CSHA were a bunch of wild goons!

The referee and linesmen were blowing their whistles and working hard to calm the mess down. The slashing maniac was reaching over officials, as well as his teammates, with his stick in the air trying to chop at Harry, who skated around in circles and kept safely out of his stick slashing range.

"Put the stick down, ya damn nutcase. Put it down, and I promise that I will flatten your face like a pancake!" Harry was screaming.

I leaned back on the crossbar and sighed. This game was going to be a disaster. The CSHA were a bunch of crazed lunatics with wild Bible thumping fans and goons for players.

Once more, a loud chant of "O-O-O-MALLEY, O-O-O-MALLEY," broke out amongst the CSHA's faithful fans.

"Two minutes crosschecking number thirty-five, and two minutes slashing over here for number eleven. C'mon . . . off the ice. You two maniacs need to cool down!" The referee was finally handing out penalties.

I watched Harry skate to the penalty box and the wild man turned and glared at me as he made his way to his seat for two minutes of cooling down. He was a player of medium-height, muscular, powerful, and stocky. I surmised that he was a little older than I was. He had jet-black hair, small, dark eyes, a ripple of a scar on his lower lip and a snarl on his face.

He warned me, "I am going to take your head off tonight, number twenty-seven. I will cut your tongue out with my stick and feed it to you for breakfast tomorrow morning. Tonight, you die!"

I just laughed and waved my glove at him and watched him skate away to the penalty box. On the back of his jersey, it proudly displayed "O'MALLEY" in block letters.

Ah, hah! So, that is the man himself. O'Malley. Their hero! I thought the Bible had something in it about worshiping false idols. I guessed that Mr. O'Malley and hockey earned exceptions from that rule.

I should have surmised as much that this slashing and wild-eyed maniac was O'Malley. The CSHA faithful were still chanting loudly for O'Malley, and interlaced their colorful chants, with an encouraging testimony and proclamations of their hardcore faith, by loudly chanting, "KILL THE DEVILS! KILL THE DEVILS!"

My goodness, this was as if it was some type of warped, old-fashioned, Christian revival meeting on a Saturday night.

We played four on four and it was ugly without Harry

on the ice. The CSHA spun around the ice as if they were little jet planes, and without Harry on the ice to neutralize them, they were free to fire off at least ten shots on net on me. My teammates were useless. One Red Devil defenseman actually had possession of the puck, but he coughed it up like a bad pill. I flew all around in the crease, from post to post, playing like a madman, and stopped the shots, but they were blasting me in the net.

We finally iced the puck, but not without great effort. The CSHA team collectively pushed and shoved and cussed and screamed at us. Their second-string, right-winger flew by the front of the crease and butt ended me squarely in the gut for no reason. The end of the stick hit into my chest protector, so I did not feel it, and I grabbed the end of his stick as he shoved it in my gut, pushed it away, and sent him toppling over on his skates.

I had to think how their behavior was anything but Christian. These were the most gross, dirty and disgusting players I had ever seen.

O'Malley sprung from the penalty box alongside Harry, and O'Malley immediately pin-balled, slashed and bowled over everyone in his way.

The crowd was going nuts, screaming for their team to, "KILL THE DEVILS!"

O'Malley was out of control as he trampled his way up and down the rink like a bowling ball. He picked up the puck at full speed, crossed the blue line and wound up for a slap shot. Harry cut in front of me, as I heard the puck hit the blade, and I yelled, "SCREEN, HARRY! MOVE!"

Harry realized that he had blocked my vision and, at the last second, he jumped out of the way.

It was too late.

O'Malley had headhunted on purpose and the puck nailed me dead on at full speed, right square in the mask. The impact blew my head backwards. I felt my neck spring back and all of my teeth rattle in my head. While I fell backwards, I was vaguely aware of the puck spinning in the air in front of me, so I reached up, gloved it, tucked it safely away and then collapsed in a heap. All I could see were stars, and I felt the telltale trickling of blood rolling down my face.

I rolled around in the crease and could hear the referee blow the whistle to stop play.

O'Malley was over the top of me, taunting and yelling at me, until Harry came over and pushed him out of the way. "I told you that I would kill you! I told you that you would eat your tongue, goalie!" O'Malley screamed.

"Get lost, you twerpie jackass. Ya are really pissing me off now. Play the damn whistle, cut the shit out, and play the game, or I am going to roll ya ass into a little ball tonight!" Harry screamed while he pushed O'Malley away; the referees were blowing whistles and clearing the crowd in my crease.

Harry reached over and the big guy picked me off the ice.

"Twenty-seven! Paul! Paul! You, okay? Geezzzz, Paul! You even made the save somehow." I stood up and flipped the puck out of my glove to the linesman.

"Shit! You are cut again, twenty-seven."

I flipped my mask up and could feel the swelling on my forehead, but I could tell that the cut was not deep. God bless my mask. It was the most awesome piece of equipment ever made.

I would kiss it later.

"You all right, goalie?" The referee asked me.

"I am fine. I am fine. Let's go." The players lined up for the faceoff and Harry was still in my face, checking on me.

"Are you sure you're okay, Paul? Ya might need a stitch or two. I think. Sorry about the stupid screen man. My fault. These guys are friggin' animals. I am sorry I got us into this one. I really am."

"Harry, please, all the times guys wanted to stick a puck

between my eyes! What do you think I am, like some old lady here or what? Please, I am standing in the net here. I need a defenseman, not some old crybaby. I am trying to concentrate on the game. Now tap my pads with your stick and go play defense in front of me, will you? And please, no screens. Those pucks dead on in my mask really hurt."

I smiled at him and he smiled at me. He tapped my pads and game play resumed. The head shot had me charged up now.

"You know, for a bunch of so-called Christian guys, youse guys are the most disgusting assholes and biggest bunch of jerks that I have ever played against!" Harry complained as he glided in for the faceoff.

"Peter cut the ear off the Roman soldier there, thirty-five," O'Malley sneered.

I had to chuckle at that one!

O'Malley continued his rant.

"I am Dr. O'Malley. The expert dentist! I only do extractions. They are quick and somewhat painless!"

He tapped the butt end of his hockey stick to emphasize his "extraction tool." Oh, geez, this chap is a real piece of work!

Somehow, we managed to hold off O'Malley and his merry band of wild lunatics and the period mercifully ended. I looked up at the shots on goal on the scoreboard and saw that the CSHA had thirty shots on our goal and we had somehow managed to place two feeble shots on the CSHA goalie. I did not even recall our team managing a single shot on net, perhaps; the scorekeeper felt sorry for us and gave us a token shot or two!

We made our way to the locker room, and while we walked up the runway from the ice surface to the locker room, the CSHA faithful pelted us with coffee cups, dumped beer on our heads and threw half-chewed hot dogs in our direction. Such nice church going folks they all seemed to be! I can only imagine what their church services were like. I surmised that an ambulance needed to standby outside their sanctuary.

The Red Jersey Devils collapsed in a heap in our locker room and the ice packs, aspirin, and first aid kits broke out. Harry sat down next to me while I applied an ice pack to my cut. Harry then assisted me in applying some butterfly sutures to the huge, red blob forming on my forehead.

He moaned, "We do not need referees, we need an exorcist out there! These guys are beyond brutal!"

The coach for the Devils piped up. Even he seemed worn out as he stated, "Yeah, man, I heard that O'Malley guy was just recently released from his prison term. Nice work, you two guys. Without youse guys, it would be ugly by now."

Harry looked up, waved his hand at the coach and said in disgust, "Oh, and this is not ugly? Shit, I hate to see what ya think ugly is there, coach!"

The coach frowned and continued his hapless attempt to cheer us up, "Great goaltending there longhair. Is your head all right?"

I did not answer him and weakly nodded in his direction. An older player came over and sat down next to us. I recognized him as the left-winger on the team, and he was definitely the only player that the Red Jersey Devils had on their roster, who seemed as if he could somewhat skate, pass and shoot.

"Hey, guys. Thanks for all you did out there. We are bad, but not usually *this* bad."

I appreciated his honest assessment.

He continued, "Look, I know we all suck and all, and youse guys are like pros, but I have to tell ya that I can beat them on the wing. O'Malley, all he wants to do is push, shove, and set screens in front of the net, and then he blasts away. I have played against him before. He is all about havoc and mayhem and luring you into fights so he can strike with a goal. He will try like hell to get thirty-five here off the ice with stupid penalties, cuz he knows he is our best player. I am telling ya that I can beat all of their defensemen. Look for me on a rebound. If O'Malley and his henchman are in the zone deep, I can break up the wing. I know we look bad, and youse guys are really, really good, but I can score."

"Sure, sure, sure, we will look for you. What is your name there? I asked him. The player spun around so we could read his name and number.

"Okay, we got it there, Cantrelli, number eighteen. Let's see if we can do it!"

The second period was not much different. O'Malley skating around as if he was an escapee from an institution, and more of the same, with pushing, slashing and brutal butt ends of sticks. We held them off again without a goal, and it was now easy to see their strategy. Cantrelli was correct in his analysis of their game plan. They had good skaters, who were all quick, and the plan was to dump the puck, then crash the net. They could skate and were physical, and they could certainly shoot the puck, but somehow, we foiled them on their set-ups and any organized plays.

It was all brawn with them and no brains.

Harry was tired, and the big guy's legs were giving out from grinding and working the puck along the boards, and for the unbelievable amount of ice time, he was logging. It was a tough game, to say the least, but by the end of the second period, our defensive stands were frustrating them, and silencing the raucous supporters of the CSHA.

It felt as if the tide of the game was turning a bit.

I came up big on a wrist shot from the lower slot, while Harry made a great play with a strategic poke check to clear the rebound, and the four fans of the Red Jersey Devils in the crowd cheered for the first time for the Red Jersey Devils. It was the first cheer that we had heard the entire night for us rather than for the CSHA! The second period still ended scoreless, and the exhausted teams came out for the final period.

With about ten minutes remaining in the third and final period, I noticed that Cantrelli was indeed correct, and he was free at times on the wing. Now that O'Malley and his line mates were tired, the same plays and routines were the only strategy of which they utilized. One of their favorite plays seemed to be that the CSHA set a smallish-sized, but stubborn winger wearing number ten in front of the crease. And then, either O'Malley or the center iceman would try to blast it through the screen.

On one of these same plays, I gloved the puck easily through a screen, and spotted Cantrelli alone on his wing position, but I could not pass it up the rink without risking an interception of my pass. But I had a plan now!

At a stoppage in the play, I said to Harry, "When number ten sets the screen, I am going to jam the blade of my goalie stick right at the base of his skates. I am going to stick it into his blades hard and at an angle. With the correct amount of pressure, he will go down like a tree! You come in and blow him away. I think O'Malley and the other idiot will come rushing in, and I will have a clear lane to pass it to Cantrelli. He might see a lane and be able to break in on the wing."

"I like it, twenty-seven. Do it. I will send his ass to North Dakota."

The other lines for the CSHA were ineffective, and we actually managed a few shots on their goalie when they were on the ice. A line changed up, Harry jumped out with the O'Malley line, and Cantrelli jumped over the boards too.

Sure enough, here was the screen from number ten and I set my stick blade hard into his skates, while Harry perfectly timed the explosion. Number ten sailed into the next county as he fell over the stick while Harry rolled him. I easily gloved the puck, spotted O'Malley and the center iceman break towards the net, and when they did, they left the center of the ice wide open.

There was no penalty called on Harry. For some reason, the referee kept his whistle in his pocket. I think he was sick of the antics of the CSHA now too. The payoff in dough they obviously gave him before the game was not worth it now.

All of my hard work, as well as the good advice from Gordon Gurney to improve my skating abilities over the past year or so, now paid off! I was quite nimble on my skates, even tied down with all the cumbersome, goaltending equipment. I deftly skated out of the net, dropped the puck cleanly on the ice, and passed it right on Cantrelli's blade. O'Malley nailed me and spun me around, but I was a lot bigger and stronger than he thought and he fell backwards with a thud. I heard his head hit the ice hard, and he did not immediately jump back up.

The plan worked! The speedy winger for the Red Jersey Devils flew down the side of the rink, broke in alone on the goalie, a quick move and a head fake, then SCORE!

Yes! Yes! Yes!

When he spotted the goal scored on his team, O'Malley jumped up and took out his frustrations on the nearest Red Devil player. He was going to make us pay for our goal! He was flipping his lid, going wild, and with his stick slashing in the air, he clipped one of our players on the leg. He then took his glove and punched the back of the Red Devil in the head, knocking him forward onto the ice. The referee raised his arm for a penalty and as he led O'Malley off to the penalty box, O'Malley gave it one last hurrah, as he groaned, hurled obscenities, took his glove off, waved his hand in disgust at the referee, and led his henchman in rants and complaints, but we had finally scored.

It seemed as if the goal had silenced the CSHA supporters in the crowd, and we even heard a few boos and jeers float down from the seats, as it seemed as if they had also grown tired of O'Malley and his antics.

He went from savior to goat. It must have been the all of the antics while wearing a jersey with a cross on it that finally turned the tide.

That was the game. We played keep away for the rest of the game, while the final seconds of the clock ticked down, with O'Malley stuck in and ranting alone in the penalty box. Finally, the game mercifully ended.

One to zip, and a shutout! I had faced fifty-eight shots on net and this was the hardest earned twenty-five dollars I had ever made! The extra money that I earned for the shutout was not worth it.

"Great game, twenty-seven. The best goalie I have ever seen! Harry, you are a brute! Love youse guys! Thanks!" Cantrelli was thrilled with our performance and he was vocal as the Red Jersey Devils mobbed us and the celebration was underway.

"Nice shot, Cantrelli. Thank you! Nice skating, good hockey sense, and shifty work there."

I shook his hand as I pulled off my mask, revealing blood, sweat, but no tears!

Harry looked at Cantrelli and said, "Nice shot, but youse guys are on your own for the rest of this tournament. Youse guys are a bunch of bums."

Leave it to Harry to burst the poor chap's bubble, but he was calling it as he saw it! I had to agree, the Red Devils needed to find a new goalie. My medical insurance rates were high enough already.

The crowd was now standing for us and clapping. Even the CSHA supporters put aside their previous horrible behavior and cheered for us.

To say that this had been an entertaining game would be a gross understatement. The crowd certainly received their money's worth tonight!

We lined up for the traditional handshake and we went through the line, greeting players and shaking their hands.

Harry was in front of me, and I was last in the line, when I spotted O'Malley, standing in line to be the final player for us to greet.

Oh, oh. I prepared for the worse.

O'Malley smiled at us as he said, "Nice game, gentlemen. Big, tough, brute of a defenseman and a truly great goaltender. It is obvious that you two are friends and have played together for a long time. Remarkable and defined teamwork. I have great admiration and respect for teamwork. You, twenty-seven, sir, are the best goalie I have ever seen. I must compliment you on a monumental performance this evening number, twenty-seven. I certainly appreciate the fine effort that your team extended to us, and thank you both for engaging us in a wonderful game of ice hockey."

Harry first looked back at me puzzled, and then he looked at O'Malley and said, "Did you take some kind of personality change-o-pills or something? A few minutes ago, you needed a restraining jacket. You were like you were a Devil-possessed, friggin' whacko, and now you sound like a refined man of high society?"

O'Malley laughed and said, "No, bygones can be bygones. After all, the game is over now."

"Sure, sure, sure, whatever. Nice game there, O'Malley," Harry shook his head in amazement. He shook O'Malley's hand and O'Malley stepped up to me, and he fervently shook my hand.

"I am very sorry about the unfortunate head shot, but intimidation is part of our sport. Usually, I knock the goalie out cold with a shot like that one. You are one tough cookie and big too. I had no idea how big you were until I ran into you and fell on my backside. I have a feeling we shall meet again, my long-haired friend. Good luck to you."

"The same to you, sir. Thank you."

That was the best I could muster up for an answer. Once the game ended, O'Malley became a completely different guy. I did not want to choke the life out of him. O'Malley actually seemed civilized. I watched him skate off the ice, and somehow, I knew he was correct. I did not know at the time that in the very near future, exactly how prophetic his words would turn out to be for the both of us.

"Hurry up, twenty-seven! Follow me! I have to find that gal whose name I cannot remember. She will shower me with love, kisses and affection after this game! Besides, there is an entire audience of hot chicks waiting for us. I bet they will be taking off their bras for us to sign autographs on them! C'mon! Now, no Mr. Nice Guy, Paul! This is not the time to be an old lady when ya are facing a screaming audience of adoring fans!" Harry waved to me to join him.

I smiled and skated to catch up and step off the ice. I looked at the screaming crowd . . . they sure were excited.

As I stepped off the ice surface and onto the rubber matting that led to the locker room, I squeezed sideways to fit my goalie pads through the narrow rink door and I was surprised when a middle-aged man, well dressed, in a suit and tie, was standing there in front of me.

Before I could even say anything, he smiled at me and said, "Nice game there, son. Helluva a damn goaltending performance. You have a name, son?"

"Sure, sure, sure. Thank you. Paul John Henson."

"Henson, huh? Yeah, yeah, yeah, Henson." He chuckled a bit, wiped his forehead, as if he were recalling something, then he said, "That is what I thought you would say. Hey, keep up the good work. Man, you are a lot bigger in person than you looked out on the ice. Big, strong, guy. You made the legendary O'Malley look bad out there. He is a wild beast, a real handful, and you and your buddy there on defense neutralized him. Impressive. Say, do you ever shave that beard or cut all that hair?"

I smiled and said, "No, it is who I am, sir."

"Good for you. I will be seeing you around. I promise." Before I could even ask who he was, he turned and disappeared into the crowd. I reached my hand up and felt the welt and the cut on my face and looked back to see O'Malley disappear into his locker room.

I met Harry in the locker room, after his greetings from a cavalcade of young women asking for his autograph, and who knows what else. After showering and dressing in our civilian clothes, Harry tossed me a black marker he kept in his bag for marking his name on his equipment. He did not say a word. He only smiled.

I knew what to do.

I reached into my equipment bag and took out my trusty goalie mask. With the marker, I drew a stitched scar on the face of the mask where the puck had hit me.

"Ya know something, Harry? I think this mask has magical powers. I really do." I looked over at Harry and he smiled.

He shook his head and answered, "You are still alive, ain't ya? Damn straight that it has friggin' magical powers!"

I nodded, smiled and mumbled while I finished drawing the scar on my mask, "Until we meet again, O'Malley."

4

The Dubious Double Date

The summer of 1978 brought us to a point in our young lives, where the circle of activity for Harry and Paul was quite small. Our circle primarily remained women, various types of automobiles, a little fishing, and lots and lots of hockey. Well, we once had a boat, but that is another story.

Oh, my, in looking back, it was wonderful to be so young, so free, and to have what you perceive to be an entire world of opportunity in front of you. We did not have a lot of money; we grew up tough and hard, but with wonderful parents, friends and families who cared for us more than we could ever imagine. Their combined support had an amazing positive influence in our lives, and it was one of the main factors that led and drove us to being successful. Primarily, because of our upbringing and their support, failure for two boyhood friends from the streets of Haledon, and the city of Paterson, was simply not an option that we ever considered. And we knew how to have fun with some "toys" and our beloved hockey, as well as work hard too!

As Harry would say, "We work hard during the day, but the night always comes, my friend, and we will be there together forever."

Those words are truly an entire other story! The adventures of these years and the summers of that time would fill many, many pages!

On the other hand, some of our wild, off-ice adventures, particularly the adventures that involved beautiful women, shaped our persona, and in a strange sort of way, they paved the way to connections for our hockey world. It was just that sometimes, the adventures that happened to involve beautiful women were always a little tricky.

It was early on a lazy Saturday afternoon in August 1978 or thereabouts, and I had a rare Saturday off from my full-time job and other than our practice skates, it was off season in the world of hockey. I was lounging on my bed, listening to the latest record from my favorite rock and roll band, "No Way," when I heard the telephone ring.

I heard the old man bellow for me to come and pick up the call, "It's Harry! Make it quick. I am expecting a call from the shop on a machine that is giving us fits!"

I jumped out of bed and made my way to the dining room, where our telephone sat on a little table. The old man scowled while he handed me the telephone handset and reminded me to keep the call short.

"Dad, I have never spoken to Harry for over five minutes on a telephone call in all the years I have known him!"

"Yeah, yeah, yeah, keep it that way," the old man mumbled while handing me the telephone.

It was true. Harry's conversations were usually short and generally involved some wild scheme or plan that he had concocted to drag me into at the moment.

"Hey, Harry."

"I need your help big time, twenty-seven . . . look, I need you at around seven o'clock tonight to go to Lord Crudley's' bar and find a gal named Mary. She looks Irish, with red hair, a big chest and long legs. She should be rather easy to find. I suspect she may have some guys drooling on her. She will be at the bar, waiting for me. Buy her a few drinks, tell her who you are, and that I am running late. Apologize and tell her I had a, a . . . flat tire. Yeah, yeah, yeah, a flat tire. That will work. Then call this number at seven fifteen. Ya got a pencil?"

Yes, I knew it. A wild Harry scheme, and this sounded like an extra special debacle!

I reached for a nearby pencil and pad, while mumbling, "Go ahead."

"Two, seven, nine, three, five, zero, nine. A chick named Linda is going to answer. Tell her it is an emergency, that your jeep is broken down and you need help right away."

"Oh, you mean for me to tell her a bunch of lies, Harry?"

"Nah, nah, nah, this is not exactly a lie, Paul, about the jeep. Chances are, your old piece of shit jeep will break down soon. Think of it as a preemptive action."

"What about the fact that I have to tell Mary you are running late because of having a flat tire?"

"Yeah, yeah, yeah, well, that one is an outright lie, twenty-seven. But someday, I will be late because of a flat tire."

"What do I do if Linda asks me how I got her number?"

"Oh geez, there ya go guessing wild, stupid stuff again! She will not ask that! Why the hell would she ask ya something stupid like that?"

"Because that is what I would ask."

"Well. You're an old lady who is shackled now and until the end of all time, with a hopeless case of Mr. Nice Guy and a dose of the ever-present Old Lady Syndrome. Geez, c'mon, twenty-seven. I am your best buddy and I need ya help here."

"Okay, okay, okay. I got you, Harry. Well, we will see. So, I am going to tell a pack of lies, for some unknown reason, which probably has to do with you chick juggling. Why do I always have to be brought in on your wild schemes?"

"Ah c'mon, twenty-seven! Stop being such an old lady and help me out here. You can go to confession and it will be okay."

"I am Lutheran, Harry. We do not do that."

"Whatever! The old man will tell you to help me out

here. He is most likely standing there, waiting for the telephone because the shop has another crummy ass machine broken down. Look, I owe you. I will pay you back for the drinks. The lies, well, you are on your own for that one. God loves you, twenty-seven. He listens to you. God forgives ya, Paul. Besides, I think Mary has a hot friend for you to date. Ask Mary about her. You know, this might lead to true romance, be fruitful and multiply. You know all that Bible stuff a lot better than I do. Call me. Thanks!"

"Click" the line went dead.

"Stop being such an old lady and help the guy out, will ya? He is your best buddy in the world," the old man said as he reached for the telephone.

Of course, the old man agreed with Harry.

"I got to use the phone. Good luck with all of that Harry drama shit! I could only hear part of that conversation, but it sounds like a winner, even for Harry to come up with." The old man's comments did not make me feel any better.

Seven o'clock in the early evening found me sitting at the bar at Lord Crudley's gin mill. I sat there thinking about the amazing things that we do for our friends.

Lord Crudley's was an old shack tucked away on a hillside just off a main road. It was nothing special; a gin joint that had a cover band, a small dance floor, and that was about it. We had both just turned the legal drinking age for New Jersey when the state lowered the age for a few years. It did not last long. The lawmakers changed the drinking age again when we both reached twenty-one, so we were unaffected anyway!

"What'll ya have dare, long-haired, pal?" A rather grouchy barkeeper with a heavier New Jersey accent than mine growled at me from his post behind the bar. "Did they proof ya ass at the door?"

"Yes sir, they did. In fact, they proofed all of me. Ass and all. Big Boulder on tap will do."

The barkeeper looked at me rather suspiciously. Ah hah, so we were going to have some fun with the long-haired, hippie guy, eh?

I could tell. I was not in the mood for this clown's games tonight.

"Describe 'em . . . ya know, describe who proofed ya."

"Why not make this easier, rather than play twenty bullshit questions? I will just show you my identification again?"

I stood up, reached in my back pocket for my wallet and watched the barkeeper's eyes while they went up and down my tall frame. I could tell that he was going to say what everyone always said.

"Whoa, big guy! Ya didn't look that big sitting dare. Nah, nah, nah, shit. We are good. A tall or a short Big Boulder?"

"A short one, please. Thanks."

He nodded and, while he filled the glass from the tap, he looked over at me again.

"Waiting for someone? Or are ya alone?"

"Well, I have to meet a gal here and tell her that my buddy is running a little late for his date with her. He, ah, ah . . . had a flat tire, so he sent me ahead to let her know that he did not stand her up for their date."

Well, there you go, Paulie. That little effort at fudging was easy now. I had to look on the bright side of this little adventure and consider my fudging right now with the grouchy barkeeper to be "practice."

The barkeeper dropped the beer in front of me, and I laid down a few dollars on the bar.

"What does this gal look like? Does she have a name? I know all the regulars and you are not one of them. If ya don't mind me sayin' that, ya are dressed like a hippie bum for meeting a gal."

I looked down at my usual attire of black canvas sneakers and a tee shirt with the famous logo of the band

"No Way" emblazoned across the front. He was correct because I did look like a bum. However, she was not *my* date.

I ignored his remark on my appearance and only answered his questions, "Her name is Mary and she has long, red hair. That is all I know. I never met her." I decided to skip Harry's overt description of her chest and legs.

"Turn around, hippie. I would say dat dare is a very good chance that might be her walking up to the bar right now. From the looks of her, your buddy would be nuts to stand her up!"

He took some bills off my stack and I turned around.

Sure enough, a stunningly attractive, red-haired gal was standing behind me, looking up and down the bar, and you could tell from the look on her face, she was surprised that Harry was not there.

Oh, oh! It is time to move quickly before she thinks that Harry is a no-show.

I jumped off the bar stool and walked over to her while asking, "Excuse me, but are you, by any chance, a gal named Mary?"

The gal looked puzzled and weakly smiled while saying, "Why yes, I am. Why do you ask?"

"I am sorry, but I am Paul John Henson. Harry M. Redmond Junior is my best buddy, and he asked me to run over here to meet you. He had a bit of a situation come up, and he was running late. He will be here, though, in just a few minutes. Something about a flat tire on his car or something like that." Oh boy, I continued to dig myself deeper into the fudge department, courtesy of Harry and my own lack of fortitude.

"Oh hi. Paul John Henson. Okay, yes, the famous ice hockey goalie. Harry has mentioned you about a million times."

I smiled and said, "I do not know about the famous part,

but yes, I do play the position of goaltender. It is nice to meet you." I reached out and gently shook her hand. I had a bad habit of squeezing people's hands too hard when I would greet them. I was becoming more aware of it as I grew stronger and stronger from my workouts.

"Hi, I am Mary O'Leary. Nice to meet you too. I must say that Harry never mentioned how large a man you are! You are very tall and lean, but muscular. He also never mentioned how strikingly handsome you are! A super hottie with a body!"

"Oh, yes. I, well, ah, I guess that I am tall. Say, I have to make a quick telephone call there on the payphone. First, why don't we sit down, and I can buy you a drink. I will make the call, and I am sure Harry will be here shortly."

Mary agreed, and we sat down together. Mr. Grouchy came over, Mary ordered a Scotch and water, and I paid for the drink. I excused myself to make the call to the number Harry gave me. As I walked down towards the end of the bar to use the pay telephone, Mr. Grouchy, the barkeeper frantically, waved me over. I glanced at my watch. It was almost seven fifteen. I had to make the call.

I leaned in and the barkeeper said in a low whisper, "Say, ah, hippie guy. This pal of yours is he a big, 'trong, guy, with red hair, kinda cut inah crew cut? A guy named Timmy O'Reilly? I know Timmy and he is a regular here. That gal ovah dare. Mary, I do recognize her now, as his gal."

Oh no! This had trouble written all over it. Harry, Harry, Harry. Why do you do this to me?

"No, no, no, my buddy's name is Harry. He is a big guy, but he does not have red hair or wear a crew cut. Harry has sort of dirty blondish hair. Kinda long, but not nearly as long as mine. He has a moustache."

The barkeeper smiled and his eyes flickered with the pending trouble that was no doubt looming on the horizon.

Saturday night at the fights.

I knew what was coming next. I just knew it from all of our adventures. Nothing, in which Harry M. Redmond Jr. ever did, was ever cut and dry.

The chances were very good that a gal as stunningly beautiful as Mary was would already have a man in her life. Harry was either weaseling in on her, or she had recently broken up with this Timmy chap, and is on the rebound from him. Poor Mary O'Leary had fallen into the Harry trap. His silken tongue had woven a tapestry of words to lure her into his web and he hopelessly tangled her, along with, apparently, a few other gals too.

I also now knew the rest of the story.

I can predict these things from years and years of watching Harry operate. He never picked any other type of woman, other than a woman on the rebound from boyfriends who were hulking bruisers, who drove fancy sports cars; they were either professional or amateur boxers, football players, racecar drivers, secret agents, bodyguards for movie stars, rodeo heroes or they were all involved in similar types of pastimes or occupations. Two additional requirements that were even more ironclad were that these former boyfriends always had to have lots of friends and piles of money.

I decided to confirm my fate and theory.

"Say, this Timmy chap, is he enormous and strong, and did he play football?"

"Nah, nah, nah, he is big and 'trong, but he was a professional rugby player over in Ireland. He never played football that I know of, at least. He has tons of dough and drives. . .."

Rugby, I thought for a second, how that was a new sport for the list!

I cut him off, "I know the drill! He drives a fancy sports car."

"Yeah, yeah, yeah, dats right. How did ya know dat?" I did not answer him, but while I walked away, the barkeeper warned me, "Timmy usually comes in every Saturday around eight or so with all of his friends. Ya know, he comes in here with all the players on his rugby team."

Yup. I knew that, too.

I dropped some coins in the pay telephone, dialed the number that Harry gave me and waited to dig myself deeper and deeper into the pit of Harry flim-flam.

One ring and a young woman's lovely voice answers.

"Hello."

"Ah . . . hello, Linda. I am sorry to bother you, but this is Harry's best friend, Paul John Henson calling, and I . . . ah . . . have an emergency. My jeep is broken down and I hope that Harry can help me."

"How did you get my number?"

I stopped short and swallowed.

One of these days, I will send Harry to the planet Mars with no return rocket ship. Yes, that might just suffice.

"Well . . . I . . . I, well, Harry gave it to me."

That question, of course, was the first thing that I had predicted she would ask me this afternoon, and Harry jumped down my throat, calling me an old lady. I decided to weave a little flim-flam of my own, but this time, I laced it with some words that might actually have some element of truth associated with it.

"My old jeep is a bucket of bolts. It has been shaky as of late and Harry said he might be here at this number if I needed help with a rescue mission."

"Oh, okay, yeah, yeah, yeah. Harry mentioned the other day that your jeep was a hunk of junk and that you are always penniless. Hold on."

I heard the telephone receiver drop, some speaking about my jeep, then some hilarious laughing in the background, and then Harry said, "Geez, that shitty jeep of yours, twenty-seven! Where are you ole buddy ole boy? Sure, no trouble, of course. I will come and rescue you."

Oh, brother, my poor jeep had to be the centerpiece for hilarity and the ace in the deck for Harry's evil plan.

"You know where I am, you big galuk. Come quickly, too. Did you know this Mary gal has a big, bad boyfriend?"

"Oh yeah, yeah, yeah. Don't they all! Sure, sure, sure, twenty-seven. Say, Linda, you do not mind. Do ya baby cakes? I will make it up to you. Paul is on the side of the road with antifreeze pouring out of the jeep. I would bring ya, but we will be all messy."

"I understand, Harry! You are my big baby doll! It is so nice that you are so caring and willing to help your best friend in an emergency. That is just one of the reasons I love you so much." I could faintly hear Linda respond to the actor of the year.

A saying that my old man always said popped into my head, "All the actors are not in Hollywood!"

Harry whispered into the telephone to me, "On my way, twenty-seven. Mary is hot, right?"

"Click" the line went dead.

I thought. No, maybe Mars is too close. There is a chance Harry would be resourceful and be able to find his way back to planet Earth. He would find a wayward space suit, float back on some space junk, land in the Pacific Ocean, find deadwood to float on and he would return to New Jersey.

"Is everything okay, Paul?"

"Oh yes. It is fine, Mary."

I picked up my beer and took a sip while nervously glancing at my watch. Ah, why not! I swigged the beer down and ordered another. The bartender quickly brought another beer over and slid it over to me.

"Harry tells me that you guys are always playing in hockey games and are very good."

"I do not know about us being very good. However, we do play in many hockey games though. We have played together for years and years. You know, Mary, I have to say that Harry tends to exaggerate quite a bit, especially when it comes to our hockey careers."

It was finally time to tell some truth tonight. My prayers for forgiveness already would take about ten hours of Heaven's time to hear.

"Oh, I do not mind. He seems as if he is a lot of fun. I have only known him for a week or so. He asked me to see if my uncle could get youse guys a tryout in a senior hockey league that my uncle coaches here in New Jersey. I told him that I would. . .."

Ah, hah! The picture becomes clearer. Harry is working an angle, not only trying to date a very lovely young woman, but he is making a connection for a hockey club.

Now, I understood the entire picture just a bit better. There is usually, not always, but sometimes, there is a method to the wild and crazy world of Harry M. Redmond Junior.

I returned from my daydream in order to pretend that I was actually paying attention to what Mary was saying. The mention of a potential chance with a senior hockey league had diverted my attention from lies, hulking rugby players, lovely red-haired gals, exiles to Mars, and other assorted Harry related schemes of intrigue.

Mary was indeed quite lovely, and very nice to look at, but she seemed a bit overpowering. I could not quite put my finger on her personality yet. I had a deep inclination that she wasn't a cupcake or a prissy pant.

"I must admit that I have a girlfriend who would love to meet a guy such as you are, Paul. She is very nice; I think she is home tonight. Maybe when Harry arrives, we can go over there and we could double date to the movies or something. I just broke up with my boyfriend last week and she dumped the loser bum she had been dating, too. We are both ready to move on with our lives and meet quality men, instead of these meatheads that we have been shackled with as of late."

"Oh well, I am sure she is a lovely gal, but I am not really dressed for a date. I just came over to help Harry out here tonight."

"Oh, I think you look just fine. In fact, I find you incredibly sexy myself. That hair, the beard, the tall frame, your muscles. I want to sit here and sip my drink and drool over you. You are a hot number, Paul. I am thinking of ditching Harry and running out with you myself."

I coughed and choked on my beer and started to stammer when the barkeeper came over and told Mary, "You have to drink to sit here. So ya ready?"

"Sure, sure. I am ready all right! In more ways than one!" Mary looked at me and winked. This was unreal. It really was unreal. I now had a better grip on her personality. Hockey league connection or not, this gal was a bit much. No sooner did the barkeeper set the drink down next to Mary, she picked it up and downed it in two gulps and a trickle of a swallow.

"Hit me again!" Mary shouted out.

Oh geez, she was going to drink me under the bar and into the poorhouse. Another drink instantly appeared, and she initially sipped at this one. All right, this is good. She knocked one or two drinks down to take the edge off, and now she will nurse a drink for an hour or so. . ..

Mary then turned to me, tugged at her already plunging neckline to reveal her overflowing cleavage, and said, "So, what do you think there, Paul? You turned a little red there for a moment. A big, rough, tough, ice hockey goalie. I did not think I could ever embarrass a man like you are. Or, can I?"

She returned her attention back to the drink, picked up the glass, chugged it, and immediately signaled for another one.

I guess she pushed the sipping-the-drink-plan to the wayside.

She downed that sucker in what appeared to be a

minute or two and quickly signaled for another.

Mary was smiling widely now, cuddling up closer and closer to me, putting her hand upon my leg while simultaneously, tugging at her neckline more and more in order to reveal her mountainous cleavage and a bit more too, and generally, becoming a bit on the sloshed side.

Oh, oh! Where is Harry? I am going broke here! This gal is a party gal! Quarter to eight. . ..

"Youuuuurr . . . nottt, still ssssshy or embarrasssssed are you there? I think it is number twenty sssssseven. Isn't it? Youuuuuu are turning a little red tttttthere."

Her words and the pauses between them were becoming a bit longer in their formation. I decided to try the laughter and humor approach.

It works every time.

"Ha, ha, ha," I forced a few phony chuckles. "Oh, nah, nah, nah, you can't embarrass me. I can see that you have a great sense of humor, Mary! Harry and I have been best buddies since we were ten years old. I would never. . .."

"Who the hell is kidding? I am not kidding. I ain't laughing either, not when I check those arm muscles of yours out. I find you ssssso damn hot. I bet you are amazing in bed. I would rip that shirt off ya, toss ya down on the floor and have my. . .."

Well, not every time does the humor angle work.

"Hey, guys! Sorry I am late! Tricky tires. Everything is good now!" I heard the big guy's voice behind me and a powerful slap on my back told me that Harry had finally made it. Thank goodness! It was just about eight o'clock on the nose and I was down to ten dollars to my name.

"Hi, Harry! It is ssssso nnnnnnice to sssssssee you!" Mary leaned in and gave Harry a whopper of a kiss.

"Hiya, Mary baby. Wwwoooo, it sounds and smells like ya went ahead and started celebrating the evening, a little early and without me, huh? I trust you and Paul are getting along well enough, and he has treated you well in my absence."

"Well, not as well or half asssssss nnnnnnnice as what I could hope for, but a girl can only wwwwwwish for ssssso mmmmuuuuuch, Hhhhhharry."

She winked, shook her head a little and seemed to recover her mouth operations. Suddenly, her word delivery improved. It was still not perfect, but improved. This gal was impressive in her alcohol consumption recovery abilities.

"I told Paul that my best friend Janet is home all alone tonight, and she would love to meet Paul. Maybe, we can double date tonight! She just bbbbrrroooooke up with her bbbbboyfriend ttttttoo. He was always playing fffffootbbbball in college or in the weight room working on his muscles and never had time for her. She is ssssso lonely."

"Does her ex-boyfriend drive a fancy sports car, Mary?" I asked.

"Yessssss! How did you know that, Pppppaawwwllll?"

"Lucky guess."

"I think a double date is a great idea!" Harry spouted as he waved to the barkeeper to order a drink. "Give me a double Wall crawler, heavy on the ice there, ya gloomy faced, chief!" The barkeeper frowned, nodded, and waved towards Harry.

"Give me ahhhhh sssssecond and I will call her," Mary jumped up, and she tilted a little here and there, as the drinks had knocked her for a bit of a loop. She giggled, steadied herself, and then she precariously propelled her way towards the pay telephone.

As soon as Mary had wobbled over to the pay telephone and she was safely out of listening range, I turned to Harry and excitedly told him, "Geez Harry, this gal is a bit over the top. She has sucked down about six drinks in twenty minutes like it is tap water, and I have to tell you, buddy . . . that she is. . .."

"She's hitting on ya right, Paul. I know. She is a party gal. A cute one, but she is a little on the wild side. It is all right. You are such an old lady that you probably turned ten shades of red. I know that she saw you at a hockey game and told me what she wanted to do with you. She is a little, how shall I say this but, she is kind of loose. How do you think I got a date with her?"

I did not know what to say. It seemed as if Harry, of course, had this all figured out ahead of time. The barkeeper came over, dropped Harry's cocktail in front of him, and anxiously waved his fingers for Harry to cough up the dough right away for the drink. This barkeeper was really testing my nerves, and I could tell that he annoyed Harry right away.

"Hold ya horses there hotshot. I got to get my wallet out." Harry reached for his wallet and plopped a ten spot in the barkeeper's anxious hands.

The barkeeper smiled and said, "Ya better save a few bucks for doctor bills once Irish Timmy shows up with his Irish rugby team and kicks ya ass for being with his chickee poo."

Harry picked up his drink, sipped it, and smiled. Oh boy, there was nothing that Harry enjoyed more than a challenge to his manhood.

"Well, look at my legs trembling in fear there, ya big jerk! Who the hell asked ya, anyway? I don't recall asking ya for advice! What are ya, his watchdog or something? Jackass! I ain't scared of jackshit! Rugby players, my ass. We are hockey players and we eat rugby guys for lunch. Bring 'em on! We will send their asses back to Ireland in coffins."

The barkeeper went away, still smirking.

I could hear him mumble, "Hah, sure, sure, sure, like I am really gonna believe some long-haired hippie is a hockey player! Irish Timmy will kick both ya asses raw."

He seemed to be a doubter in the team of Harry and

Paul.

Harry turned his attention back to the matter at hand and he sipped his drink, checked for Mary's whereabouts and told me, "Mary, being a walk on the wild side, well, it does not matter. She is hot and I am working for some other stuff as well as working the angle for her uncle to give us a tryout at a senior league. Her uncle is a big shot coach, and he is sure to get us a chance for at least a tryout skate with one of those senior clubs. It could be a big break for us, Paul. The good looks, the long legs, the big chest, those are just bonus points. Ya know, a little sun on the otherwise dark horizon, so to speak. It may cost me a few bucks for drinks and other things, but if we make the hockey connection, it will be good!"

"Mary did tell me about her uncle. I have to admit that would be great Harry, but man, oh man, she is a bit much. It is going to cost you more than just a few bucks for drinks. You had better draw down on your bank account when you take her out on the town."

"You know, twenty-seven, I got to tell it as it is, but when you are a helpless victim of the dreaded Old Lady Syndrome and Mr. Nice Guy, a hot chick like Mary might be a little too much. For me, it is all in a day's work. I have to tell you, though. I am exhausted. This is the seventh date I have with seven different chicks today. All of these women are getting tough to keep track of. That's why I needed you to call me. I needed to ditch Linda to make it here on time to meet Mary. There are only so many hours in a day, twenty-seven."

Harry smiled and sipped his drink while he raised his eyebrows at me to promote his incredible achievement.

"Seven dates, with seven different gals in one day, Harry. That is amazing, even for you."

"Yeah, yeah, yeah, I know. I feel kinda bad. You have not had seven dates in your entire life. Sorry, Paul. But if it helps you at all, you are the *best* goaltender in the entire world!" Harry reached over, put his big arm around me and squeezed me until it was hard to breathe.

That made me feel a lot better—it really did.

Mary reappeared, and she stumbled up to the barstool.

She announced in a slightly fuzzy delivery, "Janet is ready to meet Paul. I told her that he is hot, told her about the long hair, the beard, the arm muscles and how tall he is. I mentioned the goalie stuff and that he has a nice, tight backside and most likely packs some major equipment. Not hockey equipment, by the way. So, she is in!"

"Works for me! Good thing ya did not mention he is Mr. Nice Guy or an old lady at heart! Way to sell it, Mary! Great job! Let's go!" Harry dropped more dollar bills on the bar and he grabbed Mary's hand to leave.

Mary turned to Harry and asked, "Can I order one more shot of whiskey, Harry baby?"

This was too much, even if Mary could get us a tryout in a senior league!

"Sure, sure, sure, Mary."

Harry ordered the drink and Mary downed it in one shot and we were off. Harry held Mary up with his arm so that she did not topple over. I waved to the barkeeper, who did not even acknowledge me, and we headed for the door.

I glanced at my watch and it was now five minutes after eight. We were in luck! We were going to leave before Irish Timmy, the rugby player and his team of rugby thugs, arrived in their sports cars to attempt to dismantle Harry and me. Finally, something worked out right for a change.

Maybe.

We took off in Harry's car and Mary gave us directions to Janet's house. She was a little sloppy. She hung all over Harry, but she seemed to be recovering somewhat.

"Now, youse guys, I have to warn you that there is something seriously wrong with Janet's brother. He has some type of brain defect and he runs all over the house, screaming at the top of his lungs. It is a little annoying, but you do become used to it after a little while."

Harry shook his head in a display of sympathy while he said, "Ya get used to it, huh? Sounds kinda weird. Oh, a brain defect, huh? Poor kid is a loon, huh? That sounds like what my brother-in-law Ronzo does after he sucks down too many Dingleberry beers!"

"Oh, yuck! Those Dingleberries are way too sweet. I do not drink them . . . unless there is nothing else available," Mary admitted.

I thought to myself, poor Dingleberry beer, *even* Mary would only drink them if there was nothing else available. Someday, I would give one of them a try. . ..

"One other very important thing to remember, if by chance, the kid stops screaming and running around, and you get a chance to look at him, you have to remember this."

Mary had us on the edge of our seats. Well, sort of on the edge of our seats.

She explained, "Do not, and I repeat, please, please, please, do not, under any circumstance, say anything about the big birthmark on his face! Janet's mom and dad are very sensitive about his appearance, as well as his behavior, and they will get very upset and throw you out of the house. It looks as if he has a big, giant, black eye, but it is really just a terrible birthmark."

"Geez, Mary, this kid is a friggin' disaster! Seems as if nuthin' is going right for him! Sounds like he was last on line in the luck department and first in the loser line," Harry displayed a profound and sincere sympathy for the poor young man's plight. To me, it sounded like a typical adventure that Harry would somehow remarkably be able to involve us in!

"No sweat. Paul and I will not say a word! If the kid needs a straitjacket and a plastic surgeon, then so be it! You can count on us not to say a word."

We pulled into the driveway of Janet's house, which was

ironically only a block or two away from the Ice Land arena. The three of us climbed out of the car. We all walked up to the front door and rang the doorbell.

This was a typical split-level type home, commonly found in the suburbs of New Jersey, New York, and Connecticut. The homes all were the same, with a small entrance hallway that had an open foyer with stairs in front of you to take you to the upper level, and another set of stairs, which brought you down to the lower level.

This home was very nice, a fine trimmed lawn, well lit, a quiet street, all set in a well-to-do neighborhood.

A perfect setting.

A fine example of classic, successful, upper middle-class America. Certainly, this was a few million steps up from the old neighborhood where we lived.

The door swung open, and a very cute, petite, young gal with short brown hair, a wonderful smile, containing a mouthful of perfect choppers, opened the door and she smiled at us.

"Hi, Mary! Come in! Come in! This must be Harry and Paul. Please come in." The young gal almost shouted at us. I was certainly encouraged. Janet seemed very sweet, pretty, and quite pleasant.

This evening was suddenly looking up a bit. I thought about how I really needed to upgrade my wardrobe, and I wished that I had dressed a little better these days. I vowed to work on that.

Mary introduced us, "Janet Simmons, please meet Harry M. Redmond Junior and the hunky, hairy guy is Paul John Henson."

"Nice to meet ya there, Janet! You are a cute little dish! Nice choppers and a cute little tushie too!" Harry smiled and shook her hand.

"Hi, I am. Paul John Henson," I said while smiling and shaking her hand, and presenting a rather conservative introduction as opposed to Harry's slightly lascivious comments.

"Hi! It is nice to meet you, Paul. My goodness, you are so big, so tall," Janet stuttered.

"Hello, Mr. and Mrs. Simmons. How are you tonight?" Mary greeted and smiled at two middle-aged, beautiful people.

A handsome gentleman wearing a dinner jacket, smoking a pipe, stood at the top of the staircase in front of us and he was arm in arm with his lovely wife. He sipped a drink from a martini glass, in-between a puff or two on his pipe. The heavenly aroma of the pipe tobacco floated in and around the entire home.

His wife was a picture-perfect model of the perfect spouse. She was dressed in a perfectly fitting dress, which enhanced her rather shapely figure and came down to mid-length on her knees. Her hair was prepared in a perfect coiffure, in a striking flip style, and she wore a breathtaking necklace of white pearls with a matching set of pearl earrings. Very expensive and quite impressive too! She, too, sipped a drink from a martini glass.

A picture-perfect couple, calm and relaxed, successful and eloquent. Deeply in love and enjoying cocktails together on a lovely Saturday evening. They were happy, smiling folks, who waved back at us from the top of the staircase, right in front of what appeared to be a gourmet kitchen.

I marveled at how Mary had remarkably sobered up quickly. Either she just had a fortified liver, which absorbed alcohol like a sponge, or she was a gal who could hide it rather well. I was not sure which theory was correct.

"Nice to meet you!" The Simmons waved, smiled and yelled at us. An all-American family. How nice. A pretty, cute gal, beautiful, handsome, happy parents, fancy house, and a . . . lunatic little kid. . ..

Suddenly, a horrifying sound broke the picture-perfect setting. I nearly jumped out of my canvas sneakers!

"AHHHHHHHH! AHHHHHHHH!"

A small boy, about ten or eleven years old, screamed and whizzed by us while we stood in the foyer. He broke through our group like a racecar and spun the poor half-in-the-bag, Mary around as if she were a wobbly bowling pin. "AHHHHHH!" He then screamed and flew off in the other direction.

"AHHHHHH! OHHHHHHH!" Off he went, screaming at the top of his lungs, as he circled back for another round. The four of us just stood there watching this kid fly around the house screaming and waving his hands above his head. His screams were deafening and there was no use in trying to attempt to have a conversation or attempt to try to speak over his shouts and screams.

Harry leaned over and whispered to me, "Holy smokes, twenty-seven. This poor little nutcase is crazier than O'Malley is. I gotta wonder how ya sleep or watch television around here."

"AHHHHOOOOOO! AHHHHHHHHH!"

After a few whirlwind passes and deafening screams, the little kid finally ran out of propulsion.

The little kid finally stopped next to Janet. While gasping desperately for air in deep breaths, he stood at attention and he looked at us with wild tousled hair and with his eyeballs spinning around in his head.

Janet put her arm around him, smiled and said, "Guys, this is my little brother, Poindexter. He has . . . a lot of energy."

Harry leaned over, put his hand out to shake the little kid's hand and said, "I'll say there, Poin-a-roo-ski. That is an understatement for sure!"

Harry stood up after shaking the little kid's hand; he peered in at the kid's face, leaned in and then pointed at his eyeball with the very weird birthmark.

"Say, next time ya ought to duck! Ya got some kind of shiner there, pal! Ya need to calm down there, sonny. Ya musta crashed into something! Besides, ya lookin' an actin' a little whacked out there, kid!"

I felt my heart go in my throat, and Harry, realizing what he had said, stood up, screwed his mouth up like a corkscrew and said, "Oops."

Immediately, when they heard Harry's errant comments, the former all-American couple erupted into extreme fits of rage and anger. They both spilled their martinis. The picture-perfect husband hurled his pipe at us and his wife shrieked in horror while pointing at us!

Good thing that I was a goalie. I caught the pipe while it hurtled in the air toward us and handed it to Janet.

The Simmons screamed in unison at us, "OUT OF OUR HOUSE, YOU HORRIBLE, COLD HEARTED, EVIL WRETCHES! YOU HEATHENS! OUT! OUT! POOR LITTLE POINDEXTER, CANNOT HELP THE WAY HE IS! OR THE WAY HE LOOKS! OUT! OUT! OUT! YOU EVIL BUMS! YOU WILL NEVER DATE OUR DAUGHTER, YOU HIPPIE FREAK, WHACKO LOSER!"

Harry and I threw our arms up in the air and Harry screamed, "Make a run for it, twenty-seven. The whole joint is filled with whackos!"

We both turned to make a mad dash for the front door.

Mary stomped her feet on the ground at Harry's inexplicable blunder, and I could hear her cussing under her breath.

Janet's face showed her sheer disappointment as she tugged at my arm to pull me back in and she mouthed to me, "Please call me. I am so sorry."

While she grabbed me, she spun me around, and while I tried in vain to make it to the front door, Janet slipped a note in my hand. A quick glance told me it had her telephone number written down on it. She must have known ahead of time that this meeting might end suddenly. I had a feeling that it was not the first time a potential boyfriend had made a quick exit from Janet's home.

"AHHHHOOOOOO! AHHHHHHHH!"

Poindexter, the terrible was now unleashed in a display of full terror and howling. He screamed as he blasted off to who knows where.

So much for the all-American family.

We bolted out the front door, just in time, as Mrs. Simmons grabbed a dust mop to attack us with, in an effort to drive the heathens from her house.

She blew by her daughter, slashing out at us with the mop handle while screaming, "Out! Out! You cold-hearted wretches!"

"Run, twenty-seven! She must be O'Malley's sister!"

We flew down the driveway with a half-in-the-bag, cleavage bouncing, Mary stumbling behind us.

"Better hold on to them, there, chesticals, Mary! They are gonna pop out of ya holders and take out ya eyeballs!" Harry was yelling advice to Mary as we narrowly escaped the mop handle-equipped thrasher.

We arrived red-faced and panting, but intact and safe, at the side of Harry's car.

Harry turned to Mary, and he apologized for his sudden and inexplicable case of amnesia.

"Sorry, Mary, honey! I forgot." Harry apologized as we stood in the driveway. He added on the heels of his repentance, "Geez, talk about friggin' whack jobs. Ya got to admit that they do seem a bit on the unusual side."

Mary was not very pleased as she screamed back at Harry, "You forgot! You forgot!" Mary shook her head, and she crossed her arms in front of her now under control chest. "How the hell could you forget? I am the one who has been hammering down drinks. I *just* told you!"

Harry held his head in his hands and I stood there shaking my head at the entire scene.

Harry recovered and offered up a possible explanation for their behavior, "Ya sure those whackos last name ain't,

O'Malley? They seem to resemble someone that Paul and I know."

"No. Their last name is Simmons. What the hell are ya babbling about, Harry? Ya screwed up big time and now, well, I have to go in there and patch it all up. Oh well, I will go in and see what I can do to smooth this over. I guess that Janet will ride me back to my car at the bar."

I observed how Mary recovered quickly from almost every type of situation. She seemed remarkably resilient. I wondered how her liver functions were.

Mary stood up and smiled. She reached down, adjusted her blouse to "replace" things and to expose a bit of her cleavage, and then gracefully shifted into seduction mode for good ole Harry.

It did not take too much, believe me.

She leaned in and whispered, "I will fix it up. Please, call me . . . okay, there, big boy. We had such plans for later. Oh well. Ya can give my backside a little squeeze at least, and let me show ya a little of this too!" Mary leaned in and kissed Harry.

I looked the other way for the rest of it.

"Say, Mary, could you write down your uncle's telephone number for me?" Harry handed Mary a piece of scrap paper and a pen. Even under mop handle and sexually induced duress, Harry stuck to his covert hockey plan.

"Sure, sure, sure, I will call him for youse guys too. Here is his number. Goodnight and please call me. And Paul, you are a sexy dog. Please call poor, lonely, Janet. We could always meet at my house, so you do not have to deal with her whacky brother."

I only nodded, but I did not answer her. Mary waved, and she ran into the house. I was speechless as we climbed into Harry's car and he started it. Even behind closed doors and the rumble of Harry's car engine, we could hear the faint screams of little Poin-a-roo-ski.

"I will take ya back to your jeep at Lord Crudley's and buy ya a beer. Ya are looking a little pale. Like ya need some kind of oxygen boost or something like that. Are you okay?"

"I am okay, Harry. It has been quite the evening. I must say that at first, I had very high hopes for Janet. She is very attractive. And that poor kid . . . I feel so sorry for him. It is terrible. We better pick another place than Lord Crudley's gin mill for a beer. The last thing we need now is to run into those rugby players."

"Yeah, yeah, yeah. Sure, ya feel sorry for the kid because ya an old lady at heart. But you're right about switching gin joints. We have had enough excitement with irate whackos for one night. We will head for Slater's Millhouse. There is a hot chick there that I have been trying to date."

Harry looked at me in order to gauge a reaction, but I remained silent and numb.

He continued with his summary, "You had high hopes! Yeah, yeah, yeah, I did too! Oh well, I guess a night like this really hurts when you are Mr. Nice Guy, and afflicted with the Old Lady Syndrome too. After all, you are a double loser, Paul."

Harry looked at me, shook his head a little as he continued with a summary of this evening's events, "I understand how ya feel. Ya know, me fibbing just a bit. With me, having you weave a bunch of tall tales, the sloshed chick hitting on ya, my hands out in plain sight, squeezing hot twigeon's backsides and little kids who are out of their mind with weird ass birthmarks under their spinning eyeballs. It is all out of your comfort zone there, twenty-seven."

I nodded while Harry reached over; he put his arm around me and squeezed me tightly.

"You know, someday, twenty-seven, this will all be worth it, Paul, and you will thank me. You really will."

I leaned back and sighed.

I did not say anything. I only nodded. It was difficult to find the correct words, and when I thought really hard about it, there was not too much else to say.

Someday, I have to find a rocket ship and I swear. . ..

5

The Accident

Despite the pain, anguish, and tempestuous events associated with Mary and our dubious double date, it did prove to be fruitful. Harry, with his roundabout and oftentimes strange methodology, somehow produced amazing and surprising results. Often, it was an exercise in extreme perseverance, just a matter of swallowing hard and withstanding the initial impact of his wild plans until you, ultimately, reached the final goal.

The results of that rather unusual evening did surprisingly end up on an exciting note. Harry and I did obtain a tryout with a well-known senior league operating in various ice rinks in and around the Tri-State region. It remained somewhat of a mystery to me as to exactly how Harry planned these wild plots, which in the end, generally worked out in a positive manner for us. However, as he told me, someday, you will thank me for all of this.

Where, oh where, or actually, when was someday?

I had learned through the many years and countless other adventures to buckle my chin straps and just go along for the ride. There was not too much else for me to do!

I did eventually muster enough courage to call Janet for a date. My date with Janet Simmons is an adventure that is better suited for another set of words, somewhere down the road. Suffice it to say that Janet Simmons was a very nice gal. It was just that along with her, came a bit of other, "stuff."

To my recollection, Harry only dated Mary a few more times, until she faded away. She came with a lot of baggage and very expensive bar tabs! Even for the fortified and battle-hardened Harry, I think that Mary, despite her gorgeous looks, fun personality and an amazing figure, was just a bit too much to take, although, looking back, I could be wrong about that one. There was something quite attractive about both Mary and Janet.

The week after our tumultuous experience, we spoke to Mary's uncle, who was expecting our call, and after some discussion, he had us show up and skate in a practice with a senior league hockey club that was a bit short of players. Back then, these leagues were common, and although you had to pay an entrance fee in order to join the team, it was worth the money you spent on the ice time to hone your skills against some premier competition. Within the ranks of these leagues, you would find former professional players or even some current semi-professional players who were rehabbing injuries or just trying to stay sharp with their skills. Some players were looking for a chance to catch a coach or a scout's eye and receive an invitation to join a team, which might be a notch or two up the hockey ladder.

During this era, a hockey player from the United States had an extremely difficult path to travel in order to have an even remote chance to play in the big leagues of ice hockey. It was not impossible, nor unheard of; it was just that the competition from the Canadian ranks made it very difficult. You had a much better chance of success if you grew up in the colder northern regions, states such as Michigan, Minnesota, upstate New York, or some New England states. In locations where the long winters and oft-frozen ponds provided you with more ice-skating time. However, change was on the horizon. The advent of widespread ice rink construction in the United States really was just beginning to occur, and with that, opportunities to learn to skate improved. As a result of more ice rinks appearing and improved opportunities to learn to ice skate, the sport of ice hockey increased slightly in popularity.

Right for now, without the perfect background or experience, your potential path to the big league, had to include these rough and tumble leagues. In these types of leagues and by your reputation, you had the potential to earn an invitation to juniors in the Canadian leagues or the semi-professional leagues, where you worked hard to create a unique angle, or you stood out somehow. A player really needed to be exceptional and pay their dues with some bitter and hard knocks in order to attract the eye of a scout from the big time.

United States colleges and universities did funnel in some players here and there, but the advent of a college draft or American colleges providing a large influx of players, or being a minor league for the big league, was still a few decades away.

Now, the chances of two dopey guys from the streets of New Jersey to make it anywhere, well . . . that was a tough route to consider.

After we successfully made it through our tryout, both Harry and I received invitations to play for a team based out of the Ice Land arena. Ice Land, of course, was our home rink, and the location made it very convenient for our travel schedule. Most games were played early in the mornings on Saturday and Sunday, when the rink could provide ice time at reduced rates. These were perfect days and times for us, since it worked favorably into our schedules with our current, full-time "regular" employment.

It was a simple procedure to join, once the coach and team decided that you were good enough and they had an open slot for you, you paid a fee, signed a waiver form for injuries and liabilities, a form agreeing to absolve the league, teams, coaches, players, rinks and game officials of any liability due to injury. This was a "play at your own risk" type of deal! You also needed to provide proof of medical insurance and since both Harry and I had medical insurance from our full-time jobs; we were good to go. This league knew that the chances of player injuries remained high, so they made sure the burden of those expenses was covered!

This team had some big, strong players and the one aspect that we did notice right away was that the speed of the skating and game action was much faster, and the power and speed of the shots were amazing. These shots were certainly more powerful than any previous shots that we had ever seen before. In addition, not only was the speed of the skating improved, but the overall skating abilities of the players far exceeded any competition, which we had ever seen to this point in our careers too.

Goaltenders were always in demand and the goalie that had been currently filling the starting goalie position for the team had some schedule conflicts with his job and he was nursing a sore knee.

The incumbent goaltender was happy to see me show up and provide him some relief for a few games, in fact, after our first practice, he told me that he was now my backup goalie and he willingly relinquished the starting net minding duties to me. He told me that the talent in the league far outclassed his abilities and he was so sore from welts and injuries that he could hardly work at his full-time job or bend over and tie his shoes in the morning! I did not know what to tell him, but I had a strange feeling that he would not be around much longer even to provide me with backup net minding duties!

Harry seemed, as of late, to lose some of his usual confidence. This was a bit troubling, slightly peculiar, and a different twist to his personality, all of which I found to be a bit unusual. The normally, bombastic and ever-confident, number thirty-five, became somewhat subdued after a few practices with our new team, and he privately voiced a concern to me that he felt as if he could not skate well enough to keep up with some players. I noticed that Harry would hang back in the defensive zones more and more, and that he did not pinch in the offensive zones as much as he previously had in the past. He became more of a classic "stay at home" defenseman in our team practices.

Perhaps, because of his perception of his weaker skating abilities, he felt that he did not want to venture too deep into the offensive zone and that by staying back; he would be able to skate back to the defensive zones in time, in order to protect the net and defensive areas. This new style still had great effectiveness, since Harry remained an outstanding shot blocker, a beast in the corners, and a tough guy in front of the net, while moving out the opposition players, however, it took away his offensive opportunities to skate up on the point and unleash that powerful slap shot of his. Yet, based upon his defensive skills alone, he easily made the team and was an instant contributor.

Our first game with our new team came up on a Saturday morning in early November 1978. We drew a team out of Connecticut and both teams seemed evenly matched. I faced a few difficult shots here and there, but it seemed as if both of the teams were pacing one another and feeling out each other's strengths and weaknesses. Late in the first period, I saw Harry jump over the boards to take a shift. He was mostly playing right defense on a third line for now, and his defensive partner was more of an offensive threat than what Harry was.

Sure enough, the left defenseman for our team took a gamble. He snuck in the opposition zone and he became caught deep in the zone on a change of possession of the puck. He scrambled desperately to regain the defensive zone by putting his head down and biting a deep edge into the ice with his skates. He was a good skater, but despite his efforts, he did not have enough speed to make it back in time in order to assist Harry in dealing with the resulting two on one breakaway.

Harry played our usual strategy for a breakaway and I watched him flip backwards on his skates. He put his stick out in front of him; it was a classic defensive stance to face the attack. A play that the two of us had played thousands of times together over the many years.

Harry glided in the zone backwards, while yelling out, "Shooter, twenty-seven!"

This meant that Harry was going to cheat to the side of the attacking player who had possession of the puck and do his best to force the play towards the sideboards.

I leaned towards the open player, but I still kept my eyes on the puck handler. I tapped the right post with my stick and decided that I was too close to the net, so I glided out about a foot or so, and settled on the edge of the crease line.

In a surprise move, the puck carrier became a shooter. He wound up and blasted a slap shot, and out of the corner of my eye, I saw Harry stand straight up and then . . . no puck. I thought about how Harry would usually not stand upright on a shot such as that one was. Harry usually put his head down and his weight forward. He must have been surprised that the player had shot the puck so quickly.

For an instant, I thought I had missed the puck and that it had flown over my head and into the capture net mounted above the glass behind my goal. As I turned to find the puck, I spotted Harry collapse from his upright position; he dropped his stick, and he fell like a tree, straight down into the ice!

I heard the referee blow the whistle and saw him frantically wave his hands over his head in a signal to stop play. From the reaction of the player who had taken the slap shot, I knew this would not be good.

I dropped my stick, tossed off my goalie gloves and skated out of the net as fast as I could, while players, coaches, and game officials all did the same as we all rushed in Harry's direction. I prayed that this was another one of his practical jokes, and that he was just pulling our legs, but the large pool of red blood flowing around Harry's face onto the ice, and Harry kicking his skates violently on the ice surface, all told me this was some serious trouble!

In a flash, I reached for Harry, pulled my mask off, and tossed it aside. I knelt down next to him and touched his back while gently pulling on the back of his jersey.

"Harry! Harry! Harry!" I called out in desperation. I needed to see his face.

He lifted his head, and what I saw was a sight beyond horrific. Harry had taken the puck dead on in the face, and he was a sea of blood spewing from his mouth and nose, along with exposed bones. And, well, it was a horrible mess. My stomach began to turn, and I felt a little nauseous at the horrific sight.

"Twenty-seven," Harry struggled to speak, and as he spoke, his teeth were falling out of his mouth in pieces and the blood flowed and spewed in all directions.

"Get an ambulance! Call an ambulance! I need a towel! Please get me a towel and ice! Quick!" I screamed and started to panic.

Stay calm, Paul . . . stay calm . . . I told myself to stay calm.

"Don't talk, Harry. Stay with me. You are going to be all right. You are a tough guy, Harry! Stay with me here, buddy!"

"Is it bad, Paul? Is it bad? It hurts like hell."

I did not answer him, and it did not matter, as Harry's eyes rolled back in his head and he passed out from the pain.

"C'mon, guys! Hurry up with the damn help here! We need an ambulance! C'MON! HURRY THE HELL UP!" I screamed, as a player skated frantically over from the bench and he handed me a towel and some ice.

I scraped at the ice surface with my goalie skates and rounded up a good pile of snow to add to the ice. I placed it on Harry's face and stuffed what I could of the towel and ice mixture into his mouth, while making sure that I was keeping his air passages open. I knew that the swelling would be immediate and catastrophic and that the ice would be essential in keeping the swelling somewhat at bay. I could see that most of his teeth were broken out of his jawbone and blood was pouring from those gashes inside of his mouth, as well as spewing from his nostrils. He had a large cut on his right cheekbone and I could see some bones of his eye socket exposed under his eye. The puck had peeled his skin away as you might peel an orange.

I did not know where to apply pressure to first!

I applied the towel, ice and pressure to Harry's cheekbone location first, and then I tore at the towel to break it into another section, in order to work on the blood flow in the other locations.

I did not need to be a doctor to know that his nose was broken. His nose was flat upon his face, but his nostrils seemed somehow to be open. They were just severely bleeding. I made sure he could breathe through his open mouth too as I tried to clean away his broken teeth and who knows what else was coming out of there.

I tried my best to recover my senses; I was not going to do Harry any good by wimping out now, not when he needed me more than he ever had in his entire life. No one else was jumping in here to assist me. It was so horrible that everyone just stood around watching, and some guys even turned away from the sight because it was a bit difficult to take.

I knelt down on my leg pads, put his head on my lap, and I tried to control the blood as best I could. I could feel him breathing, so I did not start any type of mouth-to-mouth actions. I had no actual first aid training, just a short course given to me at my employment in case one of us received an electrical shock, but I did make sure that I had learned and knew how to do mouth-to-mouth resuscitation.

I have to say that watching my mother and Dr. Salami patch me up over the years taught me a thing or two about first aid too!

I stuck my fingers in Harry's nostrils to make sure they remained open, as the blood poured out all over the ice and me. A referee had sprinted to the main office in the rink to use a telephone, so I knew medical help was on the way.

I reached down into the back pocket of my warm-up pants under my goalie pants, and pulled out the cross, still tucked neatly inside of the cloth. I held it tightly in my hand and I started to pray.

I held my dearest friend in my arms and kept his head off the ice. While I held him, I did my best to administer first aid, and I did the only other thing, in which I knew how to do . . . I prayed.

The old man used to rant and rave that the only free things in the world anymore, "Were prayer and air. They charge you for everything else in this world these days!"

I never heard truer words than those words right at this horrible moment. Harry required both of them!

I prayed aloud, "Lord Jesus, hear my prayer. By the grace of God, send us help soon. Let Harry be all right. Lord Jesus, hear my prayer!" I sat there intermittently praying with my teammates, all the opposition's players, the goaltender from the other team, and coaches, officials, and others, doing their best to support us, pray together and encourage Harry.

Harry drifted in and out of consciousness; he would open his eyes, look at me, and then drift away.

"Hang in there, buddy. Help is coming," I encouraged him.

It was the longest minutes of my life. I thought to myself that this guy, this Harry M. Redmond Junior, has to be the toughest son of a bitch who ever lived.

The good Lord heard my prayers because I looked up to see a team of paramedics heading my way onto the ice. They must have taken jet planes to Ice Land, or time actually passed by quicker than I thought it had passed. A group of players assisted the medical team by holding their arms to help them navigate the tricky ice surface. They had a stretcher and medical equipment with them.

A paramedic rushed over and bent over to help me, while saying, "I got it, goalie. Thanks! It looks as if you controlled the bleeding! Ice and pressure! Damn, good work!"

I stood up and watched as the medical team took over. A paramedic handed me a towel to wipe the blood off my hands and uniform. It was a bloody mess. Literally.

"You have any information on him, goalie? Ya must know him," a paramedic holding a notepad and pencil asked me; while I watched, the medical teams went to work on Harry. I was still stunned; it took me a little while before I could answer him.

"Yes. He is my best friend. Since we were ten years old . . . nah, shit, who the hell am I kiddin'? He is my brother. Harry M. Redmond Junior. He lives at 20 John Street. . .."

I gave him all the information I could. My mind was a damn blur. It was like some type of terrible dream.

"He is going to be all right? Isn't he?" I asked the paramedic when I finished giving him all the information on Harry.

The medic did not answer me.

"Please, make sure you call his father and his sisters. I will go with you guys. Let me take off my equipment. It will just take me a minute and I will go in the ambulance."

They had strapped Harry to the stretcher, and we were wheeling him off the ice rink, when everyone stood still in shock, when Harry suddenly spoke, "Hell no! Stay, twenty-seven!"

"Sssshh, don't talk pal," one paramedic leaned over and told Harry.

The paramedic looked at me and said, "I can't believe that this guy is awake, nonetheless that he is talking! He must be a damn superhero!"

Harry waved for me to come closer to the stretcher, and as I leaned in, he struggled in a whisper, while barely opening his mouth to tell me, "Hell no! You had better not leave, or when I am better, I swear that I will send that whacked out kid Poindexter to scream in your ears and I will kick ya ass. Finish the friggin' game, Paul. Finish it for me. Not a marble, twenty-seven. Not a damn friggin' marble."

"Harry . . . I can't. I have to go with you!"

He spit chunks of blood out of his mouth onto the ice and said, "Stay. What the hell are ya gonna do at the hospital? Sew my ass up? We never quit, Paul. You know that better than any of us do. You taught us all to suck it up. Just a little blood comin' out of my ass. Guys from Geyer Street Gardens never friggin' quit. Never!"

He gave me a wave and a one thumb up signal as they rolled him across the ice.

"Okay, you got it, Harry. I will finish the game. For you."

One paramedic looked at me and forced a gentle smile while he said, "I do not think you have much of a choice. I think he wants you to stay here, goalie."

"Yeah, yeah, yeah, I guess. Where are you taking him?"

"He is going to Saint Joseph's Hospital in downtown Paterson."

I nodded and watched while they rolled Harry off the ice and he disappeared into a maze of police officers and the medical team.

It was still stunning to me.

I was still in shock.

I turned and looked to where the rink maintenance man scraped at the blood marks on the ice with an ice scraper. He took a broom and pan, to what was left of my best friend's teeth. I picked up Harry's stick and his gloves and I studied them while slowly skating over to our player's bench and handing them to the equipment manager.

It was disgusting and body numbing. The captain of the team we were playing for skated over to me, and he handed my goalie gloves, stick, and my mask.

He looked deeply at the shock in my face and said, "I am sorry about your buddy there, twenty-seven. I hope he is going to be okay. Do you want to stay in the game? We could put a defenseman in if you want to go to the hospital with Harry."

He was apparently not privy to the conversation that Harry and I had.

I thanked him for bringing my equipment over to me. He gave me the equipment and I held it in my hands. I held my mask and repeatedly turned it in my hands while I studied the black "scar" marks on it. Visions of playing hockey with Harry, Jeff Porter, Tags, Pooch, Big Wex, Johnny the Cho, and the rest of the Haledon Hockey League floated through my mind. The sound of those first pucks that we had ever shot gliding along the street echoed in my mind. I clearly saw my dear mum sewing the quilt inside of my sweatshirt at the kitchen table. The joy of Pooch winning the game against the Bruisers resonated through my soul.

I smiled, pulled my sweaty hair back and flipped my mask over my head.

"Bloody well, pal. I am not quitting now! Hell no. You bet your swinging ass that I am staying in the net. I am ready. Let's go!"

He nodded at me; I waved to the referee and skated back to the net. I smoothed the ice in front of my crease with my stick, crouched over in my stance, and signaled that I was now ready for the faceoff.

Harry was right, we never, ever, quit! Ever!

I did not play a very good game in the net.

I would rank it as being amongst the worst games that I had ever played; it was not my best performance. In particular, a little trickling shot with a puck rolling on its edge, I fumbled, bumbled and misplayed the puck as it rolled under my stick into the net. I should have stopped that shot with my eyes closed. It was quite embarrassing.

However, despite my lack of focus, I made sure I did not come up puck-shy, when a hard slap shot came in; I stuck my head right into it. The fear of injury due to Harry's injury remained in my head, but a puck shy goaltender is a bad goaltender.

I kept telling myself that I was not afraid. Not now, not ever.

It was difficult to concentrate, my mind was elsewhere, but we managed to win the game by the score of three goals to two. Thank goodness that we won the game! I really would have felt as if I let the big guy down if we had lost that one.

I hurriedly showered, dressed in my civilian clothes, grabbed my equipment as well as Harry's gear, bag and clothes, and hustled my way to my jeep. It was a long drive to the hospital in downtown Paterson. I parked on the city streets about four blocks away, ran into the front door of the hospital and obtained information on Harry's whereabouts from a sympathetic Catholic nun working the front desk. When I arrived on the floor, Harry's family met me. They were all very happy to see me.

"I guess you stayed to finish the game, Paulie," Mr. Redmond almost laughed as he met me and put his arm around me. "Harry kept trying to tell us, as best as he could speak, that twenty-seven is going to finish that damn game."

"Yeah, yeah, yeah, Mr. Redmond. I finished it. We won. How is he?"

"He is in surgery right now, Paulie. They have an oral surgeon, a plastic surgeon, and another general surgeon in there working on him." Ronzo was there too, along with Patty and Linda. I imagined that Harry's other brother-in-law, George (A.K.A. The Big Spike) was on kiddie duty.

Patty walked over and put her arm around me as she studied my face. She could see the concern and pain I was feeling for Harry, and she must have felt that she needed to comfort me.

"He is going to be all right, Paulie. It was an accident. It is not your fault. You know better than any of us do that playing hockey has some risk. How many times have they stitched you up, Paulie?"

I nodded and appreciated her words. I could not help but think about how hesitant Harry was as of late, with the level of this more intense competition. Perhaps I should have been more conscious of his apprehension and taken it a bit more seriously. Playing ice hockey at this high of a level is dangerous, and I felt terrible now at how this had all transpired. I wondered if my own zeal and my insistent dream of playing hockey professionally had sucked Harry up into something that he did not really want to do, or even worse, he was afraid of doing!

The Redmonds were not only my friends, but they were my second family. They had all known me since I was just a little squirt, and they sensed that I was struggling terribly with the emotions of the situation. Now, they were all doing their best to ease my concerns.

Ronzo smiled, and he motioned for me to join him, as he said, "Come on over here. Sit down and try to relax, Paulie. It is going to be okay." I walked over to a chair and sat down next to Ronzo.

Ronzo shook my hand and said in typical Ronzo fashion, "C'mon, Paul. Cheer up. Harry is a blockhead and you can dent his head, but I doubt anyone, or even a hockey puck, could break it!"

I smiled, laughed and mumbled, "I guess, Ronzo."

Linda and Mr. Redmond came over and they sat with us, too.

Linda explained, "I called your old man and Mum for you, Paulie. I figured you would just rush over after the game and they might become concerned if you were late."

"Thanks, Linny. I did not even think of calling them, but you are right. Thank you for that one. Is George watching the kids?"

Patty nodded to confirm what I had thought.

I was now resorting to small talk to hide my fears and concerns.

It was not working.

The vision of the gruesome injuries to Harry would not leave my mind. The blood, the gashes, the teeth crumbling out of his mouth, the exposed bones in his mouth and face, all of it was all a bit too much to handle right for now.

In our hockey related euphoria, I never thought of any serious injuries of this magnitude occurring. Sure, we had our cuts, stitches, a broken finger or toe, but never in my wildest dreams did the thought ever occur that one of us could suffer such a serious and devastating injury.

It had disturbed my soul and on a more serious note, I felt my spirit for the sport leaving.

We all sat for hours, mostly in silence, when a surgeon suddenly appeared in the main hallway. He asked a nurse at the front desk some questions. She pointed towards us. He nodded and he walked over to us. We all stood up, introduced ourselves, and greeted the doctor. He smiled and shook all of our hands.

"Hello, folks. I am Doctor Lentini. I performed the general surgery on Harry. He is a tough young man . . . one amazingly tough man. Harry is fine. We had an oral surgeon in there with me and we called in a plastic surgeon. He had some extensive injuries for sure, but he is going to be just fine. I have to say that this is the first ice hockey related injury that I have ever worked on, or even seen, but it was the equivalent of severe, car accident injuries that I have seen. He had a fractured jaw in five locations, his nose was broken, and he lost most of his upper teeth and a few on the bottom. A dentist will fit him for dentures before he leaves the hospital and has healed enough to take the measurements. The impact of the hockey puck pulverized his right cheekbone . . . it was powder."

I sighed deeply and put my head down; as Ronzo put his one arm around me, and with his other arm, he embraced Mr. Redmond, who was standing on the other side of Ronzo.

I heard Mr. Redmond sigh and mumble, "Damn."

This testimony was a little tough to take.

Dr. Lentini continued to describe the situation, "The plastic surgeon has reconstructed his cheekbone. In a few months, you will never know that the injury occurred. I assure you that he is going to be fine, but he will need to be here for at least ten days or even more. For obvious reasons, he cannot eat. I would suggest that you could poke your head in there just to see him, but there is not very much to see. He has many bandages on and he will be out of it for tonight. The pain of these injuries is significant and intense, so we will need to keep him highly medicated for a few days. I would suggest going home and coming back tomorrow."

We all thanked Doctor Lentini, and we followed his advice. We all looked in on Harry, and just as the doctor had told us, there was not too much to see. Harry was sleeping, hooked up to all kinds of tubes, bottles and intravenous fluids pumping into him. Large, wide wraps of white bandages covered his head and face.

It was gruesome and terribly disturbing to view.

Every one of us just kept repeating that the doctor had assured us that Harry was going to be just fine. It was the hope of which we all held on to at the moment.

"How is he?" The old man asked, as I sadly walked into the living room of our home at 182 Belmont Avenue.

"The doctor, who operated on him, says he is going to be fine. He is in the hospital for at least ten days, though." Mum came in and she sat down to hear how Harry was doing. The concern was all over their faces because they loved the big guy, too.

The old man whistled and shook his head.

"Damn, his ass got rocked, huh?"

"Big time, Dad. It was disgusting. Blood, bones, stuff all over. I was really afraid, you guys. I was afraid that he was going to die. It has me a bit shook up." Mum came over and motioned for me to sit down.

She gently asked me, "Would you like a cup of tea, Paulie? Sit down and relax. I will make the tea. Harry is going to be all right now. He is in the hospital and they will ease his pain and take good care of him. I understand how you feel."

"Yeah, yeah, yeah, please, some tea, Mum. It will taste good," I nodded and thanked Mum as she went off to the kitchen and prepared some tea.

"Did ya bums win?"

"Yup, we won, Dad. I stunk up the game, but we won. Harry insisted I stay and finish the game. So, I did."

The old man nodded and smiled.

He spoke confidently, but in a gentler tone than what my father generally used whenever he spoke, "I would not expect anything else. You had to finish the game for the both of you. You two are not quitters, never have been since you were little squirts. In fact, you dig in harder when the shit hits the fan. It is in both of youse guy's nature. Can't imagine ya quitting on that one. It is not like you could operate on his ass."

I smiled and nodded because the old man was not being cold-hearted. He was being factual.

It was also what Harry had told me.

He continued to speak, "I never played hockey, but baseball, now that game, I know. Many outstanding baseball players that I saw lost their hearts for the game due to a head beaning with a fastball. I imagine a hockey puck is sorta the same. It seems a little deadlier, to be honest. If you are going to play at that level, then you had better have the stomach for it. If not, then ya are going to get hurt even more."

My father leaned over in his chair, he looked at me sitting next to him, he looked straight in my eyes and his voice grew even softer as he said, "Ya know, Paulie, I have never seen you afraid of anything. I swear you would meet the Devil and spit in his eye. Ya may have been a little short in the brain's handout line to play this stupid ass game, but ya sure as hell were first in line for courage. You have a quiet courage inside of you, Paulie. Unassuming, deep, you do not wear it on your sleeve and go around knocking people on their asses, and yet, people sense your strength and your power. People around you, well, they can feel it too. I would watch you through the windows out there in the cold, snow, ice, shooting hockey pucks into the wall or steps in the backyard. Endlessly. The noise drove me crazy. I hoped that you would play baseball, but no, this is your sport. So be it. It is part of you now, Paulie. It has invaded your soul. You can never shake it."

The old man leaned over a bit more. His voice grew louder and more intense, and he pointed at me with his finger.

"Deep inside, it is shaping you, making you a man, facing challenges in the net that will help you deal with challenges in real life. Paulie, I am sure that hockey will teach you lessons in life that are worth a fortune. It settles conflict inside of you. I can see that it is much more than just a sport with you. I think you are up to it, but if not, and you are afraid, then admit it and hang up your mask and skates. Otherwise, you will get hurt too."

The old man leaned back and smiled at me. I appreciated his wisdom and words of advice more than I could tell him.

"Thanks, Dad. I have the stomach for it. I have this fire inside of me. When I turn it on, I can feel it burning inside of me. I do not know how to describe it, but it drives me. I need to succeed, and fear, or rather, being afraid, well, that is just not a part of it, Dad."

The old man did not comment. Instead, he only nodded in acknowledgement. He then smiled, lowered his voice and waved towards the kitchen while telling me, "I think that I would go have that cup of tea now, or Mum will be mad at you. She needs her Paulie time, too."

I nodded, stood up and headed towards the kitchen.

"And, number twenty-seven!"

I turned back to my father.

"If ya are going to do it, then do it all the way. Remember! Always remember, Paulie, how commitment to what you do, what you want, or the woman who you will eventually fall in love with, well, that makes you a man. Contribution's suck. They are for wimps and pansy asses. Bacon and eggs breakfast, Paulie, the hen, well, she makes a contribution, but the pig, his ass, made a serious, damn commitment."

I knocked on the door and walked into the hospital room the next afternoon, and Harry was sitting upright in his bed. I could only see his eyes and an opening in the bandages for his mouth. He had been sipping on a cup full of something with a straw stuck in it.

He looked like a mummy in the museum.

"Hey there, number thirty-five! You are awake, eh?"

Harry motioned for me to come close and sit in the chair next to him. He reached for the television remote control and clicked off the set. He could not speak, but he had a pad for writing notes on in order to communicate. He picked the pad up and took his pencil. He wrote something and showed me.

I read it aloud when Harry showed me, "Did we win?"

I smiled and said, "Yeah, yeah, yeah, we won, Harry."

He gave me a thumb up signal, and I have to think that if he could smile, he would have.

Maybe in his heart he was smiling.

He took the pad again and wrote something else on it. Harry wrote for a long time. He held it up and I read that one aloud, too.

"I hate this friggin' soup and gelatin shit! I am sick of it! This food sucks, but the chicks that have come in and seen me are awesome! Joyce wore something really slinky and low cut to cheer me up!"

Yes indeed, Harry was going to be just fine!

After all, you can only keep a man down for so long.

We sat and "chatted" for hours until the nurse chased me out. All Harry could have to eat were liquids that he could take with a straw; the doctors had wired his jaw shut to heal, so I promised him on my next visit after work; that I would bring him a milkshake from our favorite hot dog and hamburger joint.

Over the next few days, I visited him whenever I could. He had an endless parade of visitors, between his family, Jeff Porter and his girlfriend Debbie, the old man and Mum, his family priest, Father Mark came by, his entire seemingly endless, harems of young ladies, hockey players, coworkers from his shop, it was remarkable to experience and see the amount of people who came by to see him.

I had a game three days after the accident with the senior league team. While I stood in the net for my warm-ups, I did my best to put the accident out of my head, along with the vivid and graphic memories of the entire incident.

This was not going to be quite as easy as I thought it would be.

"Ready, twenty-seven?" A teammate shouted from the blue line as I crouched into my stance to prepare for the warm-up shots. I held my stick up to indicate that I was ready to go. One slap shot . . . an easy stick save . . . one wrist shot, easily gloved, then a blast from a big defenseman! The puck rose high and hard on me, and it was heading straight for my head. I knocked the shot down to the ice with my glove and kicked the puck aside with my skate in anger.

I held my gloves and my stick up and yelled, "Geez! One guy almost dead is not good enough for youse guys! Warm-ups, man! No headshots! Geez! Shit, I have enough issues going on here in my head. C'mon guys. We are all teammates here."

"Sorry, Paulie. It rose and took off on me. I didn't mean it, twenty-seven. Take it easy, will ya?"

I faced another shot, stopped it in my skates, and with my stick, I winged the puck up on the glass. In frustration, I skated out of the net and let the backup goaltender take over for me.

I stood on the sideline fuming in anger, trying hard to gather my thoughts, control my rage, and calm my soul. This was not like me. I never became angry, and I was not comfortable at all with the turmoil that I was feeling inside of me. It was raw emotion, it was pain manifesting in a toxic manner, and I knew that right now, I had reached a turning point in my hockey life.

A point where I crossed the line of whether my love of hockey and playing this crazy position was dying, or if it would just become stronger.

While I stood there very deep in my thoughts, I spotted a spectator standing directly behind the net. I did a double take when I realized the spectator was not an ordinary spectator.

It was my father!

To my knowledge, this was the first hockey game, in which my father had ever attended and seen me play. I stood up straighter and taller, and now I felt bad about my lack of poise and my silly outburst. The old man looked over at me, and he now was aware of the fact that I had noticed his presence. I did not pull my mask off; somehow, I wanted to hide behind it now.

There was little doubt that I was very embarrassed by my behavior.

The old man gave me a slight nod of his head and a motion to get back into the net. I nodded back, that I understood.

I skated over to the side of the net, and the other goalie looked at me and asked, "You okay, twenty-seven? Are you ready now?"

"Yes, I am. More than ready."

I proceeded to take all the warm-ups and then played the best game I had played to date with the senior league team. A shutout. My first shutout ever with this hockey club. The old man stood behind my net for the entire game. He switched sides when I switched ends, and for the most part, he did not acknowledge me or even say anything. When the game finished, I did spot him clapping with the rest of a very small crowd, but when I came out of the locker room after the game . . . he was gone.

When I arrived home, my father was sitting in his chair in the living room. I came in and smiled at him while he motioned for me to sit down.

"You played some game there, Paulie. I like how you use the catching glove there. Sorta like a first baseman. They never scored on ya. I enjoyed it. You are very good."

"Thanks, Dad. I enjoyed having you there."

"Let me ask ya, chief? Why the hell did you get all hot

and bothered when the guy shot the puck at your head in the warm-up time before the game?"

"Well, after what happened to Harry, you know, it is an unwritten rule that you warm up your goalie easily. You know, you kinda give him time to loosen up and get in the groove. A head shot right away can ruin your timing and rattle your nerves."

The old man did not say anything right away. He just stared at me.

I felt his eyes searching me.

It was very uncomfortable. I knew my father well enough to know that he thought that I was wrong.

Finally, he spoke, "Let me ask you. In the game, does the other team try to shoot at your head to shake you up? You know, see if you are easily rattled?"

"Sure, sure, sure. It is part of the game, like fighting and pushing and shoving. It is intimidation."

"Like a brush back pitch in baseball?"

"Exactly, Dad."

The old man leaned in now and spoke with a stern voice, "Then, why the hell would you not want your teammates to throw it at you right away to get the edge off? In the real world, no one is going to cut you any breaks, because ya ain't warm yet, or they feel sorry for ya winky-dinky ass, because your best buddy got hurtsy-wurtsy. So why cut ya breaks in the warm-ups to the game? That is bush league and stupid. You acted like a pansy la-la and a jerk. That is not like ya. Acting like some kinda prima donna jackass. Ya need to get the hell into the net and take the best they can throw at you right away. Spit in their eyes and play the game hard. Warm-ups or not. There are no easy ones, Paulie. Never believe that there will ever be easy ones in hockey or in life. If ya love it, then ya gotta work for it."

He sat back and smiled at me.

I smiled at him, too.

"Thanks."

I stood up, walked over to his chair, and shook his hand.

"Get some sleep, twenty-seven. If you are going to do this thing, this goalie thing, then do it all the way. Like, I told ya when Harry got hurt, ya need to make a commitment, because there really is no sense in doing anything halfway. Either ya ass is in, or ya ass needs to get the hell out. Looking at the way you can play and skate, and jump around in the net, my suggestion is to be in. Ya know, just remember, not all the games are going to end in shutouts. Even Big Foot Garumba struck out, but at least he always went down swinging."

My old man is one smart guy.

He may not have had a wall full of diplomas or wallpaper stating how smart he is, or what classes he attended, and listened to some professor's personal agendas, but believe me, he is one smart guy. Life's lessons are hard and they come to you in many ways. I thanked God every day that he sent me the father that I have because he is one of a kind. It is amazing how when you are eighteen or so, you think your parents are not too smart, but when you reach the age of forty or thereabouts, it seems as if they sure become a lot smarter!

About four or five days into his recovery, I went to visit Harry. I was eager to tell him about the shutout and about how well our team was playing. I came into his room in the hospital, and Harry still could not speak, but he no longer looked like a mummy. Instead, he now looked like a Halloween monster! When you looked at his swollen eyes, face, bruises, and black and blue face and forehead, then the impact of his injuries was quite clear and relevant.

It was still a bit rough for me to see.

Harry was still embroiled in his "photography phase" so he had asked me to bring his camera and equipment to take some pictures. Of course, he mostly wanted to take pictures of the young ladies who came to visit him. I brought his camera, extra film and one or two extra lenses. Harry spent some of his recovery time in the hospital by happily snapping pictures.

Harry was still in great spirits, even flirting with a cute nurse, with whom he took a fancy to while she administered "care." He wrote on his pad, typical Harry remarks.

Some of his remarks about her short dress and legs required a "writing pad censor." His pictures of her and her long legs, and other attributes, were also going to require a bit of a "filter."

They knocked Harry down, but I could tell that he certainly was on the road to recovery! There was no doubt that the injury had not altered his hormonal balance in any manner.

Each day, his condition improved more and more and on about the eleventh day, I was happily surprised to walk into his room and find Harry dressed in his civilian clothes, walking around and looking great! His swollen face had improved considerably and I could see that he would have some small scars, but overall, he looked like, Harry! Handsome as always!

He could now move his jaw. They had removed the clamps, and although he could speak only softly and gently in a low whisper, he could slowly gum some solid foods and speak. He had lost a lot of weight and some chest muscle, but he still was looking a lot better than he had looked the last few days.

"Wow! Looking good, Harry!"

He smiled at me and said in a low whisper, "Yeah, yeah, yeah! And, twenty-seven, ya can bet ya ass, when they let me out of this dump and I get my new choppers, you are taking me to the Greek joint for some pizza. I am dying for a slice of pizza."

I patted him on the back and Harry went and sat down on the edge of the bed. He was still weak from the lack of solid food and from staying confined to the bed and hospital room for so long.

He took a deep breath and looked at me.

"I bet you cannot wait to get back on the ice, thirty-five. All the guys are asking about you."

Harry shook his head a little, smiled, and motioned for me to sit in the chair next to the bed. I sat down and looked at Harry. It was obvious that he wanted to speak to me about something. He waved for me to come in closer. He still did not have his false choppers yet, so his voice was not only soft, but it was also a little difficult to understand.

"I wanted to tell you, Paul. It is over for me. I am hanging up my skates. I will fool around a little here and there in a huff and puff league, or a public skate, but as far as serious hockey, it is all over for me."

Harry looked at me while he carefully studied my face for a reaction to his statement.

I was shocked, stunned, in fact, and I protested a little, "Nah, nah, nah, Harry. It is just a little ripple of puck-shy stuff going on. I guess that it is normal. I felt it in the game the other day and then I pulled off a shutout. The old man talked me up, and I came out of it. You can still play . . . we are a team."

I stopped speaking when I saw the tears forming in the corners of his eyes. I then knew that this was not a hasty decision. It must have been a decision, which caused him great pain and a great conflict. Furthermore, I knew in my heart that Harry had made up his mind. After what he had suffered and gone through in the past two weeks or so, I was not going to dispute his decision. That would not be fair.

"No, Paul. It is so much more than that now. I know, and you know, that I am just not good enough. The injury and the accident are one thing, but the competition is just too good now. It has all gone by me now. Not you though, Paul. Not you. You are the world famous, number twenty-seven. And you can do it for all of us. I have seen it all of our lives together. You are the best. I believe in the long-haired, hippie goalie who wears number twenty-seven. All the things that I have seen you do on the ice and off of it, too. You have to go on."

Harry looked at me and wiped the tears from his eyes while I slowly nodded my head. I did not say a word; it was not the right time to say anything. His emotions were much too high.

In a typical Harry manner, he broke the chain of emotions with his humor.

"Besides, I cannot risk losing these good looks. The disappointment amongst thousands of young women throughout New Jersey and beyond would be crushing! You . . . well, I do not worry about too much! You are already ugly enough for both of us!"

I smiled, and Harry grabbed me by the shoulders and held me tightly. I could feel his tears dripping on my neck and shoulders while we embraced.

"Hey, promise me that you will go on, not a marble, twenty-seven. Ya can't let even a marble roll by you."

"I will, Harry . . . for both of us. I promise."

Now, only one remains.

There was only one member of the Haledon Hockey League left, and he still wore the number twenty-seven.

Geyer Street Gardens

Part Three

Number Twenty-seven

1

The Chance Finally Arrives

I had just finished a game in the senior league and was nursing my pride a bit while dressing back in my civilian clothes. It was early December 1978, and we had lost the game on a last minute, power play goal. The game was lost for us when a slap shot from the point was deflected in front of me; the puck changed directions two or three times until it finally found the net behind me. Deflections were tough to track, and even though the game-winning shot was on a deflection, I still thought that I should have tracked and stopped it. I learned to shake off goals scored on me rather quickly, but this one, I replayed continually over in my mind. Now dressed, I picked up my equipment bag, slung it over my shoulder, kept my head down and busily hurried out of the locker room, while remaining slightly oblivious as to anything that was going on around me.

It was a Saturday night; I was going to meet Harry and his latest love at a gin joint, and I was in a bit of a hurry to forget that wretched goal.

"Say, Paul John Henson! Henson! Twenty-seven! Wait up there, young man!" I turned around to see a middle-aged man, dressed in a suit, running alongside the rink walkways, trying hard to catch up with me. "Geez, your eyes are a lot sharper than your ears there, Henson. I was shouting at ya for a long time. You deaf?"

I dropped my equipment bag and pads on the rubber walkway and smiled. I thought that I recognized this guy, but I could not be sure. He seemed very familiar to me.

"No, sir. I am not deaf, just in a bit of a fog over the game. Can I help you? I am in a bit of a hurry here to meet my buddy."

"Say, I need some of your time here, Henson. I realize you are in a hurry. This will be worth it! I promise you. Can you sit down here?"

He motioned at some benches along the base of the grandstands and I nodded. I now recognized this chap as the man who stopped me outside the rink during the afternoon when we beat the Christian Skaters of America hockey club that had that nutcase, right-winger, with the last name of O'Malley as their fearless leader.

He had asked me my name back then, and as we walked together to sit down, I tried hard to recall more of the conversation. There was not too much more to recall. The conversation had been very brief, so I could not imagine what this meeting was all about now.

I sat down on the bench and he sat next to me. He was a balding man, with a round face and large, round eyes. He seemed relaxed and, for some reason, he seemed as if he was very kind.

"Hello, Paul. It is my pleasure to meet you."

I cut him off, "We have already met, sir. You asked me my name after that game, if you can call it a game, in which we played against O'Malley and those lunatic Christian skaters."

He studied my face and smiled and said, "Yes, you are correct. You have an excellent memory, Henson. You are a sharp young man. Let me formally introduce myself to you. I am Eddie Austeri. I am the general manager of the Long Island Roosters hockey club on Long Island. We are a semi-professional team in the Metropolitan League. We are, in some manner, remotely part of the Boston Bears farm system."

"Nice. How can I help you, sir?"

"What you may not know is that I have been watching you for years. In fact, since my good buddy, Gordon Gurney, dropped a dime on me a few years back, when you were still nineteen years old or whatever the hell age that you were at the time and playing in a hockey clinic for goaltenders. Gordy told me to come over and check out a long-haired kid who is playing goal in the clinic. A converted street hockey kid, who had stopped him on a backhand shot and had the best moves he had ever seen for a goalie his age. The best ever. Gordon told me to come over to the clinic, watch you, and that I would not regret it. He also told me that if you could improve the skating aspect of your game, and then, you might just be the best he has ever seen. When Gordon Gurney even speaks, nonetheless, he heaps praise and speaks. Let me tell you that you need to pay attention. He is a man of few words, and most of them are not printable or repeatable, anyway."

"Thank you, sir. Wow, that is something, Mr. Austeri. I do not know what to say."

"I can tell you that you have improved your skating, and Gordy, well, he was not wrong. You have it all: speed, strength, size and guts. I have never seen a goalie that does not back down on anything like you do." He patted my knee and said, "You should have come out a hair more on that deflection this afternoon. You might have stopped it."

"That is what I am thinking, too."

"Paul, I have to tell you that here in this briefcase, I have a contract for you. It needs to have some personal information filled in, date of birth, address, social security number, next of kin, blah, blah, blah, blah. Other than that, it is good to go. I offer you crummy pay, something like a lousy seventeen bucks a game. A shutout will get you a fifty-dollar bonus, and we offer free medical care for those stitches. You are a good-looking kid, we can sell posters of you and jerseys of yours, and you will get a few nickels from them too, the money sucks, but what I can entice you with, is a starting role as a goaltender in a professional league."

I felt a shiver go up and down my spine; this was what I was waiting for my entire hockey life. Hell, who was I kidding? It was a dream come true! A contract! A hockey contract to play professionally!

"I am up against it now, Paul. I wanted to wait until you had a few more games under your pads, but our starting goalie is hurt. We are in the thick of a playoff race, and I quickly need a solid goaltender. The league has stringent signing rules in order to prevent ringers, and I have to have your signature on this contract filed with the league office by Monday morning."

He reached into his bag, pulled out some papers, and handed them to me.

I was a bit dumbfounded.

This was so unexpected.

I felt the dreaded Old Lady Syndrome set in on me. As much as I wanted this, what if there were hidden agendas or "gotchas" in the contract? I glanced at the papers and Mr. Austeri held a pen in his hand.

"I badly need a goalie, Paul. If you do not sign, I am going with Jim Hikibin. He is still bouncing around out there. You are a far better goalie than he is, or will ever be, Paul. There is no comparison. However, I have no choice though. My current backup goalie stinks. He is a bum."

I popped my head up from the papers. Hikibin, geez, he was my coach and instructor! What a small circle this world of hockey madness really is.

I could hear Harry's voice circling throughout my brain, doing its best to ward off, trample, and overcome the Old Lady Syndrome.

"Are you crazy, twenty-seven? Sign it you, dumb-ass

dope!"

"Paul, honest, there are no tricks here. I can sense your apprehension on this situation. I know this is sudden, but I have very little time here. I am sorry to put you in a position like this, but I have been around hockey both here and in Canada since I was twenty years old. You do not stick around this long by being a jerk or a chiseler. You're a street kid, and too smart to be fooled by someone pulling a fast one."

I looked into his eyes and went with my first impression. My initial reactions served me well so far, and I sensed that Mr. Eddie Austeri was a good guy.

"I am your man, Mr. Austeri. No need to call Jim Hikibin. I will sign this right now. Please, sir, let me have your pen."

Mr. Austeri smiled and handed me the pen. I quickly filled in the missing information, signed it, and handed the pen and contract back to him. I stood up and extended my hand.

He was beaming now, and he took the contract and quickly studied it while saying, "I will give you a copy of this tomorrow. Please do not squeeze my hand as you just did, Henson. I hid it well, but it felt as if every bone in my hand erupted. I did not want you to think that I was a pansy la-la!"

"Okay, then thank you, sir. In fact, I cannot thank you enough. This is like a dream come true for me, Mr. Austeri."

"Call me, Eddie, there Henson. For a hippie, you are an awfully polite young man and a nice guy. Just do not shake my hand!"

I smiled and said, "I promise that I will avoid the handshake. Now, tell me where and when to report, and let me make a few telephone calls. I need to tell this team here that they need a new goaltender."

"Henson . . . I love it! You are one fearless son of a bitch.

Here is the address. The first practice is tomorrow at ten in the morning; your first game is on next Tuesday the eleventh. I made sure that you will wear number twenty-seven when we play the Colonials out of Rockland County in New York."

"Great! I will be ready."

"Ya better be, Henson. Better, buckle ya ass in, because there is one more piece of the puzzle that I need to tell you about for your first game, twenty-seven. The star of the Colonials is James T. O'Malley. Yup, that O'Malley. Thank God, there is only one of 'em. He is scoring goals as often as you change your socks and sending guys to the hospital one after another. The local police had to take him off the ice in cuffs last week."

"So, Mr. O'Malley, we *will* meet again." I smiled at the prophetic words.

When I caught up with Harry, the big guy was ecstatic. His joy turned to a fever pitch, and he introduced me to his new gal, "As the best, long-haired, hippie goaltender in the entire world."

I had to admit that I was a little excited, too.

Harry bought me a few beers. We laughed a lot, shared a lot, but to be honest, I could not even tell you the name of the gal that Harry introduced me to that night! I remember her being a dark-haired, beautiful, Italian looking gal, but I could not remember much more. Everything was a blur and the excitement in my mind overtook all my thoughts.

I made it a brief night. My first practice was the next day, and I had to get some rest.

The next task, when I broke the good news to my parents, was a hapless effort to contain my excitement with the old man and Mum. The old man immediately went crazy, jumping on the telephone, and calling all of his buddies from the shop and reporting how his son had made the big time! I calmly tried to explain, to no avail, that the Long Island Roosters were a few hundred steps away from the "big time," but I gave up and let the old man have some fun.

I was up early, grabbed my equipment, jumped in my jeep and made the ride out to a rink in Bridgeport, Connecticut, where the Rooster team practiced at an arena and rink there. Mr. Austeri met me there, continued to talk me up and boost my confidence, and introduced me to my new coach and teammates.

The coach's name was Jack Smithson, and he was a grouchy old timer with a thick New York, or perhaps a Long Island accent. He would not shake my hand; instead, he looked me up and down and then frowned at Mr. Austeri.

"Say, Eddie, can we talk over here? Nice to meet you, Hensworth. Get ya hairy ass dressed over there. The equipment kid is giving you a jersey and a locker for 'bout ten minutes. Then ya can ride your sorry ass back to New Jersey. Take that locker over there in the far corner . . . right over there, close to the exit door. It is number twenty-nine, right?" He pointed to a locker in the far corner of the locker room.

"No sir, it is twenty-seven. And, my name is Henson. Paul John Henson."

"Whatever. Kid, I am gonna tell you that you will not be here long enough for me to worry about it."

Coach Smithson put his arm around Eddie Austeri and led him away from what he thought was out of an earshot from me. I could hear them loud and clear, as could my teammates, who were all slowly dressing next to me.

This was certainly not the way that I wanted this adventure to begin. Talk about a bubble bursting. I may be a victim of the Old Lady Syndrome and Mr. Nice Guy, but if I was one thing, it was that I was a fierce competitor.

"Look, this kid is a long-haired hippie, Eddie. Please! Shit, ya kiddin'? A kid from New Jersey! A former street hockey and roller goalie. Shit, c'mon, Eddie. What in the hell are ya thinking here? Ain't nuthin' in Jersey 'cept the mob, thugs, drugs and trash dumps. Sure, as hell, there ain't no damn ice hockey goalies. I know that you are my boss, but I need a damn goalie, not some hairball hippie in canvas sneakers and wearin' rock and roll tee shirts. He looks as if he should be playing guitar for some wild, rock and roll band. Please go and get Hikibin's sorry ass in here, will ya? Give this hippie fifty bucks, send his ass back to Jersey and stick that contract straight up his ass."

I had faced this long-haired hippie thing way too many times. I felt the now familiar inner fire rise inside of me. It started deep from within me; it rose up and would sometimes make my ears feel as if they were on fire and turning red. I was not about to sit there and allow my new coach to trash me without a chance. Hell no. I had come too far! Too many stitches, too much pain, and sure as hell, too much pride. New Jersey, my ass!

Time to move, twenty-seven.

I stood up and walked over to where they were speaking. I stood next to the coach and flexed my muscles a little, then folded my arms across my bare chest. I towered over him. He had not seen me standing up yet. When he chose to show me his ass, and when he chose to ignore my greeting, I was sitting down and he walked away before I could even stand up.

"Excuse me. Pardon the interruption, Coach Smithson. The name is Henson. Paul John Henson. Since you turned your back on me, when I tried to introduce myself, I thought that perhaps I should make the first step in a more *proper* introduction."

Coach Smithson turned around and looked at me. He took a step back, and he carefully studied me while I stuck my hand out to shake his hand. Mr. Austeri stood there smiling a wide smile, because he knew what was coming.

The coach was a bit taken back since he now realized how large and tall a man I was. He stammered a little now;

his cockiness had suffered a bit of an ego blow.

"Yeah . . . okay, yeah, I got it, Henson. Whoa, big goalie . . . you did not look so big sitting there. Hey, I will be right with ya. Nice to meet you."

He stuck his hand out, and I grabbed it.

Here is where I was going to even the score.

One little squeeze sent Coach Smithson to his knees as he tried to pull away.

"Oh! All right now! The score is even big guy! Henson. Paul John Henson! I got it loud and clear. We are even!"

"Thank you, Coach Smithson, and the number *is* twenty-seven. So, do you like to drink beer?" Coach Smithson pulled away from me, and he rubbed his hand with a puzzled look on his face.

"Yeah, why?"

"When practice begins, then I will face whoever you feel might just be your two best shooters. Line them up. Give them ten shots at me. If they score more than one goal, I will buy you a case of your favorite beer and you can stick that contract of mine up my ass. That is, if you think you can. If I hold them off, you never will call me a hippie ever again, and maybe *your* contract, well, I will leave that up to Eddie here to decide where it lands. Deal?" The coach looked at me, and Mr. Austeri continued to smile.

"Cocky, hippie ass sucker, huh?"

"No sir, confident. That is the correct word. Cocky shows that you have no poise and shows your bare ass a little too much for my liking. My old man taught me to always have poise."

"Deal, twenty-seven. Please, we do not have to shake on it either."

I smiled and returned to my locker. There, I found a hockey jersey sitting on the bench in front of my locker. I flipped the jersey over and checked the name and number.

The name on the back was HENSON. The number was twenty-seven.

A young teenager holding a basket of practice jerseys looked at me and smiled. He set his basket down and said, "Hey, twenty-seven, I am Justin Smithson. I am the equipment kid. Yeah, man, the coach's son. Dad can be a bit of an asshole at times, but he is a good coach. I like your toughness. Good luck to you. I will skip shaking your hand, though. The long hair doesn't bother me none!"

I laughed and smiled.

"Thank you, Justin. Nice to meet you."

Slowly, teammates came over and introduced themselves to me, wished me luck, and they all refused to shake my hand. Once dressed, I placed the cross inside my back pocket of my warm-up pants, tied my hair behind my head, pulled my mask over my head, and virtually ran on my skates out to the ice.

Wow! What a rink! The ice was perfect too. No ripples, no chunks, wonderful ice that was like glass. I could skate a million miles per hour on this ice! The seating looked the same as the seating in the professional rinks that you see in the big time! This was a little larger than my beloved Ice Land, that was for sure.

Coach Smithson waved at two players and bellowed, "Starost and McDonald! Get ya asses over here and line up ten pucks and score on hippie Henson. Shoot his ass up, will you guys? I am thirsty, and I have to leave a few extra minutes to call Hikibin in time to make the deadline and adjust a certain contract! Do you need some warm-up shots there, long-haired hippie?"

"I do not need any warm-ups and I also do not mind any head shots, either. Fire away!"

"You are a weird one there, twenty-seven. Go for it, boys!"

I waved to show that I was ready to go. I heard someone bang on the glass behind my goal and turned around to see Mr. Austeri standing behind me. He gave me a wave of encouragement, and I lifted my stick to thank him. I scuffed some ice in front of the net and crouched down in my stance. I tapped the right post with the top of my stick and I mumbled, "Not a marble, twenty-seven, not a marble."

The barrage started. One-on-one breakaways, slap shots, wrist shots, and nine pucks later, I had yet to give up a goal. I was pumped and on it. In fact, dead on it!

When the player named, Starost, broke in hard, cut across the top of the slot and fired a wrist shot towards the opposite top corner of the net, I easily gloved it, and then skated out of the net to where Coach Smithson stood watching, with just a little smile now appearing on his face. I stopped hard, sprayed a little snow on his skates, flipped my mask up and gently flipped the puck to him. He caught it in midair and smiled at me.

"I think you are going to be thirsty or have to spend your own dough there, Coach Smithson. Also, you might not want to bend too far over."

"Yeah, okay. I got it. Hey, Henson, welcome to the Roosters. Where the hell did you learn to play goal like that in New Jersey? I never knew there was even any ice in New Jersey, 'cept in a glass of whiskey."

"Geyer Street Gardens, Coach Smithson. Where else would I have come from, eh, coach?"

He rubbed his chin and said, "Geez, I never heard of it before."

Coach Smithson and I were going to be fine; he was just a little grouchy, sort of like the old man when the New York Bugs lost a baseball game.

I could tell that we were going to be fine.

He would later on become, as Harry would proudly say, "Our kind of guy."

The Roosters were, so far, the best team of players and coaches I had ever played with. The talent on the team, the hockey knowledge, and the overall professional approach of everyone associated with the organization were wonderful. I soon learned that I actually was very lucky to have shut out the two shooters, who Coach Smithson chose in an effort to win the free case of beer on me and try to "adjust" my contract status! When the practice started, I did not fare quite as well on several shots.

Joseph Starost was the best defenseman of the defensive corps. In fact; he was the best player for the Long Island Roosters. He was a little older than I was. I would guess, maybe around twenty-four to twenty-five years of age. He was a big guy who possessed a powerful slap shot and an equally hard wrist shot. He was tall, a little taller than I was, and he had great balance and skating ability.

He skated over after taking some shots on me and took his gloves off while saying, "I am not afraid to shake your hand there, twenty-seven. I am Joe Starost. Welcome to the hockey club. They call me, Big Joe."

"Hey, Big Joe. Very nice to meet you. Nice shooting." I shook his hand and eased up a little, and then I realized that he was a powerful young man.

"You're a strong guy, Paul. Great saves, man, you have such quick moves and great feet. Never saw a goalie react quite that fast. I love how you stood up to Coach Smithson. He sure underestimated your ass!"

"Thank you, Big Joe. Yeah, yeah, yeah, I faced that hippie shit my whole life. Sometimes, you have to stand up for yourself. Have you been on the team long?"

"Nah, just came to the club this October. I am out of Connecticut here, near New Haven. I take the ferry over to Port Jeff for the home games. We have played well and with our starting goalie, Ace Stanley, going down due to injury and we knew we needed some help."

Joe skated close and leaned in out of an earshot of the backup goalie standing on the side watching the action. "Higgins there, I guess that he is now your backup. He sucks. He can't stop a beach ball!"

I nodded and smiled. This was going to be fun. I liked

Big Joe Starost because I enjoyed having a big, tough defenseman to play in front of me. He may not be Harry M. Redmond Junior, or Jeff Porter, but very few people were!

"You need to be ready to go for the first game. We play the Colonials, you know, and that means we have to face that lunatic Jim O'Malley. Last time we played him, damn, it was a slugfest. I punched it out with him and let me tell you, I outweigh him by seventy pounds, and he is barely six feet tall, but he is one tough hombre. He split my lip open, and I ended up just hanging on his jersey for dear life. The guy is a psychotic nutcase."

I nodded and acknowledged O'Malley and his evil ways.

"You know him?"

"Oh, yes. I only had the pleasure of dealing with him once. A tournament game a while back while he was a ringer for a team of Christian skaters, who brought him in for some muscle and who knows what else."

"Christians! With O'Malley," Big Joe laughed and seemed surprised.

"Yeah, yeah, yeah, it was an interesting game for sure."

Big Joe handled a puck as it slid by our feet while we stood on the side of the ice and watched the backup goalie take shots.

He continued to explain, "The trouble is, twenty-seven, O'Malley is a hockey goon, but he does have skills. He can shoot, score and fight too. Right now, he leads the league in penalty minutes, points and goals. He actually is a very good player."

"I am not surprised to hear that. In the game that I played against him, I noticed how he could really shoot. Although, Big Joe, I think I know some of his tricks and his eyes always give his plans up too soon. We will work together. Maybe after practice, we can go for a few beers and talk about some defensive moves and strategies. My good buddy played defense in front of me for most of my career, and we came up with some tricks. He suffered a tough injury and no longer plays, but our ideas still work!"

"I would like that, Paul. Sorry about your pal. . .."

It was Tuesday night around seven thirty or thereabouts, the eleventh day of December in 1978. I stood in front of a hockey goal net on the south end of the Skate-O-Rama ice rink in Rockland County, in lower New York State. I stood in my goaltending gear, purchased from my friends at Wurtzberg Brothers Sporting Goods Store in downtown Paterson, New Jersey. I held my trusty goaltender's mask under my arm, had my lucky silver cross stuck neatly in the back pocket of my warm-up pants, and I stood quietly at attention, while the National Anthem played.

When the last few bars of the song played, the raucous crowd broke into loud cheers and screams. I did not dare to look up in the grandstands from my post. I held my pose until the song finished. If I dared to look up in a certain corner of the seats, the flash of the Redmond's cameras going off would blind me!

It was a dream that finally had come true for me. All the way from the gritty streets of Geyer Street to this ice rink here in lower New York. My first game as a professional, a semi-professional, but hey, the Long Island Roosters were still paying me, my measly seventeen dollars per game, and ten cents royalty on each "Henson" jersey and some dopey posters of me that they sold.

Out of respect, I held my attention until the song ended. What a great country! Where a poor kid from the city streets could follow and fulfill his dreams, and I knew how lucky I was to live here.

The least that I could do was to pay my respects.

I flipped my hair back, tied it off with a hair tie, and then pulled the mask over my head. Out of the corner of my eyes, I could see the fourteen million, seventy-two thousand, and two flash bulbs going off with the picture taking madness led by my fan club in the grandstands.

My old man was there, along with the guys from his shop, Harry and his latest flame, whose name I did not know, or could even keep track of, Mr. Redmond, Ronzo, Patty, Linny, the Big Spike, all of them were there! Snapping pictures and cheering like lunatics! Despite their overly zealous approach to everything in life, I loved them all dearly, and I knew in my heart that there were no better people in this entire world.

I smoothed the ice in front of the crease with my skates and stick as each of my teammates skated by to tap my pads and wish me good luck. Finally, I crouched down in my classic stance, looked up at my fan club, and gave them a wave with my stick. It was as if a bright flash of lightning was going off in the corner of the stands.

Big Joe Starost stood next to me laughing, and he tapped my pads with his stick.

"Geez Paulie. Holy shit, that is a lot of cameras. Good luck, twenty-seven. From the glare in O'Malley's eyes, it is going to be a long one."

I nodded and did not say a word. I was too focused now and trying hard to get into the flow that I knew I would need. I cannot say that I was nervous at all; I never really became nervous before games.

It was more as if I was anxious.

O'Malley was out with his line to start the game. I did not recognize his line mates. There was a tall, center iceman with long, flowing, black hair, playing alongside a left-winger, who was one of the few players on the Colonials who wore a hockey helmet. O'Malley still played the right-wing position, and he skated around waving his stick and glaring at Rooster players. His mouth was jawing away a mile a minute, shouting threats and insults, mixed with classic obscenities to us as he waited for the puck drop. The home crowd was going nuts, the arena was packed and the homers, of course, loved their wild-eyed hero.

O'Malley egged the crowd on by waving his hand in the

air and right before the puck dropped; he picked up his stick and pointed the blade end at Big Joe.

"Here I come again, Starost. I carved a player's eyeball out last week! You are next on my hit list!"

He was such a pleasant and cordial chap. Time had not mellowed his demeanor one bit.

Big Joe waved his glove towards O'Malley and yelled, "My stick is going up your ass, Jim. Straight up your ass!"

I do not think that O'Malley even noticed me, or even had the opportunity to recognize me, but I knew that time would come soon enough.

Here we go.

"Not a marble, twenty-seven. Not a marble can roll by you," I said to myself.

I picked my stick up to signal to the referee that I was good to go and the Colonial's goalie did the same. The referee dropped the puck, and the game was off! A mad rush ensued after a clean win on the faceoff by the Roosters, and our speedy center, Greg McDonald, sped down the ice and led a charge. A nifty poke check by the Colonial's defenseman caused a shift in the puck's possession, and a wave led by the tall, center iceman charged at us.

O'Malley flew down the right wing and McDonald back checked feverishly in an effort to keep up. It was a three on two break, with Big Joe and my other defenseman, a stocky Irish chap named Willy Mulligan holding the line.

One pass, then two passes and a hard slap shot by the left-winger wearing the helmet. I watched the puck the entire way, easily gloved the shot, and held it for a faceoff. I braced myself because I knew what was coming!

Years before I had met O'Malley, I had played street hockey with Big Wex!

Sure enough, O'Malley plowed into me and knocked me backwards into the net, while butt ending me and slashing wildly at my glove, even though the referee blew the play dead a few seconds earlier.

His act had not changed too much, if at all!

It was time to reintroduce myself to my old pal, O'Malley.

"Play the whistle! Play the whistle, you slashing idiot!" I screamed, jumped to my skates, and pushed O'Malley backwards. I was a strong man and O'Malley was not expecting to receive such a powerful push. He almost tumbled backwards on his skates until he caught his balance and recover.

He looked at me and smiled.

"Hey! Shit! I know you. I knew it was only a matter of time until you made it here, too. No doubt, you can stop the biscuit, but can you handle the pain?"

"Piss off and go away, O'Malley! Just play the game," I told him as I tossed the puck to the linesman and waved my glove in the air towards O'Malley. He glided around on his skates, circling the crease like a hawk circling prey.

"So, we meet again, hippie freak! Oh, this is going to be fun! I heard your big, dopey lard ass friend, went down with half of his face smashed in and his teeth knocked clean out of his stupid head. Good, he deserved it! The big lard ass. Now, it is your turn, longhair! I am going to make you wish you stayed in those senior leagues and you can join your pal in the hospital bed and you can keep him company."

Big Joe came over and pushed O'Malley while telling him, "You're a pig, Jim. Just a sick pig. Did anyone ever tell you that you really suck?"

"All the time, Starost! Every damn day! It is what I live for. All I want is to piss you off so bad cuz, I want to win and I'll do anything I have to, in order to beat ya ass."

This was a typical O'Malley-induced melee; it was his "modus operandi." It was what he lived for, wanted and sought, in order to disrupt the initial rhythm of the game and to control the game from the onset.

The officials were trying hard to calm the situation down, but I had to admit, for the comment he had made about Harry, I wanted to knock O'Malley out myself. I knew better. Actually, he was working his magic, getting everyone off their game, getting under our skin, and then he would strike.

"Stay cool, Big Joe. That is what he wants. Let's beat him on the ice."

"I will beat your ass wherever you want! I really do not give a shit, because I will fight you here, in the parking lot, or in a dark alley! Bring it on pussies!" O'Malley screamed.

What O'Malley did not realize was that his comments had set the little fire burning inside of me. Any tentative actions or anxious moments were now gone. It was over for the New York Colonials. He should not have messed with my friend, nor tried to mess with my head.

It had a reverse effect on me.

O'Malley was now going to lose.

The fire rose inside of me and I smiled because the fire was burning hard. I watched as the linesman called the players in for the faceoff and I crouched down for the ensuing draw. I felt the flow come over me and I shut out everything else.

The game was back and forth, up and down, and it remained scoreless through two full periods. Between the periods in our locker room, Coach Smithson drew up new plays and strategies to penetrate the tough Colonial defense. This game was turning out to be an epic adventure and struggle. Arriving in our locker room between periods had been enough of an adventure. The entire Long Island Rooster team could have certainly done without the long journey to our supposed haven of a locker room. The home crowd fans pelted us with half-eaten hot dogs and dumped a rain of beer and soda on top of us while we walked up the runways to our locker room between periods. What did we expect? We *were* in the Colonial home rink!

Security made a very half-hearted effort to intervene on our behalf, but they were O'Malley fans too!

I only hoped that my faithful entourage did not partake in the melees in the stands. Between Harry, the old man, the guys from the shop, Ronzo and the Big Spike, we packed a little muscle too!

I made a number of key saves and the opposition goaltender for the Colonials was on top of his game, too. It was a heated contest between what appeared to be two very evenly matched teams. I cannot say that the shots did not test me, because I did handle a few tough shots, but I was in the flow and seeing the puck so well that, so far, the game was an easy one for me.

O'Malley ranted and raved, slashed and butt-ended his way up and down the ice. He told us, in quite descriptive language, what his opinion of each player on the Roosters was.

To say that he was a piece of work was quite the understatement. His mouth never stopped, the string of obscenities that O'Malley could put together would make a drunken sailor blush.

While he spewed hate and malice, he led the charge up and down the ice, and he, as well as his line mates, had several quality shots on me. He did not utilize his set screen play yet, and I wondered if perhaps he had moved on from that play he used when we played him in the tournament. O'Malley served a number of minor penalties. He and Big Joe ended up in another shoving match that resulted in roughing calls for both of them, but for the most part, it was a hard-fought and controlled contest.

Then came the third period.

Right from the opening faceoff, everyone in the entire arena could feel the ticking time bomb of frustration inside of Jim O'Malley. The Colonials and the O'Malley merry band of followers were being stifled, and that did not go over so well.

It was time for the O'Malley bomb to explode.

O'Malley broke in on the right wing and took a slap shot that I knew had one intention. The shot's sole purpose was to kill me, or to kill one of the defensemen in front of me. I screamed to Big Joe and Mulligan to duck; I had it tracked and both of them moved out of the way. This was a killer of a shot, a deadly shot, and one thing about O'Malley was that he could really nail a heavy slap shot.

I bet the shot peaked at one hundred miles an hour, or very close to it.

I easily utilized my stick glove blocker on the puck, reached up and gloved it. My motions deflected the rocket of a shot over the glass and out of play, and it forced a whistle for a stoppage of play. O'Malley sneered at me. Big Joe came barreling in and the pushing and jawing began once more. This was exactly what O'Malley wanted at this point of the game, and his plan was to cause a last disruption and try to intimidate us into losing a key player to a penalty.

I knew that the key player, of which James T. O'Malley sought to remove from the game, was going to be Big Joe. He knew that Joe Starost was the key to our defense, and he required more room to operate out there.

I warned my team to stay out of it.

"He can shoot those headhunters all night long, guys. Every time he does that, it is another scoring chance that he squanders! Don't let him get to you. That is what he wants!"

"Squanders . . . squanders . . . big, educated words from a brainless, jackass, hairball, hippie ass goalie. You do not often even cuss or swear, and you use big words, twenty-seven. Let me tell you to wake up, hippie ass. You are in the big time now, and nice guys like ya stupid ass are will end up with their heads split open! I am going to cut your tongue out and feed it to you for breakfast!" O'Malley came in and pushed me backwards into the crossbar.

That was it!

Big Joe took the bait and dropped the gloves. O'Malley dropped his gloves too, and the fight was on, right in front of me. I stayed in my crease because if I left during a fight; I would receive a penalty, so I stayed right there.

There was a ringside seat for me.

The crowd went nuts and the two men traded blows back and forth. Big Joe had the height, weight and leverage advantage, and O'Malley, although not a small man by any means, on this particular go around, did not fare as well as what Joe had described what had happened in their previous roo-bah-bah. What O'Malley lacked in size compared to Big Joe, he made up with sheer amounts of courage and acrimonious attitude.

Big Joe pummeled O'Malley, and blood quickly shot out of the corner of O'Malley's mouth and it spewed in the air, while I tried hard to avoid the splashes of sweat, spit and blood flying my way from the two combatants. After about five minutes of the gruesome battle, the goon covered up, and he held on since he was exhausted from his beating from Big Joe. He held on for dear life until the officials could jump in and break it up.

It did not matter.

The now bloodied O'Malley had achieved his goal.

He managed to get our best defenseman and our best player in Big Joe off the ice for the rest of the contest. His plan, of course, had worked to perfection; he was not at all stupid. He, in his own way, was quite the strategist.

The referee called out the penalties, "Five minutes for fighting to number eleven of the Colonials, and two minutes for the cross check into the goalie. Two minutes roughing, a major for fighting, and a game misconduct for being the third man in for number five for the Roosters! Hit the showers there, Starost! Ya was the third man in!"

O'Malley spit out large gobs of blood onto the ice, and then he spit out one of his teeth, caught it in his hand and tossed it over the glass. He played to the crowd, working them into a wild frenzy while he skated the long distance to the penalty box. His now toothless smile was a mile wide.

We played four on four for a few minutes, and both teams had their checking lines out. The third lines for both teams were the weakest players, and both coaches were just trying to kill time to allow the first and second lines to recover their wind and legs.

A Colonial player dumped a rolling puck into our defensive zone as a prelude for a line change, and the puck harmlessly rolled towards the net. I relaxed for just a moment . . . big mistake, Paul! Willy Mulligan went to pick it up, the puck jumped on some choppy ice, Mulligan mishandled it, and before I could even react, he tapped the puck towards our own net and the puck rolled in for a goal in our own net!

"Twenty-seven! My dumb-ass fault, geez! I am so sorry, twenty-seven! That is the only way they could score on you tonight. A stupid mistake on my part! Shit! Shit! Shit!"

I had made a last second, hopeless, dive for the puck and while I was sprawled there watching the celebration of the Colonials, I angrily scooped the puck out of the net and rolled it towards the linesman.

"Nah, nah, nah, Willy, my fault. I relaxed and I know better. Never relax, ever."

I could see Harry and my cheering section standing and rooting me onward. They were there, in and amongst the bedlam of the home team crowd that was still going crazy over the scoring of the cheap goal.

Coach Smithson and our team's bench shouted out for Mulligan and number twenty-seven to shake it off!

"It is only one goal," was the rallying cry!

As often happens in a momentum shift in any sport, after a score or a key play happens, the next few minutes are crucial. Ever since I started playing, I shook off defeat, or goals scored on me very quickly. I did not fret or dwell, but I ground in even harder.

Here we go. Buckle those pads and mask straps!

The Colonials did not disappoint us. When O'Malley escaped from his seven minutes of confinement, he hit the ice like a tornado rolling across a prairie! With Big Joe in the locker room, he was free to unleash his reign of uninhibited terror, and he set his mind to wreak havoc upon the Long Island Roosters! For the next five minutes, the Colonials threw everything at us.

I dove headfirst. I made some wild split saves. They crashed the net and Mulligan, and another Rooster defenseman, a shifty, skilled player with good hands named Van Dyke, held them off. I noticed how, in many ways, Van Dyke reminded me of Johnny the Cho. He was a good stick-handler around the net, and like Johnny the Cho, he had a wonderful and uncanny ability to lift the puck high in the air with his stick and lob the puck safely out of the zone.

Ah, hah. I remembered a play that the Buckley Park Bruisers used a very long time ago to create a breakaway opportunity on Geyer Street Gardens.

Okay, it might work here too!

After a mad rush and a few frantic saves, I held the puck for a faceoff and as we were lining up, I waved McDonald and Van Dyke over to me and whispered, "McDonald, don't back check, we got this. Ya need to hang out near center ice, and Van Dyke, when you get a chance, get under that puck and lift it high into the neutral zone. Watch for a two-line pass. Stand just shy of the red line because they leave the middle of the ice wide open! Van Dyke, lob it high and far. I just bet they will pinch and it will be a wide-open lane to their net."

They both nodded at the suggestion. McDonald won a clean draw, and after a scramble in the corner and a missed body check by O'Malley, Van Dyke lifted the puck into center ice, where the crafty and fast skating McDonald was waiting. Off to the races, a little tuck of the shoulder, a head fake, and it was a tie game! Greg McDonald was quite the shifty little player.

Our play worked!

Oh, yeah! Long live, Johnny the Cho!

The small contingent of Rooster fans went nuts, led by our gang, and it was then that I heard, for the first time, the famous Rooster fan club chant. At first, I did not understand what they were doing, and it seemed to register quite high on the stupid list.

Looking back now, I actually grew quite fond of it and later on, it factored into quite a moment in our lives, but that is indeed another story.

The Long Island Rooster fan club lined up and split into two individual groups. They joined hands and waved their arms in the air while simultaneously cheering.

One side of the fan club cheered loudly, "ROOSTERS! ROOSTERS! ROOSTERS!"

Then another group answered, "COCKLE DOODLE DOO, COCKLE DOODLE DOO, COCKLE DOODLE DOO!"

Where was the lip lady when we needed her?

At least she did not duplicate the crows of a rooster! McDonald scored another goal about a minute later on a little give and go play, and we now took a two-to-one lead. The lob play had set the tone, the momentum shifted, and we had withstood the best that the Colonials could throw at us.

I glanced at the game clock and saw that we had about four minutes to go.

Four minutes to my first win!

O'Malley led another furious charge and I should have known that he would try to pull the old screen in front trick, but this time, he added a little trickery to the play. As he fired a shot towards the net, his center iceman skated by and rather than set the screen, he stuck his blade under my goalie skates and tugged at the skate blades. It was a set play, and technically, it was goaltender interference.

The referee saw the play cleanly, but for some reason, he kept his whistle in his pocket!

I made the first save, but the trip forced me off balance, and while I landed flat in the crease, O'Malley snuck into play the puck, and he was on top of the rebound. Now, with both of our defenseman stuck in the high slot, with McDonald furiously trying to return on a back check, and with number twenty-seven now caught out of position, the net was wide open.

From my prone position, I quickly looked into O'Malley's eyes and saw that he looked at the top of the net. His eyes quickly studied the short side top corner. He now flipped the puck to his backhand as he cut across the lower slot. He was going to go top shelf with a backhand.

I guessed, knowing that if I were wrong, then it would be a gift goal for a wide-open net.

I dove to the top shelf and waved my catching glove in the air, and sure enough, the puck tipped the very edge of my glove and wobbled up over the glass. The referee blew the whistle, and I slid out of control across the crease and rolled into Mulligan's skates.

"SAVE!" Holy shit, twenty-seven! You are friggin' on fire, Paulie!" Mulligan shouted, as he helped pick me up off the ice. "That might just be the greatest damn save that I have ever seen. You can bend in ways that a person ain't supposed to bend!"

O'Malley, in his sheer frustration, chopped his stick repeatedly on the ice and then on the boards and glass, until the wooden blade and shaft shattered in about ten pieces! The referee blew the whistle and administered a two-minute, unsportsmanlike conduct penalty to O'Malley. This penalty would remove him from the ice for most of the rest of the game.

No penalty ever summed up O'Malley's attitude better than "unsportsmanlike conduct" did!

While the officials cleaned up the sections of broken wood from O'Malley's stick, and the none-too-happy O'Malley fumed on his way to the penalty box, I leaned back on the crossbar and studied the game clock.

The sweat was dripping off the end of my mask like a leaky faucet, and the sweat was running down my chest. I swear that it dripped all the way down to my jockstrap.

Since this game started, I must have lost five pounds of water weight alone. Looking up at the game clock, I realized that there were four minutes and twenty-seven seconds left in the game.

There it was again, that magical number of twenty-seven!

The Colonials pulled the goalie for an extra attacker, and we added an open net goal, but the game essentially ended with the glove save and the penalty to O'Malley. The final buzzer sounded, and the Roosters flew over the boards to celebrate.

I flipped my mask off, looked at Harry, the old man and the rest of the gang in the crowd and waved my stick in the air! The flash bulbs were going off like lighthouse beacons in a fog bank!

That one special game, years ago, on Geyer Street Gardens, when we beat the Buckley Park Bruisers, sure felt good, but this win felt really good too!

The fan club was cheering wildly in the stands, screaming in unison, "ROOSTERS, ROOSTERS, ROOSTERS! COCKLE DOODLE DOO, COCKLE DOODLE DOO, COCKLE DOODLE DOO!"

Hey, it kinda grows on ya!

I think that I will get used to it.

2

The Many Seasons of Hockey

O'Malley and I met many times during that long, long hockey season. Some were epic battles that were full of his wild antics, and some, considering the cast of characters, were remarkably subdued. One thing became certain; the rivalry of the Colonials and the Roosters was growing into a legend in the Metropolitan Hockey League. Whenever we played, the arenas became packed houses, filled with wild screaming fans and over the top celebrations. I am sure the team owners, the arena owners, and all who had financial interests in the two teams remained thrilled as the rivalry grew and grew in intensity.

The fans sure loved it! The fights in the stands were often worse than the on-ice battles were.

O'Malley versus Henson became a miniature rivalry within the larger rivalry of the two teams. I stopped O'Malley many times, but he scored a few on me too! Some games, I came out on top, but we lost a few too!

James T. O'Malley was not just a hockey goon and tough guy. He, in fact, was a special player. Sure, he went crazy out on the ice and wreaked havoc, but he actually was a supremely gifted hockey player. He was strong, a skilled skater, and smart too. He possessed a powerful and accurate shot, and above all the chaos, he was a fierce competitor who loved the game of hockey.

There was little doubt that you could not help but admire his desire, his resilience, and his incredible passion for the sport of hockey.

The Colonials were in a different division than our team was; we were the south division, and the Colonials headed up the north division, and as the season rolled on, our main divisional opponent was a tough one. Out of the four teams in our division, the best team by far, was the Rockets. The New Jersey Rockets played out of my home arena of Ice Land, and they were a formidable team. In order for the Roosters to play in the championship game, we first needed to overcome the Rockets. We fought each other neck and neck, and the two teams traded places back and forth many times during the season, while we were vying for the first-place position in the south division.

I supplanted the former incumbent goaltender for the Roosters, a chap named Stanley, who I never actually met. His injuries healed and when he was ready to return to the Roosters, he felt that there was no longer a spot on the team for him.

From what my teammates and Coach Smithson told me, he did not relish a backup goalie role, so he sought another position. Mr. Austeri remained tight-lipped about the situation, but he hinted that Stanley was from Ontario Province in Canada. He was terribly homesick anyway, and he returned to play in his homeland. That left just two goalies remaining on the active roster for the Long Island Roosters, Henson and a chap named Higgins.

Mr. Austeri and Coach Smithson both shared their thoughts on my backup goalie, Michael Higgins, for being less than competent, and they asked me to work with him all the time.

I did not share their views.

In my opinion, Higgins was a solid goaltender. He was older, around thirty-five years of age, and Higgins was a seasoned and battle-hardened goaltender. His pads looked as if they went back to the era of Gordon Gurney or even earlier. His pads were more than broken in!

We roomed together on the road trips, and he was a

quiet guy. He kept to himself and studied goaltending. I always thought he would be a wonderful coach someday. We worked on the finer points together and he would jump in for a mop up duty, when we were far ahead in a game, or occasionally, he would jump in when we were losing by a wide margin.

During this season, was also when I met a magical and captivating gal named Miss Renee Gorman, and my life changed for a short period of time. We shared something very special, incredible, unforgettable, and all too soon, because of reasons out of our control, our brief, yet powerful, romance ended. She was my soul mate.

Retreating from the pain, I hid behind my mask once again.

Despite the pain off the ice, overall, on the ice, I was doing very well. I led the league in goals against average and in shutouts, and when the end of February in 1979 rolled around; it looked as if the team was in a very good position going into the end of the season.

As we slowly gained victories, we finally overtook the New Jersey Rockets. We landed in first place by seven points; it appeared as if the Roosters would settle in at the top slot and win the south division for the 1978-79 hockey season. The picture was now clearer for the Long Island Roosters to play the New York Colonials for the championship showdown in March 1979.

Along with Harry and his revolving cast of girlfriends, his family, my family, and the guys from the shop, I did slowly acquire other followers in a fan club of sorts. I had to admit that it was indeed an ego booster, whenever you would spot a fan wearing your hockey jersey, with your name and number on the back of the jersey.

There were even a handful of fans who called themselves "Henson's Hippies." They were a group of Rooster fans that wore long-haired wigs, black canvas sneakers, "No Way" tee shirts or my jerseys, and they would root and cheer for me at games, while all of them were dressed as fellow hippies! It was comical, and I did pose for pictures with them, and sign autographs. It was a different world for sure! Leave it to people who hail from New Jersey, New York, or Connecticut for the best in wild innovations and strong opinions!

Behind the scenes, the rough and tumble world of semi-professional hockey was not very glorious. Locker rooms were dank, dirty, and dark. The buses that we rode to the games in were glorified school buses, and the characters that you met along the way were quite colorful and unusual. I grew accustomed to the lifestyle and the fact that I held down a full-time job, and played and practiced hockey too, left me very little time for any other activities.

I was indeed living my dream.

March came, and the showdown of the Colonials and the Roosters came to fruition. As expected, the best of seven playoff games, to determine the champions of the Metropolitan Hockey League for the 1978-79 season, was a frenzy of fan activity, O'Malley's now legendary antics, and pure, competitive hockey. One could say whatever you wanted to label the hockey player known as James T. O'Malley. He was a lunatic, a hockey goon, a wild man, but if he was one thing, it was that he was certainly entertaining! He was the one player that the opposition fans throughout the league would love to hate, and the Colonial fans would erect a shrine in his honor after each game.

James T. O'Malley became a legend.

The playoff series went back and forth. We won the first game, and then the Colonials won the second game. The Colonials had a better overall league record than our team did, so they had earned a home ice advantage. Therefore, we had desperately wanted to avoid a seventh game played in Rockland County, however; it was not to be. We ended up after six games, tied at three games each, and the two teams were now set to meet in a classic showdown on the Colonial's home ice.

The game was all that my old neighborhood talked about for days and days, and if some of the old timers knew where Rockland County, New York was, I am sure they would have shown up in mass numbers. A caravan of support rolled out of John Street on the night of the big game, and the old guard carried all the old stalwarts that they could carry. Thank goodness that Cliffy McWhiffy was too half-in-the-bag to make the trip! He would have given O'Malley a good run for it in the cursing contest. Of course, there would be no lack of picture taking this evening! Harry and the Redmonds must have shot two hundred rolls of film before we even left the end of John Street.

A packed arena, full of wild, O'Malley incensed fans, local radio, local newspapers it was the culmination of a season's worth of historic animosity between the two hockey clubs. It was so fitting that it needed to come down to a seventh game and to a final, epic battle.

Even my dear mum made this trip. She was fully prepared to cover her eyes when the puck came my way, but there she sat in the grandstands, trying hard to still figure out the difference between this game and English football.

Harry had told me he was meeting a new gal tonight, and that his new gal's best friend wanted to come and see a hockey game too, but I paid him very little attention when it came to his constant evolution of lady friends.

It was too exhausting to keep track of these days!

I remained intense, and I tried very hard not to allow the diversions of this game and the preludes to it to cause me to lose my focus.

O'Malley stormed up and down the ice in his usual madness, and he fired everything that he and his fellow line-mates had at the Roosters and at me.

We remained scoreless through the first period and through all the second period too.

The flow was strong, and I was spot on during the game. There was no doubt that I was feeling well. I had better be into this. It was the biggest game of my career to this point! I was moving quickly and loosely, but as always, a single moment can change everything.

I took a hard shot in the mask on a screened slapper in the last few seconds of the second period, and it knocked me backwards a bit. I kept my wits about me and covered the puck up. The blood ran hard from under my mask, but when I noticed that there were only a few seconds remaining in the period, I waved off any assistance from the trainer, and I stayed in the goal until the period ended. When the referee blew the whistle signaling the end of the period, I skated hard to the rink door. I kept my mask on and my head down, and I hurried up the runway to the locker room. The blood ran down my face and it dripped off the end of my mask and all over my jersey, so I moved along as fast as I could, at least as fast as I could move, while being hampered by wearing goalie skates. I did not want Mum, Harry, or the old man to see any injuries, so I made sure they did not have a chance to see me while I made my way to the locker room.

"The doctor is a half hour away, twenty-seven. You need a few stitches above your right eye. That mask of yours is magical. I swear it is amazin' that you were not cold-conked out like a friggin' light," the team trainer and equipment manager, the young Mr. Justin Smithson, told me as he stared in at the cut.

"Half an hour will not do. We do not have a half an hour, youse guys. Why the hell was the doc not here for a championship game!" I was a bit angry and I yelled out my frustration to the walls and my teammates.

Coach Smithson walked over and put his hand on my shoulder while telling me, "Calm down, twenty-seven. We can start, Higgins, and then switch ya out. Butterflies won't hold the blood back. It is too deep."

"Nah, please stitch me yourself, Coach Smithson. If ya can't, then tell your son to stitch it with that needle and thread over there!"

Justin told me, "Twenty-seven. Geez man, I just used that on a tear in those dirty ass socks!"

"Wave the needle over a match to sterilize it, and then stitch it, Justin. Numb it with that ice and then stop it from bleeding. If your gut is too queasy to do it, then I will go get my old man out of the stands to do it for you. He has had a lot of practice. We can always have the doc touch it up when he arrives. C'mon! Please, Justin, the needle is a thin one. Shit! I have never won anything in my life. I am not going to lose this one over a cut! Stitch, the bloody thing!"

Coach Smithson nodded to his son to do it, while my entire team cringed at the mere thought. The truth was that the old man had done it more times than I wanted to count.

Coach Smithson said, "Wait. I have something better than ice to numb it." He then rubbed my head with some whiskey from a flask he stashed in his back pocket; a small nip of the whiskey went down my gullet, a few deep, deep breaths, and that was the end of the bleeding!

I may have played a better game here and there, but they had all started to blend. I do remember making a ton of saves in this championship game. Some were spectacular, some were not so spectacular, but we held them out. My defense bailed me out on numerous occasions, and I made a few key stops in wild scrambles in front of the net.

The most intriguing aspect of the game turned out to be that when the frustration set in, and O'Malley resorted to his usual wild tactics of trying to bait Big Joe and McDonald into a battle to lure them off the ice—we resisted!

We were as if we were teen-age virgins, holding out for true love.

It paid off too.

At the nineteen-minute mark, when overtime seemed to loom on the horizon, Big Joe Starost got a clean look from the point with his slap shot and buried the puck in the top shelf of the net, high on the stick side of the Colonial's goaltender and we went crazy! The lead was now ours! Something deep inside of me felt as if that was all we needed, just one goal.

The Roosters could smell a victory, and the championship was so close now! We held off a mad rush, a breakaway or two, and victory was ours! The loud chants from the Rooster's fan club grew and grew in intensity.

"ROOSTERS, ROOSTERS, ROOSTERS! COCKLE DOODLE DOO, COCKLE DOODLE DOO, COCKLE DOODLE DOO!"

Yes, it had grown on me.

I had never won a championship until now and the feeling was something which I could never describe or ever try to duplicate! My teammates mobbed me and the wild celebration was on! Looking up in the grandstands, I spotted the wild hugs and tears of joy that came from my cheering section! The Rooster chants filled the arena. Sad-faced Colonial fans put their heads down, and then they too cheered for the game and season we had all witnessed.

It was indeed something special. An epic struggle between two ultimate foes.

We lined up for the tradition of the congratulatory handshake, which is so unique to the sport of hockey. Here we were, former, bitter combatants who just battled in a literal war on ice, sharing their mutual affection and admiration for one another.

I made my way through the lineup of Colonial players and when I reached a certain man named James T. O'Malley; he completely surprised me by warmly embracing me. His one eye was black and swollen, and he had a few stitches in his lower lip. It had been a grueling series for both teams.

The flash bulbs went off in the background. He looked at me deeply in my eyes, as he released me and said, "Twenty-seven, let me tell you . . . I despise you and love you all at the same time! You are a goalie for the damn ages, a warrior, of which I have never seen or faced before. It comes from deep within you, twenty-seven. A fearless son of a bitch, you are! I swear that it comes from your genes. Your relatives must have been incredibly tough bastards. However, I will tell you, I am coming back, my long-haired friend. I will be back."

I smiled, hugged him back and said, "Jim, I am counting on it! I would not want it to be any other way. Would you?"

O'Malley smiled. He shook his head and tapped my pads with his stick while saying, "Hell no, twenty-seven, hell no."

Later on, in our lives, our paths would cross again, in a unique and different manner. I am sorry to say it again, but that, dear reader, is another story!

There would be many more hockey goons that I would meet along the way. Some were pretenders, some had no hockey skills at all, and some were just escaped criminals or professional boxers, who were posing as hockey players. When you shake it all out, you can say what you want about James T. O'Malley. He may have acted like a nutcase, cursed and despised all of your relatives, and the day that you were born, but he was certainly no pretender. Jim O'Malley was the real deal, and he never backed down from anyone or anything.

He was a fearless son of a bitch.

I learned an awful lot from O'Malley; I just did not realize it at the time!

The on-the-ice celebration was underway. The league

officials awarded us some type of obscure championship trophy. It reminded me of the famous Tremont Cup, and we paraded it around the ice in celebration together.

Gradually, we all left the ice, and I made my way up the runway towards the locker room. I looked up at my family and Harry and waved to them.

They were all going nuts in the crowd and started chanting in unison, "Twenty-seven, twenty-seven!" Ronzo and the Big Spike were both down in the lower grandstands standing with the fan club, leading them in the Rooster chant; they were wearing hippie wigs along with the group of Henson's Hippies.

I think beer was only fifty cents a glass during the game.

Then my mind left the hockey world.

My world was about to be put into perspective in two very different manners. It is amazing how life is so full of twists and turns.

As I directed my attention away from the fan clubs and fans screaming at me from the stands, I heard a man yelling out at the top of his lungs, "Mr. Henson! Twenty-seven! Twenty-seven! Please, over here! Twenty-seven . . . please!"

He called out to me while waving frantically with his arms over the line of security officers who had lined up to control the crowd. Security was working hard to keep the hallway from the edge of the rink to the locker room, clear of spectators and fans. The frantic man yelling at me was a middle-aged man, dressed in one of our team sweatshirts. He caught my attention with his pleading calls and when our eyes met, he walked closer to the line of security officers.

He took a few steps forward, when one of the security officers held his hands out and gently showed to the man, "That he was sorry. He needed to stay clear of the players and the hallway."

Something told me that this man desperately wanted to

speak with me, and it was not in order to congratulate me on winning the championship. I walked closer, and it was then I could see that he had his hands firmly on the handles of a wheelchair. Seated in the chair was a young girl. She was looking in my direction too, and she was wearing not only a Long Island Rooster's ball cap, but she wore a matching jersey too, and the jersey was a number twenty-seven jersey, with "HENSON" emblazoned upon the back of it.

"C'mon, Paul! Where are you going? You can't get involved with fans now. We need to meet Coach Smithson in the locker room," Big Joe pleaded with me, and he tugged at my arm.

"Yeah, yeah, yeah. I will be there in a second, Big Joe. Hang on."

I needed to see what this man and young gal wanted with number twenty-seven.

I waved at the security officer and said, "Please let them through. I cannot walk too far in my skates and this equipment. Please let them come over here."

"Are you sure, twenty-seven? It might start a shit storm of a mad rush, ya know—if I let some people come through."

"I am sure, please."

I saw both of their faces light up when they heard my words, and the security officer waved and allowed them to pass through the wall of officers.

The man grabbed the handles of the wheelchair, pushed the lock off the wheels, and he quickly pushed the chair through the line. He wheeled the young girl closer towards me and it was then that I could see she was a young girl, perhaps, about ten or so years old. She was a beautiful little gal, with long brown hair neatly tied into a long ponytail, which was about as long as mine was. She smiled an ear-to-ear smile, and she wore huge plaster casts on both of her legs.

"Oh, thank you, twenty-seven! Ah, ah, ah, I mean, Paul or actually, Mr. Henson. It is our pleasure to meet you! My daughter here, she is your biggest fan. I am James Macklin and this is my daughter, Allison."

The girl smiled a little more, and she shyly laughed as her blue eyes sparkled.

"We came out from the island to see the big game. All that Allison has wished for was to meet you, and after the game, I told her we would give it our best shot. Congratulations, you are the greatest goalie we have ever seen and Allie, well, she loves you! Tonight, we all love you for beating the Colonials and that scoundrel, O'Malley! I have been around hockey all my life, and I have never seen a goalie play better than you can. I mean, even stitched and cut and all! You are amazing in the net and so big too! My goodness, I never realized how large a man you are."

"Thank you. Please, you can call me twenty-seven or Paulie. Not too many people ever call me Paul. Only some special folks, on rare occasions. Please, there is no need to call me Mr. Henson either. You are very kind, but I have to tell you that my mum might be my biggest fan."

I reached out and gently shook his hand while being cognizant not to squeeze his hand with my usual zeal. I took a few steps, put my gloves and goalie stick down, and tucked my mask down inside of my leg pad. Mr. Macklin held out a program from tonight's game along with a pen, and I took it and signed it for them, and scrolled a number twenty-seven under my autograph. I then knelt down on my pads next to the wheelchair and gently spoke to Allison, "I am sorry, I am bleeding and a little sweaty here."

She giggled and finally spoke.

I could tell from her spirit that she was an amazing little girl.

"Oh, I don't care. I still think you are the most handsome

man in the world. I can't believe that I am really meeting you. Wait until I tell my girlfriends! I love ice hockey, and all of my girlfriends in school love you. We all have your posters on our bedroom walls, too!"

I smiled at her and said, "Thank you for being a fan of mine and wearing my hockey sweater. May I ask why you are in casts? Did you have an accident? I hope you are healing fast."

Her smile faded a little, and she looked up at her father, as if she did not want to answer my questions.

Mr. Macklin intervened and explained on his daughter's behalf, "Allison was born with some birth defects, twenty-seven. She has never been able to walk. She had an experimental operation a few months ago, to try to put some rods in her legs, straighten them out, in hopes that she can walk on her own someday. It has been rough and a little painful. . .."

I felt my heart sink. I stumbled a bit for words, searching my heart for a few seconds, in order to say the correct thing to such a courageous little girl. Here I was a goalie, a fine-tuned athlete, a man who was able to ice skate better than most people could walk; I was now a professional hockey player, and I had to admit that I now took my abilities for granted.

This little girl just wanted to be able to walk.

It put it all in perspective for me.

I pulled the hair tie out of my sweaty hair, tossed it aside, leaned in closer to Allison and found some words from deep within my heart to say to her, "Oh, I see. Well, Allison, it is all going to be okay. You will walk. I can tell, because, well, I just can tell. Please, never, ever give up. I can tell you to dream as much as you can every day, because dreams do come true. A long time ago, I dreamt that I would be right here, in this place right now, playing hockey and winning a championship game. Do you know something? Here I am, living my dream. Please, listen to the doctors, listen to your parents, listen to your school teachers, always, no matter how many O'Malleys that you have to face, always stay positive, and never, ever, give up."

I reached out with my hands and she grasped my hands eagerly. While she smiled at me, I asked her, "Do you promise me that you will never give up?"

She had some tears forming now in the corners of her little eyes and she whispered to me, "I promise, twenty-seven. I promise that I will walk someday. Maybe even ice skate too!"

I let go of her hands, stood up, smiled and gently took her right hand while saying, "Of course you will. I am counting on it. You will not let me down now, eh?"

I then reached down into my leg pad and pulled out the old mask.

It was time . . . it had served me well. I tried very hard to convince myself, within a few meager seconds, that it was time for a new mask.

I would miss it, but right now, she needed the magic more than I did.

"Here, this is for you. I am sorry for the sweat and blood. You can wash it up. When it gets tough, and the pain comes along, or you want to give up and feel that you cannot go on, hold it in your hands, and believe with all of your heart that it will protect you. It will. I promise you that it will. Better yet, if it really becomes rough, then maybe even put it on. It has magical powers. Believe me. It really does."

"REALLY? I CAN HAVE YOUR GOALIE MASK?"

"It is yours. I am sorry, but I have to go now."

"THANK YOU!"

"No, thank you, Allison."

I handed her the old mask, shook hands with Mr. Macklin and turned to make my way towards the locker room.

Big Joe had been watching the scene unfold. He was waiting for me and he smiled, put his big arm around me and said, "You are friggin' amazing. You really do make all the saves, Paulie. You really do!"

"It was the right thing to do, Big Joe. Sometimes, ya got to be a pig, rather than a hen."

"Not sure what in Hell that exactly means, but I will take ya word for it, Paulie."

We made our way up the hallway and once more, I looked up into the crowd where my friends and family were still celebrating the victory. My life was about to change for a second time within a short period.

I stopped and stared as I noticed a young woman standing next to both Harry and another gal. I assumed the one gal was his date for the evening because Harry had his arm around her shoulders. Harry's date was a short-haired gal who looked Italian in her heritage. The Italian gal was not the object of my focus. The gal on the other side of Harry, however, caught my eye. She was stunning. She had long blonde hair and sparkling blue eyes that I could see, even from this far away.

Her figure was perfect, her features captivating. She was beyond gorgeous, and she astounded me.

I smiled and waved to her. She returned my gesture with a little wave. The beautiful woman gave me a little wave back and then she winked at me. I felt my knees wobble a bit, and I strained to capture another look at her just as Big Joe Starost picked me up and hustled me into the locker room.

Who was that woman? Ever since Renee left my life, this gal was the most beautiful woman that I have ever seen!

I gave a wave to dear Mum and the old man, and my teammates caught me up and pulled me along.

Still, I could not even imagine how such a beautiful woman could even exist.

"Hm, well, I do think that young Smithson has a future

career in medicine, but until then, next time, please wait for the actual doctor to arrive, Paulie," our team doctor said as he finished putting doctor approved stitches in my head and cleaning out the cut.

"Sure, doctor. Thank you."

"It is not going to be too large a scar there on that one. It will be red for a long time, but by the end of the year, it will blend with the other ones on your face. You are a good-looking guy, Paulie. You should invest in a better mask!" I laughed at the doctor's uniquely timed comments and continued the celebration. A little cut on my head bone and a new mask were the last things on my mind right now.

The team owner (who we never actually met!) bought out a local tavern near the rink, and the celebration was on in full swing. Coach Smithson told us to bring our friends and families, and the Henson and Redmond contingent alone packed the joint wall-to-wall.

Between beers, hugs, and celebrations, I managed to catch Harry one on one. He was strangely without company. The young Italian gal with the short hair did not accompany him, and I still had in the back of my mind the gorgeous blonde woman that I had spotted in the grandstands.

"Twenty-seven, that was the greatest game I ever have seen ya play, and I have seen a ton of 'em!" Harry gave me a bear hug, and he was smiling ear-to-ear. I never received the impression that Harry ever missed playing the game, even on a night, such as this one was because he was involved enough in the sport through me to still feel connected.

The terrible injury took more than just healing power away from the big guy. I am afraid it also took some of his hockey spirit because he was strangely content to be a spectator.

"Thanks, thirty-five. But you did miss that first game we played against the Bruisers."

Harry frowned at the memory.

"I have to say this feels good. We never won the Tremont Cup, but this sure makes up a little for those games. Say, Harry, ah, no twigeon with you? What happened to the pretty gal, with the short hair, who was at the game with you?"

"Nah, nah, nah, the gal I was with, she had to go to work. She wanted to come and meet you and the team, maybe some other time, ya know, when I can fit her in my schedule! She works in a store on a late shift, restocking the joint or doing inventory or some crazy shit like that. I like this gal! She is hot. She is like one of those Italian gals you see in the foreign movies. Say, Paul, get in there with Starost and let me snap a picture or two."

I posed with Big Joe, and Harry snapped away. "Just remember, Big Joe, ya are the third best defenseman twenty-seven has ever played with! Ole thirty-five is first, Jeff Porter is the second, and we will allow your sorry ass to hang out in third place!" Of course, Harry had to get a plug in for the Haledon Hockey League.

After the picture taking, I leaned in and asked Harry, "Thirty-five, do you know who the gorgeous blonde gal was that was sitting up next to you and the gang? I can't get her out of my mind. She was gorgeous."

Harry smiled, and he took a sip of his Wallcrawler.

"Oh, yeah! She is unreal. She is a friend of the gal that I am seeing. What a body on that gal! She is a bit unusual, but she is unreal. I think you caught her eye too, Paul."

The old man and Mum came over to join Harry and me. I lost my thoughts, and my mind drifted, as I greeted my parents.

Coach Smithson suddenly began shouting and tapping on a beer mug with a spoon to get our attention, while he shouted across the tavern, "Hey, now listen up! Listen up!" The coach was trying hard to quiet us down and catch our attention. "I just got word that our own number twenty-seven was not only named the most valuable player of the playoffs, but he also won the league MVP, and the damn Rookie of the Year title too!"

My teammates mobbed me, and Big Joe Starost doused me with a full mug of beer.

These were the times of your life which you never would forget. I would travel a long way from home, play for a few more teams, share more special moments, but I always considered myself a Long Island Rooster!

It was a special team, with special players and special memories that I will hold near and dear in my heart forever.

Little did I know there would be more celebrations, but none of them would ever exceed that extraordinary night in March 1979.

That year of 1979, dear reader, went on to include more events, incidents, and times than I can tell you in one story.

The many adventures of Harry and Paul reached a fever pitch during this year. It also marked the passing of a Redmond phase when they all hung up their cameras and moved from "photography phase" to "country and western phase."

This new phase, in which they all wore cowboy boots, hats, belt buckles and western garb, and tried hard to ditch northern New Jersey accents to speak with phony western accents, transformed our lives for a long time. I felt as if it would never pass over!

Yes, these were great times, roaring times, but some sad ones too.

My beloved English grandfather passed away a few weeks after we won the championship. He lived a very long life, and he meant more to me than any words could ever describe. He was a great influence on me, a tough guy from England, who always stood for what he believed in and taught me more than I realized at the time. He also passed along to me many traits, some of which Mum would proudly proclaim to be, "From her side of the family!"

I think the one trait that Gramps passed on to me that I valued more than any other value and became a huge part of my life was the love of reading. And I mean that together, we read everything, from newspapers, to books, to magazines, to the classics. All of this reading taught me more than all my formal education combined ever did.

My grandfather, well, he was the smartest man I ever met. He mostly taught himself, because in England during his youth, there was a big war raging and life was a bit difficult. Therefore, his education stopped at what we would call eighth-grade elementary school. It did not matter, by reading; he figured it all out himself. He gave me the classics to read when I was about ten years old or thereabouts. Dickens, Stevenson, Conan Doyle, Kipling, Fleming, the Bible—you know all the names and titles.

I read them all, and I never stopped reading.

Just before my hockey world took off, I had the bug to write a manuscript about one of the humorous adventures of Harry and Paul, and the crazy Redmond family. Gramps loved it and he let an English friend of his, who ran a bookstore and was a bit of a literary critic, read it too. They both encouraged me to keep on writing, and I vowed that someday that is what I would do.

I tucked it away for safekeeping. And now, dear reader, you are a part of those wild adventures too.

My grandfather was a cool guy, and I loved him with all of my heart.

That year of 1979, also brought the year in which I fell in love with a gal. Not an ordinary gal, but a gal who changed my life. Only my very brief romance with Renee Gorman had made me feel the same way that I felt around this woman. After Renee left me, I had lost hope of ever experiencing that intense amount of love with any other woman.

I was wrong. In this life, I learned that you could have many soul mates.

When I first met Binky Hobnobber, it did not go over so well. Our initial meeting was a bit rocky for the first few minutes. We smoothed out a little as the night went on, but at first, it was a bit rough.

It was not until many days later that I actually made the connection! Harry, with his revolving cast of young ladies, had captured me in the shuffle too. It was not until my memories became clearer that I realized Binky was the gorgeous gal I saw in the stands at the finish of the championship game.

You would have thought that Harry would have told me!

The long, love story of Binky Hobnobber and Paul John Henson is for another set of pages, but suffice it to say . . . that just when I felt something inside of my heart that pushed hockey to another place, a secondary place, then she left me. She took off to "find herself" and attend a university on the west coast. It was now a consistent pattern of rejection with all the women that I grew close to now in my life. I must admit that it became a bit difficult to handle.

At first, I brushed it off; I tried very hard not to let anyone know how deeply I loved her, and how her loss affected me.

However, her observation, "That we met too early in our lives, and that I was the kind of guy a woman wants to marry and not to date," hit me especially hard.

Harry had always warned me of the dreaded Old Lady Syndrome, as well as my tendency to be Mr. Nice Guy, and it turned out that he was correct.

Nice guys do finish last.

The realization of that as well as the impact of the loss of my girlfriend had changed me.

She had crushed my very soul.

As often as these types of emotional events tend to go in our lives, there was actually a productive byproduct to the emotional pain that I felt when Binky left my life. It actually was the final, missing piece of the puzzle, in which I required to reach the pinnacle of my hockey ability. The pain manifested a new attitude in number twenty-seven. My approach to goaltending became more vicious, more intense, and I became a goalie who attacked shooters rather than hang back in the net and allow the action to come to me. It gave me a chip with a hard edge for me to wear on my hockey sweater, and I liked it. No more Mr. Nice Guy!

I remember one of the first games the Roosters played after Binky had left me; there I was in the net, equipped with my new mask, a new set of goalie gloves, new leg pads and a different attitude. During the first period of a close contest, I even came skating out of the net, taunted O'Malley, dropped my gloves and challenged him to a fight. I would have beaten his ass silly, and O'Malley knew it, too. I was a big, powerful man, and you best not rile me up too much. My teammates, coaches, Harry, the old man and the guys from the shop, the fans, the game officials, and even O'Malley, were all shocked!

We were separated before we could battle, and I was assessed a two-minute penalty for delay of the game. The officials let me ride on the fact that I had left my goaltending crease, which should have been an automatic ejection for a game misconduct, but the point was that my new edge gave me what I needed to achieve my goal. Until Binky left, I was missing the aggression you needed to climb to the top, to challenge shooters, to dive into the melee in front of the net, the hard edge to do whatever was required, in order to win games.

I now had only one dream left in my heart, and that was to be a professional goaltender in the big league! It now gave me an outlet to hide the pain, the loneliness, and to release some of my bottled-up emotions. I could hide behind the mask, and no one could see who I really was. All they ever saw was number twenty-seven. When I played goal, Paul John Henson no longer existed. That is exactly the way that I wanted it to be. It gave me comfort to know that I could not be physically penetrated, hurt, or pushed around; I stood up to whatever an opponent could throw my way. As I had told Gordon Gurney, when you play the position of goaltender, you can be the good guy and the bad guy all in one, and that remained an intriguing aspect of the game for me.

However, off the ice, emotionally, it was a different story.

Halfway through the following year, the upper management of the Roosters lent me to a team in Kansas City, Missouri, called the Kansas City Hawks. The owner of the Roosters had an interest in that team and due to an injury to their starting goalie; they were in dire need of a goaltender. I was to be an emergency injury replacement, a short-term loan to the team, and my tenure there would be limited because of stringent league rules to prevent "ringers."

Higgins took over for me in goal for the Roosters, and from thereon, my life changed. I became a full-time professional ice hockey player; I left my full-time job and moved into a full-time life of game after game, with the bus, the train, and the plane rides and endless practice, gym workouts and training.

In Kansas City, I made more friends, contacts and connections. I had a new friend, a defenseman on the team, a Canadian prairie guy named Henry Jazkot. I always bonded most with the defensemen; they were my protectors, my allies in defense of the net. Hank was a great guy, and we established a connection that has lasted until this very day. I became somewhat of a celebrity, the hard, New Jersey accent, the story of a kid from the streets of New Jersey, the background, the long hair, the hippie lifestyle; it was becoming a bit overblown and pretentious.

I did radio, television, newspaper and magazine interviews and told the story of Geyer Street Gardens so many times that I became tired of hearing it. It was stupid media hype, and I did not enjoy being involved in all the madness. There was, however, no escape. The team required media interaction. This, after all, was all a business.

This league in the center of America was very good. The competition was a step up in abilities, and my skills developed more and more. My coaches and Mr. Austeri assured me a big contract with the Boston Bears loomed on the horizon for me.

They told me that I was on my way!

I returned to New Jersey early in the year of 1980 to wild celebrations with Harry and the Redmonds, along with many new surprises in my life. Harry had met a gal, a special gal, and the man who would never get married decided to settle down.

The world would never be the same.

As wonderful a year as 1979 was, I was about to learn that life was full of twists and turns, and it can change so quickly. You see, sometimes, a moment can change everything.

3

Life is Full of Twists and Turns

Harry married his dream woman, Sky Blu Redmond, in the spring of the next year, and his wild behavior and wayward ways became part of history.

A few weeks later, I signed a contract to play in Albany, New York, for a team within the Boston Bears organization called the Flying Dutchman.

The Flying Dutchman was the name of a ghostly ship in a legend about a ship that sails the oceans of the world forever, but can never make a port, or something like that! All I knew was that the logo on my new hockey sweater was very striking and I was continuing on my way up through the Bears organization.

How life had changed in the period of just a few short years!

I loved upstate New York, and it was my favorite place that I had ever lived. You would think that I would be happy, with a great team, many of my dreams coming true, big signing bonus money, a wonderful setting, tough league to play in and people telling me how I would shortly be the starting goaltender for the Boston Bears in the big time!

Somehow, the glory mixed in too often with too much pain. The memories of those good times, the simple times and of a lovely gal named Binky Hobnobber, never left me.

Now, my fate was sealed. The famous team of Harry and Paul no longer existed. He had a wife now, his own life, and I had mine. My dream to play professionally had come to fruition, and we both moved on with our lives.

On the other hand, so I thought.

Sky Blu Redmond passed away in December 1980, of a horrible disease that tragically took a lovely, gorgeous woman way too soon.

It tore our lives apart. Harry fled in grief a few days after his wife passed away, and there was nothing that I could do to stop him. He had to leave it all behind because the ghosts were too powerful.

I was beginning to feel the same way.

For the first time since I was around ten years of age, I no longer had Harry to speak with, to lean on, and to enjoy wild adventures with, and it was all very disturbing to my mind and to my spirit. These horrible events created incredible loneliness in my life, which at times, I felt as if it would tear me apart. I could not wait to get back into the net to forget it all, to hide once more behind my mask. To make the saves in the game, the saves, which I could not make in real life.

I felt as if there was a void in my life now that would never close again. First Maureen left, then Renee, and then Binky was gone. The tragic culmination was when Sky Blu passed away, and of course, now Harry was gone too.

That season, despite all the personal turmoil, I played well in goal for the Albany team. We won a league championship that season; I won the league's MVP award, and I moved on, rather reluctantly, to the next step up in the system. I was now one-step from the big league and was now the starting goaltender for a team in Norfolk, Virginia.

The Norfolk Navigators.

I took with me from Albany, more fond memories, more wonderful people. My coach there was a man who I particularly enjoyed playing for and he and I continued to be friends all of our lives.

I did not want to leave. I could have been happy there

forever in Albany, New York.

During my time with this hockey club, I had encountered a peculiar incident. A strange event, in which I had no proper explanation for then, and even now. It was an incident in an old Irish public house in New Hampshire after a road game, with a strange man who predicted that I would go off in another direction in my life. He indicated to me, in a roundabout manner, that hockey was a temporary career and that my true destiny was off in an entirely different direction. The evening, and his words, haunted me. It was so peculiar, this stranger telling me that hockey might not be what I was supposed to be doing with my life, and his prediction bothered me terribly.

I ended up in Norfolk, and let me tell you, it was not my favorite place. It was hot, sticky, and generally nasty. The mosquitoes were as if they were tiny helicopters flying around. This hockey circuit was unusual; it did not seem as if it was even a hockey environment. Even the fans and media were not the same. These were not avid hockey towns and cities, filled with screaming fanatical hockey fans waving banners, cheering, wild team chants and dumping stale beer or tossing half-eaten hot dogs on the visiting team's players. These towns and cities seemed as if they were primarily baseball and football fans, and hockey was more of a novelty sport.

Off I went, on more train and bus rides, a few airplane rides, lonely apartments, and musty hotel rooms. The nights after games, we filled up with meals and beer in stale gin joints, where "lounge lizard" women prowled and pursued professional hockey players hoping to make your acquaintance for dubious reasons.

I steered clear of those meetings; nothing but trouble written all over them!

I met an entirely new collection of want-to-be hockey goons, suffered more cuts, stitches, assorted injuries and the games all rolled on into one another.

It seemed as if I never had a place to call home.

The apartment there in Norfolk was small and cramped, and let me tell you, I was, and still am, the world's worst cook. I could handle spaghetti, I could make scrambled eggs and toast, and after that, it was brutal, and usually not even close to being edible. You can only eat so much pizza, or eat in so many restaurants. After that, your very soul cries out for a home-cooked meal!

This was now a grind, as all jobs are. The sheer grit and intensity that you required were remarkable. You required mental toughness; you had to possess physical toughness; you had to take care of your body and work out constantly, or you could suffer some serious injuries.

It was not as if I had not suffered some injuries over my many years of playing. No, that certainly was not the case, all the way from my first stitches sewn in my head from good old Dr. Salami, to my mum's first aid, to my old man's stitching attempts; to my treatments now with excellent athletic trainers and doctors, it was just that I had yet to suffer a *serious* injury. I had come along a difficult route, a long route to arrive where I currently was. I was an American in a sport dominated by Canadians; I was a former street and roller player, and I had many, many games on my pads. Most players at this point had played in a quarter of the number of games that I had played in; they did not have to navigate such a long road to reach where we all currently were. That long road was now taking a toll on me.

Let's see, several broken toes, every single one of my fingers broken at least once. My pinky finger on my catching glove hand shattered and reconstructed with cadaver bones in the off-season, and my real bugbear—persistent groin pulls and tears in my groin muscles from constant split saves and over stretching of the muscles.

By my best count, (unofficial, I had run out of room on my new mask for those marker stitches) I had over two hundred stitches in my head alone. This count included a recent injury that required thirty-five more in my upper lip, when a shot through a screen hit me in my mask and drove my front choppers clean through my upper lip. When the doctors repaired that damage, it was the first time that I had been clean-shaven since I was fourteen years old! I was missing a few choppers, but they were in the back of my mouth and not a big priority right now. I could do without the floating bone chips in my right elbow, which the doctors told me that it was just not worth cleaning the chips out or operating on my elbow, until someday, I hung up the skates.

The constant impact of various parts of my body falling upon the ice tended to "loosen" my parts! The bones on my legs had taken a beating over the years, too. If you would run your fingers along the front edge of them, they felt as if they were old wooden logs, with some chunks carved out of them. And the list could go on and on and I was a fortunate player. There were players on my team with a longer list of injuries than mine!

Oh well, injuries are a part of the game.

The endless monotony wore you down too. It grew quite tedious. All the rinks and cities started to look the same. Nothing was bright, or shiny, or new any longer.

My dream became a grind.

The competition level here kept me sharp; the skaters were by far the most highly skilled that I had ever seen. The abilities were all elevated; it was easy to see that at this level; most players could easily make the jump to their parent teams in the big league. At this point in our careers, a chance at the big league was just a matter of some roster slots opening.

"The word is to keep your bags packed there, Henson. Next week could be when the call comes in. The general manager from Boston was here the other day watching our game with Memphis, and they feel it might be a good time to move you up, and let you backup Henderson there for a time, before getting a start or two. How do you feel, Paulie?" My head coach, a man named Jimmy Wheeler, sat down on the bench next to me in the locker room as he provided me with the latest information from the parent club.

He spoke to me while I dressed for the game this evening, and I carefully listened to Coach Wheeler update me on the latest news while I tried hard to focus on the upcoming game. For the last few weeks or so, the rumor mill had been churning with my pending call-up to Boston, and although I did expect the news any day now, I still felt a tingle go up and down my spine.

I was so close now that I could feel it!

"I feel good, Coach Wheeler. Really good. A little soreness in my left shoulder from that ding from the other night, but. . .."

"You know, Henson, you are friggin' amazing! I don't think I ever met someone who thinks more about hockey than you do! I do not mean how you feel physically. I mean, how the hell do you feel about a call up to the big league? I swear, all goalies are weird and eccentric, but you, my long-haired hippie friend, you take the cake."

"Oh, sorry coach, yeah, yeah, yeah, it is very exciting! I am good," I chuckled a little, and Coach Wheeler looked at me suspiciously.

"I hope so, Henson. You are the best goalie that I have ever seen. You seem so distant at times, Paulie. As if you have a different direction that you are leaning in or something else on your mind all the time."

Maybe.

I reached down into my thermal suit under my goalie pants, and felt the back pocket of my pants, to make sure the silver cross was still there.

It remained there, still tucked in those same, now very worn and tattered, cloths.

"Nah, nah, nah, I am, good coach. Really good." I finished dressing, and I paced alone in the locker room, thinking about the game, my moves, and my strategy. I reached into my equipment bag and pulled out my usual pregame snack of a banana. As I paced and chomped on the fruit, I swore I looked up to see Harry sitting on the edge of the bench, watching and laughing at me.

"You are a weird one, twenty-seven. Geez, man, there is no manly way for a guy to eat a damn banana! Can't ya switch to oranges or tangerines?"

I smiled at his ghost.

The coach was quite perceptive in his observation of his starting goalie. As of late, I had become a bit preoccupied with something other than hockey. I had to admit that the game had become to me, "Just a job."

A way to make a living that was indeed what hockey had become for me.

Recently, I went back to reading.

I went back to writing.

At first, it was out of sheer loneliness, an escape, a means to reconnect with my memories, a way to chase away the ghosts and spirits of the past that haunted me everywhere I went. However, they always returned, and when I put down some of the other books and picked up my Bible, I felt some type of reassurance, some type of motivation that there was indeed a plan, so much more than what I had initially realized.

Sky Blu's tragic death changed me in many ways, but one way, in which it had changed me for the better, was to allow me to see that there was a spiritual plan for all of us, right there in front of our eyes.

At first, I read the Bible to pass time, then I read it to learn, then I read it, to fulfill my spirit.

After Sky's death, and because of certain changes in my soul, I never read the Bible to entertain myself. I frown even to this day upon religious music, teachings, worship services and readings, which entertain us. I do not think God's plan for worship should be entertaining; we should be humbled and molded, but not necessarily entertained per se. I am not ashamed to say that I had at the time, and still do, to a great extent, have a problem fitting in within the man-made confines, rules and regulations of organized religion. Considering the profession that I chose later in my life, that is a somewhat bizarre and profound statement.

Once humankind becomes involved, they sure can foul things up.

It was late in the second period; we were in our home arena in Norfolk, struggling to hold off a poorly playing hockey club from Charlotte, North Carolina, and cling to a two-goal lead.

The Norfolk Navigators were not too swift a hockey club, but we did have a smattering of a home fan base, with a small, but somewhat loyal following with military families from the nearby naval base.

It was not anything like hockey up north was.

I do suppose that some of the lack of fans was because our team was not very good. We were very good offensively, but the team was awful on defense.

It was the one team in which I ever played for that I felt no actual connection to. Not with the players, or the area, the coaches, or the fans. It was not that I was aloof with anyone, I always was polite, and actually had another fan base, albeit small, but it was complete with wild wigs once again promoting my long-haired status. My emotions and lack of connection were a little hard for me to describe, but it was as if I was just passing through here to who knows where.

Our game plan consisted of outscoring the other team, not in playing any kind of actual defense! Right now, we fought day-to-day with this Carolina team to see which team would occupy the last place in our division.

I did not mind. I usually faced at least fifty shots on goal in each game and the number of shots all kept me loose, sharp, intense and they helped to prevent my mind from drifting too much.

Early in the first period of the game, a routine shot came my way. I made the classic mistake of steering a routine stick save into my own corner, and it bothered me as soon as I did it.

I could hear the echo of the entire collective group of all of my coaches that I had ever played for, going all the way back to Ray Edelski, screaming at me, "Clear the zone, twenty-seven! Never throw the puck in your own corner! At least put the puck behind the net!"

It was a lazy error because when the puck is behind the net, at least the opposition has to capture the puck and bring it to the front of the net, in order to have a scoring opportunity. When the puck is in the corner, the puck is already halfway home.

Sure enough, the opposition center beat our defenseman to the puck and my stupid error had unwittingly unleashed sheer chaos. He tossed the puck in front of the net, where a mad scramble ensued. I made one wild split save, and the puck licked off my skate blade and then it rolled straight out in front of the net. I then reached to glove the puck; however, it was out of my reach and I missed it.

A defenseman fell down in the crease, and the puck dribbled to the low slot where a Carolina player shot it high and hard. I made that save too, and as I gloved it off my chest protector, an opposition player crashed into the side of my lower right leg, while my own defenseman hit into the same leg from the soft spot behind my kneecap. The human leg does not bend both ways like that, at least not easily, and even with heavy leg pads on, the powerful push from behind my leg, caused a loud, audible, and somewhat sickening, "pop" to be heard from my right knee.

I held the puck in my catching glove, and after the

players finished crashing into me, we all fell into a large heap in the crease. The referee came in, blowing the whistle, and the pain shooting up and down my leg caused me to cry out.

"Get up! Get up off my leg, please!"

I knew that something was seriously wrong with my right knee. I had never felt pain like anything I was now experiencing. I rolled around on the ice, and one of my defensemen stood up and immediately waved for the trainers to come off the bench.

Everyone heard the disgusting popping noise and heard me crying out, too.

At first, the small home crowd did not realize that I was injured, and they chanted in appreciation of my saves at the top of their lungs, "Twenty-seven! Twenty-seven! Twenty-seven!"

The chants stopped when the crowd realized that I was not getting off the ice and the trainers were rushing out to assist me.

I tried to stand up; the trainer put his hand on my shoulders and held me down while telling me, "Stay down, twenty-seven. Just lie back and relax."

It was very strange, but I could not control my lower leg. I did not think my leg was broken. It felt as if my knee was an uncontrollable hinge of some sort, with terrible pain shooting all over my leg. When I did lie back on the ice, the trainers carefully took my goalie leg pad off, and they carefully moved my knee and lower leg. The head trainer shook his head as the pain caused me to scream out, and I tried to stop them from moving it.

"Ligaments, Paulie, all the ligaments are blown," was all that the head trainer said.

"What do you mean? Let me get up and skate it off. I can skate this off. I have skated off worse shit than this. Once they even stitched me up with a needle they used on my socks. Let me the hell up!"

Old war stories.

He shook his head and said, "No, you can't get up, Paulie. You are a tough son of a bitch, but this goes beyond being tough. You have torn all the ligaments in your right knee. The reverse impacts twisted your knee like a pretzel and popped all the soft tissue. You will not be able to control your knee and it will cause even more damage. We are putting a soft cast on this to hold your leg in place. Then we will get you up and to the hospital."

It was stunning; I had only missed one period of a game in my entire career, when I broke some toes on my foot while playing in Albany. That was also the horrible time when Sky Blu passed away.

"No! Get me up. I am going to skate it off. I am going to the Boston Bears next week. I, please, I need to get the hell up."

"Twenty-seven, stop! You ain't gonna be able to stand or move. There aren't any intact ligaments left in your knee to connect the bones. You are going to need an operation."

When I heard the words, "You are going to need an operation," then I knew in my heart that the dream was dead.

From there on in, it was all a blur. The trainers put some type of cloth brace on my knee; they helped me to my skates; my teammates supported me under my shoulders as the opposition players and the crowd cheered for me while I left the ice. I remembered a ride in an ambulance and some pain medication going into my arm, and that was about all.

It all became a haze, a blur in my mind's eye, a nightmare of irony that seemed too unreal to rationalize.

The doctors confirmed the injury in the local hospital, but the team management of the Boston Bears consulted with their team doctor for my final treatment. They had a large amount of money invested in me at this point! The team doctor in Boston asked the Norfolk medical team to bring me to the Bears orthopedic specialist for the operation. The doctor worked out of a renowned hospital in Boston, and his reputation for his outstanding surgical skill level was well known.

I called my parents, and they were horrified. The old man insisted on making the trip to the hospital in Boston for the operation. I told them to stay in New Jersey. Not only did I not want any visitors but also, there really was nothing that anyone could do.

I recalled Harry's words of so long ago, "Stay! What the hell ya gonna do at the hospital, sew my ass up?"

Nothing against my parents. I love them both dearly, but I had been alone for so long on the road that I was more comfortable being alone.

My life was better when it was just the ghosts and me.

The plane ride to Boston was the longest plane ride that I had ever experienced. It was brutally long, and the Bears had to purchase two seats in an exit row to provide me with more legroom, because of my leg captured in a cumbersome cast. Walking was a chore, sitting was a pain, swallowing pain pills sucked, the plane rides and taxi rides were an adventure, all of it was damn misery.

I sat in a hospital bed in a hospital in downtown Boston.

I stared out the window and watched a mixture of rain and snow pelt the glass. It looked cold, drab, and dreary out there.

An utterly bleak horizon.

The door to my room swung open, and a doctor walked in. He held a metal clipboard in his hand and some papers in his other. He glanced at the papers while he stood next to the hospital bed, then he took his eyeglasses off and perched them atop of his head. He was bald, short, maybe in his mid-fifties or so. I could tell he had a gentle demeanor because he had a kind smile.

"Hello, Paul. I am Doctor Dennis O'Brien. I am the head orthopedic surgeon for the Boston Bears. The nurses will be in here shortly to prepare you for the operation, but I wanted to sit with you for a minute and explain some things to you. Do you mind?"

Doctor O'Brien looked towards a guest chair positioned next to the bed and then back towards me. I forced a weak smile and nodded as the doctor sat down.

"Hi ya there, Doctor O'Brien. Most people, they call me twenty-seven, or Paulie. Not too many people call me, Paul. Only some very special people call me by my real name. Those special people, I trust, but I guess that I damn sure have to trust you right now."

"Okay, gotcha. I hope you trust me, but until I gain that trust, I understand. I will refrain from shaking your hand, number twenty-seven. The coaches and players warned me how strong you are, and I earn a very good living with my hands." He smiled at me and once again, I weakly smiled back, but I did not answer him.

The doctor sensed my sadness, and he leaned in a little closer and said, "Look, Paulie, I will be very honest with you and frank, too. You are a goalie, you have to be a little crazy to do what you do, but seriously, I know that you are a very tough young man. I have watched the films of you, and above all, I am a hockey fan, too."

"Thank you, doc. The truth is what I need. I am not a real fan of sugar-coating shit at this point."

"I understand," Doctor O'Brien said, as he leaned back in the chair and he relaxed. It was obvious that he was working very hard to put me at ease.

"Twenty-seven, I have to tell you that this is a serious operation for a professional athlete. You have torn both the anterior cruciate ligament and the medial collateral ligament from the bones in your right knee. It is a grade three injury, which is the worse of its kind. It is a difficult operation. I have to open your knee wide open and reattach everything. To come back from this is a tough one. It is not unheard of, but a long road back with painful rehabilitation and hard work. I have some goals here. My first goal here in this operation, is to allow you to walk uninhibited and normally for the rest of your life, and my second goal, is to try to protect the investment that the Boston Bears hockey club has made here in a spectacularly talented, young goaltender named, Paul John Henson."

"Understood. Thank you for the compliment, Doctor O'Brien. Please, let me tell you that I am prepared to do whatever it takes to make it back to the game."

Doctor O'Brien cut me off and said rather abruptly, "Paulie, you are looking at a full year's worth of brutal rehabilitation here. You will not be able to even skate for four months. I want to be honest with you here, son."

I did not cry easy, in fact, I had only cried once in the last twenty years or so. It was when Harry told me he was leaving and taking off to who knows where. I stood in the street in front of the house that he and Sky Blu lived in and watched through a rain of tears; the taillights of his van disappear into the night.

That horrible incident was too much to take, and this was shaping up to be a close second.

The tears welled up in my eyes, and I spoke up just above a whisper, "In a year or so, it might be too late, doc. I do not have a year to take off. You know how quickly they replace you these days."

Doctor O'Brien stood up and he placed his hand on my arm. I was correct in my assessment of him. I always had the ability to judge people as to their character by looking at their eyes and face, and I had been correct in my initial judgment of Doctor Dennis O'Brien.

"Twenty-seven, I know this situation sucks big time. However, I have to tell you that you have paid your dues. Looking at your medical chart, the list of your injuries is as long as if it is an eight-year-old kid's Christmas wish list. It goes on forever. Everyone has read about, or heard the remarkable story of, the kid from New Jersey who was a street hockey player, from a gritty, tough neighborhood and made it this far. If you make it back, then that is great, wonderful. In fact, maybe it makes me the greatest sports surgeon in the country, and I ride it to a fortune operating on torn up knees. Good for me and good for you, too. Because, if you make it back, there is no doubt in anyone's mind that knows the sport of hockey, your ass will be in the Hockey Hall of Fame. No doubt."

He laughed, and I managed a chuckle too, while I wiped my eyes. I was slightly embarrassed at my display of tears.

Doctor O'Brien pointed his finger at me and became serious as he spoke, "However, if you don't . . . then you have nothing to be ashamed of, Paulie. You will still be number twenty-seven. No one can ever take that from you. Ever. A legend in the ranks. What? The most valuable player multiple times, some championships. What is there to be ashamed of, twenty-seven? Life is full of twists and turns, and who actually knows what your destiny is, or what your future holds? You are young, with a lot of living ahead of you."

He now gripped my shoulder tightly while saying, "At one time or another in our lives, we all feel as if we have lived an unfulfilled destiny. The truth is, however, that when you stop and examine your life, it is exactly quite the opposite. If you did the best that you could, treated people with respect and gained the respect of others, played the game fair and hard, then you have fulfilled more than you can ever imagine."

He smiled at me; he patted me gently on the arm as he picked up his clipboard and papers and turned to walk away from me.

"I will see you in the operating room, twenty-seven. You are not the only one who specializes in saves, you know."

I gently grabbed his arm and said, "Doc, hey, thanks. Please, *you* may call me, Paul. I trust you and know that you will do the best that you can. Thank you."

He smiled at me, gripped my arm tightly, then Doctor O'Brien let go and I watched as he left the room.

Deep from within the recess of my memories, it all came rushing back to me. The strange words that the unusual stranger spoke to me outside that Irish pub in Concord, New Hampshire echoed in my head once again. In that strange encounter, a complete stranger who I had no idea who he was, and never met before, told me that, "Sometimes the direction you think you are going is not really where you will end up."

I smiled, and suddenly I relaxed, as I knew there might just be a lot more here than just a hockey career. Perhaps there was a deeper meaning to all of this and what I perceived to be a cruel blow in my life was actually part of a plan, a purpose.

Doctor O'Brien was indeed correct.

Life is full of twists and turns.

4

You Can Never Go Back

The operation was a major success. I had my knee restored to full operation and motion, and within seven months, I was back on the ice and skating. The trainers and therapists had all been impressed with my dedication and the fact that I was ahead of schedule was a credit for their inspiration and my own hard work.

A major factor in my success was that I was in prime physical condition at the time of the injury, but nonetheless, it had been a long and painful road back. Doctor O'Brien had pulled no punches or fudged the rehabilitation process at all. It was painful; it was long, and it was hard work.

Once the doctors cleared me to resume play, the Boston Bears assigned me for a rehabilitation stint. There I was, playing for an obscure minor league team in western Pennsylvania. The team played in a league that I never heard of, in an old coal town or city that I did not care to be in, and in a dark, dingy, and horrible old hockey rink for a home arena that brought me nothing but bad vibrations and memories.

While my knee had fully healed, something was missing. I was slow in the net; my knee did not move quickly enough, and my reflexes were not sharp enough.

It was not a physical problem; no, it was much deeper than physical.

The trouble was in my spirit, in my heart.

The dream was dead.

I knew the end had come. The coaches knew it too, and when it came time to make the fateful decision, I knew in my heart that we all were making the correct choice. The management of the Boston Bears was straight up with me, as they always had been, and offered a full buyout on the remainder of my contract to dump me off the rosters and their books.

They gave me a generous offer. I also collected a nice sum on some insurance I had taken years earlier for a potential injury.

Number twenty seven had earned a large sum of money in actual salary, more money than I ever dreamed I could earn. It was such a long way from lugging refrigerators to earn a few extra bucks.

In addition, I never spent a dime of my bonus money throughout my career, lived rather frugally, still drove that same old jeep and banked all of my money under the watchful eye of dear Mum.

Mum turned out to be quite the wise investor, and I had quite a tidy sum of money in the bank! On that money alone, I could live very easily for the rest of my life. I did not retire to a life of ease, by any means, oh no, quite the opposite.

I had full intentions of returning to upstate New York. In my mind, I had a few options. Perhaps I would go into coaching with the Flying Dutchman and rejoin the hockey world or take a full-time job and simply return to the semi-professional ranks in order to obtain my hockey fix.

I could still play on a lower level. I knew that I could.

I might even be interested in taking a radio or television job as a color commentator during hockey game broadcasts. I had some general inquiries already, with some probing about my interest in such a career. After all, I could try hard and recall Gramp's efforts at lessons in "Proper King's English!" On the other hand, I could keep my hard Jersey accent and it would be so unique.

No, for reasons that became much clearer later on, I returned to the old neighborhood and, well, once again, it is a whole, long story, but you know how I began to read that old Bible that Gramps once owned?

Well, I became a Lutheran pastor.

Yeah, yeah, yeah, I know. It was quite the career change.

In addition, that gorgeous gal named Binky Hobnobber who took off on me, well, she returned and I married her this time around!

And that crazy, wild number thirty-five? Old Harry M. Redmond Junior, he returned too, and we are still the greatest of friends to this day. Ah shit, who the hell am I kidding? We are brothers.

Oh, and one more thing, Jim O'Malley, well, he also entered the ministry! He renounced his former evil ways; I guess we really did have more in common than what we had realized.

Yeah, yeah, yeah, life is full of twists and turns, but dear reader; those stories, I promise that I will leave for pages and pages down the road some other time.

They say you can never go back or that you never should. I disagree; I do it all the time. I always have, and I always will.

My dear wife, Binky, had tried for so long to purge the memory of number twenty-seven from my mind, but she still allowed me to go back occasionally and not to forget. She had done an exceptional job of helping me to move on and embrace the new life and career that I had chosen. She had a wonderful oil portrait painted of me, a portrait that together, we hung in my pastor's office at the church where I was serving as the head pastor. It was a portrait, depicting my many careers, with number twenty-seven crouched in a classic goaltending pose in front of the net, superimposed upon a backdrop of me preaching at the pulpit and repairing an electrical panel. She baked cakes commemorating my first game, and she hung a framed picture containing my number twenty-seven jersey under glass in our living room in the parsonage.

I felt that I had moved on.

I had given it all I had, traveled farther than a poor kid could ever have imagined, met more people than I could even try to remember. I achieved more success than I ever dreamed that I could; I was interviewed on television and radio and even been featured on the cover of a hockey magazine. They were all fabulous memories, and my life now was wonderful. We had amazing and beautiful children; I had a wonderful, gorgeous, caring wife whom I loved more than life itself, a wonderful career serving God and my church, great friends, the entire package of joy all wrapped together.

I was indeed a lucky man.

Binky knew better, though.

She sensed the turmoil deep in my soul, and she wanted more than she would say for me to seek closure. She loved me and she supported me, yet she knew me better than anyone ever could.

Even more than my own dear mum could.

You see, she could tell by the look in my eyes when I watched a hockey game on the television, or by the way that I moved in the chair when the goalie made a save, when the tears that I would try very hard to hide from my wife would come. Or, when I came across a picture, or a trophy, or an old piece of my hockey equipment that I found in a box tucked in the corner of a closet.

I could never hide my eyes from my dear Binky.

Despite all the efforts, there was one more thing I just had to do, in order to close the book forever on number twenty-seven.

I walked up the road, and it loomed in front of me.

Full of potholes, full of cracks, and strewn with trash, broken beer and soda bottles, and urban grit, Geyer Street Gardens was there, right in front of me. I ran the rest of the way and stood where I thought the net would have been. I spun and turned and tried as hard as I could to find my bearings.

Nothing, to me, looked the same. You see, the street had all changed.

The dead-end was still in front of me. It still ended in a factory, although I am not sure exactly what business they might have been involved in now. The rich guy's garages they were now all gone. They had mowed them all over and replaced them with dirt and stones. Or maybe, the garages had burned down.

The lip lady's house still stood. It was vacant, boarded up, and abandoned, but it still was there.

It was so sad, such a shame, how urban decay sets in.

Then as I stood there, the tears came, and they rained down upon my cheeks, dripped off the edges of my face, and fell upon the asphalt of Geyer Street Gardens.

The sounds of a hockey game returned, and the ghosts came alive before my eyes. There they all were. Big George, Big Wex, and Jeff Porter with his hat on backwards. Jeff was blocking shots and sliding on his pads! There was Harry and Handsome Mike the Italian kid! Ray Edelski pointed out the defense and called for a play, and Johnny the Cho put the puck in the net! Pooch stood on the sideline, waiting eagerly for his turn, and Tags encouraged him with a pat on the backside.

"You will get in someday, Pooch. Honest you will," Tags told him.

The lip lady appeared in the front yard; she shook her fist at us and warned us to stop ruining her fence! In the meantime, she secretly snuck back onto her porch to watch the action.

They were all there, even a long-haired kid, with the

number twenty-seven and the name of HENSON, written with a black marker, on the back of a sweatshirt with an old quilt sewn inside of it.

Yes, they were all still there!

They were just as I was.

They, too, had never left.

I had traveled far and wide, and had come within a few days of the big time, but in reality, I never left Geyer Street Gardens. It was what made me who I was, and what I dreamed that I could be. It was a part of me. A group of teenagers turned from boys to men here and we learned that with teamwork, hard work and heartfelt desire that you could achieve almost anything that you set your mind out to do.

Some people would look and see an old, dead-end street, but to a group of young boys who grew into men here, it was anything but that because to us; it was actually a hockey rink full of joy and memories.

It was indeed sacred ground.

A shrine.

I walked over to the lip lady's fence and lined up as best that my mind could remember, exactly where the net would have sat upon the goal line. I reached in my back pocket and carefully took out the old cloths. Carefully and respectfully, I took the silver cross out of the folds of the cloths. I held it in my hand for a long, long time. I then reached over a post on the fence and carefully hung the cross over the top of the post.

"Hey, buddy! This is not exactly the kinda neighborhood to be wandering around in, ya know!"

I spun around a little; I was startled at the sound of a voice. I had not even noticed that a truck had pulled into the dead-end and that the driver was hanging out the window of the truck yelling out a warning to me. You would have thought that I would have heard his truck come up the road.

"Oh yeah, thanks! I will be fine. I know exactly where I am. In fact, I know it better than you might realize."

The driver seemed puzzled, and he said, "Well, okay, but many people get hurt while wandering around here! They cut you up and mug ya around here."

Well, I do know about the cut part.

"Especially well-dressed people like you are, with fancy cameras around their necks, and who look like they do not belong here."

I smiled and stood up straight. Now, that particular statement, I was going to dispute.

"Oh, I belong here all right. Been here longer than most anyone who comes around. In fact, I have never left."

You could tell by the look on his face that the driver was now clearly puzzled. He reached for his gearshift and put the truck into gear.

He must have figured that I was a nutcase.

His eyes caught the cross I had hung on the post and said, "That will not be there too long. I do not know why ya hung it there, but someone is going to take it."

"That is exactly why I hung it there. You see, my friend, I no longer need it. It now signifies a buried memory."

He smiled, waved and yelled out the window, as his truck started to move, "Okay, pal. Be careful and don't say that I didn't warn ya. Hey, good luck, you might need it. After all, Geyer Street is just an old, dead-end street, full of troubles and potholes!"

I mumbled, "Not a marble, twenty-seven. Not a marble can roll by you."

I then waved to him while he pulled his truck away and said to myself, "No sir, you are wrong. It is not just an old, dead-end street. It is actually sacred ground. By the way, the name of this street, well, it is actually called Geyer Street Gardens."

THE END

Epilogue

"Dear, Father! Please do not cry! We all love you. We do not want you to be sad!" Heather Sarah jumped up from the floor and squeezed in next to me on the sofa. It was quite the crowd on the sofa now!

I looked up, placed my beer mug on the end table next to me and realized that there were indeed some very rare tears forming in the corners of my eyes.

I felt foolish.

The storytelling had caught me in my own emotions.

My family and friends surrounded me and gathered around. They all realized that this story had hit a nerve with me and unleashed a mountain of memories for me.

"Oh, geez. I am very sorry, everyone. My . . . I went on a bit too long. The ghost of number twenty-seven chased me into a corner. I do apologize."

"For what, Paul?" Harry asked and smiled at me.

He had stood up from the sofa and walked over in front of me. He, too, had tears in his eyes. While I looked around the room at everyone, I noticed that all of us had tears in their eyes and were crying a bit.

I guess I hit a nerve with everyone tonight.

The big guy came over. He held out his hand and I shook it.

"You are the world famous, number twenty-seven. You always will be. Not a marble, twenty-seven. Not a marble can roll by you," Harry said with a smile.

I smiled back and said, "I guess, thirty-five. I guess. You know, sometimes the direction you think you are going is not really where you will end up."

Harry nodded in agreement as Rose came over, hugged him, gave him a kiss, and Blue Cloud joined her father and mother in a group hug. Cocoa Two came over and barked, and then he smiled at me, too. I guess even in his old age, he heard enough to enjoy the story, too.

My dear Binky came over. She gave me a kiss on the cheek, and she wrapped her arms around my neck, while she hugged me tightly. Paul William joined his sister on the sofa, and my two children and my lovely wife scrambled to find enough room to all fit next to me.

"We have a little surprise for you today. I guess it might be a late Boxing Day present. Here, this box came in the mail today for you, twenty-seven," Binky reached over behind the sofa and she handed me a medium-sized box with a shipping label that clearly had an address made out to number, "Twenty-seven."

I studied the label and read it aloud to my family and friends, "To the great number, twenty-seven, in care of Reunion Lutheran Church." I looked up at everyone and asked, "Oh my goodness, what have you all been up to?"

I then studied the label a little more carefully and saw that the return-address was from Ms. A. Collingsworth with an address in New York. The name meant nothing to me.

"I can assure you that none of us sent it, Paul," Binky said as she motioned for me to open it. Everyone was now anxious, and I could tell from their faces that they might not have sent the package, but they somehow knew what was inside.

They were all eerily quiet, even Harry.

I shrugged my shoulders. Binky handed me a pair of scissors and I cut into the tape. The gang all leaned in to watch me open the box. It was all so mysterious.

I opened the flaps to the box, tossed the packing material out of the way, stuck my hands down inside the box, and as soon as my hands hit the item buried down inside of the box, I knew what it was. I had felt it so many times before in my life that the feel of it was something that I could never forget. Ever!

I didn't even have to lift it out of the box to know that my hands were holding my old goalie mask!

I lifted it from the box to screams of joy from everyone and a few loud barks from Cocoa Two.

I felt as if my heart was going to stop. I held it in my hands, turned it over, studied the marker scars, the straps, the memories, it was as if a piece of me had returned, a void inside of me refilled, and despite my best efforts to resist the emotional wave that was overwhelming me, the tears, rained down again.

Binky put her arm around me and held me tightly while I buried my face in her chest and sobbed.

She whispered, "Allison called a few days before Christmas and asked to confirm that Pastor Paul John Henson was actually *the* number twenty-seven. She said that there would be a letter in there too."

After a few minutes of comfort, I recovered, now really feeling quite foolish at my behavior, nodded my head and picked the box back up.

Why did this affect me so badly? It was just an old goalie mask, full of marks, nicks, and black marker scars.

It was more than thirty years old now.

My goodness, such emotional behavior from the man who usually holds his emotions inside. I imagined that I had kept it all bottled up inside of me for a long, long time.

Too long.

I pulled out the letter, composed myself and read it aloud,

"Dear Twenty-seven,

I wanted to return this to you for many reasons, but most of all, because I no longer need it. You see, it has magical powers. It is now time that I returned it to you, in order for you to give it to someone else who might need it more than I do now.

I want you to know how much it has meant to me. It was just as you said, when the pain became too much, and I wanted to give up. I took that mask and stole some of its magic. It protected me and gave me something to believe in when my life was so difficult.

I always did exactly what you told me to do. I kept dreaming. I never gave up, stayed positive, and when I faced my O'Malley, the magical mask helped me to defeat him.

My operation was a success. It was a long road, a hard road, but I can now walk, run, jump, and yes, even ice skate. To top it all off, I am now married too!

In November, I gave birth to my first child and that, along with me being able to walk, are the two greatest miracles in my life. I will be able to play, walk, swim, ice skate and run with my little girl. I can do all of these things now, just as normally as any other mother could, because of the magic.

It does not surprise me that you are a minister now. The kindness in your heart is something that I will never forget. You might be a minister now, but in my heart, you will always be the great number twenty-seven.

Please never forget that the kind gesture you performed for a disabled, ten-year-old girl with stars in her eyes at meeting her handsome hero changed my life forever. You gave me courage, strength, hope and, most of all, magic. It is with great joy in my heart that I know the magical old mask has now finally returned home. There are no words to say thank you enough, but from the bottom of my heart, I simply say thank you. God bless you and your family.

Sincerely,

Ms. Allison Macklin Collingsworth"

I folded the letter, and I held the mask tightly in my

hands while I studied it once again. The memories were astounding to me. I looked up at my family and friends through bleary eyes.

I did not know what to say, and I think no one else knew what to say either.

The old mask's magic had stolen all of our words.

The spirit in my heart revived the words of Doctor Dennis O'Brien, and the memories of his words shifted inside of my soul as I recalled him saying, "At one time or another in our lives, we all feel as if we have lived an unfulfilled destiny. The truth is, however, that when you stop and examine your life, it is exactly quite the opposite. If you did the best that you could, treated people with respect and gained the respect of others, played the game fair and hard, then you have fulfilled more than you can ever imagine."

I relaxed, held my wife and children tightly, and pulled them in close to me.

I knew that right now; I had indeed fulfilled more than I could ever begin to imagine, and it felt good.

It felt really good to be the pig rather than just being the hen.

In fact, it felt really, really good.

Pictures and Afterword from the Author

Many actual experiences, as well as a large amount of inspiration, went into the creation of this novel. There is no doubt that hockey and a small, dead-end street known as Geyer Street in Haledon, New Jersey, played a large role in the development of my own hockey career, my own personality, my spirit, my courage to face life, as well as my love of the sport.

When you carefully examine your life, it is amazing how the subtle influences, both good and bad, can have in helping to chart your journey through this strange thing we all call life.

It was just an old, dead-end street. Or was it?

In addition, we all have our heroes growing up. In sports, mine were Joe Namath, Mickey Mantle, Walt "Clyde" Frazier, Willie Mays. However, in hockey it was Bernard Marcel Parent.

Bernie Parent was the goaltender for the Philadelphia Flyers, the goaltender on the teams in the mid-seventies, which won multiple Stanley Cup titles. He won a unanimous election to the National Hockey League Hall of Fame, won multiple Vezina trophies, MVP awards, and was the dominant goaltender of his era.

I patterned my style of playing the position of goaltender after Bernie Parent's stand-up style, and I even wore the same equipment, in which he wore as well as the identical goalie skates. He was also the inspiration for the character of Rumblehowser mentioned in this book, as well as some of my other work.

I still think that there was never a better goalie. Ever!

One of the greatest thrills that I ever had was when my Uncle Dave, my Cousin Dave, and I attended a New York

Rangers hockey game at Madison Square Garden. This was a very rare treat for a poor kid from Paterson, New Jersey, but my uncle had seats, which he could use occasionally, through his employment. This was at the height of the dominance of the Philadelphia Flyers, in or around 1975, or thereabouts, and the game for this evening was the Flyers versus the New York Rangers.

My Uncle Dave and Cousin David were loyal New York Rangers fans, but I did not care. I was going to root for my favorite goalie and for the Flyers!

Sure enough, we were lucky enough to have seats right behind the net, in which the Flyers were set to defend for the first period and I watched in awe as my hero, the great Bernie Parent, skated into the net for warm-ups.

Now, Bernie (as all goalies are, including myself, they are all a little weird, eccentric, and unusual, as well as a bit quirky in their beliefs!) had a particular superstition of never removing his goalie mask while he was on the ice.

Once he flipped it down, it was down, and he would not take it off while on the ice.

When his warm-ups ended, he took to skating around the ice in a drill and I jumped at my opportunity. I walked down closer to the ice than our seats were, and I stood on some steel rails within the seats. Much to the heckling and chagrin of the multiple nearby Ranger fans, as well as my own family members, I cheered at the top of my lungs while simultaneously waving my arms as if I were a madman over my head.

I cheered, "Bernie! Bernie! Bernie!"

I screamed as loud as I could while wearing my Bernie Parent hockey sweater. The local fans let me have it with full barrels. They pelted me with beer cups and hot dogs, but I did not care. They may have been New York roughnecks, but I was a Paterson, New Jersey kid and nothing shook me up!

At first, Bernie ignored me, so I shouted louder, and

waved with a more intense fervor.

Another pass, nothing, two passes by the glass, nothing, then, Bernie Parent must have felt sorry for me, or thought I was a total nutcase, because while he circled around the net for one last pass, he pulled his mask off his face, held it over his head, smiled at me and waved. He then pulled the mask back down over his head and skated away! My life had now reached a zenith. I was now in hockey euphoria!

That simple gesture lasted an entire lifetime!

I wonder if Mr. Bernie Parent would remember that gesture? Perhaps I will send him a copy of this book and see if he does! Regardless, my hero acknowledged me, and a simple joy has lasted all of these years.

It is funny how life is. The simple things are so special. As they still say in Philadelphia to this very day, "Only the Lord saves more than Bernie Parent!"

In March 2013, and again in early May 2014, I visited in person the old neighborhood in Haledon, New Jersey, where Harry, Jeff, and I grew up together.

My purpose, and underlying hope for the site visits, was that it would assist me in the gathering of memories and some information as a prelude to writing this book.

The entire process of writing this novel had grown somewhat frustrating for me. I had started and stopped the manuscript a number of times. They were both emotional visits for me, visits, which did indeed; provide the spark that I required to begin and then finally complete *Geyer Street Gardens.* After my second actual site visit, I felt the framework, in which I had previously set within my mind would work and I set forth in earnest to write the novel.

I decided to divide the book into parts, with each part of the book having a clearly defined progression within the individual and collective character's involvement with the sport of hockey.

I must say that the first part and most of the second part are primarily nonfiction. Part three contains mostly fiction, but with a factual overlay.

Number twenty-seven, did indeed rise from playing street hockey and roller hockey to playing on the ice, and while I never reached the level of playing in leagues that the character of Paul John Henson did, I did play against some very good competition.

Yes, one time, the trainer did stitch a cut of mine with the same needle, which we used to repair tears in hockey sweaters and socks!

In another stroke of nonfiction, my career did end due to a right knee injury. However, it was a broken kneecap, not a ligament injury, which caused my career to end. The kneecap broke due to the impact from a slap shot that slipped behind my leg pad, and never healed correctly until I finally underwent surgery to repair the damage.

The old neighborhood is a bit on the rough side these days. However, in many ways, it still is home to me. Not unlike an awful lot of inner-city urban areas in our country, the urban cities of New Jersey, and the outlying locations of Paterson, New Jersey, all have suffered terribly.

While refraining from political statements, I must say how intriguing it is that we can spend so much of the American taxpayer's monies overseas to rebuild other countries, while our own, wonderful, older neighborhoods fall into ruin and decay.

I decided to take a few pictures during my visit, and I must say too that the condition of Geyer Street is a little difficult to handle. It is now full of potholes and torn up asphalt, and to play a street hockey game there now would be impossible!

The lip lady's home is abandoned and in decay, and many things have changed. However, as I wrote in my own words within the novel, to me, and many other guys, it is very much sacred ground.

All old neighborhoods are, and they tend to stay in our hearts and minds forever. It will never leave me, and I am very sure it will never leave any of my friends and all the other folks who lived, and in some cases, died there. No, there are too many ghosts there, echoes of hockey pucks, visions of kick saves and, most of all, laughter. Laughter, which I could still hear very clearly, when I stood in the middle of Geyer Street Gardens, when I closed my eyes and I tried very hard to recall all that happened there.

Long live, Geyer Street Gardens and the Haledon Hockey League, forever more in my heart and many other hearts!

Yes, forever more, now, and until the end of all time.

30 John Street—home of the Pierce (Porter) family.

John Street at the corner of Geyer Street, looking towards Belmont Avenue.

Geyer Street, where the large potholes are located, is about where the south goal net would have stood.

The lip lady's house. Now abandoned. Very sad indeed.

The actual site of Geyer Street Gardens - circa 2013.

The iconic 20 John Street—home of the Rogers (Redmond) family!

The corner of John Street and Geyer Street, looking past 30 and 20 John Street, towards Belmont Avenue. Notice the old pair of sneakers hanging from the electrical wires! A weird New Jersey pastime!

The iconic 182 Belmont Avenue in Haledon, New Jersey. Fictional home of the "Henson family" and the actual boyhood home of the author.

A picture of a street hockey game of the Haledon Hockey League versus a team from the city of Clifton, New Jersey—circa around the winter of 1979 - 80. This game is on an outdoor rink in Clifton. Note, the snow piles and some ice patches on the rink and on the sidelines.

Depicted are:

3 Jeff Pierce (Porter - note the hat on backwards!)

65 Aldo Iacovo

18 Raymond Bossard—player and coach

#1 Martin DeVoogd

#27 Paul John Hausleben (Henson) is the goaltender in the goal making the split save.

ABOUT THE AUTHOR

If you ask Paul John Hausleben, he will tell you that he is not an author, he is just a storyteller. His mission is to continue to write and tell stories to warm your heart, make you laugh, and sometimes make you cry, just a little. Most of all, he deals in memories, and helps you to remember the good times of your own life, and the special people who touched you along the way. Paul was born and raised in Paterson, and then nearby Haledon, New Jersey, and began writing at an early age. He revisited a writing career later in his life, and he now is the author of a number of novels, compilations, short stories and audio and video works. Most of his work touches upon nostalgic remembrances of simpler times, and tells the stories of heartfelt, humorous, and special human relationships. Other than writing, among many careers both paid and unpaid, he is a former semi-professional hockey goaltender, a music fan and music reviewer, an avid sports fan, a photographer and former military and current amateur radio operator. He now resides in Somewhere, U.S.A., but his heart always remains along Belmont Avenue in good old Paterson, and Haledon, New Jersey.

Titles by Mr. Hausleben that you also will enjoy:

The Time Bomb in The Cupboard and Other Adventures of Harry and Paul

The Night Always Comes, Another story from the Adventures of Harry and Paul

Reunion, A sequel to the Night Always Comes and Another story from the Adventures of Harry and Paul

The Autumn Collection

The Christmas Tree and Other Christmas Stories. Tales for a Christmas Evening

The Miracle Tree, Another story from the Adventures of Harry and Paul

Heaven's Gain

The Adventures of Harry and Paul Series

The Summer Collection

Special Edition: The Time Bomb in The Cupboard and Other Adventures of Harry and Paul

Tales of the Quiet Stranger in the Black Hat

Coming soon?

You may write to the author at ctte27@gmail.com

Published by God Bless the Keg Publishing
Somewhere, U.S.A.

You may write to the publisher at
godblessthekegpublishing@gmail.com

"Life's simple pleasures are so often the best ones!"

www.ingramcontent.com/pod-product-compliance
Lightning Source LLC
LaVergne TN
LVHW020657110826
845149LV00012B/2021

9780990697923